CW00859610

Preferred Lies

Graham Pryor

If the individuals portrayed in this tale are thought to resemble real persons, whether living or dead, it is evidence of the conspiracy between draughtsmanship and coincidence.

Copyright © Graham Pryor, 2007

ISBN 978-1-84753-370-8

The right of Graham Pryor to be identified as the author
of this work has been asserted by him in accordance with the
Copyright, Designs and Patents Act, 1988.

Memory is an unreliable
witness to the truth - M.R.P.

- ONE -

WHEN THE ROOF FELL IN the late afternoon sky was filled with early stars. There was a heavy pall of smoke in the air above the house and, below, the flicker of leaping light made masks of staring faces. For a moment he breathed the excitement of bonfire night, but it was only an inappropriate instant before the shock returned and a shattering of hot glass stunned the complacent summer garden. He glimpsed a figure all in white racing away from the house but the billowing smoke was playing tricks on his grasp of time and place and the image transformed into a spectral procession of shimmering fumes that coursed around the house in its own whirlpool of heat. He was alone.

A whoop went up from the crowd gathering at the dusky garden wall and for the first time Stephen realised that the tail end of his afternoon adventure was no longer contained within the boundaries of his private childhood realm. There was a tautness of excitement in the voices he heard, a sound not only of thrill but apprehension too. And accusation. A house doesn't explode of its own accord. Not even a wooden house.

Reality rose up in front of him as showers of bright red sparks erupted over the brim of the smoking wall, floating up and winking across the sky, the roof going softly down in a slow breath of flame, the windows darkened as the descending ceiling snuffed out all the light from the burning rooms. But with the house no longer held together by the span of oak above there came a terrible cracking, with heat and smoke pressed to the floor by the weight of rafters and shingles, and the curved walls straining against the sudden plunge of immense weight until they burst open in several places, the flames tearing through and the garden lit anew with brightness like midday.

"Run! Get out of there!"

He was dismayed that they should see him, crouched under the living room window, so petrified by his loss of invisibility that he failed to grasp the more immediate terror that loomed above his head.

"Get away, boy! Run! Run!" There was no hint of condemnation now in the shouts that rose above the renewed cacophony of breaking glass.

He saw his reflection in the movement of the smashed window pane as a last remaining shard caught the fire's glow, the staccato pinging of clout and nail like a machine gun as the clapboard wall unravelled and the window frame was finally liberated, tumbling forward towards him. He felt the sting of hot metal splinters in his cheek and hands and heard the sun-bleached staves tumble away all around the house.

"Run!" They were voices daring him to survive.

"Run!" He sprinted across the flickering lawn, his throat tight from the raw taste of ash and the sickly aroma of steaming grass.

"Run! Here! My hand!" There was a firm grip around his wrist; he was passed to another, swung urgently along a line of clutching fists, dark figures in shiny uniform, a white hose snaking along the path from the gate.

The air was cooler at the road. Scraps of red light lit enquiring faces, shadows swallowed looks of consternation and curiosity. Stephen ducked beneath the cloak of a large woman who leaned on the bonnet of a car. Men from the hire car firm across the road were taking no chances and anxious drivers in peaked caps were attempting to manoeuvre their small fleet through the crowd and away to a safe distance from the fire. He slipped around the boot of a Humber Hawk and gulped great draughts of air from the quiet on the other side. Large drops of rain fell without warning and he imagined rather than heard the hiss of steam from the burning timbers of the house. The garage doors were open wide and the empty darkness within suggested refuge. He stumbled against the bulk of blackness, confused by its unexpected resistance, another hand at his wrist now, the restraining fingers confident and easy.

Stephen heard the car behind him edge away and in the relief of light he made out the shape of silver buttons and insignia, white chevrons hovering in the murky space before him, a broad face softened by a thick moustache.

"OK, Sunny Jim", said a not ungentle voice, "seems you're not too keen to stick around, not like these other good folk. Perhaps you and me need to have a talk about what's been going on here."

"But do you realise...do you realise the gravity of this situation?"

The voices were removed from him now, talking over his head, and the focus of blame had transferred from where it wouldn't steady. His shoulders were too young to bear the weight of his crime.

His father cleared his throat to postpone the thought, he was not yet out of his heavy working shoes, those shoes that seemed to have been cast from iron, creased in a single relenting gouge across the toe above the deep-drilled holes of brogue. He was not yet sat at his supper table although the kitchen had long since blossomed with steam and his bicycle remained propped under the parlour window, despite the rain. He had been snatched from the refuge of his front hall, carried somehow or transported and set down standing, still amazed, disbelieving that he had been apprehended by the gloved hand of the law. How ironically gentle was that strong arm of the law, so assuredly it had turned him from his glad anticipation of rest. But he was still not believing.

He knew the man in the uniform who faced him across the empty desk. Sandy from the Tuesday evening domino club. Not a threatening face, not threatening anyone at all but still he was frozen, uncomprehending. It was all too unexpected.

"Dead?"

The word was like a log that he let fall into the room, he felt it pitch heavily and awkwardly upon the floor between them.

"Dead?"

It was a soulless thing he stumbled over in the dark of the ill-lit enquiry room and would skin his ankles in disturbed dreams across the years, his iron shoes denting the soft dead bark as he fell against the word.

And he - the boy, his son - sat watching from his seat, his panic subsiding at last when the conversation was lifted from him. It was a discourse meant for adults, X-rated. He was too slight in years ever to have been given a ticket to the auditorium and heard only the edge of their embarrassed and shocked exchange of sighs and whispers as he watched the shifting of the imposing shoes he could barely lift to polish on a Sunday evening, the shoes he was allowed to address with the mock suede buffer and the sample dark tan kiwi tin from Kleeneze, always wondering if ever he would have the strength to carry shoes like that, they were so weighty and unyielding.

"We don't know that yet"; a large hand smoothed the red moustache. "But it'll be touch and go."

Sandy in his disassociating uniform and no doubt the cycle clips he would not have had time to remove, hidden behind the desk. Better they were there than placed upon the desk between them; better they were concealed along with his own private sense of their inauspicious risibility. On the desk their presence would have held him like leg-irons to the shared humour that bound him with this unfortunate man, the humour of more propitious times in the Rose & Crown. But so it was even in that other place that he kept them on, unquestioning and unremarked, Tuesday upon Tuesday evening, his incongruous uniformed legs bound tight in preparedness whilst he dealt the wooden blocks and supped, always ready just in case the call came, the call that never came to this quiet seaside town until tonight.

He was always prepared but tonight found himself wholly unprepared. The two men had been set suddenly against one another then joined again in mutual resentment of this incision, this disturbance, this calamity thrown up and then descended into the reflex of their cupping hands. But there had been no-one else to call upon to catch its fall.

And the boy was made blameless by their presence. This was an adult thing, a matter for which only they were prepared, parent and policeman. It was the rôle to which they had committed when swearing under the King's badge and at the altar – the bondsmen of law and sovereign and marriage bed. It was not the responsibility of unharnessed childhood; it was not fitting for the undeclared and tolerated child who was but a gentle savage in that epoch before teenage was invented.

But there was no resentment nor even anger toward the boy. He was just the clumsy embodiment of their misfortune. There was no approbation, no more from the father than from the town's objective representative of the law. There was no word for him as he sat upon his hands, bare thighs in summer shorts prised from the cold of the felon's bench, his sandaled feet short of the floor, swinging free of purpose or of statement even, as children's feet will, like a doll or a puppet at rest until borne up once more by command or opportunity. He watched his father shift again uneasily, informed less by the moment than by those heavy iron shoes which he now realised he'd always worn for such a moment, or to mark his presence at least. Wearing the shoes furnished an acceptance of his presence and his adult right to be there. Responsibility alone had been the due he'd paid for those shoes. Responsibility had been the currency of the exchange he'd made, the purchase of the right to wear them. They grated in the quiet of the room.

Only the simple black and white clock on the wall offered any other sound in that room. Its insistent and measured ticking held them, marking out the geometry of the space they occupied, inch by inch and second by second, striking the space of that otherwise quiet room and urging the appalled dynamic with which they were required to animate it. It reminded them that yes, they were really here and yes, this was all happening and they had no choice but to deal with it for, yes, time was truly passing and this time they were required to attend to it. They were under the watchful eye of time itself and this event was its gift to them. There was no-one else. Nothing else was in motion except the waves against the nearby shingle beach.

It was still outside, still in the street past the police station where it was too early in the passage of progress for many cars to have filled those waiting seaside streets, streets that in not so many later years would ache with vulgar tourists in Ford Cortinas and, later still, when the first surprise of post-war wealth matured, and in an attempt at an assumption of style, the ubiquity of mile-hungry Golf GTIs would throb like an ironic plague upon the land made small. Five wasted years, his father would remark, seeing this German invasion.

But back then the long-shoring sea was all else they could hear, through the high window. The rain now was as light as mist, it was not heard but only felt as a pervasive coolness at the window.

They were waiting for the telephone to ring, repeatedly hearing it when it didn't ring so that they could pass the moment to someone more qualified to deal with this. They were like Home Guard, so unpractised were they in the warfare of juvenile crime. Words like mugging and vandalism were alien and unspoken, they had meaning only in the tongues and in the vocabularies of those foreign places to which they were linguistically attributed.

Between the two men none of this was spoken. It was not their way. But neither could they handle silence and they struggled to appease its threats.

"So it may not come to that; it may be only a misdemeanour. Serious, mind, but not murder."

The bond that held the two men strained at the mention of this crime, a crime which may not have happened at all, but causing them to shift around the desk, they were moved by a surge of rawness that roiled against the walls of the room, exposing them as accuser and father of the accused, both embarrassed at these words of false hope and transparent self-delusion that were spoken only to preserve their old amity. Then, the moment subsiding, they were confederates again.

"You'd best be home, Harry. Nothing to be done here now. I'll be round to see you. When I hear. I'll be sure to hear before the morning."

All this the murdered man was unaware of – he would have given his life quietly not to have been the unwilling instrument of it – and worse, he was not dead at all. He was made a counterfeit corpse, more dreadful in its inconsequential consequences for the innocent father and the hapless official, their friendship called fraudulently to account for its honesty when friendship makes no allowance for interrogation, since all must be assumed or lose its value.

"I was not hurt at all. Not burnt, leastways, not fried or baked in the way you feared."

His thin face was streaked with the white hair of a mandarin beard, not burnt with the scars of flame, not hurt in that way, although it was a face scorched by the ordeal of fire all the same, another more enduring fire for which that burning of his house had been yet an instance of visible and public excoriation, working as fire will, no servant of propriety and privacy, no respecter of clothing and cover. That fire had bared him and burned him when he had long believed himself invisible, his own raging inferno of shame and guilt and anger for years contained and concealed, now made naked again. Naked to himself more than to any other disinterested or passing stranger, of course, who would have seen only an old man smitten by rude catastrophe.

"I'd thought I'd forgotten, you see, young man. Only there is no forgetting, no denying yourself."

They were alone together in the curtained day room. The old man sat with his legs drawn up under his institutional white robe, his bare feet red and bony, the toe-nails cut neatly, just visible. It seemed he had been carried from house to hospital bed and thence to this place, having never dressed again for the outdoors. A decade since, like he'd been cleaned and tidied then wrapped up with purpose, once and for all, and kept packaged ready for his eventual departure from life. That's how it seemed to Stephen. Or he'd been parcelled up with no address, waiting for this day ten years and no less but a month or two, waiting to be claimed by someone who could identify him, perhaps that only someone being the boy who had wiped clean with fire any sense of the address or belonging with which he had been allowed residence in a place or time where people did not – and need not – have cause to question, a place and time in which he might once have said this is me and I am known thus. As if the boy, Stephen, owned him by that act. Like a huntsman who in piercing the stag with his arrow lays his mark and out of the anonymous herd says that is mine, through this gift of death I realise your identity and claim you as a part of me. But it had been unfinished, the *coup de grace* suspended. A decade had passed with the old man waiting for him to come and confirm his claim, so that he might be released from confinement and the boy would be unleashed from the straits of a history defined by cataclysm.

The curtains were drawn against the afternoon sun and hollyhocks cast tall grey fluted shadows against them, Stephen hearing traffic sighing on the hill outside, imagining the heat of the choked crossroads at its summit, the taut heat of a southern summer's day transmitted by the passing cars to the waving flower stalks that leaned and peered against the inscrutable window. But all that was shut outside, the garden and the thoughtless cars blind to their exchange, for they were as yet not ready to open up to time, a time which had not yet caught up in this room, the room in which a long pendulumed clock ticked on the wall next to the door with the same unbroken rhythm as the plain black and white clock above the desk in the enquiry room, keeping a pattern set and handed unbroken down the years.

It had always been present, an echo behind his heartbeat, never ending. He'd heard it there and been strangely reassured. It reminded him there was a tale that had not been properly finished, that there was a punctuation left unplaced. Mr Fazakerly heard it too; Stephen knew that. The old man had been watching the clock constantly although his eyes were fixed upon the younger man. He could tell from the way that he spoke into a wider distance than was afforded by this room that Fazakerly's attention was taken by the infinitesimally observed movement of the hands across the face of the clock, wanting to stop it and not wanting it to stop until he had properly done and emptied all he had stored up into that space. The tension made his voice come out dry and squeaky.

"So tell me, when did you hear of my not being dead? Your father, did he say...?"

These questions in the quiet of the visitors' room recalled the heavy silence of that other place, those ten years before. Only that had not been a place of death, just a confined space where the concatenation of misdeeds had shocked the peace of the living.

The man's - his father's - numbed tread across the floor had been an unconscious response to his acknowledgement of living, of time inescapable, of knowing that there would be more time, more days, a future still not entirely unfolded until there were no more wraps to be unfurled from around the mystery. There was no paralysis. Instead, time's demands took him on to the door where the worn brass handle did nothing to prevent his going nor that of the boy, since they were free to go, the charge unable to be spoken just then. It was enough that he belonged to the town that he could be set at liberty without fear of absconding.

"I didn't....No-one... Nothing seemed to be made of it at first."

His recollection was childlike, he had been unaware of the larger tremors around the epicentre, and he was at that centre, so why would he have believed or considered that there was damage all around him, that there was worse destruction in the fall-out at the edge? Everything he saw was so close and clear and focused right then, it seemed as if his hand was still upon the very torch that had lit the moment and the light remained bright around him.

They had walked home in silence through the rain, taking their time. There was no hurry. They had walked hesitantly at first, thinking that before they turned the corner towards Ladies Walk bridge, long before they might place the canal between them and the police station, the solid blue door behind them would open, a shout or cry, maybe even a whisper confidentially calling them back to the telephone. But they had reluctantly gained the canal path and no such command had been heard. Neither did they speak between themselves, the man showing nothing more than his customary contemplation, the way he used to hum between his teeth, lifting those heavy shoes as if they were inconsequential and marking his pace, never hurried but always undaunted, making that wincing face that was not pain but his way of concentrating on the problems of the world and blowing them out in the meandering medley of hums and whispers with which he ordered his abstractions and measured the progress of his path.

No, nothing was said, well, nothing extraordinary anyway. They'd passed the library - almost halfway home and not having spoken - before they met anyone. Two friends with whom he'd have normally spent that day, just arrived off the last coach from London, separated from him for that day alone. He'd been reluctant to join them in their treat and the mother who always made him feel that he was being offered charity. They all walked together loosely through the familiar back alleys, his friends uncomfortable but acting superior in their smart school clothes, full of what they'd seen and where they'd been. He didn't have to speak except to be phatic. Until they'd done and had no more glorious adventures to impart, inquiring then what had he been doing and "nothing...nothing special!" he'd replied, "you know...", his reply serving only to see them along the road to their doors, leaving them not curious but wishing they too had been doing just that, better than wearing school clothes on a holiday and wearying around the untouchable dead things in a museum.

His father's eyes were hidden in deference to propriety and the darkness; he didn't snort or remonstrate, he made no comment or explanation or argument of that slight reply, just propelled his son on by the shoulder as the others turned off into their front paths, taking him on to his own door and retrieving the bicycle, shaking it as one would an umbrella and easing it carefully over the threshold into the long hall.

"No, they didn't seem to want to talk of it at all. They were waiting, you see, preferring not to say until they knew for sure. Shocked, I suppose, and not wanting to admit how shocked when they didn't know the extent of it."

There'd been nothing before to make them fear anything like this, nothing inauspicious, not an inkling, nothing he'd done or threatened to do. Not a single dark inclination had he shown them, not even in jest, and no earlier circumstances could they dredge from the depths of family recall with which to compare. There had been nothing out of the ordinary. Indisputably. Nothing at least that he had shared with them. They played conversations over and over in their heads, words with friends and neighbours, searching for traces, knowing that any suspicion, any at all would have reached them. But there had been no reports from friends, neighbours or townsfolk in this small seaside town where the simple banging of a door after midnight was remarked upon over the choosing of fresh skate at Furlong's morning market stall.

"It was just so very, very quiet in the house, so much quieter than normal, the sort of quiet when no-one knows how to break the silence without creating a disturbance. You see, they'd allowed no room for something like this."

"So you really had no idea...? No concern for me, for what you'd done?"

Even now, in the cocoon of this quiet room, away from the concussion of events it was hard to recall that night coolly and objectively.

"Somehow...you weren't a part of it."

He struggled to reassemble recollections that were at best impressionistic.

No-one had known what to think, that's what it was. It was alien to us then. We had had no training for this kind of situation. It was instead the kind of thing that belonged elsewhere, or so it was imagined, the sort of abhorrence that was commonplace on the council estate. At least that was what I imagined. I had no evidence, of course, it was only an atmosphere, only a sense of how those people lived, a prejudice inherited from a generation with aspirations and codes which caused them to suffer their integrity rather than accept that they, themselves, were only a side-step from the welfare.

Pride. It sustained them and itself was nourished by the distance of comparison. After all, where was the pride in those rows of featureless brick maisonettes only a half dozen streets away, with their every door painted the same dull green; what pride had there been that left broken gates and gardens turned to wild turf, where rusting prams were cast up the abandoned flotsam of their unwed daughters' broken voyages? After all, what cause had we with the intolerable tribes of Teddy Boys who strutted that uncouth labyrinth of unimaginative streets bearing the presumptuous names of local Labour dignitaries?

It was injury to their pride as well as shock that silenced them. It was their being unable to handle the shame, to face the rude and glaring physiognomy of shame that their own son had donned without leave or explanation. Now they too would be expected out of the natural passage of implication to wear it for all time. So it was the absolute and unmistakable mask of tragedy that they made of it.

That and their understanding of position was clear, of the duty of the parent and their expectations of the child. And they had to fit all of this into the limited framework of their ordinary experience, a framework that until now had served them unquestionably well, even sustaining them through the lengthy dislocation of a world war. But it was too simple and fixed to allow for the truly extraordinary. There was no measure to be found there that would help them make sense of that, so the extraordinary had to be altered and seen otherwise, made something else before it could be interpreted.

So it was that they stole the responsibility for my crime, making it theirs, their fault, they the reason somehow for this startling conflagration of waywardness. The evil must have seeded within themselves, a worm they had passed between them, unknowing. Something that had lain beneath the unmarked cheery skin of this child, the precious arch of their love. And now it was a chancre irrupting suddenly and without warning to drench them with reproach for their neglect of the dark side of their souls; they had been too glad to be happy as man and wife and son to acknowledge its presence, to believe that they may have been wrong in some way.

Their son, the keystone to their aspirations had fallen, and they knew not how they had come to build the structure of their lives so inadequately, only that they were left standing in the rubble of misfortune with all those others from those hapless nearby streets, and the only thing that remained to serve as their salvation was their tragic pride. Their pride, not mine.

So it had to be theirs, didn't it: their crime, their wrongdoing; and they would deal with it.

She didn't ask. My mother. It was enough that the police had called. Not unlike the shadow of death, she'd thought, his outline against the parlour window, when he apprehended the home coming craftsman. As unexpected as death. Almost safe, her husband, after his gruelling dawn to dusk, then collared at the threshold to his modest haven.

She didn't need to ask, the entrance of the burly corpulence of the law into our lives was sufficient evidence of disaster.

They whispered in the quiet of the kitchen, ignoring me. I was merely the instrument of misfortune. Only a brief catching in her throat when first we came home, a disbelieving "Oh, Stephen, Lord save us!", but no reproach. Only conviction. The simple presence of the law had delivered unto her all that was required for it to be confirmed. There could be no quarrel with that. Otherwise, normality, and in the resumption of normality came my own undoing. I was despatched to my bed with no more than a wry, possibly (but only possibly) tearful smile, the mug of warm milk proffered as it was always given, no trial or inquisition, just the mug of warm milk and a digestive biscuit to help me sleep tight; my room with the door open so that I could see it was empty and safe, the curtains drawn against ghosts and gremlins, and the sheets turned back for a quick entrance before the reach of childish nightmare might catch at my ankles; a soft hand on my head to calm my fears as on any other night. All normality except for the tension of silence and her smile of rue – and that could have been taken for fatigue on any other night.

No. There had been no concern felt – leastwise, not for the old man.

"Somehow there was no opportunity for any of that. It was nothing to do with being callous or not caring, but it was in some way all stifled."

"So I was removed from the equation. I was never there for them. That's how it was, wasn't it?"

Fazakerly's long thin face ran at last with the rivulets of a grimace, wry and suddenly contented a little by the ironical continuity of the game he had played in life like a consummate draughtsman, one that he had so satisfactorily seen drawn out for him into apparent death. He'd achieved that then; he had played a convincing hand – whatever that meant now. He sought the entire landscape, not challenging any more, with false innocence wheedling:

"Tell me, what did they say of me? Did they speak of me at all?"

The door bell rang once before the morning was light. That Stephen could recall as if it were still ringing, piercing and peremptory.

He had been awakened as he was often awakened by the popping of the milkman's Norton struggling to prove a worthy successor to old Grace the dray horse, the weight of the side-car loaded with crates causing the motorcycle to lean so far that its kick-start grated against the road. There had been a faint salutation as it turned the corner by the Co-op and seconds later the ringing of the bell. He knew that at this unpropitious hour it could only mean the sergeant's promised mission, an association confirmed by the heavy and reluctant clearing of the large man's throat as he stood awkwardly before the front door. Yet, it was still enough to make him sit bolt upright with dread when the bell rang.

The tread of iron shoes was quick to respond to its summons, they'd been awake all night, his father's hand at the lock, the rattle of the safety chain clumsy and nervous; it would presage the clinking of handcuffs and the opening of a stiff cell door, manacles set cold and unrelenting in the stone wall above a rude pallet, just visible in the dim shadows cast from a high barred fanlight.

It would be all darkness from now on, dark and brittle and heavy with the iron and rock and polished wood of Her Majesty's pleasure, the traditions of law and obedience an edifice of magnificent, unavoidable, immovable weight to whose lower fastnesses he would now be consigned forever. He felt the reaches of its inescapable darkness flood into the hall below him, the bulk of the blue-black uniform night itself, stood up tall and eclipsing forever the waiting, welcome light of a summer's morning; unending night present now in the house, hearing the crackle of the sergeant's stiff cape in the hall beneath his room and knowing it was still raining outside, that there would be no relief at all from the darkness of his wrongdoing.

Soon there would be footsteps on the stair and he would be taken in the shrouding mist, removed from the world under a mantle of cape and drizzle, stolen away so that there would be no evidence remaining but their sadness and brave shame.

He had waited and waited, wondering whether he should be dressed rather than seized humiliatingly from his bed, but knowing that to be ready would be to assent, to speed his journey into darkness. The kitchen door was closed and no discernible sounds came up to him. They were in there, huddling, in consolation of each other, agreeing the best way to dispose of the matter with least pain or trauma, deciding who should extract him from the safety of his childish room with the flying saucer wallpaper and the Airfix models suspended by cotton from the ceiling. It would be a violation, whoever drew the short straw.

But once removed from there it would be simple. Out under the cloak of darkness to the cell that had no pity or desire to understand, to the courtroom where the impassive gavel would deny all further argument and come slamming down with the finality of the door that would swiftly bang behind him; as would the trapdoor as suddenly fall away in front of him, but which he wouldn't notice, being in total darkness now inside the black silk hood and with the noose around his young neck all that was left for him to feel. He would be blind from now on; there was no sense to see at all, just the colourless sky of oblivion, which he thought he recognised, a sightless glow, fed from the flames he had watched springing from within the writhing black anarchy of sparking smoke that had been the Round House.

The memory of those tearing flames would be all the light he would know from now on, and he realised at last that it was that wall of flame that stood between him and both pity and condemnation; it had sealed him in to an exacting and distant isolation from where he could see only their wreathing, mocking light, seared upon blinded eyes that looked out into the darkness of time stopped.

"No, it was bigger than you," he replied at last, knowing that he was not insulting the old man; he was opening another door out of the room that had held him cocooned for ten years, one month and thirteen days.

"No, they didn't mention you at all. You were never meant to be a part of it – not by me anyway."

- TWO -

THE EARLY RISING SUN was so bright he could feel its cheer through closed eyelids and, opening his eyes, he peered gladly, even hungrily at the golden welcome. As he awoke, he became aware that it filled the entire landscape in front of him with a brave and undeniable light, his head on his forearm raised level with the brilliance of its benediction, although his ears were ringing yet with the hissing, gonging rush of sound that the last assault had bequeathed him, still ferocious and unfinished in the aching perforations of hearing despite the earth no longer shivering, so that he'd at first thought it was but a pause, a catching of infernal breath between the reloading of cannon, a brief interstice of peace in the clouded fabric of the smoke-drenched afternoon that mortar and mud and scream had every intention of filling when next the ghastly turmoil was resumed. Except that this light told him otherwise. It was perhaps all over.

Lance-Corporal Fazakerly, Thomas, 6874..... He couldn't remember all of the number they'd given him, only his name; he'd never belonged to that number and it was the first casualty of his shell-shocked memory, so lightly had it been imprinted upon his notion of himself. But what he did remember was enough to open his eyes upon the light of morning, feeling his legs cold and numb, as he'd grown used to feeling them. His boots were too heavy to lift, he'd worn them sodden with mud for so long he feared that to remove them would mean taking his feet away as well, there was no telling any more where the rotten dead clumps of shapeless leather ended and where began what remained of the sunken, withdrawn warmth of his own life. But opening his eyes wide, tensed and ready to wince at the brilliance of the light yet finding it gentle, he forgot immediately the cold in his bones. The golden orb was huge and perfect, undiminished by wakening, suspended there right in front of his face. He thought he was truly dead that he could have come this close to the sun and not be burned.

Then, his sight clearing, as though the smoke and hail of wasted soil had stuck up his eyes for a moment and he had to blink it away, or maybe not from his eyes but from his floundering, rheumy sanity, and seeing that it was not the sun at all but a flower, a single flower, a buttercup next to his reclining face, he was no less gladdened by the discovery. It must be the last and only buttercup in the world, here of all places, just beyond his nose. He dared not breathe, for this was the most perfect thing in all creation but a fragile inch or two from where he'd fallen hopelessly, felled by despair.

He closed his eyes again and saw the flower's yellow light pressing through his wondering lashes. Not wanting to relinquish the image, and at the same time afraid to accept it, all he knew for certain was that he couldn't have imagined it, it was beyond the wit or craft of a man to have dreamed or to have fashioned such a thing of wonder. Yet, however astonishing it was to him that he should have discovered it here, alone in this fastness of utter desolation, his intoxicating awe fed its own rapture to the phenomenon. For here was found glory in this terrible place, where not an inch of virgin soil remained. It enthralled and then steadied him. As a paradox it was without doubt beyond the wildest mischief of a sane mind. To have so rashly placed that thing of simple beauty in this sickening mire lay far outside all but the most diabolical calibrations of the surreal, and only the cynical handiwork of a madman may have tried this work, in celebration of some inhuman lunacy. That was his comfort, knowing that all the madmen were far away from this field of death, far and safe away in the war rooms of merry England.

If not mad, alive then. Survived. He had lived to tell the tale.

He was emboldened by the sheer and insistent glow of the flower to look again, to raise himself on his elbows and look beyond over its brave, chaste golden insolence, finding there was just the two of them, just him and this tiny goblet of sunlight in a wasteland of grey and glistening mud, an expanse unrelieved even by the stump of a tree or the presence of earthworks. Men had raged upon it for far too long to allow a single feature any further residence.

A contrary thought intruded, bringing its own unexpected feeling of relief: perhaps he *was* dead, caught betwixt heaven and hell. But if this was purgatory it had nothing on the days that had furnished its entrance. Then, if not dead, maybe insane? Was he the madman after all? In that case this place must easily be of his design, it belonged nowhere better than in the nightmare of his depression. All grey: the sky, the earth, the skin upon his bared arm, all colourless and grey. Only the tiny bowl of gold, suspended where the sun should be, offered the last preserved reflection of his soul.

He slept, in sleep careful not to reach out and crush the flower, desperate in sleep not to spill the shallow residue of his spirit from that shiny yellow bowl, this spirit awakened how many hours or days after what event he did not care to measure, as there had been no good reason for it to awake. He could never crawl from this place when there was no place of safety he might gain, and in any case he could not leave knowing that his soul was planted here, in the mud.

He was awakened again at a point where he had no desire to awake, when he had already found a solution that was fitting. Having awoken once to find the shining buttercup, his desire to sleep was nourished by the promise of entering a dream of living; it was all a part of the larger expanse of contradiction that seemed natural to him now. So, disinclined to wake, he heard none of the slopping and attenuated progress of his approaching salvation, two weary rescuers who had trawled the field expecting to find only refuse, but were committed to looking all the same; it was all they could do to prove their consciences in this filthy, futile war and he, Fazakerly, could not be allowed to deny them that.

The man's boot was uncommonly gentle in his gut; there must have been an expression of life still in his sleeping smile.

So was he brought back again, but with such a depth of resentment at this redemption. He could not understand the cruelty of it, his deliverance just another example of undecipherable inhumanity, nothing more than a motiveless desire to disturb him and break his last and ever-lasting slumber. Worse, he found the sun had truly gone out this time. He opened his eyes a little, afraid of the renewed gloom, and searching found only the mud-encrusted boot of the second stretcher-bearer filling the short, wan, poorly lit distance between his face and the rude sled they had fashioned out of a piece of corrugated steel. The buttercup had gone, an ooze of grey slime erupting from beneath the man's sinking boot as he stood for a moment, the ground no longer ground but a suspension of dirt and rancid water upon which one might stand still only long enough to consider where next to place one's step, and where only the supine might be borne grudgingly without fear of drowning.

He was lifted hurriedly, the two men eager to move on. They folded his arms upon his chest to prevent them from tearing on the bare metal edge of the sled, loosely binding his wrists together with a rag. Their voices sounded kindly enough. They rummaged quickly in his pockets, pulling at his undershirt to discover a name tag.

"Well, that's something," he heard one say. "Good on yer, mate." The man bent over him. "He's wearing metal tags. Fibres wouldn't have lasted five minutes out here." He felt a tugging behind his left shoulder and the man stood up again, breathing huskily, spitting on the name tags and wiping away the dirt.

"Fazakerly? Hey, Fazakerly, you with the Twenty-fifth, then, eh?" They spoke encouragingly, familiarly, mouths close to his ear.

But he was no longer disposed to talk of those things. A blackness had descended that rendered them all unspeakable, unreadable, voices from a Babel of darkness, and they accepted his silence with pity, he being the only survivor found in a day of searching.

The two men hoisted the sled a little, first to waist and then back to knee height as they accustomed themselves to his weight, their breath close in his face as they stooped momentarily. Then he felt the world tilt sharply and movement begin. It was so long since he'd felt real motion his stomach turned over and he stiffened, crying out until they halted, lying rigid in the centre of the sled until a hand was placed on his brow to steady him and he stared up at the man who bent to calm him, the man who was holding a crushed and bruised buttercup between his fingers as one dangles a trinket before a stricken child.

"Look Fazakerly, look!" urged the man, his large round face weathered a deep red. "Here, c'mon lad, we're off now. Going home! Hold on."

The man's hot palm was smoothing the grime from his forehead, but Fazakerly was unable to feel it because he was watching the dead yellow thing that drooped from thoughtless fingers on its slight green thread of stem, his eyes so tightly focused, their grey stare straining to reach out as if to grasp it yet, aghast and horrified to touch what it had become, they were blinded by seeing.

"Here, it's all right now," his rescuer declared, Fazakerly's frozen rictus producing an anxious moment with its mask of death. Fatuously he waved the broken flower in his face, brushing it playfully at Fazakerly's chin, with the intention of good-naturedly teasing his spirit to sorts, watching his eyes all the while and glad to see the pupils steady. He glanced aside to reassure his comrade.

"Yeah, he'll make it".

The uncertainty of this thought made them both look around the stilled and smitten landscape. By no means were they safe and sure here in this place. The first man peered again at their prize, chuckling, suddenly pressing the limp, bruised petals against Fazakerly's neck.

"Hey, Fazakerly, do you like butter?".

Thomas Fazakerly's eyes remained wide open but were no longer seeing; he didn't want to watch the torn weed as it was twisted and twirled between thumb and index finger, nor feel himself flipped away with it like a dog-end into the sloshing mire. It was all too dark and colourless to watch.

Later, when he'd fashioned his house, his fine wooden Round House, he cared not for the tidy expectations of polite England but made the garden a wasteland, a wild place full of winking speedwell, fescue, rye and clouds of Yorkshire fog. Around the warm circumference of the wooden house deadnettle made a velvety shade for cats to slumber undisturbed all summer long, their warm fur glazed with the powdery lace of pollen that made them seem garden ornaments, and the larch lap fence burgeoned with the brilliant white bells of nodding convolvulus, whose ringing would wake them only when they closed to silence against the first suggestion of cool rains from off the sea. But when the sun truly shone it was the buttercups that caught one's eye, their bright golden carpet unbroken and dazzling all the way from the road right up to the house. Not a soul or footfall had disturbed their upward gaze and they filled the space completely where once there had been an arid lawn.

It was enough in those times to make him a marked man, a man of some diabolical means in his own house, no less excused by the eccentricity of the house itself. It was a house that might have argued wealth and fashion and as its dissident master he would have been afforded the usual genuflection bestowed on genuine rank by a tradition of toleration and obedience; but the house had been left to the wind and salt sea air to weather white and bleach to the smoothness of bone, leaving him naked with no camouflage of polite convention. A disgrace, to let a place go like that; a shame indeed when decent folk who haven't two brass farthings to rub together can manage to keep their doorsteps clean and their front paths free of moss.

But even that indignation was transient and ambivalent, secondary to the gladness that this recusant was theirs, here in this town, hidden and secure in that single storey tower between the funeral director's curtained window and the safe tree-shaded anonymity of number ten Oak Cottages. He was absorbed into the patina of their local geometry and coveted jealously for his difference, where to covet was to worship unknowingly, with some awe perhaps or, at the very least, unconscious respect, where he sharpened inspiration like a tuning fork to their idle conversation whenever he appeared, without which they were dull harmony.

So it was more curiosity and a sense of possession than any resolve to resentment that he excited in the town, as well as some undeserved pity. To see his still, thin face peering like a bird's from behind the drawn lace curtain, his intent not to be deflected by the passing onlookers but fixed upon the golden fleece of buttercups where he had hidden his dissipated and subversive passions, they would smile and tut and shake their silly heads, feeling good about themselves and the way of the world, not really seeing him at all. If they had followed his unwavering stare, which admitted no-one, they would have realised there was none inside that house to receive visitors anyway, for he was out there in front of them, basking in glory under the sunny sky. He had gone there years ahead of himself, but time had taken a while more to bring along what remained of his humanity.

The distance of their route back over the fields of stinking mud had been multiplied a thousand fold since they had set out at first reveillé, or so it seemed to the wind-chilled stretcher-bearers. There was little appreciable sunlight that day and the air remained heavy with a dense layer of blown smoke that could find no further space in which to rise. It was cold and dead air, which they breathed in deliberate, short gasps, not wanting to fill their throats and lungs with its foul flavours. Progress was possible only by way of a meandering course between the fluid tracts that striated what once had been a moorland of chalk and clay; their footholds were more often than not the tiny islands of corpses that rose almost imperceptibly above the surface mud. And these were not without hazard. In that darkened light as the day drew on it became less easy to identify the true orientation of these treacherous bodies, whether they were simply floating or would they offer a more reliable purchase in the slime. The risk of putting their stretcher-weighted tread upon a swollen belly instead of finding a firm trenchcoated shoulder blade beneath their feet slowed their passage increasingly once night threatened, when they could no longer watch for the warning beacons of upturned bloated faces. One false step and they'd be through the tissue of putrid skin with the filth of entrails lashing around their legs, each eviscerating gulf of putrescence more terror to these battle numb non-coms than the avenues of mine and wire which they'd nimbly traversed for more than a year now without a wrinkle of loathing on their faces, only watchfulness.

For Fazakerly the whole affair of that miserable afternoon was of no consequence. He had renounced it, and the day after and the day after that. Even his ride in an open box-car two days later was remembered (when he eventually conceded some recognition of his own consciousness) as nothing more distinct than a flight through some featureless and uninterrupted vortex of icy wind, a journey that had no purpose or outcome other than to parch dry the skin of his tear-drained eyes. His passage from the sore and wounded landscape south of Torhout had no form or features except the anonymous and desolate hand of the heavens that beat at his face all the way from Arras, the sky lowering with a smoke that seemed to cover the world over, a shroud of cold shame that did not lift until the train that dragged him uncomplaining through its torment finally desisted and, steaming from the cold, subsided into the rail yard at Étaples. Since setting out on the road at Roeselare, their truck edging through the secretive darkness around occupied Lille, and onward until his rescuers felt they might relax a little in the comparative safety of the provisioning centre at Arras, he had been numb to the world; and when the reality of his escape was eventually signalled with the next morning train's departure for the coast it meant nothing to him, for he felt he had been torn out of himself and left behind on that wasteland. There was nothing left of him to save.

Even then he did not admit to any further participation in the world to which he had been delivered; not even with the modest sun revealing its glory at last when the heavy cattle door was torn back, where there were steady hands to help him down, warm hands that had not at that point yet shivered with a bayonet in their grasp nor felt the heavy tearing resistance of muscle rent so unwillingly when the callous blade was forced home. These hands belonged to men who had no sense yet of thee or me, only of us and them, and their warm, strong hands held him gladly, for to them he was a messenger of hope, evidence that there was always the possibility they too would be coming back from the front.

Fazakerly's expeditions in France and Belgium had scarcely begun but he had already construed them an interlude of nightmare. That foreign bit, he referred to it dismissively, feigned contempt removing its shadows from recollections in wiser years, when he had recognised its unreality. That's how he introduced it to Stephen over half a century later and it was an easy way to tell the truth without having to explain it: a nightmare, the elapse of a bad dream that would be followed by a morning and an awakening. His admission that "we got our just desserts, attacking a military hospital like that", was his only concession to complicity. But that was also the torn edge of his error in false humility, and the carpet of gold where the front lawn had been burned with the lie became a roaring duplicity, bold and brazen and defiant, his loss of faith in himself rolled out under the sun for all to see. Seeing the stuff of himself so unashamedly displayed, not hidden in shame, one might never think to make the connection, that blazing out from this garden was the real unconcealed truth of his nightmare. Its brilliant overstatement in nature blinded all deeper curiosity.

But of nightmare, such indeed was his recollection of consciousness during that time in the hospital bed at Étaples. Then came his gradual awakening, long slow months of mornings when, little by little, he recovered himself from the enervation of dreams.

His recovery was not welcome. As clarity and colour returned, he found himself emerging from the suppression of his senses into an ensuing bombardment of his reason by forces of reality that seemed intent on punishing him for his retreat into somnambulism.

"It sometimes seems that I never left that place and here I am now stretched out on the same blanket in the same bed. But of course that is foolish, just the wandering fancies of an old man. Then again, perhaps it is all a part of the same thing, all the loose ends of life so tangled up together I haven't been able to unravel my true place in it, or in time itself - until now, perhaps." His eyes widened momentarily. "But it is all so late."

Fazakerly reached and caught Stephen's arm, his face brightening a little. "But for you of course, my young friend, it is not so late at all."

It was their third afternoon together. Fazakerly had become so consumed by this accidental resumption of their association that he could entertain no other thoughts. He had not dressed, but lay motionless in his bed until the young man arrived, all of time suspended and without meaning until he reappeared. Perhaps it was his way of not wanting to use time ill any more, not until he had formed an understanding of time past. He felt so much joy and respect for the change of time. His greeting upon Stephen's arrival had been like that of a father to a long lost son, not a prodigal but a welcome innocent mislaid through his own negligence, like a treasure he hadn't valued until it was misplaced and he had feared it gone forever.

From the first moment of recognition there had been no malice or antagonism in their meeting and Stephen was aware only of a sense of immense relief spilling from the old man. For him too, there was relief, as well as surprise, discovering his victim alive. It was as if he had opened his bedroom window in the middle of a winter's hollow night and found Santa Claus sorting through his sacks before taking off for another part of town, and calling out 'Hi there! Good to see you', excited at proving him at last but knowing he'd never ever doubted him now that he'd seen him, his rush of excitement being a confirmation of that knowledge rather than the welling of mere childish glee. For Stephen it was such a moment of comfort, as if in that sudden instant he'd never questioned that Fazakerly remained flesh and blood, even whilst knowing that his substance had been composed only of the stuff of his personal and local mythology, and that his towering familiarity with the man was the dark consequence of richly woven repetitions of childhood fable, draped with the inventions of memory.

Fazakerly was dead and he'd never needed to question the impossibility that he'd ever actually see him again. But in the moment when they met, or in the ensuing hours when in solitude he could interrogate the reflections of that moment, he began to recognise that his belief in this condition was founded largely on trust and a willingness not to disbelieve.

It was the ascendance of evidence over faith that explained his own easy acceptance when first Stephen discovered Fazakerly in the nursing home. He knew that intuitively. All the same, to say their meeting came as a surprise would be an understatement of gigantic proportions, although it was the overwhelming comfort of the moment that hit him rather than the shock of finding this dead man alive.

There were other, deeper needs that would be satisfied at last and knowing this filled him with an unconscious sense of joy. Things he had crammed into the unlit back of his mind, that had waited there unresolved, over time becoming something else, changing form but no less powerful because of their evolution; questions, doubts that had no appreciable cause, whispers where there was no evident desire for secrecy; a suspicion that, despite the certainty of his life and the assumed clarity with which he recalled his passage through it, a blind had been drawn whilst he looked the other way. His consuming uneasiness about the memory of his, as yet, short past was formless, yet his own life had become a source of scepticism for him.

He recognised echoes of this vein of suspicion in his robust rejection of religious faith, his scorn towards the Christmas story itself, unwelcome in a town that reverberated with Sunday bells, a story which everyone else seemed to want to believe simply because it was so extraordinary and unlikely that the weight of faith it generated had created an avalanche of hope. But for Stephen, without evidence, hope had always seemed a dubious carriage for interpreting and plotting his life's course. This, he knew, was his own contradiction, an indefensible position, for if he had seen those wounds, heard the nails driven through flesh, he would have been doubtless and never having doubted. But there was no substantiation, no consummation, only a story older than Santa Claus, and no awakening in the dead of night to hail Christ as he distributed the gift of mercy to the world. The world in which he lived. His world. Was mercy due to it out of pity or as consolation for its lack of certitude?

It had always been that way, or so it seemed. He had unconsciously acknowledged Fazakerly's presence as some kind of personal totem for the most part of his childhood. In his more reflective teenage years the absence of the old man had become a more conspicuous but no less elusive motif for something momentous that had happened or seemed to have happened but had somehow been hidden away, all but removed yet having left an aura, a deep shadow of terrible but untouchable and unconfirmable proportions. It was a memory that he could no longer quite grasp, recalling it only in brief glimpses, allowing him some sense of familiarity and presence but no ability or data to assess the full import of it all.

Only now, that opportunity had been given to him. So unexpected was it and without preamble that he had been allowed no option but to get on with it, to deal with it as if it were a natural commonplace, as if there had been no hiatus, finding himself in denial of all those questions and mystery that had left him through all those intervening years and unable to focus on the scale of what had happened. Unless he simply walked away, of course, and that was no option at all. Not after all these years, not when he'd been rendered so impotent of consciousness it was as if there had been wholesale surgery done on the natural development of his soul.

He laughed to himself. Such was his extravagance of thought! What unashamed hyperbole! It was his first true awareness of those extremes of expression with which he had become used to countering his flimsy visions of the past. It was also a tenet of the Sixties *zeitgeist* and his collision with reality would lead to further intrusions of unfashionable self-consciousness.

Old man and young man were hungry to fill in the gaps of their respective pasts, both of them compelled by an unspoken necessity to begin from the beginning, or at least from that first collision with fate that had sent them ricocheting right out of the groove they had believed was carved for them. From here, quite unexpectedly, they might rebuild the structure of their lives with all the missing pieces put back in place and the connections and bridges that had become obscured made visible again. From the vantage point of renewal they would be able to make sense of the view from the parapet and realise where indeed they'd been and just how far they had come.

"I'd got left back on that wasteland south of Torhout. Finished, I thought. Done for. Perhaps that's what was supposed to happen, but you can't make plans against all eventualities. Not even our Maker, it would seem. Seems like even He couldn't prevent those two fellows coming along like that. And I was saved, wasn't I? Thought I was past saving, too. Didn't really want salvation by then. Well, you can't choose your saviours. They did what they did, and for the best. Maybe it'd be different today; it's impossible to break a leg without a whole army of do-gooders coming knocking at your door. They come in here, too." He glanced towards the door with an expression of genuine apprehension.

"They turn up with their arms full of salvation, their faces a picture of practiced care and consolation, all usually wrapped up in a tissue of saintliness. Guilt or the politics of dependency, who cares?"

Fazakerly relaxed again.

"Anyhow, they did their best. They weren't there to save my mind, after all – or my soul. I was just another casualty of war and I was lucky.

One of them came to see me in the hospital. 'Here you are, then', he said to me. I remember it clearly: 'here you are safe and sound', and he propped me up in an old wing chair against the window so that I could look out into the garden. 'That's better. You like flowers, don't you.' I remember his big, bright red-faced smile. 'There, that'll cheer you up.' He was all matey and conspiratorial. 'See', he said, 'I remember you, old chap, I know what makes you tick'. He'd already missed the point of course, but then you can't choose your saviours."

His view through the window would have cheered all but the terminally depressed.

The sun had shone the whole week long since he was lifted down from the cattle truck, with the door hauled back to admit a low early morning light he hadn't known was there. He'd been pinched by the wind into a coil of aching limbs, hunched against the wall, aware only of the oppressive glow above from the reflexive shadows in which he sat, his eyes closed and stuck raw at last against all reproaches for his bodily survival.

He'd distrusted the light at first, it could have been just another chimera, another hallucination of the nearly dead, and he had the conviction that, like a miserable copy of Faust, he already given his soul in exchange for its brief wealth of gold. But gradually he found himself coming back, confronted by pieces of himself he knew, only changed;

motes of existence gathering in the sunbeams through the window. The person he saw seemed a little out of focus just yet, there had been a loss of that clarity and dependability of meaning he had known before the war, and he felt uncertain about himself or what he thought about it all.

As the months passed this ceased to bother him and he became at one with the light itself, the warmth of the sun drawing him to the window early each morning, from where he watched for hour upon hour, patiently nodding and craning his neck as if he were looking for something that might have been set there just for him but which had been placed awkwardly and out of sight. It would come right if he waited.

The medical orderly observed his distractedness as he studied him peering out into the neat pattern of flowerbeds where men broken in body had urged a brave pennant of defiance from the soil. It was no heraldic perfection, but no-one denied that the azure field of viola, planted square and densely at its centre, made a fitting quarterly for the blazing bars of marigold d'or raised there. The unbroken discipline of these measured borders with their regiments of manicured privet made a barricade in miniature against the foe. Fazakerly gazed expressionless upon these glorious and sterile gardens without emotion, motionless and unmoved until he was turned by a nurse and laid out for inspection upon his crisp white bed. The orderly diagnosed shortsightedness and he was prescribed spectacles.

At first having suspected concussion, but finding no trace, they determined that he was simply a patriot who was concealing his very poor sight. There was nothing else physically or visibly damaged to be found, just the scabs and bruises of fatigue and shock and fear, which would soon mend now that he was away from the front. And his eyesight, which they could deal with in no time at all. There was a charity box full of spectacles for such difficult moments as this.

They were probably right but no thanks to them all the same he did begin to mend. The view through the window was indeed a cheerful one, but not on account of the labours of the walking wounded. Fazakerly never went out into the garden except to tiptoe barefoot over the cropped spongy grass each morning, putting on loose slippers to shuffle up the dirt road as far as the wide main gate where he peered for ages back up the lane toward the rail yard, looking like a man awaiting delivery of his luggage sent after him. But he did this less frequently as the weeks passed and no deliveries were made, his eyes being drawn instead to the near aspect of the bustling town, a happy confusion of leaning, clambering walls and orange tiles where the demands of a long war had left no time to press order upon its streets and structures, and where birds, beasts and mankind darted amongst passageways brimming with the disorder of wild nettle, fireweed and thistle.

Instead of maintaining his vigil at the gate, increasingly he spent his time in conversation with the nursing staff, so hungry for conversation it seemed it was a facility he had just learned and found so fascinating and absorbing he could not bear to lay it aside for one moment, he'd been without it for too long, and with this transfusion of speech he became animate once more. He would sit forward, the fingers of his nurse or an orderly grasped between both of his own scrawny hands, his head slightly to one side but his eyes wide and expectant, like that of a child entranced by a favourite fairy tale. Only when their conversation was exhausted could he release them, continuing to sit, transfixed, hearing over and over the words that had passed between them.

His manner had all the appearances of a recovery from trauma but it was more serious a pattern of behaviour than their practiced goodwill would allow them to comprehend: he was looking for something, trying to find himself amongst them all, knowing unconsciously that if he touched enough hands he would at least have many to hold on to when he finally gave up, having never found his own hand amongst the crowd.

Unconsciously, but no less certain for that, he was aware that he had to go on looking if he was not just going to give up, and in looking there was hope that he might find another view of himself. For the man that he had been was no longer available to reassure and inform him; he had left him behind in a febrile cup of gold in the mud just outside Torhout.

"So you were ok, then, not wounded?"

As soon as he spoke Stephen knew the inadequacy of his words.

"Listen. That wasn't why I was there, was it? I wasn't wounded. It was just a necessary period of adjustment. That's when it all started. You understand that, don't you?"

There was an unexpected trace of panic in his voice.

"It was all new and I needed first to recuperate. I hadn't felt the need before. Everything had always been so sure, and then suddenly it was blown away. It felt like *I* was blown away. It seemed to me that someone had stolen my very being, or I'd dropped it in the confusion of battle. So I wasn't wounded at all; it was just a coincidence that they should find me in that place when everything else was so torn apart, just when I'd reached that point from another direction. It was the natural sequence of things, I suppose."

Fazakerly gave a sigh of relief.

"Everyone falls at some time or another; it's just that I'd got caught up with all those bigger carryings on. At least, that's what I thought then. That's how I explained it to myself. But it didn't last and I don't know why I'm telling you now. We have to see things through, I guess, right to the bitter end, come what may and all those other platitudinous aphorisms it galls me to admit are true."

He fixed Stephen with a meaningful glare.

"When they're cold and remote we have to turn them over and see these things for what they are. It's the only way to move on."

The young man, severely discomfited, stumbled again with a repetition of his same trite words of commiseration, but Fazakerly let it go this time.

"Well, it didn't last anyway. What I was experiencing was a mere symptom of the phase I was going through.

That's why I explain it the way I do. So, you see, I've known all of this since long before now. But, you know, it's really helped me, this; us meeting this way. I might never have thought to rake over such old coals as this; I'd have gone on waiting and waiting for someone else to blow upon the dull embers, my lungs full of ash and my eyes blinded by the heat, waiting for death as the only certainty. And that would have made it all such a wasteland. Like Torhout."

And like the Round House all those years later when he was plucked unprotesting and unmarked from the smoke-filled living room, sitting bolt upright on the wheeled stretcher the firemen had to douse with their hose to keep from igniting, fallen yet pathetically commanding in his distress like a deposed raja on his palanquin, unbelieving at the insurrection and indignity and still afforded safe passage.

He was wholly and entirely stunned.

But more than that, hearing the crack of the stained glass on his veranda and the sky roaring with fiery stars, the crowd at his gate going 'ooh!' and 'aah', like it was Guy Fawkes night.

The mystery of sedition singed the air, for he was being whisked away, he was leaving them disappointed, not having truly been a burned effigy. Only not disappointing them, if truth be told, for he maintained his secrecy in flight. Just as he had always been their secret, a conspirator sanctioned to dwell in their midst under a cloak of eccentricity that didn't fail them when the myth was given grace to linger amongst them in the smoke from his escaping chariot. Instead of being dead and still and silent and lifeless, where they might gawp momentarily at the story's end, as they would stare at the conger eel speared and bravely faced in death upon the deck of their wooden boat, only briefly enjoying the knowledge that they'd exposed a monster from the dark side of the day, instead of that he was author to them of the inferno from which he was retrieved, author and character and plot snatched from glorious incineration and removed to safety from the indignity of oblivion, to be reprised on further occasions.

But more even than that, it was more than an outrage for him, much more.

'At last', spoke the words in his head; at last, when the flames had been lit, so swiftly did those yawning gaps appear in the fabric he had woven about himself, so swiftly he felt cold despite the rage of fire; and finding just how flimsy a barrier he had constructed, more than an outrage: he could see through those burning walls the unremittingly desolate wilderness that he would have given anything to deny.

"That's how it felt after you burned me out. When the roof came falling in upon me I thought: this is it, it's over, it was all a sham. I was reduced to being naked again, exposed to all with the sky appearing where the ceiling had been, just as I'd always known it would. And I was already old by then. I couldn't face it all again. But I still breathed; I still passed water. It wasn't over yet."

He waited expectantly, not for Stephen but for his own agitation to settle, waiting for the moment of calm that would free him, enabling him to reach out finally and surely for the conclusion that he sought. But with his breaths coming fast, unable to contain his hunger any longer, he blurted out again through the hard red bars of taut fleshlessness that ribbed his face, in his haste already having made the move that would drop the key to his quest.

"So tell me, for I know you can't want to hear any more of this, tell me and let an old man die at last: was that all it was, was it just another episode of outrageous fortune, or did you have a reason for what you pulled off that day?"

- THREE -

THE OLD MAN may have been desperate for an answer but Stephen was consumed by an overwhelming desire not to hurry. Whether the fire had been lit by mere fate or malice, he was in no way ready to offer any answers on that score. Despite Fazakerly's impatience with the sense of a past that was no more lucidly comprehended than his own, the memories he had shared that afternoon served as an introduction, not a conclusion; a preamble nonetheless, out of which Stephen could feel the whispers of instinct growing, soft and unformed but promising, where before there had been nothing. He did want to hear more, whatever the old man claimed, for all he had learned so far was that there was a long tale to tell. How and why it had first led to him, a decade past, he did not know. As for explaining himself, if he'd had a reason to give for the narrative of his actions all those years ago it would have consoled him long before this belated rendezvous. Even if it had been a wicked or indefensible reason it would have provided a conscious frame to which he might have attached some anatomy of meaning. As it was, the expectations of providence, no less, had been defied - robustly, and for a good many years now - and he, although with a happier balance of time on his side, was as much in search of answers as the old man; but he was not yet ready to select one and, in any case, he was too absorbed by savouring the agony of choice. All the same, whilst relishing this new experience of dilemma shared, neither did he dare break the connections they had newly made.

He'd spent that morning working through the obligatory research methods programme, aware that it was only a month or so now until he resumed his student life. Until the unexpected had happened and his remote and inconclusive past had confronted him with a spectre that was very persistently alive, he'd been eager to commence his postgraduate studies. Here would be found order and focus, and he would be able to look away from the uncertainties of the larger world, where life was unstructured. Faced with the challenge he found diversion from Fazakerly's question in his present preoccupation with academic argument, oblivious how much such an apparent *non sequitur* might irritate.

"I remember at school, it was in one of those general studies classes they thought would leaven the narrow diet of A-levels, we were examining the conflict of science and religion – you know what I mean, evidence versus faith, all that kind of stuff – and someone of course put his hand up and said that science could explain the cause of all things, eventually that is, and that nothing happened without some cause or other. He (it couldn't have been a master, the thesis was too heretical), he said this proved that there was no God, the argument being that, as the Creator, God would have had to exist prior to the Creation, which of course we think of as the first causation, but as there was nothing greater than God then how was he caused? So, QED, he did not exist!

"The argument was pure sophistry of course, schoolboy stuff and designed principally to be argumentative – in the worst sense of the word, I mean. I hope it's not the kind of thing I'd grant room in my own research thesis, but whilst it was an argument full of holes, I was attracted by its simplicity. I hadn't time or the sophistication to refute it then and I guess maybe I didn't mean to because I was trying to find another answer to it, something that had nothing to do with reason. I just felt at the time there was something lacking that would have made sense of it, something small and just a little way out of my grasp but reachable. It wasn't necessarily something rational, either. Not that it makes sense now, as we are wise enough to think back beyond the Creation, at least scientifically, but wasn't it that kind of something that happened to us? Something beyond the edge of reason?"

Fazakerly hunched silently over his knees. They were drawn up defensively as a prop to the stalemate he so wanted to break. He was clean shaven and his face looked sharp, almost commanding.

It had a contrary effect on Stephen, who felt himself pitying him, he felt responsible for the old man, something he had never felt before at all. It was an uncomfortable thought that had not occurred to him until now: despite his new, somewhat stalwart air, the old man was evidently resigned to hearing him out, whatever spurious yarn he might have to spin, fearful that only at the end of patience could he hope to find what only time would tell. But Stephen was not moved to inventing an answer just to suit him; he owed both of them more than that.

It was Fazakerly, unexpectedly, who expressed a kind of pity, seemingly impervious to irritation but quietly enraged, asking simply:

"What happened to you? Was it my so-called demise that turned your head to all this… these verbal complications?

Stephen stood up to leave.

"Look, I'll come and see you again tomorrow and I'd like you to tell me some more about the war. It doesn't mean I won't think about all of this other stuff but it's not easy, don't you understand, I've been as much in the dark as you, and for longer in a way – it's been half of my life."

It had in fact seemed like forever, as though there had been no existence before that fateful evening ten years ago. No wonder, he sighed. If he prevaricated now it was as a consequence of seeing all the stones laid down over a lifetime about to be turned over. It was perverse of

Fazakerly to expect that he'd behave otherwise. Surely. From the glimpses he'd offered of what *he'd* lived through, how could this old man imagine that he, Stephen, might flip over the whole of his life with one easy sentence?

All these years, he thought, I've been living in a half-light; I've been continually listening and watching for a sign. Some visible change, just a slight sense of movement would have been enough. He recognised how considerable had been the consolation of his imagination. I've been like all those folk who eke out their lives somewhere on the precarious edge of swift and sudden extinction, like the beekeepers who spend their lives on the smoking slopes of Mount Etna. That's what it's been like. Surviving always under a sense of threat that, as the years passed, I risked believing I'd imagined. And it's a way of being that becomes unremarkable; it becomes just the way things are. It was worse for me than it was for him: there was just no explanation, no name for the terror, not even a denial of it, but it was there all the same and I have managed to live a life in spite of it. And now, without warning and when it seemed perhaps that everything was settled, my watchfulness has been vindicated. It has all been brought back again.

But these were inappropriate thoughts to utter with a dead man listening, the corpse behind the shroud that had screened him from his childish misadventures, no longer a corpse but an insistent question.

The old man's eyes watched him, accusing. "My world changed once, twice, maybe three times. The first time," he shrugged, "who really knows the reason why, but I woke to find the landscape so torn and scoured, without even any colour to define it, it was just a flat, featureless nothing; and I knew the cause was a simple misunderstanding of what that world meant to the men who made it waste. The second I have yet to come to, but if you don't know why you did what you did, I tell you, it will prove a stranger story than the one I have yet to finish."

The young man reddened, edging to the door.

"Look, let's say that ten years ago I discovered... it was like I discovered an uncharted fault line, in *my* world."

He was well away now, swelling with the metaphor he had caught from Fazakerly, his tone defensive but secretly hating himself for the ease with which he found himself slipping into self-conscious academic arrogance.

"The whole topography of life around me was altered."

Did he really say that? Wash your mouth out, Stephen. He took a deep breath.

"Finding it should have changed the course of everything. But they wouldn't even look at it; they wouldn't acknowledge it as mine. How the hell then can I begin to explain what I was forcibly, yes forcibly, no less, prevented from understanding?"

He would never forget the beginning of that great and calamitous occlusion, not now, not even another decade hence...

There had been no footfalls on the stairs. He had waited and waited on the edge of his bed with his clean clothes hastily pulled on, wearing long socks hoisted up so tight his toes pinched and with his school shoes tied neatly; it all felt unnatural in the early summer morning and the feeling afforded him a sense of further remoteness. Dressed that way during the summer holiday he could have been up early for an excursion, but his gut had been full of lead instead of the cotton wool of excitement.

And no-one came.

There was a light on outside his room and he peered at long last around the half-closed door, not with courage but wanting it all to end, to end the anguish of suspense and expectation, expecting to find his nemesis creeping silently along the landing but seeing only the bathroom door ajar and the silver sparkle of water dripping from a tap into the basin. It made him yearn to pee. Would there be time to go? Should he go now before someone came for him or would they find him out of his bed and unprepared for seizure, stopped in his tracks on the red patterned runner where he would have lost the composure so necessary for him to see this through? It wouldn't be fitting. The minutes ticked by loudly from his Timex watch with the luminous dial that a jealous friend had warned would give him cancer. The thick green minute hand made the whole room grow phosphorescent as he stared at it and stared at it, urging the minutes up towards the hour and wanting the kitchen door below to open now, at twenty to six, at a quarter to, now at ten to the hour, now, now! The drip of the tap in the bathroom grew louder, even louder as the discomfort in his bladder jabbed at him for attention, so that at last he slipped quietly from off his bed and, blinded by luminescence, felt his way along the banister to the lighted room.

And no-one came.

He sat on the edge of his bed until six forty-five when the day was quite apparent and he was ready for sleep. Did he sleep? He was soon awoken at seven with curiosity at his being fully and formally dressed, his mother busy at the curtains and with tea in a mug, tea and a single biscuit on a tin tray with a spoon for the sugar that she always brought him in a little china bowl, even knowing he did not take sugar, and being overcome with mock foolishness for her mistake, as she was every morning. She did not pursue her enquiry about his state of dress and he heard her a moment later at her own dressing table in the adjacent room, humming quietly and fixing her hair with pins. His father passed his door without entering - he smelled the rosy passage of Cussons aftershave - and the sound of his mother's preparations diminished as their bedroom door was closed. Voices murmured low, seeming distant. Then two pairs of footsteps on the stairs, down to the hallway, retreating wordlessly.

He heard the front door open at seven-thirty and his father's bicycle wheel bump against the boot scraper, the handle of the small attaché case holding his bright clean tools tapping against the carrier as he rode away to work. The mist of fine rain was already evaporating under an early sun and he was drawn to the window, called out by the new effulgence of a fresh summer's morning.

Was he free to go? Was that it? Or was it all a trap? They were making it easy on themselves, leaving him alone, with the whole house pacified by normality so that they wouldn't hear, wouldn't see, wouldn't even have to imagine him being dragged wriggling and screaming to the Black Maria by the large policeman who waited sombrely for him downstairs.

The sound of spent coke being raked out of the grate told him that she, his mother, was still at home. She'd have let the fire die overnight, there being sufficient hot water made for a warm summer's day.

It was all right then, strangely it was all right; he could venture down and not be taken.

Stephen changed quickly out of his serious clothes and into his customary shorts and sandals. It would be ok. Somehow, at least for the moment, there was to be a reprieve, the words of the policeman not meant for him but resonantly ameliorating in the back of his mind: 'it may not come to that…'.

The kind rumour of housework proceeding downstairs was a comfort, and momentarily he imagined that it had all been dreamed, he'd passed in the night into a parallel universe where white was black and good was bad. He'd been his dark side for the brief flickering seconds of a dream and was now awake, secure and out of its reach, the memory of what he'd done in that short and demonic adventure as real only as the imagined landscapes he'd conjure when reading a favourite book.

But the hollow feeling in the pit of his stomach would not fade. Even the echoes of a woken dream did not ache like that, and tall shadows from the previous day rose at his back with the great sword of justice poised, steady, tantalising and terrifying in its long pause. Why would it not fall and let all be done? Whose word had stayed its momentum?

He dared not ask his mother and she did not offer to tell. She gathered plates and a cup from the breakfast table, not speaking, not questioning, gladly distracted by the importunate discussion on the wireless, which buzzed with talk of the test match, of cricket and all things England. Her movement around him at the table was too busy with the paraphernalia of a studied housewife for her to be his confidante.

Her silence is too self-conscious today, he thought; but maybe it was always so, he'd never had cause to question it before.

"I..."

Her eyebrows lifted to beseech him more. A light smile played across her face. Was it for him or for Freddie Truman, England's promised glory heard trumpeting from the wireless, some exaggerated rage at an arcane plot involving silly mid-ons? Her ear remained tuned to the BBC.

"I... has anyone called?"

"It's a bit early for callers, Stephen."

A bit early. Did she mean that news of his crime would not have been circulated yet? He'd imagined a roving pack of newshounds having quickly got wind of the desperate events in this quiet seaside town, they'd have been drawn the mere seventy miles by the scent of curious calamity. No question about it. It might not be their back yard but this was just an easy rural landscape from the outskirts of London. They'd surely be out there right now; they ought to be licking their pencils, sketching out a story in their notepads in readiness for a word from the juvenile monster himself to lend it some authenticity. If not already jostling on the front path he couldn't believe they weren't at this very minute racing towards his house in taxis from the station, first arrivals fiercely disputing command of the red telephone box at the end of the road, pennies hot in their hands, eager to be the first to relay their reports of evil uncovered in the Garden of England.

"So, no-one..."

She shook her head. "It's barely eight o'clock. Weren't your friends away all day...yesterday?"

She was staring out of the tall casement window now, she seemed far away, speaking about his uncomfortable friendship with a boy whose mother measured out her welcome like Maundy Money. He had declined to join their excursion.

"Mmm, weren't they out for the day?" moving with her arms full of clean towels from the clothes-horse and tottering out into the scullery, one hand fumbling in her apron pocket, her fingers tight around the wet handkerchief she had stuffed there hastily when he had come down for breakfast. Her teeth were clenched around the hard sobs that she forced back, gulping them down like hot food in her throat. She couldn't answer him when he called out to her, she wouldn't admit the shame of her grief.

Her face was flushed but composed when she returned; it could have been steam from the laundry in the copper, the back of her hand wiping the long strands of hair away from her face where they had stuck, and only a sniff at swallowed tears giving any clue to her discomfiture.

"Stephen? Sorry, I couldn't hear..."

"Oh, nothing. I was just wondering. Yes, they went to London for the day."

"So there'll be lots to talk about."

"Mmmm." Lots to talk about. There would as a rule, or there should be.

Normally he would have constructed an entire catalogue of events, an elaborate and kaleidoscopic feast of racontage, which grandly he might exchange with his friends in compensation for the day spent alone. Not that he had wanted to go with them to London, but it was an opportunity he had missed all the same; so he would have had to balance their gain and produce better tales to tell in retaliation for the extravagance of their own adventures. It would have been a really special day he'd had, a day when by odd coincidence or unlucky fortune his friends would have missed the most amazing and serendipitous incidents they could ever have imagined might take place during that whole, long and safely tranquil summer, reserved by fate for him alone and never to be repeated in the rest of those placid, shared days before school began again. They would be expecting nothing less. They would be in ready anticipation of hearing what his nonchalant "nothing special" had really disguised, what extraordinary exploits he had been into whilst they were away. It was always so, with any of them, and no-one ever cared to question the bombast and exaggeration of deeds said to have been done in the inventive hours of childish solitude.

But he could say nothing of yesterday. Not that. Is that what she meant? Surely not.

"I wasn't planning to go out today. I thought maybe you might like some help with something. Perhaps we could have a chat."

"No. Really. You go on out." She was hustling away again to stir clothes that bubbled in the copper. "It's a fine day," she called, "a shame to waste it after all the rain we've had this past month."

So was that it then? Whether it had been done or not, whether a dream or a nightmare, that was it. All over. The words took up a circular dance in his head. Never mind, it's all over now; there, there, never you mind. They were echoing comforts, dizzying stereotypes. Don't worry yourself, don't cry, don't fret, poor child, poor thing. Over and over. He'd have to accept their words. They wouldn't stop until he did.

But his mother offered him none of those tireless and timeless maternal panaceas. All over? Meaningless echoes of normality were all she offered him. It was the *lingua franca* that defined her.

This was a first experience he was not ready to admit, confronting the yawning gulf between them, and he found himself on a high cliff with nothing at his back and no stairway down. "Mother!" he screamed.

She was too far away to hear his cry for help.

As much as any family he knew, hopefully more, he'd thought of them as close, closer even than he would be too embarrassed to tell without sounding soft. It was the way things were and always would be. It was all he knew and so too it was unquestionably the way he imagined it to be elsewhere, in other families. But thinking about it now, when thinking had become a matter so urgently compressed, so unusually focused, maybe he'd had it wrong all along. Maybe everything he'd believed he'd known was…well, wrong, misunderstood. Was it that he'd been asleep his entire childhood and missed the telling of the true story? Deaf. Yes, that's what he'd been and he hadn't known. Or his thoughts had been elsewhere. Sleepwalking and deaf too, unaware of the real nature of reality passing close by for an astonishingly numb eleven years. He shook with the chill of that thought. Wouldn't that explain everything?

He thought then of all those secret things he'd done, those childish thoughts and deeds he'd tried or dared and not always liked but believed that once back behind that front door at the end of the day, whatever they had seemed like, away from the street and the world outside they did not matter, they were separate, apart, just a sequence of events that he had looked upon from a distance without ever really having become a true participant. Perhaps they had been more real after all, and this, this place, this home, this was more the fantasy.

And not only the dubious and distasteful things, for they were only incidental and he had covered them quickly, displacing them from their insistent presence with preferred images of domestic familiarity; but what about all the rest, the strange and exciting taste and touch and sound of juvenile perception, the daily thrill from first knowledge and discovery with which he knowingly indulged himself, for he knew it all self-consciously? Real, yes, but only privately so. Not the stuff of reality.

He would describe in later years how keenly if perhaps unusually aware he had been as a boy of the buzz from his young and undulled palette of senses, every day bringing him a torrent of vibrant tumult that, like the synthesis of a stimulant, gave accent to his experience. To Stephen's ears the volume of the world was turned up to maximum, there was always a clear, blood-thumping immediacy that could invest even the most insignificant detail with glorious richness. He knew the rush of pleasure that followed as his own way of defining experience; but real, lasting truth? Indeed, it was because of that inhesion, because of the sheer, dazzling, roaring clamour to his receiving senses, that none of it had ever actually picked him up or drawn him in to its embrace. Life was over-defined, like a play dramatically limned under limelight or the crisp distinction of cinema, large, brilliant and, more to the point, remote, so that despite its force it remained unthreatening and, eventually, quiescent. It was a game he played.

The flood of light and colour and the thunder of sound that accompanied his journey through those early years were so extraordinary that it would have needed only a simple turn on light feet to have taken him to the world of the phantasmagorical. And so it was that as he lay upon his pillow at the end of a day's distance he could close it away like the glossy plates in a book. It had been seen, done, passed through and safely enjoyed.

All that then was real to him, the child, but at the same time unreal as he reflected upon it from the small and safe reality of the house to which he turned each night for assurance; the pages straining open, bursting upon him so that the images he'd captured in a sense quite passively were set free to jostle and race in his brain, a riot in his head from where they would not be expelled. Ever. But he could move on, with his trawl a store of memories and his flesh unbruised.

But now, oh what had become of reality now, when the book where he had filed all those episodes from real life was just a silly autistic fancy?

His family offered no retreat at all from the disorder that bayed beyond their solid front door. Some part of it had followed him in last night and was now insisting that white was indeed black or black was white, or both, and this place that he lived *was* the parallel universe of a nightmare that wasn't a nightmare.

This chaos of his thoughts would not easily settle but in the unrestrained jumble of their new liberty it was easy to believe a new truth might be found. Like an intuitive solution achieved without the hard grind of logic; an impression of truth made from the tumbling grains of thought that whirled and clung together.

Stephen's head spun. He felt nausea. A spiralling vortex of receding light hummed with the images he had set loose. His mother's arms were quickly around him, holding him close, so tight he felt his head might be pulled off as he half knelt on the kitchen chair, half tip-toed on the bare floor, suspended at an awkward angle and dependent on her clasping him to her breast.

"Lord save us Stephen," came her steamy breath next his cheek. "What a dreadful thing. What a terrible, terrible thing. It's all been such a shock."

He slid onto the chair, alert again. At last, here was something he wanted to hear. She was brushing the front of her apron smooth with the backs of her hands, her eyes red, but smiling.

"But we must thank the Lord that all's to be mended, Stephen, all will come to rights in the end under his gaze. I had no doubts from the start. No doubts in you."

She leant back into the scullery, catching up a bowl of rice crispies from the draining board. "Now, you eat that and you'll feel a lot better." She poured milk and sliced a banana onto the cereal. "Lord knows, this has been a terrible thing for us to deal with – all of us – such a shock. What you have made of it God only knows. But time will mend."

He spooned rice crispies and banana into his mouth, slowly, thinking rather than eating, not tasting at all. So that was it? Nothing was going to happen. They'd decided. They'd heard from the police and they'd all agreed amongst themselves. They'd keep it to themselves. Nothing to be done. No point. Perhaps he was too young. He didn't know anything of the mysterious adult calibrations of justice.

He was, then, perhaps free. The town would let him pass amongst them for it had been agreed: he was unexpectedly free and judged blameless.

"OK then. I'm going out."

He waited. He gave her time to relent but she did not reappear from the scullery where she had gone to wring out his father's steaming shirts. See: nothing was going to happen.

"I'm going up the beach." Like yesterday, just going in search of innocent adventure.

"See you." He swallowed the last of the milk and slid down from his chair. Free. He couldn't yet grasp it. It was contrary to all his expectations but it seemed he was free to go amongst the world. It was over and he would not be called to account. He'd misunderstood the rules, that's all.

"See you about lunchtime." He waited in the doorway but there was no recall. He walked noisily to the front door and made a great play of opening the latch. "'Bye."

"Good-bye, Stephen" came her reply, made distant by the sound of water running in the sink..

This then was reality and there was indeed no structure to it at all. The dire events of the previous day had become a riddle to which no solution would be found using his old rules. Having been their unprotesting instrument he had expected simple retribution, but no, it would seem that his act had joined him to them; it was all a part of the same thing, something elaborate and more complex than he could for the moment unravel. Something wiser, adult, clever. Which explained why, of course, they had understood and he had not. His parents. The policeman. They had access to some other kind of code that would make sense of it all. The realisation that there were possibly no hard and fast rules made him feel giddy again.

He couldn't readily grasp something as momentous as that; the revelation was too huge to take in at one gulp. Moreover, even after all that thrashing about, at the back of his mind was a deposit of recent memories that was still burning, and whatever the contraindications, he would not easily believe that yesterday's wickedness could count for so little. Stephen shut the front door quietly, now that he'd been let go he had the feeling that he was stealing away.

The surprise of a fine morning had caught everyone unawares and he found the promenade all but deserted. It was in any case too early for sunbathers. The large grey pebbles of the upper beach had been ramped up dark and cold by a succession of tides, and the shingle where the waters had recently receded was black and rheumy with salt. Later in the day it would be a warm, bright place, the rank smell of seaweed burned away; but right now, as he jumped the three or four feet down from the sea wall, it felt as if he was trampling over the unhealed wounds of a shore that had been licked open by an irritated ocean.

He had sat there for much of the previous morning, waiting for the sky to clear away the chill of unseasonal drizzle, the puddling lift of the sea swelling powerfully around the breakwater, its invitation to swim darkened by the sinister hue painted upon its surface by the cloud cover. The sea became a dangerous place to his imagination when the sun was not shining and, if bold enough to try it, he would swim with a great unease. Under a bright, clear sky he might go carefree for a hundred yards, two hundred, perhaps even more, out where the water became a deep, cobalt blue and the muddying swirl of sand and human slops at the shoreline where bathers crowded would seem little more than a far, milky hemline to its glittering mantle. Out where it became suddenly very cold, in currents that passed by the flotsam of the beach without ever touching, he could look back, feeling himself swept past the land on an arc that would take him all around the low headland of Dungeness and on, until after hours of drifting he would be delivered into the distant Atlantic, never having touched at the shore again.

Out that far there was serious swimming between him and the land, out there where he could look back as he climbed the curve of the world, seeing the hill behind the town rise up over the tops of the tall fringing hotels that lined the sea front. The hill rose up directly north, with its church tower a mile or two distant, watching him from the mass of its narrow, cobbled passageways; and, if he dared to tease out more the space between them, splashing further into the buoyant sea, he could see the impressionistic blur of the far North Downs peering down at him from above the forest at Saltwood, and making a second tier to his new horizon.

At that point he would feel both a frisson of fleeting panic and the delight of self-determination, having almost lost touch with the land, out of earshot of the bathers on its edge and totally at the disposal of his own resources, where a suspicion of cramp in his shins called for urgent and immediate attention and the pounding of his heartbeat was a motor he listened to attentively for the assurance of its continued and regular rhythm. But knowing he could swim back, under the sun, he could make it, in time. It was a fair challenge to his young strength and skill, not without danger but with the risks open and seemingly honest under the brightness of the sun.

But not when the sun was absent. For just as the sun spanned the sea and the earth, making a bridge between both worlds, when the sun did not shine he fancied that the sea would be free to exert its hold upon him. It would begin merely by vexing him, by confusing his course with spattering crests of white water thrown in his face, then sending spirals of freezing currents up from the far depths to numb him, stealthily weakening his sure pattern of forearm, breath and forearm as he trailed across its surface. And having unseated his confidence it would despatch unrecognisable shapes of weed and stinging jellyfish, flotsam made into the appearance of serpent and shark's fin, unexplained shadows brushing his legs, all to terrorise him and cause him to flounder. Thus caught in the chaos from its darker waters he would find its seductions laid bare, the swell shifting and opening to reveal the entangling mess of old breakwaters and the rusted scaffolding that had once supported a wartime minefield, no longer armed and explosive but a web of broken pipework where he would struggle to avoid the torn steel, and in struggling he would be entrapped and devoured by the maw of the rising tide.

Today there were no such terrors. Where the phantoms of the sea had thrashed on the wet beach in the night, the rising heat of the morning was already sending their traces skyward in a haze of tangy steam. Besides, there would be no more such terrors ever again now that he had begun to decipher reality. They had already been relegated to the patina of an imagination with which he had once decorated the dreamscape of his waking hours, but which was now looking colourless and discredited. If only he had known all this yesterday.

But without the events of yesterday there would have been no knowing. In company he may have ventured into yesterday's leaden waters. Together with his friends no words would have been spoken of their cold and awkward emergence into the cool air. Theirs were the thoughtless pleasures of bathing, for it was summer and they would swim as a matter of right whatever the weather, sitting afterwards huddled under tar-stained towels, foolishly tweaking the hair on each others' goose-pimpled flesh, sneaking a cheap *Woodbine* beneath the sea wall and feeling brave and unmastered. They would have sat for hours in rude contemplation of the future, where they hung slowly overbalancing towards the edge of adolescence, absorbed by their poignant consciousness of the process itself, and in such a state safe from the consequences of actual participation in the rough ravages of the grown-up world.

Warren was the oldest and increasingly irregular member of their group, a naïve fourteen, but already tutored in the scurrilous imagery of the secondary schoolyard. His startlingly lewd postulations enthralled and frightened them all. For Stephen, a whole day spent in his company as well as that of his priggish mother had been too unattractive a price to pay for a day trip to London. He would goad Stephen, calling him a nutcase, a spastic, and feed his eager imagination with dark untruths, later to be exposed of course, and leaving him humbled, but somehow prospering from the jealousy the others felt for the older boy's apparent ease with the world. Yet even with the elder Warren to cajole and cackle at them, in their huddle on the beach they would have made sense of their confused interpretations of the world simply by not attempting any confrontation with logic or half-understood fact. They would pass the morning away unharmed and harmless, their hours filled with stories of female encounters imagined, persuasively embellished with alley images glimpsed in passing, leaping with equal fervour into consummate descriptions of the sail-karts they were building in back yards and who had nicked what and how often from the open counters in Woolworths. Consumed by the confusions and illusions of child and adult, they were on the brink of both ages where it did not matter whether they were looking back or forward, they were cocooned mid-times and journeying without cause other than the journey. In their company Stephen felt resilient and safe from unfamiliar temptation.

He chinked pebbles in his hands, feeling the sun warm on his neck and the dreamy curl of the surf soft and reassuring. But there was another taste to the air now, a new presence he could not name, a freshly astringent layer revealed between the flavours of indolent summer that made him feel edgy and unsettled. It was all coming apart, his world was unravelling and had been since this past night and this morning. He was alone again, with no-one to share the discovery, none to admit it with him and acknowledge the difference that had been wrought.

A decade later Stephen paused at the door he had a moment ago needed so urgently to pass through, finding himself caught on the broken edge of an idea and demanding: "What was a sham?"

"Why, the way we were then of course," came the old man's reply, unhesitating. "The way we were to ourselves. The stories we'd tell – agh! Do you know, after the war – not my war that is, but your father's – it's said we had a period not just of austerity but honesty. We were all come together in the land of hope and glory. Social justice for the heroic nation, that's what we were told to expect. Equality. There would be harmony in adversity. Well, I don't know, it didn't seem any different to me. It was all a sham, a pretence. And I was no different. Thought I was, mind, but no. Worse than most, I don't doubt."

"And that's it?"

"It was enough, wasn't it? One great big pretence. A cover up. A sham. That's what we do, though, isn't it? That's how we get by. Otherwise," he made a quick slicing movement with the edge of his hand across his throat, "finito. Couldn't handle it. Only, sometimes the pretence becomes too huge to bear. It's all still there, all the hidden truth, all the muck back of your eyeballs. There's no denying what's what and what's been, whatever we might say about it. No-one can pretend forever."

"And that's what it felt like when I...when your house was burned?"

"It seemed that way. Something like."

"And before, in France? When you were rescued. That was all pretence too, I suppose."

"Mm." Fazakerly screwed his face up tight. "It was different then. Too much was uncovered. Much too much. But it was wartime, wasn't it, and you can lose yourself in war. The rules all change, see. That's why, pardon my French, everyone is so fucked up by it. All the cracks were opened up and we spent the rest of our lives papering them over."

- FOUR -

ON VICTORY IN EUROPE DAY he took down the blackout from his ten circumferal windows, shaking out the dust and desiccated insects that had accumulated there over the past six years, the concealed lace curtains behind them rotted away and the brocade of the heavy drapes faded. With all ten casements thrown wide, the Round House resembled a buccaneer's rig with its gun ports agape, the flaking panels of its curved flanks matted with the scum of battle and a never-ending journey, it had been unpainted for so long and buffeted by successive winter south-westerlies. But this was a day not designed for fighting, nor for embarkation on distant voyages, and the only artillery to be heard was from the rise of scrub and gorse behind the town, where men and boys sought rabbit and pigeon for the pot to feed the day's celebration of peace in our time. The clatter of shotguns, infrequent and stuttering, echoed across the quiet streets and gardens right up to the sea wall, where it was discharged upon the sea, having first passed through Fazakerly's north-facing windows and been despatched thence to all points of the compass east, west and south, through the array of open and unencumbered chambers.

When Fazakerly had built his house he commissioned an architect from London. Not that he shunned the local men for their professional inadequacy, not that he resented (as he knew he would) their questions about the motive for his design and what he was doing in their midst, constructing such a folly, and why. All that would come anyway, he knew, for he could not ship in from distant parts all the joiners and painters and divers other trades that would necessarily make a house, and he was in any case by now deceptively artful in the cause of maintaining privacy in the face of enquiry. His London architect was a military man, most recently engaged in the design of trench fortifications, limited by materials and time to deal in simple ramparts, escarpments and subterranean fastnesses, but with a penchant for the more splendid tradition of his craft and a relish for the language of fortress, machicolation and counterscarp. It was his fascination with the work of his forebears that had brought him to the Kent coast, and it was during one enthusiastic exploration of the Martello towers that calibrate the reaches between Folkestone and New Romney that he encountered Fazakerly, a wild-haired, angular figure who had climbed to the roof of tower number 15 with a telescope and considerable disregard for his own safety. It was here that the architect first discovered him, sprawled dangerously close to the edge of the downward-sloping parapet, his right elbow jabbed into the tarred surface to provide purchase and a prop for the telescope, with the viewfinder of the extended instrument pressed into one eye, his other eye screwed up into a tight red knot, muttering loudly and drawing in sharp breaths as he scoured whatever horizon he had reached on the French side of the Channel.

Prompted by shocked concern and a fair understanding of these Napoleonic defences, the architect immediately set to persuading Fazakerly, with as much beckoning and cajoling as he could summon in the face of looming disaster, that he should give up his surveillance, for he was all too expertly aware that the angle of the parapet had been particularly designed as that least likely to afford prolonged advantage. But his attempts to explain this aspect of the building to Fazakerly served merely to frustrate his evidently unwelcome rescue bid, a patient description of the rationale for these coastal forts as a means of deterring incursions from France only alarming him further, on account of its startlingly dramatic consequences. The rising pitch of protestations it engendered, together with Fazakerly's frantic jabbing of a bony hand in the general direction of the Pas-de-Calais, described a state of mounting frenzy that was frighteningly inappropriate to their perch at the top of the building.

But success came at last and it was with Fazakerly's thin fingers firmly clasped in the grip of the astonished architect, and with the telescope folded away, that fate moved the pieces on the table that day, these two strangers unpredictably joined for a while in realising the ambitions of one and preserving the conscience of the other.

Fazakerly's single storey Martello was constructed entirely from wood. He would admit no brick or stone save for the chimney and hearth. Wood, he explained, was alive. Long after curing it would continue to sing when the wind pressed close against its curves, and the warming and cooling of the sun would cause the shingles of the low vaulted roof to tick and shuffle through an endless cycle of tumescence and deflation. The house resonated with the natural life of the world from which it had grown. Its construction would be a source of comfort.

"More than that", he'd exclaim, with a look of secret satisfaction, "you can hear who's coming. Not so with stone, nor brick or concrete. But with wood I can know what's what."

From this Round House, this pillbox, this weatherboard rotunda, he would survey the years. As it spun through the seasons nothing and no-one could approach it without first being spied from its eyeing fenestrations. The tradesmen or travellers who out of necessity or guile approached the house would be bewildered by its geometry, for where in a round house sat mid-point in a half acre of grass should they find the door, with no path to guide them, and he could pick them off at will with declining waves of his hand as he passed elusively from window to window. His alliance with the dreaming architect had produced a fastness that would deter all manner of fascinated inquiry, save the inquisitive glances and stares that became commonplace from the safe distance of the low wall at the road. But as the glee of this mischief paled – mostly in the face of thwarted officialdom – he fetched fifty cubits of pebbles from the beach and pricked a way with them through the grass from the road to his single door, flush in the east facing wall, where he set bright watchful eyes of coloured glass, strung on wires from a gazebo over the platform he made out of bleached driftwood. No-one and nothing would reach his door without shivering the bones of this ivory veranda, its reverberations aspirant in the crystal tinkle of coloured lights that would unfailingly flare discovery.

Little of the world beyond the block walls reached his ears in the military hospital at Étaples. Men marched in uniform groups upon the garrison square; they marched alone to the slamming front entrance, bringing packages in to the medical staff, arms swinging, their pace unbroken by the stiff, spring-loaded doors, left right, left right, uninterrupted, shiny boots tight on the track they'd been set upon by order and the desire to be ordered. The sudden and conclusive concussion of a dozen soldiers coming to attention on the parade ground outside described a punctuation that Fazakerly saw rather than heard through the window, a movement at the periphery of his vision, a summation of prescribed coincidence, nothing more, not even alerted by its singular echo as the arriving messenger delivered salutation and messages to the nurse by his bed. All the comings and goings in the military compound were matters in which he did not share.

After little more than a month he had ceased his regular excursions to the gate and no longer dodged the rattling traffic of trucks, wheeled guns and motorcycles that seemed to be permitted a necessary frenzy of purpose between dawn and dusk, with men offloading armfuls of weaponry and munitions. If he was of a mind to, he could still study them through the window: crated mortars lifted down in heavy green boxes with rope handles, engine parts wrapped in oil cloth, bales of wire on short turning posts heaped next to baskets of fresh bread, vegetables tumbled in old canvass wraps and light hessian sacks stuffed full with cheeses. The crates, ironware and baskets would all be recycled during the day until by sundown the flow of vehicles and men was slowed until it had imperceptibly ceased, with trucks, field guns, bikes and trailers stood at ease in regimented silence in the twilight, ready only to start up their earnest motion again at first light and new orders. But none of this he heard now. The determined energies of the day beyond his window were not matters for which he had any criticism; they simply belonged to somewhere else, a place he had no thoughts of visiting and he had forgotten to ask himself why he might.

Activity for Fazakerly was concentrated in the flicker of an eyebrow as his nurse glanced briefly towards the advancing messenger, her slight grimace barely visible and as soon replaced by a smile for her patient, the quick shuffle of her stiff apron that she used to conceal her womanliness like the mark of an apostrophe separating her from the messenger's onward passage. Her face was light and open, rendering a constant sparkle of gaiety from eyes that suggested to Fazakerly an almost child-like presence within, although the form that was bound tight in her military uniform implied that another, more luxurious spirit might dwell there. He had no wish that it should be disclosed.

He was afraid. She had been assigned to him for three weeks now and he was afraid that one morning she would be gone, posted on. That was the way of impermanence that informed all life at the base. And with her departure the small warm brightness that had begun to grow in his head would be extinguished.

Her name was Hermione and she did not belong in this rough, rude place. She was of good family, not aristocracy but people with enough unbroken lineage for them to enjoy an assured and quiet belief in the eventual triumph over chaos, not disposed to be intellectuals but blessed with a natural discernment that they seemed to draw from the air itself, sustained through generations by a solid sense of what then was middle England, and they knew it without crowing or broadcast to be right and sound and lasting.

Fazakerly feared for her. Sensing that he was in the presence of an inviolate purity made him ache with dread. Her gentle and profoundly sincere interest in his recovery had filled him with a new sense of hope, but he also found himself hating her in a way that he could never describe, even to himself.

The other nurses, there were six of them in all, were sharp young quines thriving in that brief period of ragged bloom before they would adopt the bloated demeanour of menial and drudge. They were fatuous of conversation and noisy without import, although no doubt all believed themselves to be well meaning. He watched them lean in the frame of the ward doorway when no tasks were required of them, smoking and preening themselves, chattering like birds in full display before the drilling squaddies; he studied them in the ward where they were hopelessly and shamelessly abashed by the passage of the young medics whose routines they trailed with unconscious servility, a gaggle of red-faced nudges and whispered laughter to which Hermione did not belong.

Fazakerly was not touched by them. They were of no more substance than poppies blown against a window in a storm, where they would thrash and tear like red and purple tissue and then be snatched away. They were an irruption from a world whose offerings he had declined. But Hermione, he quickly resolved, was of another world altogether; she had been sent to him, he was sure, sent as the bearer of that same restoring golden light he had briefly known as he floated to consciousness in that slurried field somewhere on the outskirts of Torhout. He had noticed that first, the light in her face, before any features came into focus, and he constantly wondered if others saw it too, wondering that she might be taken from him, snatched away for the prize to be found there.

She sat with him daily, reading from a book, never with news from home or reports of the action at the front - which he refused to hear, clapping his hands over large ears, fiercely shaking his head whenever it was offered by an orderly or visiting messenger. It wasn't important what she read, at first; it was the tone of her voice that mattered, the shadow of her hair across her neck, her eager expression of concern as she touched him awake at his wrist, he having sat watching through half-closed eyes, drawing on her presence with deep, silent breaths. He read her movements, storing them in the deepest, safest places of his restoring mind; he knew her like a camera knows its subject, every angle of every day together framed and filed away, so that he might replicate her in his mind's eye when she was gone, as soon he feared she might be.

Yet whilst she was the stuff of his recovery he wanted also to take her up and dash her to the tiled floor, to smash her pure form. It was too much for him to bear, too dangerous to look upon and endure. This was the agony that taunted his regaining senses.

Staffing in the hospital had been reduced as more urgent assistance was required closer to the enduring futility of battle, and Hermione had become Fazakerly's sole ministry, the other nurses being less eager to confront his invisible mental trauma than to wrap amputations or bathe contusions, which services required only passing dedication, but she seemed not to be daunted by the more expectant demands of a fractured psyche. Such, he supposed, was the confidence of a sure soul. When not reading from a book she would engage him in animated conversation, and the inchoate discussions with nursing staff that had first raised him from his trauma all those weeks past now became focused, he was no longer indiscriminate and devouring, and the words he returned to her were thoughtful, increasingly philosophical and carefully, gradually provocative.

"But I couldn't dare to take it to the edge, of course, she wasn't up to that. It was just a bit of jockeying for position, a bit of fun, really. I could tell her limits; I'm pretty sure she thought she knew mine too."

They sat in the afternoon sun on the green painted bench under the window, the hollyhocks that crowded there showing signs of drying out, they produced lazy knocking sounds whenever the two men moved against them. Fazakerly had dressed and seemed more alive in an old but brilliantly white suit of linen, a green plastic card player's visor pulled down over his eyes. Stephen smiled at the harmless incongruity and wished he could offer a cigar to the old man.

"She was no fool though?"

"No, no fool." He sighed, rather painfully Stephen thought. "But she was an innocent, true enough. That's what I loved about her, her genuine and unpractised innocence. Hated her for it too, of course."

"You hated her?"

"Not her, really. Me. I knew it was wrong for this world, you see – it was unsustainable. Didn't tell her that and I still don't know if that were right or wrong. But yes, I suppose I did blame her for being that way." He sighed again, visibly troubled by the memory. "It was unfair of me, course it was; she was so good to me, made me whole."

"But, when you were whole, as you put it, you didn't let her know, did you, what you were thinking?"

"Like I said, she was easily capable of handling the thrust and parry of lively conversation. She'd been raised on it like the good country stock she'd come from. Her father wasn't typical though, being a painter – not an artist as such, but a commercial painter, worked on signs, illustrations for books, all that kind of stuff – but he was educated, that's for sure, she knew from him all about the great movements, art and literature, plenty of history. It hadn't spoiled her, mind, all that learning. Just filled her with wonder, it seemed to me. What a picture she was, she was happy just to be able to tell me about it all, pleased to have someone to listen – well, not just listen either, someone with whom to look at it all again, from other angles, and not defensively. That was her father in her."

"A modern woman, then? Liberated."

"Aaaah", the old man sighed, his teeth clenched hard together. "No. A modern woman? No, you see she was a true ingénue. No sophistication at all. No real critical thought when it came down to it."

"And that's why you hated her?"

Fazakerly glared at him from under the broad green shade, his hands tight and white around the open slats in the seat.

"Fool! Listen, will you! Observe."

They were no mind games they played during those weeks of his recovery; it was more akin to what in present day parlance might be described as a process of normalisation. He found Hermione's calm, intelligent infusion of thoughts and words the perfect antidote to his trauma; it set him apart from the horrors of war and the rigours of social combat. But she was not armed for battles either military or intellectual, and he respected her non-combatancy, never taking their discourse to the serious limits of disputation. Instead they spoke of books and writers that had made their mark upon them, marvelling together as they exchanged thoughts and words from works long forgotten, now rediscovered in a time that itself demanded the suspension of disbelief. There were few books in the hospital that might command their interest for long, but a copy of Poe's *Contes de Mystère et Imagination* had been rescued from a burnt out cottage in the town and as they pored over the blackened pages they both thrilled at the author's skill in summoning images that could both unsettle and delight.

She shared memories too that were new to Fazakerly, of paintings seen in galleries across the cities of Europe, and they both wondered with easy concern whether they would still be there when the war was won. Her recall of these cultural encounters was rich and seductive but, he soon realised, she was untutored in the consciences, the often bloody deeds, the narcotic and tortured lives from which invariably sprang the remarkable artistic creations that had captivated her. When their thoughts engaged their present situation she spoke with great regret, knowing the war itself to be a tragedy, but she accepted its mysterious inevitability as if it were an act of God, not the consequence of the crushing fallibility of men, and Fazakerly was in no doubt that it would be fruitless for him to pursue with her the motives of those who had sent so many in sacrifice to this foreign field.

Life for Hermione was intriguing; unfailingly it brought her a series of magical tales to tell, feeding and delighting her with its feast of fine flavours. It was also danger and fright; but the lungs, lights and liver that heaved and pumped and boiled beneath its surface, the calumny and counterfeit and conspiracy that gave rude seasoning to its expressions of existence, these were not spoken of between them, for she could not admit such unnecessary injury to the store of wonder that was her knowledge of the world.

She was goodness personified and, whilst he basked in the light she had awakened, Fazakerly could feel the corrosive lustre of her sweet innocence.

"It suited me, I suppose. Jesus, it was what I needed after that other place, and I'm not going to deny it now. She was a treasure."

All this time and still he could recall the intensity and the fragility of her presence. The ambiguity of her nature was plain but he had felt no desire to open the doors to the world beyond their private conversations. She had sealed him within the bounds of her restorative embrace and whenever he blundered against them he recoiled from pushing them back.

"Now, d'you see?"

"Mmm." He didn't of course. For Stephen it had all the remoteness of another man's dream.

"But I'd never expected to get that far. Not after all that death, and thinking I was a goner. Then, all this....peace. It was unreal."

Fazakerly took a folded handkerchief from his top pocket, pushed back the visor, and patted at his brow. He squinted, not against the sudden sun but into the distance.

"It was reality of course, I can see that now, but it scared the shit out of me, knowing that, that it was all part of the same thing."

The daily hubbub on the parade ground had dwindled rapidly over the period of the last three or four days. Military trucks were leaving and not returning and the routine delivery of provisions had been relegated to the occasional and infrequent farm cart. There hung over the whole base a sense of impending departure that reached even Fazakerly in his sequestered convalescence. Food rations were conspicuously spare and other supplies seemed to have dried up. He caught snatches of complaint from the remaining members of the medical team, whose strict clinical regime had faltered; they were having to leave dressings unchanged, and a spirit of neglect was beginning to settle where previously the ward had functioned as an exemplar of order and duty.

"We'll be moving you soon", whispered Hermione, passing swiftly now that she was needed to share the routines of the smaller nursing party, only three of them left from the original team. "Get you home at last."

She hurried on, crisp and alert in her uniform with the starched white apron and the ruched scarlet belt. This sudden incursion from the world beyond and the stark reminder of the nurse's fundamental business of bandage and blood sent Fazakerly into a deep silence. But he sat patiently for the day, and several more, and there was no preparation made for his exit.

One morning he awoke to an unbroken rumbling, grumbling like far thunder that drummed in his ears, but not in his ears. He knew it for the sound of warfare. Throughout the day a monotonous fog of bombardment stole up from the distant horizon, its resonance peaking with the clack and clatter of small arms, but having established itself as a permanent background din it grew neither louder nor faint. The words *retreat* and *withdrawal* were no longer hushed by senior staff when uttered in their presence, yet no orders arrived to decamp and, after a while, with the distance of fighting seeming not to have shortened any further, there was a general resolve to stay put in the absence of any new directions to the contrary.

But there were no more lengthy and animated conversations to inspire Fazakerly, or to console his new isolation, for everyone's attention was consumed by the feeling that they had been abandoned. There was little movement beyond the hospital building save for the squad of uniformed engineers who were marched dutifully, all day it seemed, upon the square of the parade ground, out to the main gate where all eyes were turned right to peer down the empty road and back to their place beneath the union flag. They were extras suspended in an act with a role to play but where the curtain stayed down: men who had been wounded, repaired, refreshed and ready not to return home but to be turned to the front once again, to mine the mud and brace the wheels that bore the great guns, trapped in a trial from which they could not break and which would eventually break them.

But for the moment they were on hold, had been for many weeks now, resting, recuperating, charging their energies for the engines of a war whose theatre had at last left them behind. Forgotten. Left, right, left, right, wheeling past the ammunition compound, empty now but sealed with brass padlocks; left, right, along the hospital wall, eyes left to scan for the nurses who would make their own manifest parade, but they had been too apprehensive to venture forth since the barrage of ordnance had begun; left, right, boots gruff on the gritted paths between the box privet and marigold beds, gone to seed, no-one caring to notice the passing of their bloom. Left, right, dull, right, tedious tread, around and around and back again. Atten'shun! Cigarettes, almost gone; orders, orders, when would they arrive and release them?

"Can it be that they have forgotten us?" Hermione brought him water in an enamel cup. To Fazakerly her question was immediately abstract, it threw him back to that cold place of mud. She waited, attentive eyes watching him, but he had no answer, only a thirst for the source of bright animation in her face.

"Miss! Miss!" Shapes looming at the window, knuckles rapping at the glass turned her away from him. "Spare any tea for us, love?" The quartermaster-sergeant holding a caddy painted with images from imperial India, up-ending it, shaking it, pointing with his other hand. "We're out." He spoke with exaggerated movements of his mouth so that she could read him through the glass, pointing at Fazakerly's cup: "Spare any?"

The window went up and the cold, smoky afternoon air rushed in to the ward, Hermione on tip-toe. "Sorry, no, it's just water. We're out too, it would seem."

"What a pretty pass, eh love. No tea for Tommy. They're not going to be a happy band, my sappers, when I tell them that. Still, you're a sight for sore eyes, ain't you darling." He winked, staring past Hermione into the ward. "Never mind, all you've got are a few poor loonies to deal with, not like me. Hey!" he called to Fazakerly, "you're all right in there mate." He winked again, nodding his head toward Hermione. "OK love," stepping back from the window, "didn't mean to startle you. Best be off and see what they're up to now. No rations you see. Getting a bit Bolshie. I wish …" He frowned, suddenly serious, then he was away, the caddy folded in his left forearm, his right arm swinging stiffly as he marched.

She saw but did not hear the barrack door close behind him, the ward window had been sealed tight again against the foul air and echoes from the front.

As evening drew in and darkness suppressed the noise of gunfire, routines were followed as best they were able, temperatures were taken and pulses read; a sparse meal of chicken and potatoes was mustered, which Fazakerly ate in silence in his chair next to his bed.

"That's it, I'm afraid," said the orderly who came to take away his empty dish. He reached for the tray. "Your last supper. We'll have to send the MO out hunting tomorrow!"

The crack of a rifle barely preceded the dull thud of his skull shattering beneath the skin, the tinkle of broken glass that accompanied it, like applause, somehow delayed by the shock in his eyes as he struggled to stay upright. A roar that was not applause came through the broken window, a bright flickering of orange flames, the random rattle of pistol shots liberating the fire that now reached out through the stricken barrack shutters, and the voices of agitation and grief, all came in a shockwave that burst into the ward before the orderly could complete his lifeless and futile dive to the floor.

There was scuffling in the dark of the parade ground, shouts, commands, boots running off into the distance. A momentary silence was broken by voices chanting outside, close by in the darkness, rough laughter accompanying a counting down from ten, then screaming in his ear as Fazakerly watched the head of the quartermaster-sergeant burst through the web of crazed window-pane, eyes black and aghast, launched like a missile from the trebuchet of a dozen vicious hands and impaled at the throat on the spiteful shards of glass. The screaming went on and on. There were hands pulling at the shoulders of the young nurse who had run to catch the felled orderly only to face the exploding blasphemy at the window, and who shrieked and shrieked without seeming to catch breath. Hermione's hands, clasped around trembling shoulders, hands that fell away to her sides as the ward doors crashed open, not raised in supplication toward the swift motion of men, raptors, who swooped with a lethal economy of movement across the floor as they grasped and gathered her up, her legs flailing, her broad red belt snaking across the wounded room like a great skein of blood.

"But these were our men, our soldiers?"

"Yes. England's finest."

"I don't believe you." Stephen felt the cold, black sickness of outrage rising in him that always accompanied discoveries like this, desperate anxiety moving swiftly to imagined heroics and deeds of rescue. Images of the cenotaph, proud men marching, poppies, berets, some in wheelchairs, extraordinary arrays of medals won, and the clusters of honourable old soldiers in their strange crimson coats, down from London for a day at the coast. No, it wasn't so.

"I don't believe you."

"It's the way of the world. Mind you, I couldn't have said that at the time. Not at all."

"But you, I suppose you are going to tell me…" – Fazakerly would have been the warrior restored, galvanised by the moment, rising up with avenging fists flying and guns blazing – "surely you…"

"No. Not me. It was all too big for me then. Besides.."

"You said you hated her."

"No, not that. You're confusing cause and motivation. Surely you of all people will see that. No, I was useless."

Stephen shifted an inch or two back along the seat. He leaned away. This old man; there was something unwelcome come amongst them; there was some taint now. Why should he owe him any explanation of his own unproud deeds? He ought to go now. Go and not return. There would be more of this, he was certain, and he wasn't interested to hear it. But he needed to know.

Fazakerly grinned. "Face it, young man. What are you really expecting? To live a life like mine?"

The squaddie shook, his whole body in spasm; Fazakerly could see the deep tremors running from his waist to his neck. His naked buttocks heaved and thrust again. He roared, his head back. He laughed, standing, reaching for the rifle that leaned against the wall, dropping it, instead catching up his braces with his elbows and easing them in one jerking motion over his shoulders, buttoning his fly.

Hermione's head hung over the narrow mattress of Fazakerley's hospital bed, her stiff white apron turned back so that it shrouded her upper body, held taut by the two young sappers who sat on each side of her. They too rose, pulling back the hem to reveal her face. One bent to kiss her lips with a loud sucking sound. They all laughed this time. They smacked her bare thighs as they passed around the bed, one of them pummelling Fazakerly lightly in the chest as they passed, familiar, jocular and merry. Then they were gone, a jumble of heavy footsteps down the corridor, the spring-loaded doors at the entrance to the building slapping against each other for a while, then silence.

All was silence. The heavy corpse that still hung at the window blotted out the oppressive distance of the night guns on the front line. No-one moved in the hospital building. All dead. All gone. Fazakerly let out a long quiet breath. His eyes moved, the rest of him still frozen in the act of releasing his tray, hands raised as if about to pray. In the still silence he felt the tension relax and shifted at last, leaning forward on cramped limbs.

Hermione lay across his bed unmoving. Her naked legs were apart at an awkward angle as though she had begun to be torn in two, the remnants of her skirt raising up her body on a wadded tangle beneath her. It was all such disorder. Her bright red belt had become caught in the sheet and he reached to pull it free, as he bent to retrieve it finding that he had been beguiled by a weeping of blood that slowly congealed down her inner thigh. He flinched, shuddering, but aware too of the insidious torment that began to lick through his veins. Her sex was open and visible to anyone who would see, but there was only him. He was alone. The silence in the ward was beating at him and he could feel its echo in his loins. He was fumbling at the buttons of his long johns, the surging ache at his groin going *chock, chock, chock* in his ears, the urgency of the pulse in his blood showing in trembling hands as he touched the fine line of hair that smudged the base of her belly. She moved.

Fazakerly froze, a long howl of madness whirling in his head, the throbbing in his ears become a ratcheting, numbing racket that robbed him of all sense or purpose and he fell, as senseless as lumber, heavy beside her, the close dead leer of the quartermaster-sergeant large and swollen in his face as he rolled off the bed, clutching at Hermione's apron that came away in his hands, still stiff and white and miraculously unmarked.

He lay for a long while on the boards beneath the bed, the bare floor cold, the unshaded glare from electric bulbs casting sheer shadows. She hadn't moved again and, eventually, looking up, he saw her face just above him, turned upside down, her hair hanging loose and mouth just slightly open, her eyes wide but unseeing. There was no longer any light in that face. It was just another face, another stranger. If ever he'd thought she was his, she was nothing to him now; just one more pretence at naïve virtue and always going to be yet another hopeless captive of desire. Didn't he know, that long moment of impossible flawlessness was never going to last; but how dare they take it from him like this?

The faint susurration of her breath belied the vacant expression on her face. It was a complication he did not want. It made him sweat, the noise in his head starting up once more. It was over. It was all over and there was no way forward. It was all broken. All ruined. The dark tumult in his head would explode and he would be free at last. He would run. He would run out of here and down the road, back down the road to Torhout. No matter how far, he would peel it all back. The rattle of gunfire would drown out the raging battle in his head. He'd be back there, safe, yes safe.

His leg struck against the rifle that had been discarded by the bed and he recoiled. Then he was on his feet, the gun in his hands, looking down at her face, her expression blank, absent, the muzzle of the gun pressed to her temple, which was pale and inanimate, the report of the quick combustion surprisingly clean and short, leaving a dark bruise but very little blood.

- FIVE -

A CAR STOPPED on the hill, its engine left running. A window was down and they could hear Procul Harem's tale of teenage seduction swirling from the radio. It was 1967, the Summer of Love.

Late summer dozed and the harvest season hung heavily tumescent. Tomorrow, or the day after, would begin its inevitable tumbling of excess into the basket of autumn. All around the town the air hung heavy with the drone of pollen-wadded bees and a sticky anticipation of thunder; the sea, only a mile or two distant, glittered near the shore, but became rapidly indistinct under a haze that had erased the horizon. The older man gazed into it in silence with his light-coloured eyes just inside the edge of the green visor's shadow, the noisy interruption from beyond the hedge putting some imagined partition between his recently recollected history and whatever next might befall. Whether such respite was welcome or necessary there was no telling. His adopted expression of rigid inscrutability was impenetrable until a door slammed at last and the car slipped the light fandango into gear, drawing away with ease, away up the hill, the serial scale of *A Whiter Shade of Pale* streaming behind it on the buoyant summer heat. He exhaled dryly but continued to stare into the filmy distance.

"I just can't believe you. It's too awful." The younger man sat upright on the edge of the long garden bench. "Disgusting". He wanted to spit out the bile that wrenched like a hot fist in his chest. "Just unbelievable. Didn't they catch you, put you on trial or something? I mean, this was, well, criminal, heinous, it, it…" For once he struggled to produce a rhetoric that would match his enlarged sentiments.

The older man seemed not to hear; or hearing, he was resigned that all would now have to be given up. His guilt was out and there was no hurry, no necessity to speak further for the time being. It had been a part of him for so long. He seemed untroubled.

Not so the younger man, insisting: "Weren't you punished?"

Fazakerly turned his head at last with a strange look of tranquillity. "Punished?" he wheezed; he was laughing now, his voice squeaky, tricksy, his dry lips curled back. "Punished? There was plenty went unpunished anyway. Plenty of men in the trenches who'd give their comrade a bullet in the head rather than see them walk around for the rest of their lives with their guts on the outside."

He held Stephen suddenly and firmly at the wrist, his dry breath uncomfortably close in the young man's face, who until that moment hadn't been aware just how stale the old man smelled. His breath, his skin, the clean white linen jacket, all silently issuing an intense mustiness, the palpable smell of perishable things long shut away in airless rooms, the taint of rooms left locked and unlit spaces underground, which the heat of the full summer's afternoon had begun to sweeten with an edge of decay. Now it was Stephen's turn to sit rigid, some of that old fear of this most singular character returning, surprisingly immediate recollections of the childhood dares he had been given, no less vivid for being unbidden. Memories of stalking the solitary old man, he seemed old even then, sneaking up the clinking path to his Round House, hoping the big blue eye that watched over the front door would not turn his way, the boards of the veranda would not tell of his approach, the door handle would not turn…

"Punished?" hissed Fazakerly, his laughter gone. "But you'd know all about that. Isn't punishment everything that we're talking about here? Or the lack of it."

The effusion of fustiness rose and fell with his short breaths. The slow summer air let it hang. He folded one thin leg over another, the crisp white linen supple where Stephen had imagined it would crack like superannuated newspaper. No, it was the man himself, Fazakerly, who, despite his scrubbed clean appearance, was withering and perished. Outside in the air for the first time in ten years he was exposed once again to the processes of corruption. Long suspended, for all intents and purposes inanimate as he'd lain like a mummy on his swaddling bed, he was once more engaged with the forces of decay.

His claw's hold on Stephen's wrist was, nevertheless, vice like, and his piercing stare burned uncomfortably bright.

"Listen. What else are we both doing here?" He made a sweeping gesture with his free hand that begged answers from the air around them. "What else except to unravel this tangle of atonement that binds us?"

And before Stephen could ask what he meant he spat out: "life, boy; our lives. That's what I'm talking about. The conduct of our lives. Look at it all, all the fortresses that we've built around us, and here we are fetched up in our very own houses of correction."

Then, quite seamlessly, he was away again, his grip released, easing back, his grey eyes searching for something far away across the misty distance of sea, speaking only to himself now.

" Punishment? Pah! Don't we punish ourselves? And there's no more reason for our deserts than there is blame for our crimes."

The younger man too, disconnecting, speaking under his breath and more to himself than in retaliation.

"But you killed her. I never killed anyone, well, not any more…"

Taking a packet of *Consulate* from his shirt pocket he carefully extracted a cigarette. It was true, finding Fazakerly he now had a conclusion of sorts to all those years of wondering and suspense, but there had been no real answers. Not yet. He tapped the cigarette on the end of the packet, tamping it for no other reason than that he had often watched his father do the same before lighting up. The match flared into the tobacco and he inhaled the cool menthol smoke, the unpleasant odour from the old man blotted out for an instant.

His father had smoked Player's *Navy Cut* untipped. His vivid memory of the packet with the sailor's head was of a familiar ritual they would share after a swim on summer Sundays. The salt water still beading their arms and legs, the wind often brisk and chilling despite the season, he would be given a sixpence to go over to the Marine Hotel, where there was a small seafront café, and he'd stand at the glass-topped refrigerator, unconsciously dripping salt water onto the yellow linoleum, thrilled to choose from the wonderful new selection of ice creams that, it seemed to him at the time, had been invented just because it was his childhood that had imagined them. *Raspberry Split* was his favourite. Or, if he could be bothered and the day was warm, he'd run over the shingle sharp tarmac of Marine Parade to the Four Winds kiosk, an octagonal outcrop of the white-painted tea room that served as a refuge for weather-stricken seasiders, where they sold *Orange Maid*, the drink on a stick, strawberry *Mivvis* and the twisty, humbug shaped *Jubbly*. Then he would race back to the beach, the gaudy coloured ice melting down his wrist, raising the salt crust from his skin, watching as his father deftly cupped cigarette and match in the cowl of his hands, the wind off the sea catching a billow of smoke as he inhaled deeply with obvious satisfaction. Stephen's recall of the fragrance of ice cream, tobacco and the damp pebble beach all mingled together was intense: sweet and sharp, aromatic and ambrosial. And something else, the indefinable aroma of his father's presence, powerful he had thought, safe and enduring. They had been special times together. Man and boy at liberty for a day.

He offered the open packet of *Consulate* to Fazakerly, but the old man had resumed his contemplation of the indistinct distance. Man and boy. It was all so close and far away. Despite the clarity of the pleasures recalled, there were many aspects of that time that remained opaque. Had it stopped abruptly or simply faded away?

He started when Fazakerly's voice came to him, sharp and oddly irritated.

"So what are you waiting for? Go on. Just sling your hook, will you."

Stephen had scraped his ankle climbing back up the sea wall. The unseasonable dampness of the night before had dribbled through the conduit that in winter returned the foam of storm waves from where they'd crashed on the coast road; it oozed in a green and slippery trickle from the drain hole that was his customary foothold halfway up the wall. The graze chafed against the rough edge of his sandal but walking carefully with his toes clenched together he could avoid opening up the wound. Yesterday, missing his friends, he would have adopted an exaggerated gait as he walked the length of the promenade in search of another audience.

He passed the Gregorys' blighted house with caution. They were always an unpredictable proposition. Paul and Marcus. They kept snakes in an old aquarium under the front room window and a lizard in an orange box. They had an air rifle too, and were not secretive about its ownership; it was said they it carried about quite openly. Stephen had seen it on their kitchen table. Paul told him it was for hunting cats, to feed the snakes, but he'd never seen them use it that way. They'd shot at the postman, though, and were able to prove it. Paul had proudly pinned a letter of complaint from the Post Office on the back of his bedroom door, next to the promotional poster of the Lone Ranger, the large coloured picture of the masked man astride Silver, his horse, which had mysteriously and triumphantly parted company with the toy section in Woolworths. But more extraordinarily, to Stephen's mind, was that he had heard both of them swear openly in front of Mrs Gregory. More extraordinary still: they'd sworn and not been cautioned.

It wasn't just the singular nature of the rules that governed their lives that made them different. The fact that they were stepbrothers was itself enough for Stephen to regard them as having a whiff of strangeness, for in his world their quasi-fraternal status was unique and the notion of divorced parents unimaginable, made stranger still by their attendance at a small private school when everyone else he knew in the town went to the Church of England primary. 'He's Gregory and I'm Lane', said Paul, usually when Marcus had beaten or insulted him, which he could do quite brutally, being three years his senior. 'But actually we're all Gregorys now', added Marcus, confirming that they were a team and everyone outside it did not belong.

Nonetheless, Stephen had swelled with delight when included in adventures amongst their exclusive company. They were outsiders, avoided by his friends for no other reason and interesting to Stephen for the same reason. And too, whether in the sea, upon the beach, or further afield in the ancient reaches of the town, they had their own unique and curious formula for mayhem and a rough scorn for the usual rules of engagement with orderly adult society. In the right frame of mind it thrilled him. A recent hour on the canal in a hired canoe - an expensive treat at any time, and one to be used carefully, with serious and gainful feats of paddling over impossible distances before the hour was up - had become an invitation furiously to blight the restful afternoon of retired gentlefolk who sought to snooze along its banks. These were not Swallows and Amazons but anarchic river raiders invoked with a crashing and splashing of paddles and a cruel pelting from catapults. And afterwards, when they were herded into the ticket cabin by the boatman and a huddle of drenched pensioners, Stephen had been both mortified and jubilant to hear the stepbrothers cut down their captors with a defiant and liberal tirade of the worst expletives he had yet heard.

Only, in subsequent days, where previously there had been such delicious camaraderie, he could as easily find himself the target of their vicious, hurtful tongues, or running from their deadly catapult shots, without obvious cause or reason for his sudden descent into disfavour.

This troubled him deeply; on occasion it gave him a reason to let go. There were some adventures when he felt horribly out of his depth, some excursions into mischief that became harsh and beyond fun, when he craved Warren's crass and harmless scatology as an antidote to Marcus's relish for proposing and undertaking ventures that callously scorned all limits of law and morality, and threatened to be followed by consequences that could not be erased, unlike bad dreams, with the light of a new day. Some of the things they'd done had made it difficult for him to stay around and he'd looked for a way to drop out, inconspicuously, guiltless but also saving face. The brothers' capricious changes in mood, turning him from friend to foe on the passing of a mere glance between them, or so it seemed, gave him an excuse to distance himself, make the break, play safe and stay away. Why he didn't use it, even when he was uncomfortably colluding with them in kicking over traces that he'd always respected or regarded fondly, he couldn't explain. But the Gregorys' otherness, the sense he took from them that, after all, he was merely being allowed to dip his toe in their world, and it was just another part of the world he inhabited anyway, the place that, all said and done, he was doing no more than just observing and tasting and filing away, safe in the vault of his memory, this worked for him.

Yesterday, after a long and dreary morning alone he had been looking for company, spurred by a growing irritation at himself for rejecting the London trip into seeking adventures of his own. He'd had his own sense of being an outsider yesterday, convinced that he'd placed himself at the edge and it was going to be a good feeling. Coincidentally, the Gregory brothers had been there to welcome him.

Their house was set back from the road. A one and a half storey building that seemed to want to be elsewhere but had been put down clumsily in a surround of unkempt grass on the corner opposite the Four Winds. Still with the appearance of newness, it had been planted at the southern extremity of Queen's Road in the space made by a doodlebug, and was out of line with the rest of the high Victorian terrace that had survived the war with its façade to the promenade. From the back wall an alley led down into a deep wasteland overgrown by a storm of fireweed and thistle, the flowery footprint of another block of houses that had once backed on to the seafront terrace, so that the squat Gregory house was like a floating island, and the length of mouldering terrace, with its ramshackle balconies, tall steps and steep slate roofs, represented a tottering old pre-war world from which the occupants of the island had escaped. Gulls roosted in the top floor of old Marble Gamble's house, the witch woman who lived midway along the block, and they would glide down from her broken third floor windows with piercing cries and laughter, their constant wheeling about the whitewash walled buildings reinforcing the impression of the terrace as a huddle of cliffs.

Just three streets away from his own house it all felt peculiarly unfamiliar, almost uncertain, the feeling of strangeness made more acute by the unsettling presence of old man Fazakerly's wooden refuge, the place they knew as the Round House, with its glinting look-out and staring windows, which filled the narrowing perspective at the opposite, northern end of Queen's Road.

He'd passed the Gregory house, drawing close to the end of the sea wall, the broad area of the Stade where there were ramps down across the beach and the promise of boats to watch, when Fazakerly came wheeling around the bend on his bicycle, long thin legs pistoning him up the slope to the promenade with no apparent effort, as if he and the bicycle were all one and the same machine, with the function of lung and muscle and heartbeat transmitted unbroken to the whirring spokes and the rubber tread upon the road. Always at the same pace, whether uphill, downhill, or on the flat, unswerving, knees high on the upturn of the pedals, heels almost touching the road on the downturn. His pale unblinking eyes looked out and ahead through perfectly round spectacle lenses, giving the impression he saw only the road ahead. But Stephen was sure he had registered him, knew him, recognised him as one of those hateful creatures who crept into his garden and pointlessly stole the green figs that hung from his gazebo.

Man and bicycle wheeled smoothly into Queen's Road, heading for home, and Stephen followed, for no other reason than that he was at a loose end. As he turned the corner a small, round figure darted from the alley behind the Gregory house, huffing and puffing as it ran, an incoherent stream of muttering vented in an apparent mixture of fright and warning. Startled from hiding by Stephen's approach, the child, a boy with long dark hair and skin the colour of saddle leather, leapt away after Fazakerly, stumbling on bare feet in the trail of the bicycle and, as soon became evident, not in flight but quite determinedly in pursuit. Despite his obvious bulk and stumpy legs he was impelled by a simian-like rolling gait, and quickly drew near to the old man. Fazakerly continued on his way, staring ahead and seemingly oblivious of the impending ambuscade until, drawing level, the unbroken splutter of gibberish became a roaring deluge that was hurled at the old man, so sudden and potent that he swerved as if struck by something heavy, his front wheel at a right angle to his general direction and his feet tip-tapping on the road in a frantic scraping effort to maintain balance.

By the time Stephen caught up, Fazakerly had regained his momentum and begun to pedal away, a black boot on the end of a long bony leg occasionally striking out at his assailant, who was bouncing fearlessly close in the middle of the road, the old man's usually impassive face red and taut as he hissed through his teeth, eyes screwed up tight and not looking at the child, rasping "get away, will you, you abomination. Go. Humphrey, fuck off".

The child's inarticulate babble coursed unabated, refreshed by the sight of the bicycle managing to edge away from him, they were nearly at the end of the road now and the Round House was rising up from the centre of its golden haven; but as Stephen ran up the storm of unintelligible ranting broke off, leaving just a tinkle of spokes in revolution and the rough slurring of rubber on tarmac to remark Fazakerly's escape.

Humphrey froze, his dull brown eyes wide, his large head hunched all about by his shoulders as Stephen faced him down, fleetingly tempted to believe the child could be quelled so easily - but he wasn't looking at Stephen.

"Hello, Humph," said Marcus, looming quietly over Stephen's shadow, "wanna play, eh?"

"Wah!" The sound of an imbecile it may or may not have been, there had been much debate about the state of Humphrey's mental capacity, but it was plain how that simple suggestion struck deep and sure, plainer still when he took off again on his bare feet, invisible around the corner by Blackman's sweet shop before Marcus had drawn breath to laugh.

Yesterday, they had laughed together long and loud. Today, Stephen knew, all might be reversed and he could so easily be the target of that laughter. But there was no sign of movement in the house. The windows were all closed, the garage door down. Further along the road he caught the momentary flutter of sunlight on a smooth metal surface and fleetingly anticipated that it was perhaps the Gregorys, returning in their mother's Ford Prefect; but the vehicle he could see had been reversing, it was a large fire engine, which then slid out of view around the corner, leaving the road empty. That's when his eye fell on the changed prospect it had left in its wake.

He shivered. So there it was, the blackened stump of the Round House. Even from this distance, a couple of hundred yards away, he could make out the extent of its ruin, the way it had collapsed in upon itself, the walls reduced to a sooty mille-feuille of charred wood. How was it that he could have come here and not remembered where his footsteps were leading him?

There were few people about. The excitement of yesterday evening had begun to dull even as the flames were being extinguished. Some small boys hung around where the gate had been, hoping that the thin wisp of smoke the firemen had missed was the promise of a fresh conflagration. They retreated when Stephen approached and dared to climb the pile of mud and bricks, the section of the boundary wall that had been pushed aside to allow closer access for the fire tender.

So there it was. And how could it be that he was still at liberty, free to come here and see it?

A trap, he thought, it's a trap and they'll come for me now. I've returned to the scene of my crime, as they say all villains will, come back to survey my accomplishments. It's what the Sunday papers would describe as a fatal fascination and the entire world would know it as an admission of guilt. That's what they had been discussing in the kitchen, of course, conspirators around the big old kitchen table where long ago as an infant he had scratched his name in the white scrubbed wood. They'd let him run, allowing his pretended innocence free rein, there to beguile him into putting his signature under the deed. Then they'd waylay him, right there at the crime scene, as if he'd been caught in the act itself. Oh Mother! Father! The web of their cunning weighed on him with its suffocating blanket of disappointment.

A rush of cool air, moist and salty, which had swirled all the way from the sea, snouted and stirred the debris that smothered the wrecked half-acre. He started, then recognised the sudden motion for what it had been, not the surprise and arrest he had expected. The garden and its sea of gold had been consumed not by the fire but the actions set in train by the fire. Where once there had been bright constellations of sunny buttercups was a mesh of ash, mud and the drying flakes of retardant foam. Furniture and other movable items had been brought out through the windows in the early stages of the fire, but as the heat built up in the centre it had reached out and kindled these chairs and cushions and other treasures snatched indiscriminately from smouldering rooms, whiplashes of flame cracking open the darkness, producing quick echoes of startled applause and fearful congratulation from the gathering audience marshalled at the partially demolished wall, and so the blaze had danced from point to point across the entire plot from the house to the road.

No-one could have escaped this, he thought. No point kidding myself.

He moved around to the side of the garden where the pebble path had been laid. It still afforded passage through the mess of broken household paraphernalia, then he was stepping through the soft charcoal that had once been an idiosyncratic gazebo.

A crunching underfoot suggested he had arrived at the front door; it was the shattered remains of the stained glass that twenty-four hours previously had flashed and twinkled in the morning light. Fazakerly's arcane sentinel. Looking down, Stephen saw a hundred blue eyes staring back at him, his own face reflected as many times, captured in miniature by their cold, reproachful gaze.

Just as he had waited in the early hours of that morning, held tight as a watch-spring, he tensed again expectantly, shocked rigid by the accusative stare from those watching eyes, waiting for the clap of a hand on his shoulder, guilty as charged. *Mea culpa.* Take me and have done with it.

For several minutes he stood there, numbed by the physical enormity of the house laid waste, until at last realising that his feet were cold and wet, a fine liquid powder of ash having invaded his sandals, he awoke to the fact that he was alone.

What to think? What to do? The evidence was plain for all to see.

On the other hand, he remained free. Free and unpunished, and above this scene of desolation it truly was a fine day, as his mother had said. But old man Fazakerly? Dead, surely. No doubt about it. It might well be a fine day, but how that might turn out for him, after what had happened here, that was all a mystery, and he wasn't sure he wanted to ask for any answers just now. Doing that might just tip the scales a little more sharply. He looked around again, sure that someone, someone official, was watching from behind him, someone poised to leap and clap him in irons. But he was alone, just him alone with the bones of an old man somewhere under these heaped up cinders.

Somewhere in there, in that great grey mound. No doubt about it. He surveyed the undulating pile of ash. It was impossible to detect what lay beneath. That would be it of course; they couldn't do anything until they had a body. No body, no crime. Wasn't that it? But that wouldn't be the end of it.

Stephen walked briskly back through the greasy blackened grass to the road. As he emerged through the broken wall a woman burdened with a clutch of shopping bags passed, rocking as old women do from side to side, tut-tutting when he stumbled out in front of her. She fixed him with her one good eye and gave a fearsome stare.

Old Marble Gamble. She knew, of course she did; that witch knew everything. But then they'd all know by now. Whatever happened now they'd all know and he'd be shunned. Cursed by the town's witch, he'd be cast out like a leper. He might be free but, whatever they said, however they smiled and asked how'd you do, he knew he was marked. When he transferred to the Grammar School in the autumn his infamy would travel with him; they'd know even before he arrived. No new beginnings for Stephen. He was known and they would be ready for him. He had cast himself out. And, however secretly his new classmates might wish they'd had the balls to do what he did, no matter the fascination of his presence amongst them, most of all they'd fear him. He could be sure of that. No-one would want to come too close to the shroud of guilt he wore; no-one would dare to share that infamy. An orgy of crime, that was his brand, an excess of misrule that would fascinate and repel.

That would be his punishment then. So that's what they'd decided. He laughed, his eyes filling and with wet-throated desperation.

So now he was bigger than Marcus. What an achievement. An outlaw, no less. It didn't feel so good. He never felt that good anyway when he was with Marcus. Not really.

"So how did he know his name was Humphrey?"

"Eh? How did who know?" Marcus was fumbling for a match in his jeans pocket.

"The old man, Fazakerly. You know. I heard him; he was having a right fit, saying 'get off, Humphrey', and kicking at him like he was something poisonous." Stephen gestured with his thumb towards the Round House. "What was all that about?"

"Aaah," grinned Marcus. "That old cunt was just getting his comeuppance. You know, don't you?"

"No. Know what?"

"Then I ain't telling you, you dick!"

"But Fazakerly don't know any of us really. He's just a hermit, isn't he?"

"Hermit? You're such a spas. Well he knows Humphrey and Humphrey seems to know him. But I ain't telling, not unless you buy me some fags – and I don't want *Woodbines*, neither."

"No money."

"No explanation, then. But think about it, where does he live, Humph the Lumph?"

"I don't know. You just see him around."

"Think, Spas. Where does he always seem to appear from?

"The hotel. And I'm not a spastic."

"Yeah, the back of the hotel. Lives in the bins, with his mum."

"What?"

"Nola. She works in the laundry, sleeps in the laundry. In the bins, with the sheets and stuff. Oh, I get it – no, not the pig bins, you dick-head, the laundry bins."

"She's simple."

"So's Humphrey. In fact he's a real mongol. Anyway, ask Nola why Fazakerly hates Humphrey. Not that she'll be able to tell you much. Fucking zombie. Never speaks – not so's you can follow what she's saying anyway. Tell you what," he grinned, "since you aren't going to buy me some fags, let's find Humphrey and get him to nick some. He won't have gone far. And you are a spas; you should just listen to yourself sometime."

The trail left by Humphrey proved to be a short one. He'd gone around the corner by Blackman's and doubled back over the wall that made a sink between the shop and the pavement, where the shop lay at an angle to the corner. It was a common hideaway for kids who'd had to make a quick exit from the shop after sending old man Blackman out to his store to fetch something they could see was not on the shelves. It was too high for him to climb over with his gammy leg and anyone might remain there unnoticed for as long as it took, especially when sustained by blackjacks, flying saucers or the fascinating contents of jamboree bags, whatever spoils of the day they'd managed to stuff in their pockets.

Humphrey would not easily be coaxed out. The presence of Marcus clearly terrified him but it was Marcus who eventually lured him over the wall.

"He's a fucking addict. Baked beans. Give him baked beans and he'll do anything. I told you he lived out the back of the hotel. Well, he doesn't get proper food, just leavings from the restaurant. Baked beans on toast must seem like a real treat for him."

They didn't need to send Humphrey on his tobacco mission; he had a full pack of *Du Maurier* that he'd filched from the concierge at the hotel, and Marcus was elated at having something decent to smoke.

"Posh fags. I bet you those posh farts on What's My Line smoke *Du Maurier*, that ponce Gilbert Harding and Lady Isobel Wossname, bet they do. That's why they have them in the hotel. In case they turn up. They're the sort to stay in hotels." He coughed bravely. "Quality!"

The cigarettes were traded for baked beans on toast (two slices) at the Gregory house, although Humphrey was not allowed over the front step. In fact, the prospect of beans on toast seemed to dispel his obvious fear of Marcus and he sat patiently on an old oil drum in the garage until the feast was brought on an enamel plate.

Marcus's stepbrother, Paul, had been rigging up a rope ladder when they arrived. It hung from a platform that had been slung across the rafters to provide extra storage. His explanation of the ladder sounded deliberately opaque, it had something to do with an assault course he'd visited with Mr Gregory's TA colleagues, and according to Paul it was going to help him train for the army, it was part of a strategy he had devised so that he might leave home at an early age. All the kids who knew anything about Paul were aware of his obsession with the trappings of soldiering, and it was a passion that was easily satisfied in a town that sustained a large number of army barracks. Mostly it was badges he collected, these and manuals describing the most economic means of inflicting bodily harm, or how to conduct guerrilla warfare and concoct explosives from household goods. If asked, he would proudly explain the contents of his tins of survival rations, and he had several army knives with the legendary and anachronistic spike for removing stones from horses' hooves. To Stephen, it was all pretty mundane stuff. But the younger stepbrother had also amassed a frighteningly large cache of live ammunition, all garnered from careless foxholes on the firing ranges that abutted the public beaches, about a half-mile from the end of the promenade. From his furtive manner, Stephen guessed he'd been inspecting his boxes of shells when they arrived. It was clear Paul was not pleased at the interruption and he retreated into the shadows of the rudimentary loft, from where he scowled at Humphrey.

"Have to put up a red flag when I'm busy," he snorted.

"What?"

"A red flag, like they have on the ranges when the army's firing. Anyway, why'd you bring him here, that fat mongol," whined Paul. "He stinks. Look at him, he's filthy."

"Hey, Junior Leader, shut it," snapped Marcus, "we brought him for an interrogation." He whirled on Stephen. "Didn't we Spas?"

"It's really not important."

"Well, *I* ain't going to tell you what you want to know, not when you can get it from the horse's mouth."

"That's no horse, that's a fucking pig." Paul's resentment was quickly turning to sweet anticipation. "Squeak, Piggy, squeak!"

"So, how are we going to interrogate him, Junior Leader? What would your TA pals do, then?"

Humphrey gobbled obliviously. His grimy T-shirt of indeterminate colour, already streaked with oily daubs from top to bottom, had been brightened by fresh wet patches of tomato sauce; his long hair shone where it had been sucked into his mouth along with some of Heinz's very best beans, and between each mouthful he stared into space with a distant look of satisfaction until the very last bean had been licked from the plate. He ran a thick black forefinger around the rim, gathering up the final dribble of tomato, and slurped it from his hand. His appetite unabated, he reached into the crate of bottles that Marcus had made him use as a table. *Silver Spring* was written in black letters on the side of the crate, each letter *i* represented by a bottle with a drift of bubbles in place of the dot. None of the bottles in the crate had labels but this did not deter Humphrey, who was unlikely to have been able to read them anyway. He pulled one out and deftly sprang the stopper with his thumb. It looked like cream soda, it smelled like…

"Holy shit, Marcus, he's got the Molotovs!"

Paul was down the rope ladder with a display of agility likely to have guaranteed him a cadetship, but Humphrey had already gagged and dropped the bottle. It landed right way up with a sharp clunk, a small fountain of clear liquid shooting straight up then cascading back down the sides. The rest of its pungent contents seeped from the cracked heel of the bottle and spread across the concrete floor with an infernal hissing sound.

"OK, Humph, you're for it now," chortled Marcus. "Look what you've done to my dad's garage floor. He'll have your balls."

The brief heaven that had been the baked bean feast was eclipsed by sudden terror, and Humphrey backed against the closed door of the garage, the metal plates making a low gonging sound under pressure from his fat buttocks.

"Come on Piggy, clean this up," commanded Paul. He had Humphrey by the hair and was pushing him onto his knees.

"Fucking mongol, I'll teach you to leave my weapons alone. Go on, lick it up you greedy pig." He pressed the child's head at the wet patch that was swiftly evaporating. "Go on, Piggy, lick it up."

Humphrey had gone rigid, his limbs locked, his face hidden by the lank hair that had fallen forward, through which came a deep grunting noise and the quick breath of fear.

"Leave it Paul!" snapped Marcus. "Conduct unbecoming. Relegation to the ranks!" He flicked the dog-end of his cigarette with deadly accuracy and the dampness in the concrete floor flared briefly with a blue flame. There was a shocked squeal from Humphrey, strangely deep-voiced, and Stephen caught the acrid whiff of singed hair.

"Paul! We have a guest," Marcus bowed towards Stephen with a mocking flourish, "let him decide what we should do with this infidel. Go on Spas," he sneered, "ask H your question, and if he can't answer we'll make him squeak. If he answers you, you can decide what happens next."

This was one of those moments he dreaded. Stephen wanted desperately to go, but in going he would shut himself out forever. He'd be a pansy, a spastic like they called him, and next time it could be him who was locked in the garage. And if he went, what about Humphrey? It was ok to tease him, he was too soft in the head to realise, but Paul, and more particularly Marcus, they had a different view of things.

"All right. If he doesn't answer properly he has to squeak like a pig."

Humphrey was still on his hands and knees, his filthy T-shirt ridden up around his shoulders and his bloated belly shivering. His skin looked coarse, dark and too weathered for one so young.

"Looks like a pig," scoffed Paul, "or a gyppo."

"Go on then," said Marcus, "but he'll need encouragement."

"Humphrey." Stephen leant towards him, trying to peer through the mass of hair. "Humphrey, look at me. Why did you chase old man Fazakerly?"

On his hands and knees, Humphrey trembled, his face hidden under his hair. He gave no indication that he'd heard Stephen's question.

"Humphrey!" Stephen stooped and put his lips at the place where he thought the boy's ear might be, as near as he dared but resisting any thought of parting that long greasy mane. "Why did you chase old man Fazakerly?" He felt a surge of fear, hearing the pleading tone in his own voice.

Humphrey's wrists began to shiver as the tension of remaining frozen in one position stole down his neck to his shoulders to his arms, but still he kept his silence. He'd hardly moved since Marcus had lit the spilled petrol.

"OK, squeak, Piggy, squeak." Like his stepbrother, Marcus did not share Stephen's squeamishness and had hold of Humphrey's hair. He gave it a sharp yank. There was no sound.

"Fucking squeak, will you!" He pulled again, harder.

"Fucking gyppo, let me do it. Here you fucker, look!" Paul had the boy's head back, a handful of long hair held taut in his left hand, and he was shaking his right fist in front of Humphrey's nose. "Squeak or I'll flatten it! I will."

There was no squeak. Instead, they all gaped at the long low rasping sound that stole out from Humphrey's rear end. Paul and Marcus were running around the garage now, rocking with laughter, punching the air, prodding Humphrey with their boots as they wheeled about him.

"Go," thought Stephen, "get up and go now", not sure whether he was talking to himself or the forlorn creature that crouched in the centre of the floor, leaning away from a pummelling by leaping toecaps. He reached for the wire that would release the garage door's locking mechanism and there came the scrape of metal on metal as the door started to lift.

"Oi! We ain't finished yet. He hasn't finished singing for his supper, so to speak." Marcus slammed the door shut.

"I need to go. Really."

"You need to go? Sounds like Humph needs to go." They shrieked with laughter once more. "That's what beans do for you. Isn't it Humph?"

Humphrey was getting to his feet now, shaking his head furiously, his large eyes black and wide with fearful expectation.

"Time to resume our experiment, eh Paul?"

His younger stepbrother had hold of Humphrey by the neck and hauled him upright; he was already pushing his head through the rungs of the stepladder.

"He's always like this. A plate of beans and, bingo! To every action there is an equal and opposite reaction. Hah! Isn't that it, Professor Spas? Watch this. Our own experiment in the cause of military science."

"But he's just scared, that's all. He's only just had the beans. It doesn't work that quickly."

"Shut it. You'll spoil the game."

Humphrey was as fast in the ropes of the ladder as a fly in the grip of a spider's web, his head bent forward under the sixth rung from the top, his hands bound to the vertical cords with insulating tape, and his bare legs through the bottom rung, which had been wound back around his ankles so that he stood with his feet at a sharp and unyielding angle to his body. The whole device hung away from them under the imbalance of his weight, so that he leaned on tiptoe, his head craning forward into the darkness at the rear of the garage and his backside pushed out toward them

"Ta-ra!"   With a single deft movement Marcus whipped down Humphrey's shorts, his plump dark buttocks shaking free.

"Naaaaa!" Humphrey's fear came in a deep moan. "Wah!" He tromped and shook in the ladder's embrace but could not break free.

"Come on Humph, one big blast and we'll let you go." Marcus's voice was cold, his face no longer smiling. He crouched behind the stricken boy. "C'mon, we're waiting". He struck a match and held the flame upwards towards Humphrey's quivering backside. "Come on, a nice big blue flame like last time. Hurry, I ain't got many matches left. And you, hey Spas, what are you waiting for? You can fuck off. Shut the door behind you too, there's all sorts of perverts about.".

- SIX -

DEATH. There was nothing to be found there but death, and Fazakerly looked only briefly towards the town. One glimpse was all that he needed, finding the remembered promise of comfort and well-being of its tightly packed dwellings turned into the simmering fear of entrapment. Not that he could see much in the darkness. No movement was visible, but occasional gunfire interrupted and seemed periodically to stoke an indistinct but unmistakeable murmur of activity into the more audible hubbub of shouting and laughter and the frantic desperation of screams. Nothing escaped from the corral of turmoil sealed within that knot of crowding buildings, only a draught of sour smoke floating on the air that stung his eyes. He turned quickly in the other direction, away from the sickening heat of inhumanity.

It was a company of Gordon Highlanders that came upon him, though there were in truth few enough of them left to make good company, and they were jumpy enough to let off a round at the appearance of this spectre in a dressing gown and flapping slippers.

"I was a sight, I can tell you. But they were good enough to take the trouble not to shoot me. Fired over my head. A warning. They'd heard something was up but weren't sure if it was the Hun. Not that I'd have cared. It was nothing to me when the captain held a skean-dhu at my throat while I was being searched, but soon as they found I was unarmed, that and the army issue long johns, it was all easy, and I must admit I was glad not to have died. Don't ask me why. But they were good enough lads. Even gave me the knife, for my own protection they said. Anyway, I was glad they were Scotch. Straight dealing people: you always know where you are with the Scotch."

"So, these…upright Scotsmen – they didn't arrest you or anything?"

"No. You know it's funny how we speak of the inhumanity of Man when what we are really talking about is the doings of Humanity. Well, they understood that, sure as eggs is eggs. They went straight down to the town and cleaned up. They had a couple of these new machine guns, you see, mounted on their trucks, and it was quick. No recriminations. No prisoners. No point, was there? Straight dealing, like I said."

"And the base; the hospital?"

"The same. All dead before they got there. Nothing more to do. They burned it. It was easier like that to say it was the opposition. Easier to blame the squareheads' artillery than set hares running about who'd done what and when and upset a load of innocent folk back home. It was done. Over. Couldn't be mended. This kind of thing happens with people. They knew that. Who back home would want to hear about our lovely boys having a mutiny?"

"So, you got off Scot free, if you'll excuse the pun."

"No need for sarcasm, young man. Live through something like that and you're never free. Who's free anyway? Soon as you first draw breath you're connected, signed up for a lifetime. Try to keep out of it; well you can try. But look at me. Start breathing and all the world knows you're there. Thought I'd copped it, back at Torhout, and they still came for me. Heard me breathing. I wasn't excused, I wasn't free to go. Pah!"

"But that's rot. They saved you, those men with the stretcher, them and...Hermione. You didn't have to...you could have stopped those other men. She'd – she and the doctors – they restored you. You didn't need to be like the others."

"Put a sock in it, will you. You haven't worked it out yet."

"But you did get away with murder."

"Were you free to go after your own murderous little adventure? Eh? Tell me that and bugger off, will you, or are we going to sort this out together a little further? I assume that's why I have been blessed once again by your presence."

It was over a week since they had sat together under the oppressive heat of a southern summer's afternoon. Stephen had fancied he might not be welcome but Fazakerly had grasped his hand eagerly, pulling himself up out of his chair, and here they were, in the seclusion of the garden beneath the nursing home window. The air had been cleaned and cooled by two days of rain and for comfort they had spread a blanket along the moist green painted bench. Fazakerly looked refreshed too and, remembering their last meeting, Stephen resisted a temptation to sniff for those strange odours of decline that had poisoned the atmosphere between them. But, as easily as he had been granted company, and as if no time had passed since they'd last sat together, Stephen had quickly aroused the old man's irascibility. He struggled to repair their meeting. There were answers he needed.

"I'm sorry. But yes, there are things I need to know."

"Good. Time is short. Go on then, fire away."

"Well, first, can I ask, what is it you want from me? After all, you weren't killed, not like I thought; so, when we met, after all those years, what was the big excitement about meeting me? It was almost like I was family."

Fazakerly didn't pause. He had thought it through.

"Resurrection, son. That's what it was, a resurrection. I'd had as much of a time outside of it all as you. Probably what I thought I'd always wanted, but I was wrong. Talk about death, well, I sure as have been dead these past ten years. Some might say longer."

It had been a quick execution. He remembered with terrifying immediacy the roar of ignition as the entire south and east facing section of the Round House wall erupted in a blue-green flash, the explosion of glass from his shattered windows making an instant steaming frost of his front garden, then the rushing din of bells and sirens, the firm hands on his arms, at his back, propelling him on a hurtling ride through heat that trimmed his beard and in his wake parted the shimmering wall of faces that he passed overhead, his passage unbroken all the while, a momentum handed to the lurching ambulance and on again to the resolute snip, snip, snip of hurrying scissors rendering him naked and noumenal on that curtained hospital bed. How many breaths had it taken? In what seemed a moment he'd become a moth in formaldehyde, plucked in a trice from his hiding place under the tarred shingles and made safe from predators and the pernicious march of the seasons. Clean, secure, still; untroubled and untroubling. Released from the tangles of the world. Wasn't that what he had craved all his lifetime?

"It was dark in there. Safe but pointless. You know, all those years, I actually kept thinking about the fire as if it was the last adventure I never had. Like I'd been snatched away before I could appreciate what was going on – with me at the centre of it all too – bundled away into the night whilst everyone else could stay and warm their hands and enjoy the show. Well, when you turned up like that, the first time, last month, it was like you'd come to turn the lights on again. I'd been brought out of the drawer at last and it felt good. Better than good, it was bloomin' marvellous."

"And now?"

"I'm at your service, of course. I can help you fill in your gaps. It's not enough just to watch the show, you know. You do know that, don't you?"

"That's it?"

"Well, like I said, we have things to sort out. Me included."

"I can see now why you wanted to know, that first time we spoke, why you wanted to know if, as you put it, you'd been removed from the equation – their equation, that is. My parents."

"It's no fun being invisible. I've learnt that. Better late than never."

"Well, I recall now that she did sometimes mention you, my mother, before and after the fire. Not in any way of explanation, but it seems she had a fondness for you. After the fire she said how you'd been a real character and how after the tragic events of that night the town really missed having you around, how you used to give her herbs from your garden and how you'd feed the stray cats that lived in the sheds behind the funeral parlour. Stuff like that. I'd never known about all that before. I thought you kept yourself to yourself. It just goes to show. She said it was all such a shock, what had happened. I assumed at the time she meant that *I* was such a shock but I'm not so sure now. Maybe she was just sorry for what you had gone through. Shocked that it had happened to us - you know, in our town - that she might have anything to do with it. Through me I mean."

"Things were different then. All this peace and love malarkey we get these days: phoney. Just kidology for greed and lust. But then, it was different. Well, there was as much sham about then as there is now, I give you that, but there was also an honesty, an innocence. It made it hard to keep oneself to oneself. There were good people. I had to admit a little. Good people like your mother."

"Like Hermione?"

"Let's leave that one, shall we."

"Like me? How they dealt with me - was that honest? Ten years of it. How are you going to fill in that gap?"

"I can't. You'll have to do that. You have to understand the way it was then. I can help you with that. You have to understand it was all done for the best, of course, no doubt about it."

"Whose best? Theirs, their pride? Can silence be best?"

"It was a national characteristic not to make a fuss. They'd have been thinking of you, I can tell you. You were a child then, more than you would be today at that age. There were things only adults dealt with, not kids. I expect they were trying to protect you. There was always the thought that some things were best left unsaid. How old were you after all? Ten, eleven? Just a kid. Still in short trousers."

"You then. You were an adult. What about that great big hole you left in France? How did you deal with that?"

The foul waters of the Canche that trickled down to the sea resembled the drain from an abattoir, the blood and stomach of Étaples voided into the black night that encircled and overspread all of the town, the river mouth and even the roaring gale offshore that protested at this new and inexorable uncleanliness. La Manche was made a sump, a sink of corruption once more and Fazakerly looked out blindly into the hollow of darkness, listening for the cries of accusation that he knew would come after, knowing the crunch of the keel in the shallow waters to be the sound of dead men's bones as they rode away over their pit of oblivion, away to some kind of freedom, abandoning these souls to the consequences of poor causes and human instinct.

"No more. No more."

His unspoken words filled the spaces between the transfer of his weight from one foot to the other, as first the bows of the small boat and then the stern lifted high over the grey waves, filling the sky before and aft in turn as they rose up so high he thought they would all spill from her decks into the heaving waters.

They were going home and the spirits of Captain Aberdein's mortally reduced company could not be quelled by the storm that strove to prevent them leaving behind the shores of war. Most had gone below decks but animated voices swelled from the galley, tones of relief and gladness; faces lit from within by the prospect of returning home, alive, glowing in the shadows cast by match and cigarette. They were going home, and home was itself a far country yet, a long safe way north from the conflict that suppurated all along the coast from which they had fled. The sound of gunfire reached out to them but it could have been thunder, or maybe the crashing of the sea against the bulwarks of their craft, or the rumble of the engines as they laboured to climb the steepening surf. Which, it no longer mattered.

"No more," whispered Fazakerly, alone at the rail. "This time I am no more a part of all that." The wind caught at the lapels of his borrowed greatcoat and he was deafened by the drumming of heavy cloth, but the voice inside was insistent and unmistakeable.

"No more."

He had renounced it all once before, given it up to the golden light that shone over the wasteland at Torhout. That should have been the end of it. He had left himself behind in that place, gladly if not deliberately. Huh! - if only.

Later, he had been made to pick it up again, reluctantly at first, roller-coasted by military process; then, and with scant protestation, he'd been suborned by the seduction of a sweet voice, through the beguiling conduct of virtue finding his old self patched together anew. Different of course, he had gathered some changes along the way, but he'd caught up with himself, no doubt of that. And the veneer of civilisation had been barely set.

"Fool," whispered the voice in his head. "Fool!" he shouted into the wind, shaking angrily at the rail. What folly to let it all back in like that; was it really so inevitable? He'd been made a blank canvas all over again and still it came out the same. Instinctively, it seemed. Was it all really the inescapable but logical necessity of being a man? They were going home, but for Fazakerly going home could never take him far away from the phantoms that drove him.

He slipped over the side under the cover of a cloudy dawn, his clothes stuffed inside a tarpaulin bag that he'd emptied of grenades. The grenades he had slung in a piece of net, dropping the whole cache quietly into the water so as not to be discovered trying to stow them safely. The water felt colder than freezing and his legs soon ached. He took comfort that the wind had dropped as they'd neared the English coast, backing West to South-west, and while the roiling waters struck so chill they were subsiding.

Using the skean-dhu, he'd cut free a lifebuoy from its bracket on the wheelhouse wall and now he looped one arm through it, struggling with his other to keep the bag of clothes afloat. It had perhaps been a mistake to bring the greatcoat.

They'd been heading for Dover but navigation had been poor. In the dim early light he had thought he could make out the coast further west, the long flat curve of Romney Marsh barely visible as a grey pencilled smear along the distant ridges of white-topped breakers. That elevation disappeared as soon as he was in the water, as did all sight and sound of the boat.

The surge of the driven seas and the rising tide brought him ashore about a mile west of Greatstone, and he crawled all the way up the high hump of shingle on his knees and elbows, his legs too weak and numb to bear him, the tarpaulin bag making a hump of his back so that he resembled something primeval come on land for the first time. A black-tarred fisherman's hut was all that broke the featureless expanse of pebble and gorse that stretched away across the early light on the marshes.

"I am no more," he whispered, looking out from its single window upon the empty wakening day. "Truly I am no more this time".

"Now that's a place in itself," said the old man, fondly. "Come up out of the sea like a leviathan. I suppose you know it was once the western arm of the entrance to New Romney, from the sea that is, when that was a port. Nothing but a pile of stones - I liked that. It took years, of course, but it felt to me then like it was still freshly risen from the sea. It's all that way around here, which is why I stayed. It's all about life on the edge."

"So you remained free then. No-one came after you?"

"Free? In a manner of speaking. It was a good place for a new beginning. Like I said, I had a special feeling for the place, for the way it started, the whole marsh in fact. And talking of me getting off Scot free, as you did so sarcastically a moment or two ago, although I won't dwell on the hurt, I deduce that you don't actually appreciate the appropriateness of your criticism, seeing where I ended up."

"What?"

Fazakerly smirked. "Scot free. For your information the *scot* was a tax paid by folk down there on the marsh who had the benefit of the public drainage system. Quite a benefit in that place too, you know how low the land is, below sea level. If you lived on higher ground you didn't pay. So your house was *scot free*."

"Oh. I see."

"Well, don't let me bore you, Mr Brainbox, don't let me tell you anything faintly instructive. I can tell your thoughts are consumed by matters much more metaphysical."

"They are?"

"Listen. That's how I dealt with it, before you ask me again. I hid away in that fucking little shed for two whole years. No-one came near. I had just the sheep for company. Just the sheep back of the dyke and the gulls. Not even the boot-leggers who ran a tidy trade on that beach, spite of it being wartime; they didn't bother me. Why would they? I was as much an outlaw as them and they guessed it, I don't doubt. I had all I needed in any case. There was water enough, it seemed like we had horizontal rain once a week to depend on, and no-one missed the rabbits I could snare. I even managed to pull some veg from the smallholdings around Romney, not to mention the odd free range egg. There was oil left for the lamp too, and matches, though in time I had to liberate some more. The fisherman never came."

He nodded, looking out across the garden, screwing his eyes up as he peered knowingly at the sea.

"Gone over the way, I suppose."

"But it would have been pretty uncomfortable."

"Not compared to the trenches it wasn't, and I wasn't having to worry about the Huns crumping about with aerial torpedoes and whizz bangs, to say nothing about gas alarms. Fresh air, that's what I had. Cleaned me out, the wind and the rain, and I hung myself out to dry when the sun was warm. Gave me an idea, living in that little hut. It was like it had grown there, quite natural, just pushed up out of the shingle, like a little black periscope on the edge of the land and the sea. I knew I might be seen from away off, there was no cover to speak of, but I was all seeing myself on the edge of that flat land. The beach was my guard dog, no-one goes unheard on the stones, and the wooden walls told me whether to stay in my bunk or get out and enjoy the seaside sun. They were like a barometer. That's when I got the idea. I couldn't stay there forever, after all."

"The Round House."

"That's it. The Round House."

"So, all of it, the war, Hermione, Étaples, you were able just to forget it all."

"You haven't been listening. It didn't start with them and it won't end until I drop. Jesus, lad, you sound as deluded as was I."

After two years he felt not so much born again as cleansed. He was leaner, fitter, quick on his feet and quickened by the natural world that for such a long time had been his only companion. Yet to anyone who had known him those years before, the changes wrought in him had not made him in the least bit unrecognisable nor would they find him strange to behold. After two years he was refreshed, not replaced, and however desperate and sincere had been his wish, that first morning on the ridge of Greatstone's high shingle bank, without the intervention of death he knew he could never be free.

"Keep it simple then. Keep out of it. That'll do." It became a mantra.

The smell of grass warming in the spring, the sheep spilled across the marsh from safe home farms, all the presence of a renewing year reached him in his salty outpost, the morning sun inspiring a sweet breeze from landward. It was in the spring of his second year that increasingly there were men working in the fields, where the expanse of shingle cast up from more recent seas gave way to a fine fertile landscape. He could see cars and trucks, too, moving freely on the coast road where only a short while ago there had been little sign of anything except military traffic.

He judged that the war was over. The world had moved on. No-one had come for him.

"Good. Yes, I can say it is good." He spoke to himself, a running conversation that exerted his presence over the tumult of birds and the smug community of monosyllabic sheep that had been the more constant neighbours of his adopted home.

"OK, I know, I said no more. Well, all right, I'm here aren't I?" He ground his teeth and clenched his fist. "I'm here. There's no denying that. *Je pense donc je suis*, as the wise Frog said. But keep it simple. That'll do it. No need for anything too dramatic."

He brought his clenched fist up to his face, slow but hard against his cheek, his jaw quickly aching from the impact, tasting the rilling blood in his mouth. His strength surprised him. It felt good.

"OK, maybe it's not all gone but I can still make it different. Just need to keep it simple. It may be all *cogito ergo sum*, that's undeniable, that's ok, but I just have to stay out of it, stay away from all the other cogitation that's going on. Don't let any of my wires cross with theirs."

The awakening land buoyed him up and he was restless. More to the point, someone was bound to come. If the war were indeed done someone would come and discover him. It wouldn't look good.

One morning, before the sun was visible in the lightening sky, he set out across the marsh, a great fan of green with its fulcrum at Dungeness and its spreading folds held apart by the towns of Haven in the east and Rye in the west. It was not just a place, it was another place altogether, with an atmosphere all of its own. He imagined he might close it around him and be it, breathe it deep inside him. He fancied it might even make a parable of the desire he had to step out from the driving passions of the world of men, out of those bonds that sweep one on regardless of the exercise of reason; he would break free and be vanished into another existence with its own easy chemistry of tranquillity, timelessness and self-determination.

The Royal Military Canal ran a custodial ribbon around its curved and open perimeter and, following the ancient course of the Rhee Wall, the old Roman road that ran directly inland from Greatstone, he crossed it at Appledore, where his edgy mood soon softened, the generous morning light reflecting from the streets of hanging tiles making him feel warm, relaxed and resolved. Hitching a lift on a coal merchant's lorry going to load at the railway depot, it was still early when he reached Ashford and traded his skean-dhu for a ride in the guard's van on a slow train to London.

"I'm sorry, I don't get it."

"What don't you get?"

"All this hiding away, this self-contemplation. After what you had seen and, more to the point, what you had done. You make it seem so easy to shrug it off. Make it seem like it was somebody else's fault. But you killed her and one minute you sounded like you were totally shattered and – and the next it's all new worlds and new beginnings, give or take a couple of wretched years in a hut on a beach in the most raggety southernmost bit of the country. Well, I guess *she* would have rather that, rather been there than be snuffed out. Didn't you feel the least bit bad about what you had done?"

"Of course I did. No-one with any trace of conscience or pity running in their blood wouldn't have. But that wasn't why I had to get out. It wasn't about Hermione. I wasn't moved to sorrow, if that's what you're wanting me to admit, to say I was sorry. She was just a casualty. Of war. Of life. There was nothing she or I could have done to prevent what happened over there. I was sorry that I'd been the instrument of her death, though – and that's what I was running away from, don't you see? And though I knew then I could never forget what had happened – that I had been what had happened – I really thought I'd got away. One has to try."

Fazakerly took hold of Stephen's chin and raised his face until their eyes met.

"How did you get away, lad? Or is that it, your problem – you didn't make it?"

- SEVEN -

"HARRY, DID I EVER tell you about that time in Dover, during the war – I was a trainer for the War Reserve Police as you know – there was this crowd gathered in front of a house that hadn't properly screened its upstairs windows. No blackout. They'd started pulling stones from the ornamental rockery and lobbing them at the windows. Getting very ugly. Could've been a lynching if we hadn't come by."

"Hmmm."

"That incident's always stayed there, just at the back of my mind. To think how quickly honest God-fearing folk can turn nasty. An hour or so previous they'd have been all pals together, repairing an air raid shelter, doing salvage duty. It was fear of course. It always is. That lot in Dover were afraid that Jerry might see the light and drop a ton on them all. But it wasn't just that. It seemed to me there was something just a bit less obvious at the back of it all. I worked it out later. What was going on there was the impossibility – and, you know, I do mean impossible - that damned nigh on inescapable impossibility always of never being able to duck the prevailing mood, that's what hit me. No room for deviation. From the moment war was declared, everyone was signed up, willing or not. And if you didn't go along with it all as expected...well. But it doesn't have to take a war."

"That's people for you. Community. The will of the community needs to prevail."

"You've got it, Harry. Anyway, that's what worried me about this business with your lad. You don't want any rocks through your windows, now, right? Bad for trade too if all this got about."

"Mmmm. Well, it seems that everything's not as we thought…"

"Maybe. May well be the old chap didn't peg out - and there's more to this than first met our eye of course, him included, always creeping around on his own - but young…your young fellowmelad, he's certainly mixed up in this somewhere. Hard to say where."

"So…"

"Well, I won't be making any arrests, that's for sure. I'll be keeping an eye out though; it's been a terrible business and I suggest you keep a lid on it. Like I say, there's no telling when things can get ugly."

"Just go on as normal, then, stick to the rules."

"That's it. Here, I would say that, wouldn't I?"

"There shouldn't be any trouble, just keeping the peace."

"That's all we have to do. Anyway, you can't lay all this on the kid. He is only a kid after all. No harm done, I suppose; well, not unless you consider the house."

His voice lowered. He looked around the low-ceilinged public bar and leaned forward, his lips exaggerating the whispered import of his words in a kind of flabby, elastic semaphore.

"But it was a bloody eyesore all the same, I reckon. Needed a good lick of paint."

He chuckled and there was a sense that the serious words for which they had met outside of their usual weekly schedule had already been delivered. There was no sting to be had from the tail of this conversation.

"Who'd have built a round bloody wooden house anyway, in this day and age? Good riddance, eh? Perhaps we've been done a good turn."

The large policeman shifted back in the shiny wooden chair, where he sat as tight as an egg in an eggcup and scrutinised the dark coal-like pieces spread across his palms.

"I shan't shed a tear, I can tell you. There we are, double six."

He placed the smooth black domino on the table and sat back with a sigh of satisfaction, his chest and cheeks puffed out, both men reaching for their pint jugs and raising them in unison to their lips. It was the closest either would come to apportioning blame. More to the point was how they might deal with the imbalance that had been threatened. How to preserve the earned respect for a hard working man, his family; how to protect the deserved equanimity of a town that had survived the indignities of war, whose desolate broken places had begun to heal under the balm of rose-bay willow-herb and where the wartime spirit of all hands together drifted among them still like ether.

"I'm not even going to treat it as a misdemeanour."

"Aah."

"As for you, well it's not for me to dictate. You and your good lady wife, you've had worry enough. I'll leave the boy in your capable hands. But as far as I'm concerned, least said the better. These things can grow all out of proportion. He's had his fright. Her too. Enough said. It's not easy bringing up a family."

"So, you think it will all pass over, then."

"Just a fire. No-one needs to know how or why. Some old recluse come to the end of his tether. Better off where he is now if you ask me. What more is there to be said? We've had plenty of worse fires in these parts not so many years since, as there's a number of folk still around will recall. You weren't here during the war, were you."

"Gunner. Wellingtons."

"Yes, I remember. Poor you. Still, folk hereabouts will always wish you well, turning the heat back on those bastards over there. You've seen what a mess they made around these parts. Flying bombs mostly."

"Mmmm. But we're all friends now aren't we? Isn't that what they say? Christ, we've even got the French and the Germans joining the same club – wasn't it in March this year?"

"True."

"– and there are those who want us to join, you know, Britain, join this EEC thing. So what was it all about? All those lives lost and they turn round and say *oh no, actually we're friends now*. What was the point? Strike me, I don't know."

"Well, I won't forgive them."

"We have to stick together."

"Like I said, I'll pass on this one. There's been no harm done. All those boys from the Press, did you see them? – like vultures – but nothing much will come of that. I did my best to keep them away from the boy, and there's no scandal there for them, I suppose, you know what they like. Like I said, just carry on as normal. I've enough on anyway what with sorting out these Teddy boys and all their tomfoolery. You heard what they've done down at the Ritz cinema, of course. Animals. You know, people don't want all that nonsense. But that's where there'll be a lot more trouble, mark my words; there'll be fighting in the streets next."

So they were to be released from blame. Though he did not enjoy the relief of blamelessness, this father of the felon too young even to be termed delinquent in a time when Juvenile Delinquent was a badge proudly worn by Sandy's troublesome Teddy boys, in an age that would soon lionise the cult of angry young men and eventually be turned gladly upside down by the youthful dismantlement of every social and moral code upon which society would stand or fall. Or so it was thought.

So the old man lived; but draining the last drop of ale from his jug this blameless father of the putative recidivist tasted again the sharp dead brew of gall that had settled in his gut, the numbing presence of death that had come so close in that simple police station, where he had fallen against it in the quiet of the enquiry room and which he had carried with him since.

What had it all been for and why had he struggled so, to make good his place amongst these people, this town, this life? What was the point when the fortress of endeavour and propriety that he had built could so unexpectedly and completely be wrecked from within? With his own hands, he had built it with his own hands, gladly, generously, according to all the rules written and spoken and exchanged with neighbour and officer and even the air they breathed, accepting and accepted. Now it was torn open, exposed to view, they would see the full spectacle of his true standard planted in the ruins, they would stand and admire and fear his colours of crime with the banner raised high above the debris of his proud achievements. Look, see, the dark cloth flapping, hear it crack in the bleak wind, the shroud of death aloft, no less. The terrible act perpetrated, it was said, by the only son of this fallen house was no less terrible for want of worst consequences, the guilt not mitigated by an absence of proof. Yes, true, it was just association, the finger that pointed, just association; but it was enough. He might as well raise the Jolly Roger from their roof.

He rode home on his bicycle, the whirr of the dynamo pacing the thrust of his feet on the pedals as he concentrated on keeping the lamplight steady; his mood was uncharacteristically anything like constant.

"Is he asleep?"

She nodded, his wife, the mother of their misfortune. Was it her that had loosed her hold, slipped the guiding hand and glanced away for that fatal moment? Had she let the boy fall? He shrank from the cold accusation that had insinuated itself, thoughts unworthy and unsolicited given audience in the flaw of his relentless devotion. No, it had come from outside, from beyond them, something monstrous that had entered unbidden into the fold of their domestic certainties. It was much larger than them. It moved amongst them all.

They sat at the kitchen table and he cleared his throat. He stared for a moment into the open firebox of the stove where amber coke seemed to slumber after having warmed the water for his bath. He was unused to speaking his thoughts.

"Well, it seems no-one was killed."

She caught her breath, her hand at her mouth, eyes wide.

"So that's something at least."

Her hand moved to the sleeve of her jersey, fumbling with the cuff. It was suddenly uncomfortably warm in the room.

"And", he exhaled heavily between closed teeth, "seems also that no-one saw how it started. Well, Stephen, of course, and then shortly after... What I'm saying is that there's not enough for the police to prosecute. At least, that's what Sandy was telling me. Not at the moment and...well, seems we ought not to expect..."

"Oh!" She brightened, touching his wrist. "So, that's good isn't it?"

"He seems to think we should just go about our business as if nothing's happened. But it has, hasn't it? There's an old man up in St Eanswythe's hospital with his skin taken a good browning and round the corner we've got a pile of cinders that used to be a house."

He stood up, drawn to the open stove. The room was warm but he was shivering. The shifting of coke in the grate gave off a bright flurry of golden sparks but no smoke. No, there it was, he could smell the ash of Fazakerly's ruin; it was in the chimney, it hung upon the town, cold and damp.

"Why us?" he asked. "Everything was going so well. He's not a bad boy. I never thought of him like that. Plenty worse."

"We must have done something wrong," she offered. She refused to let go the message of hope that he had just carried home to them. Whatever they'd done they could identify it and make amends. "But..."

"No. It's not us. It's not even him."

"You mean they have found someone else who.."

"No. I mean it's something else."

"Some *thing* else? I don't understand."

How could he explain? His own perceptions had changed. All those dreadful years spent dealing and dodging death, looking down and imagining the yells and screams a thousand feet below him as cities burned, the stabbing light that fought back and found him, limned him and his plane against the clouds, a spidery outline waiting to be swotted by the brisk hand of death, in retribution. So many times, so many fears, the routine goodbyes, thinking this time it will be forever. Only he always came back, one of the lucky ones, back with his dreams and his hopes and his plans. Ready to make his way in a land fit, once more, for heroes. And so it had been. So why now? Why not then?

"Neither do I. But we've got to deal with it. You're right."

"We'll be all right. You have respect in the town. We're not Council people. Word might get out but no-one will believe anything, even if they hear it. It's him we must be thinking of now. Mustn't let this upset him."

"For Chrissake, woman..! No, leave it. I'm sorry, Sandy said there was no evidence."

He lit a taper from the fire and touched it to the cigarette at his mouth.

"There's something not right here but I don't know what it is. I cannot explain it. But that boy has been caught up in something that feels, well, terrible."

"Harry," she had her arm around his waist; "we can deal with it."

"I dare say."

"As long as we keep it to ourselves. Mustn't let it take over. Probably nothing. You know kids."

He felt he no longer knew anything, nothing that would help him move on anyway. It left him no option but to carry on as before. Only now there was this darkness too, this coldness at his back. He had been first aware of it there on that night in the police station, when it was suddenly made known to him. Unbidden, it had introduced itself and it had taken great courage for him to recognise it, to say its name, to hear it tumble forth from his own mouth, to give it presence with his own breath. It had acknowledged him at last, after all those years, after all those sorties when it might so much more easily have jumped up and snatched him for its own.

"Dead?"

"Harry?"

"Mmm? Oh, nothing. Yes, we must take care of him. I dare say it'll all just pass over him like a bad dream. He'll forget it in a day or so. You've had words, this morning?"

"Well, not really. I mean, after we'd been told to expect the all clear, it didn't seem right to go on about it. I really think he's suffered enough. Being made to go down to the police station like that, at his age, and you know how sensitive he can be, it must have put the fear of God into him. No, I thought it best just to act as normal, put a brave face on everything."

"I see. Probably the best. Didn't he ask...?"

"No. Nothing. Seemed quite perky. Offered to help me around the house. I wasn't feeling up to much myself, of course, I was so sorry to hear about poor Mr Fazakerly, it was a real shock. Horrible. I encouraged him to go out. It was a fine morning."

"So, no need to clear the air. He's all right then?"

"He's all right. But what about you? You look half dead yourself."

"It'll pass. A shock, like you say. Just so long as the boy is ok, we can deal with this. There'll be talk, mind, but no-one's going to have anything really, well, you know, not in the way of evidence. It'll all be talk. You might get some sharp looks when you go down the High Street, but I'm sure it won't last."

But it would never go away, he knew that. The die had been cast, resmelted.

They'd be the family who used to live in that nice Victorian three-storey, came down from London not so many years after the war. Just the one child. Nice boy. A bit strange, a bit of a loner sometimes.

A bit of a dreamer, I'd say.

Something happened there. Don't know why. You remember the old chap, don't you? Mr Buttercup we used to call him. Not related, least I think not. You remember him surely, he had a dreadful old bike, a real bone shaker, lived in that peculiar wooden house opposite the end of Queen's Road. Remember?

Fazakerly, I think his name was. Someone set fire to it, that's what I heard.

Yes, it was deliberate. The son was taken down the police station, I know that. My Arthur saw him, he was in delivering paraffin. Pink they use there. Never proved anything though.

Really? You mean, the boy?

I remember all too well. There were men from the papers in asking questions at reception; I was cleaning at the hotel.

Oh yes. Nice looking kid. Decent people, they say. She was always well turned out, wasn't she, very tasteful. Well I never.

But then, I always thought they might be a bit swanky, a mite standoffish, and him only a barber too. A gentlemen's hairdresser, she used to correct me!

Hah! Well, there's no knowing what went on there, not with folk like that. I'm surprised they got away with it, all the same. But wasn't the father pally with the local bobby?

So they say.

Well, there you go.

"St Eanswythe's, did you say? Fazakerly is in St Eanswythe's? Perhaps I should…"

"Oh no, you stay away. It has nothing to do with us. We have ourselves to consider."

More than that. It felt like they had the whole world to consider now. This shadow at his back, the weight he could hear clunking and dragging its dark and pitiless form, it had harnessed him, it had hung its dull burden from the very bonds it had lashed about him, binding him to the world with his own moral sensibility.

"When I stood there, with Sandy sitting behind his desk, hearing those terrible things, hearing that this man, this old man was dead, and it seemed like it was because...of us, I went cold. I thought, that's it, put your head in the noose Harry, it's all over. Well, he isn't dead, thank Christ; but it's still over. For me. For you. I'd thought that coming here, living here and doing quite all right, thank you, well we could just get on with our lives. No need to worry about other folk. Live and let live. Well, that was all a load of pie in the sky. Folk just can't leave you alone. Not even dead men, if you had your way. What do we have to do, I ask you? No, you stay away, do you hear me? Just stay away."

- EIGHT -

His house in Tollington Park was boarded up. It didn't surprise him. Last word of his mother had been the brief report from a neighbour concerning her sudden decline and anticipated removal to a hospital. He could not recall the probable location. The letter had taken two months to reach him. That it found him at all when his address was an anonymous pit in the lee of an upturned tank was something of a miracle.

Besieged on a rise of shattered copse, the only natural feature remaining in that particular middle of a grey waste of mud in southern Belgium, he had reflected with a certain wryness upon his short-lived impulse to seek compassionate leave. In all reality there was no way out of that place. They had reached stalemate months before. The barbed wire that separated friend from foe also fenced them in, they had traded positions with the enemy so many times all were now equally lost in a maze of unfamiliar fortifications whose identities had been blurred by the seemingly continuous rain. Even if they dared to raise themselves over the shifting ramparts of their trench encampment, in the expectation of plotting a course out, they had no reliable co-ordinates to map the myriad mines and buried tripwires with which both sides had laced the all but liquefied landscape.

There was no certain way back across the flat shiny expanse that now stretched all the way to the horizon, a smudgy ring of grey that started in the west and eventually stretched round and merged with the brighter mist the morning made of the distance in the east. Only the passage of the sun each day, and the occasional small plane that buzzed over the putrefying gutters of the front line provided any reliable sense of orientation. If it were hostile the plane would shower them with a flurry of implacable explosives, gas canisters and a hail of rapid fire; if it was friendly, and so long as the pilot himself could distinguish enemy from comradely earthworks, a light swarm of small silk parachutes would descend with inappropriate grace, bearing medicaments, military orders and packets of mail. By matching the roundels on a plane's wing and fuselage with the direction of its enviable retreat, it was possible to deduce the general position of both enemy and British rearguards. It was such a flying visit that had delivered news of Mrs Fazakerly's own misfortunes.

She was in a better place than him. At least she would be despatched with dignity, and some comfort, clean and dry in a warm bed. In any case, it was because of her that he had enlisted, to get away, and the completeness of the break the war had enabled still struck him as preferable to continuing with the way things had been at home. What would it profit anyone if he should return, the dutiful son, except to give her one final opportunity to rob him of his singularity? That and service to the less threatening but insistent charade of keeping up appearances.

Two, no nearer three years had passed since he'd read that note. She had been a determined and wealthy woman, but he was sure that she must have succumbed by now to the insidious disease that had already confined her to the house for some years prior to his departure.

Concerned not to announce his return to London to the rest of the street he crept down the side passageway and forced open the door to the rear garden; it was overgrown with brambles and the hinges moaned grievously to the rotten wood as it was jolted back. Pushing his way through this little wilderness he found that the windows and scullery door at the back of the house had been secured by stout timbers, the nails that held them rusty but resolute and hammered firmly into the sound wood of the frames. The key to the coal cellar was in its lock, as always, but there was no sign that this door had been moved either, not for a considerable time. A fine drift of leaves from the silver birches, which made a boundary between the garden and the small patch of waste ground beyond it, lay undisturbed in the recess around the two shallow steps leading down to the door, piled up in a soft brown slope against its panelled surface, deep and damp. At least two autumns had passed and no-one had cleared the back path.

He smiled: all well and good. As anticipated, he would be saved from having to give an account of himself.

The cellar key turned in the lock and, kicking away the detritus that had gathered under it, he could reach inside for the shovel that was always left leaning against the wall. In no time at all his passage into the cellar was cleared and he slipped through, closing the door on the drop catch behind him.

There was no light in the coal cellar. With the outside door open, normally one could see well enough to fill a scuttle. More to the point, a short flight of stairs led up to another, interior door, which when held open with something heavy - like a magnum, he thought - let in the light from the main hall of the house. How familiar it all seemed, and what luck that no inquisitive vagrant had thought to explore this unguarded but unexpected rear entrance. Fazakerly sprang up the stairs. He had no need of a light but the shadow of an anxious thought was barely suppressed, even as he reached for the door handle, desperately wanting not to find his successful homecoming finally barred. No, it too had been left unlocked, it was a folly that had become customary, and the door swung in soundlessly until it knocked heavily against the huge empty champagne bottle that he had left there years before.

There was no light in the house but he wasn't planning to make himself at home. He closed the cellar door and placed the empty magnum against it, then hauled an antique coat stand down the length of the hall and shimmied that too against the door. They might not keep determined housebreakers from making their way in, and it seemed that the open passage had never drawn unwelcome attention, but he would receive fair warning if his own entrance had been noticed and someone came after to apprehend him. After all, he reasoned, if I'm not missing presumed dead I suppose I am likely to be classed as being absent without leave. Had anyone come for him already, and did they shoot deserters after the cessation of hostilities? He didn't care to find out.

In the front parlour he found boxes of candles. The onset of his mother's systemic sclerosis had rendered her sensitive to even the smallest artificial light and she had found it preferable for her evenings to be lit more primitively. With the boards over the windows it was almost pitch dark in the room but treading forward carefully he was gratified to find the candles were still there, where she had always kept them, three full boxes stacked on the mantelpiece. Fortunately, it seemed that no-one had been in to rearrange the room. If that were the case, there were also matches to be found in a tiny leather drum on the sideboard, with a striker stitched into the interior of the lid. He hesitated before reaching for it.

"Don't touch", she had always snapped at him, it was a memory from way back in his earliest years, "you play with fire and you'll be burned".

The match drum went into the right-hand pocket of his coat and a bundle of candles into his left-hand pocket. As he turned, something rolled onto the floor and clattered against the wainscot. Damn. It would be a candlestick, one of a pair that sat at the back. He stood for a few seconds. No matter. He would do without. Out in the hall a faint grey glimmer filtered all the way down from the fanlight in the ceiling at the top of the house but he knew the way to her office on the first floor like the back of his hand and had no need of light.

The office was a converted box bedroom that, otherwise ordinary enough, hung out, by way of a small triangular vault, over the front steps to the house. Kneeling on the window seat that filled its base one could establish the identity of callers without the necessity of going all the way downstairs and drawing back the heavy curtains that hung over the vestibule, finally opening the ponderous half-glazed door on the off chance that this would be a welcome visitor. My ne'er-do-well's observatory, his mother had called it, without humour. The lower panes of this crow's nest had been covered on the outside with boards that were as secure as those he'd found at the rear of the house, obliterating the view beneath, but the decorative floral glass that made a frieze of amber and green along the top edge had thoughtfully been avoided. The two centre sections of the frieze had been made to slide open sideways, allowing ventilation without prejudice to security, and Fazakerly eased them back. As a child this had been his room and he had often lain in bed watching the evening light filter through the coloured glass, imagining that the bird song he heard through the tiny open panels was coming from within the vines etched into the glass. There was no bird song today but someone coughing nearby broke the silence and he climbed up on to the window seat and peered down at the street. A neighbour he did not recognise was leaning against the wall opposite, rolling a cigarette. No cause for alarm, not for the moment anyway, but it gave a new haste to his endeavours.

He lit a candle, made a puddle of wax on the edge of the desk and held the candle until it was firmly planted, before lighting another from its bright wick and fixing that to the opposite side of the desk. That was light enough, and within the hour he had discovered sufficient of his mother's business papers to know that he might leave never to return. He had them spread out on the desk between the candles, an array of contracts, deeds and bills that in one short sift he had identified as a convincing account of her business and property. The green and red postage stamps with over signatures, wax seals and sundry ribbons gave the impression of a lawyer's archive. The many-folded marriage and birth certificates that he took from a vellum sheaf in the false bottom of his mother's precious scroll chair gave their own history of his lineage, providing sufficient authenticity to the claims that he planned to establish. She had sat in that chair every day since his father died, until her illness took hold, looking regal - quite powerful, he had thought when a child - dictating instructions in foreign tongues that would almost literally, it seemed to him, bear fruit, when the cases of wine were brought on carts to the front gate, bearing mysterious labels decorated with the proud images of vineyards and rustic foreign charm, the majesty of grand and classical sounding places written in swirling gold script, the promise that from those bottles one might uncork a taste of endless summer and gain entrance to another place where there was a freedom and space that was unknown to him and which, he feared, he was being prevented from knowing.

That thought returned to him now and he felt the house become a prison once again. Quickly, the candles were extinguished and he had bundled the papers together, rushing blindly down the dark stairs, trusting to memory.

"Thomas, is that you?"

He faltered at the parlour door, documents spilling from his arms.

"How many times have I told you not to run on the stairs?"

He froze in the act of stepping past the door, waiting with his breath held down in the bottom of his throat, his ears awake to every tick and whisper the old house might make. It couldn't be her.

"I'm sorry, I..." – his voice came out in a pitiful squeak. Fool, damned fool. What was he thinking? He waited. His legs were beginning to go numb. Voices in the street outside percolated through the small openings in the office window on the floor above, birdlike female voices offering salutations that seemed to fill the whole house with sound. He heard more coughing, a man and two women arguing jocularly. He had mistaken them for something, someone else. The house had beguiled him. Ridiculous. He was aware of his face glowing with embarrassment. But it had hold of him, that he was sure; he'd have to go back up, to close those two tiny panes. Mustn't let the rain in, Thomas.

He was hot with rage when he came down again. How dare she do this to me?

Fazakerly strode into the parlour, impelled by anger yet still restrained by an uncertain feeling of suspense. Just supposing, just supposing...

He held up a lighted match and the shadows jumped up at him, clawing, reaching, frightful shapes leaping over the high ceiling to drop upon him where he stood with his eyes and mouth wide open to their assault. The match dropped from his fingers and he found himself stomping on the carpet. Is it out? Is it out? Must be careful. Don't you play with fire Thomas!

He scrabbled in his coat pocket for a candle, feeling along the sideboard with his other hand until it touched the familiar shape of the second candlestick. Oh, please, let it not be all bunged up with wax. He pressed the candle home and struck another match, the light giving life to all those terrors that sprang at him again, poorly disguised as the legitimate occupants of the room, making him step back into the tiled grate, from where through half-closed eyes he glimpsed the anorexic forms of chairs that scrambled on wasted limbs across the carpet towards him, the looming stare of a pair of Chinese humidors and a rearing standard lamp with a great triangular head. Its blind gaze made him recoil again and he went stumbling over the fireguard, falling into the sprawling embrace of a dead aspidistra, still erect in its porcelain pot, which clutched stiffly at his neck. He cried out, once, sharp and clear, eliciting a brisk reply:

"Thomas! Thomas! You are so immature. It's nothing but your own imagination."

The grim theatre ceased at once. He knew this time the voice was in his head; he recognised the complaint from long ago in his childhood. Later, she had turned to other, more sophisticated means of chastening him, each given currency as she had deemed it consistent with his progress through the years during which he submitted to her instruction.

Fazakerly opened his eyes again, the candle held up high, his gaze darting about the room. It was clear. He was alone. Nothing to worry about, then. Well, he knew that, didn't he, it was obvious from the start there was going to be no-one here; the whole place was closed up. Well, almost.

As if drawn by gravity, his eyes came to rest on his mother's easy chair, a high-backed plump affair in brocaded old rose, with maroon piping and tassels that swung from its stiff wings and ruched skirt. There was an ornate antimacassar too, in Venetian lace, and matching frills and delicate pom-poms adorned the quilted pouffe that stood on the floor next to it. Though not to his own taste, the chair had been bought less for its aesthetic appearance than the comfort it would provide to someone whose musculature was wasting away. This chair was the antithesis of the proud seat of office upstairs, where harsh rectitude had been tempered by a firm belief in the frailty of humankind and both business and private affairs were dealt with in a spirit of fair dealing. By contrast, here was the artless throne of a lingering tyrant who throughout her years of descent into decrepitude had exercised impenitent and bitter thrall over her few remaining subjects - her only son, the live-in nurse, a daily woman and Mr Crieff from the bond, but mainly her son - with the sole purpose of reaffirming her power over them. Always out of place in the otherwise traditional disposition of this room, the chair now served as a grotesque and stark totem for Fazakerly's last memories of his familial home. It was stuffed with extra cushions and a grey striped pillow and, with no effort at all, he could make out in the light from his single candle the deep indentation left in the pillow by a hunched and withered human form.

"Do you know, I even reached out to see if it was still warm. How's about that for crazy? Well, that's how she got to me, even after she'd gone. D'you know, I was twenty-one years old when I enlisted and I was terrified more from being by myself - I mean not having her there - than I was by the German guns. Yet it was her I'd run away from! What do you think of that?"

Stephen leant across unconsciously and patted up the bolster that kept Fazakerly erect in his armchair:

"Sounds spooky. But what had she done? I can't relate to that."

"No? You surprise me."

"Hey – "

"Never mind. We'll come back to that. As I was saying, it was a godsend for me, the war; well, that's how it seemed at first. Twenty-one years I'd been stuck with her. Do this, do that; no, not that way, like this, like me. Watch. On and on and on and on. And more than that. It was like I had nothing of me left."

"But you said she was fair."

"She had rules, sure. Her rules of course, not mine."

"A formidable lady."

"Formidable? You're not keeping up at all. Yes, she was better educated than most women of the time, and she had a formidable grasp of business, you're right on that score, but she was my mother too. That's what fucked me up well and truly. I was never allowed to have my own view on things. Never allowed to discover anything for myself or if I did then I was corrected. It was always her, her, her. Every minute of every day, arranged her way. I tell you, I wasn't allowed to go to school. She had a tutor come to the house. At first I thought, great, someone I can talk to, someone who'll open doors, I was so cloistered I felt I was choking. But of course he was instructed by her so, well, when he was lecturing me it was like listening to her all over again. Worse than that, she'd test me afterwards, just to make sure some unapproved thoughts hadn't managed to insinuate themselves between our breaths."

"I'm beginning to get the picture."

"Oh, hurrah! But I'm making it sound simple. It wasn't. I just grew up thinking that being in this kind of mental straitjacket was normal, that that's what happened to everyone, not that I got to meet many other people, especially not kids my own age."

"What about books? You'd find different opinions in books."

"I did. My father had quite a library and, oddly, she didn't keep me from going in there, not even after he died. But she dismissed them as lies, collections of lies, fabrication and distortion. She said that they were responsible for his failures, why in effect she'd had to rescue the business – they were wine importers, you know – all just time wasting nonsense. I was supposed to learn from them, though, by learning not what to think."

"God!"

"Oh, there was plenty of that too. God. Religion. The salvation I could look forward to with a glad heart. That wasn't lies. Apparently."

"But all this sounds just like a typical Victorian household, surely. Just a carry over from her own childhood perhaps. It doesn't explain..."

"She made me feel I didn't exist. Me, my inner self. Absent. And that's what you must understand. It's important. I suppose it got worse when I was older, particularly when she started to feel unwell and I had to be at her beck and call all day and night, though I'm sure she made up a lot of her demands just so she knew where I was. I ended up just thinking that all we're here for is to serve, and that wasn't enough. I had a brain in my head. It wasn't enough just to do someone's bidding. I wanted to do something that was an expression of me, not because it would contribute to the well-being of the world, not because it was expected or kindly. I didn't want to be a part of someone else's plan. And I did learn from the books, funnily enough, not in the way she expected perhaps, but not that different either. But all that came later, of course. When I'd had time to think – first in France, and then in my little abode on the beach in Kent.

You see, when I said I was terrified to be away from her you may not have got my meaning. It wasn't that I needed her to hold my hand; no, what I meant was, I was scared of myself, or for myself. I was so sure by then I had no purpose other than to be used in someone else's plan, it was truly terrifying, because she wasn't there to tell me what was going to happen next. And suddenly I found myself in the midst of a whole host of strangers. I didn't know who was going to make the call. I could just hear all these voices going on around me, trying to make out which ones I should be heeding, who was plotting my course, who needed what and when."

"Sounds like hell!"

"It was.   Still, I was in the best place I suppose, considering."

"What, the front line?"

"The army, stupid. Huh! That was a paradox. Here was me not wanting to be owned by anyone and then I go and enlist, ready to take orders. Well, it had shape, you see, the army. Of sorts. To start with it did, anyway, and I couldn't just make my way alone in the world. I'd had no experience. In the army I had no choice but to do as I was told."

"Out of the frying pan…"

"It suited me then. So there you are. Why hadn't I gone sooner, you may ask. Well, that just goes to show how accomplished she was. My view of the world was, well, that house. Everything outside was insubstantial.   I reckon I thought I'd sink through the tiles on the path if I ever made it out the front door on my own.   Or there'd be someone waiting behind the privet to snatch me away for his own devilish purpose. It had to be better in the house. And if all the books were lies, well how could I trust anything I might read outside.   It would all be written to trap me, some machiavellian device to fetter me to some other man's needs. I know, it sounds crazy. Perhaps I was."

"Mother. This is not you. This is just an impression left by you and look", he turned over the pillow, plumping it up, "now you are gone."

He found himself grinning. A fucking madman; I've become a fucking madman, talking like that. No, he thought, she did that to me. Well, I'm here and she is not. And I'm free of her at last, free of everything.

His knuckles rapped against something hard in the fold of the seat cushion. A key. He held it in front of him and brought the candle closer. It was a key he knew well but had never touched before. Many's the time she had waved it in front of his nose.

"No Thomas, I cannot risk it. What would your father say?"

But she would risk old Crieff, passing him the key like it was the crown jewels, and he would stalk off down the hall, returning with his plain black shoes sprinkled with dust and bearing a bottle of crisp Bordeaux or a Médoc, perhaps a long bottle of Soave Classico or sometimes a dark, fat port, what ever suited her mood, the key returned ostentatiously to the closet of her bosom. Ever dutiful, under her watchful eye young Fazakerly would be petitioned to uncork the bottle and pour her a glass. But there was no glass for him.

"This is business, you see, not pleasure. I don't drink for pleasure. And neither shall you, Thomas. That's the devil's work."

Crieff had not visited for almost a year before Fazakerly's escape from the house and she had not relented. It seemed she would rather forgo the pleasure herself than extend the burden, admit the lie.

The door to the wine cellar was built unobtrusively into the slope of the stairs: four panels over a crossbeam, foreshortened by the diagonal of the stair tread, and two larger panels below. There was no door handle. The key turned a quiet lock and the door fell open soundlessly under the weight of its asymmetry. Wooden steps descended into a space that, in the light from the candle, seemed to occupy almost the entire breadth of the house. The walls were painted white but were darkened where they had been draped with dust-laden spider webs. The rear wall was bare brick, and he guessed that it divided this larger portion of the basement from the coal cellar.

All this he could view through the shoulder-high racking that filled the room and lined the walls, racking that was secured by metal rods bolted into beams running the length of the ceiling, that was divided into upright sections the width of his extended forearm, with diagonal wires crossing each other, each half the thickness of his pinky, and describing a pattern of squares that stood on their corners like diamonds and, it gradually dawned on him, was a purpose built wine store that was now totally devoid of the prized reserve of vintage wines his mother had been laying down for as long as he could remember. There should have been hundreds, more likely thousands of bottles nestling between those wires. He had frequently seen the list on her desk after a consignment was delivered. Wines from Bordeaux, Burgundy, Rhône and Alsace; there had been cases of Piemonte, Toscana, satchel-like containers of Rioja Gran Reserva and more, from all over Europe. Not only had he seen the list, he had watched Crieff carry the newly arrived bottles in hessian baskets down to the cellar, his mother's special selection. He remembered in particular the colourful and richly decorated labels of the German Qualitätsweins, whose garlanded script alone excited and enticed one to sample the flowery harvest within.

All gone. Was this her last strike against him? Had she really disposed of it all before she was removed to the hospital? None of the devil's work for Thomas. Such spite!

It was only then he noticed the pile of lumber heaped against the stanchions that held the steps in place. The candle guttered momentarily and he lit another from its flame before descending to the cellar floor, holding it precariously in his hand but oblivious of the spattering wax. Yes, it was a rough tumble of planking and heavy duty plywood, the same materials as he'd seen fixed to the windows of the house, not a lot but enough that a disinterested workman would want to avoid having to drag back to the yard, especially when he had other, more precious assets to cart away. Now he was down on the cellar floor he could see that the thief had indeed dumped his tools, a claw hammer just thrown down, a small leather bucket spilling nails into the dust. Who could blame him, the bastard? He would need his hands free if he were to carry this treasure away.

He found a cork and cage from a champagne bottle perched on the edge of the third step. Yes, it would be thirsty work, emptying a cellar. How long had it taken? There must have been a gang of them. Too much for one man. But Fazakerly was already losing interest in the scale of the crime, for it hadn't escaped him that there was a wonderful sense of schadenfreude in all of this fiasco. To think of the years his mother had spent carefully selecting and hoarding this wonderful, expensive liquor, case by case and bottle by bottle, and it had been stolen away to be glugged, straight from the bottle no doubt, by some barbarians or tinkers who would have no appreciation of the finer points of the hierarchy of vines, of appellation and vintage, most likely the sort of unmentionable nobodies his mother would have spied from her office observatory and decided were unworthy of her going down even to open the front door and enquire of their purpose. Good grief, this was better than if he'd been able to have the wine for himself.

His perverse euphoria was quickly gone. On the fourth step he had discovered a small bundle of papers, seemingly gathered up at random and set down all higgledy-piggledy in an unsorted pile. He'd kicked it in his progress down the steps and an envelope had almost detached itself from the rest. There was something vaguely military about the franking on the envelope that attracted his attention. It was unopened, addressed to his mother. So, they had come seeking him then, as he had feared. He tore it open, his mind no longer on the purloined wine. There was a single sheet inside. It was a letter from Hermione.

Étaples, July 18th

Dear Mrs Fazakerly,

I was so delighted to learn of your approval of the course I have been taking with Thomas, especially your advice with respect to the kind of reading material that would appeal to him. It is really quite special to have a mother's insight into what best will serve to rehabilitate her dear son. As I explained in my earlier correspondence, he has been dreadfully traumatised by the situation here and I feel that I am almost dealing with a blank slate. But do not worry, the wounds he has suffered are not physical and I am sure our ministrations — mine and yours — shall bring him whole again.

Do not doubt my endeavours on your behalf. I shall have him brought home to you from this rough place as soon as passage is permissible and the moment he is passed fit for travel.

Sincerely,

Hermione Pickford

Shit! Shit, shit, shit! The unease he had first felt when seeing the envelope was fast churning up a rage in his chest and he puddled frantically with his hands in the loose sheaf of mail, church newsletters and tradesmen's lists.

The second letter had been sent two months earlier and was an evident postscript to an earlier introduction Hermione had made of herself, being a description of Fazakerly's suddenly improving condition, with a plea that her original request for advice about his likes and dislikes, and some particular childhood history, was now more urgent if she was effectively to develop her programme of nursing him back to health. It had evidently crossed his mother's reply in the erratic wartime post.

There was a third envelope addressed in the same elegant hand:

Étaples, August 23rd

Dear Mrs Fazakerly,

From your latest I fear that the exigencies of war have once more interrupted the normal flow of our postal exchange. Indeed, you would be horrified perhaps by what passes as normal this close to the Western Front. My letter of July 18th appears not to have reached you but I am glad to confirm again that the prognosis continues to be promising and dear Thomas is making excellent progress, not least thanks to your own, very special advice, for which I thank you again.

It is not possible to say much on the situation here, but I am sure you will have heard that things are not going frightfully well at the moment. This may be to Thomas's advantage, however, as they plan to remove non-combatants from what is called the theatre of war. We already have a contingent of Royal Engineers in the camp, a jolly bunch of fellows who are here to improve the roads to the coast, amongst other things of a rather more hush-hush nature.

I know it will be regarded as very silly of me, though when we live in such uncertain times I am sure you will be kind enough as to extend me the license to say it, but I feel that I have come to know Thomas so well these last few months. As my own special patient I have a very particular interest in his recovery, and he is proving to be a receptive and sympathetic companion in a world that one might dare to suggest has gone mad. You must be very proud of him.

Respectfully yours,

Hermione Pickford

Oh God, oh God, oh God, what have you done? You stupid woman. He scrunched the letter into a ball, for a moment in his anger dabbling with the thought that he would burn it, light it from a candle, and use it to set flames to the heap of lumber left by the workmen. Let him scourge this place. Oh God, oh God, she'd had her hooks into him even as he lay exhausted in a hospital bed. You stupid woman. Why write to his mother? He hadn't asked her to do that. He must burn the place, cleanse with fire the immense wound that was his life, erase all memory of her presence. He dropped the wadded letter. No, she'd have won then. He needed to take it all for himself, to make it work for him.

He made his way back up to the hall, not caring that hot wax from the candle held in his bare hand had coated his wrist. Perhaps there were more letters sent from Étaples. But he could find none in the hall; there was nothing on the doormat except the key to the front door. One of the workmen must have swept up all the mail when they entered; he imagined them running in when hailed by the expeditionary force that had discovered the treasure below stairs. The letterbox had been sealed up from the outside before they left. Work completed.

Fazakerly gathered up the documents he had retrieved from the office, placing them neatly on the floor next to the coal cellar door. Nudging the coat stand with his knee he eventually moved it across the hall until it more or less blocked the wine cellar door, which hung open. He wet a thumb and forefinger with saliva and extinguished the two candles, dropping the warm wax stubs into the neck of the magnum, which he slid away into the centre of the hall. The heat from the wax made the glass ping as though it would crack and he started.

"Thomas! Be careful with that. It's not a toy."

He fled through the door into the coal cellar where a thin line of light around its upper edge guided him to the back entrance. Feeling for the key in his pocket he found only the drum of matches and once again wondered, was this the best way. Why not burn it and be done, all his connections severed? No, it would not serve his plan. *His* plan. To think that he had a plan of his own at last gave him courage. He took a deep breath, patting his pockets. The key, where had he put the key? Of course, he had left it in the lock. He lifted the latch and stepped outside, pulling the door shut and turning the key until he felt the locking mechanism shift. Done; all done? He made a quick mental inventory of the documents he had removed from the house. Yes, all done. He pressed against the door to check it was secure then withdrew the key from the lock and hurled it over the birch trees into the grass on the waste ground.

"There, you bitch," he laughed, his head thrown back, "stuff you. That's you locked in there for good."

- NINE -

"Go on."

"Eh?" Fazakerly had started to daydream, his chin in his chest.

"Don't stop."

"Seems like it's me doing all the jawing this afternoon." He rubbed his stubbled cheeks with his palm and then smoothed away the smarts left in the skin of his throat.

"Well?"

"Well, there's still a lot I need to get from you, lad. I still need that answer – you know what I'm talking about."

Stephen shrugged.

"No, don't give me that look. It's important. I need to know."

"What, exactly?"

"What it was all about, of course. Why me? Who'd reeled me in this time? That's what I want to know. Who it was trying to claim me. Don't tell me it was an accident, my house suddenly going up in flames. Oh whoops, Mr Fazakerly, look what's happened, your house has just burned down. Me too, near as like."

"I don't know what it was all about. I really don't. It didn't have to be about anything."

"We'll see. We'll get there. Anyway, what I wanted to ask you – not *the thing I need to know* – is what brought you here anyway. I mean, are you training or something? They don't all wear uniforms here, it's hard to tell."

"I'm a student. A postgraduate. I'm just about to start my research."

"Ah. So I'm a head case am I, someone you're going to study and produce a miracle cure."

"Not at all. I'm not studying you. I'm not that kind of student. This is just a summer job, to get me some extra cash, just helping around the place."

"So what are you going to study, then?"

"Iconology. I'm researching English iconology in the Twentieth Century."

"I see. Well, I don't see actually. What's it for?"

"Well, I'll be able – I mean I hope to be able to demonstrate that modern culture can't be understood in purely textual terms. In the Twentieth Century we have all these new media that…" He caught sight of Fazakerly's look of disdain. "It's all about the meaning of things."

"Oh. So it's not science then. No cure for cancer in that, eh!" He shook his head, braying, a forced unmirthful laugh that seemed too loud for his frame. "Keep you off the dole I suppose. Hey, perhaps I can help you after all; I'm really into the meaning of things. Like I was saying, when my house went up in flames, how about the meaning of that…"

"So, you found out just what Hermione thought about you. What you meant to her. Didn't that make it all worse? She obviously had a thing about you, and what did you do?"

"Ach." Fazakerly gave a sour look. "We're back on that track, are we? Well, that was the least of my worries. Fancy her drawing that old tangle over me again, though. When I had the chance of a fresh start too. Fancy her writing home, closing in the net like that."

"That's a pretty hard hearted way to look at it. I haven't forgotten what you did to her."

"I paid for it. Later. I paid for it good. Are you sure this isn't going into your research?"

Settling his affairs had proved to be a comparatively uncomplicated matter. There was no other family to speak of and the Fazakerly estate had not been subject to any claims. The business had waned without his mother's hand at the helm, but there was still a business to be had. To the canny investors to whom it was offered it didn't seem unusual. Many enterprises had been mothballed during the war, or just kept simmering on the back burner, and a number of them were being brought to life like new now there was sufficient confidence that hostilities really were at an end.

He sold the lot: the house, the import business and a wine shop in Aldgate that he hadn't known existed. No loose ends, he had insisted, and for a premium his mother's lawyer had not delayed in disposing of the entire demesne of Fazakerly assets.

"I reckon he'd twigged about all that wine going missing. As soon as I saw his face, I knew. Near as scared the pants off him me turning up like that. It was his firm had sent the jobbers round to board up the place. That's why he wanted shot of it, sharpish, and me out of the way. I let him know my suspicions, subtle like. You should have seen him twist and fidget in his shiny leather chair. Just wanted rid of me, the smarmy git. A public school bum boy, I reckon. Well, it suited me. He wasn't going to snitch on me to the military whilst I had that little bit of *prima facie* on him. Anyway, I was ready for him and his like, after I'd had all that time to think. You know how I was telling you the way I learned from the books, and the newspapers, come to that. Even before I went away (there wasn't much to read in Kent). And from listening to the politicians; we used to get a barrage of nonsense from them when I was dug in over the Channel. And then of course from the law – especially the law - and... what else, let me think. Well, everyone who's trying to tell you something. You have to remember, whatever name they go by, however many letters they have after their name, they're just people. Human beings. And they're all out to be the one at the top of the heap, pulling the strings, with you and every other bugger on the end of them. That's what I meant by coming round to my mother's point of view concerning books, though she wouldn't necessarily agree. By the time I came back up to London, after my little coastal sojourn, I was darn sure I could see things the way they really are. I'd had plenty of time just to think, and I'd thought about all the stuff I'd read, as well as all the things I'd seen and heard in the military, in France. Me being new again, as it were, it was as clear as daylight. Now I don't believe...well, any of it. What they tell you - you've got to beware of it, lad. All of it. Beware. You've got to ask yourself, what are they really saying. What's it for, then, and how will it turn the tables on me?"

He leaned forward, sagaciously and with a confidential tapping of his nose.

"I tell you, you have to look out for the disguises too. Savile Row suits - pah! Fancy dress. All those bowlers and wigs, helmets, badges and braid, grand titles, all that paraphernalia. Anything they can hold up in front of themselves so you can't see what they really look like. That way you end up dealing with these god forsaken chimerical things as if they are real, as if they have real meaning. But they're all masks, and underneath: just people. Human beings, like I said. All walking around got up in camouflage. And they're the ones even now writing the books and speaking on the wireless and making up all the stories in the papers. That's why we ended up having a war, wasn't it? Christ! How tempting was that? All those really big strings they could pull, across all those countries. Look at the way we fell for it. All those bastards telling all those lies and us running proudly to the slaughter. Time and again. Mmm, you ask your father."

Fazakerly sucked in his cheeks, drew on a deep breath, closed his eyes tight and exhaled a long draught of prescience.

"No, I reckoned I was out of it for good. I'd said my goodbyes to the lot of them."

He took the train from London Bridge. Scrubbed clean after a diligent hour in the public baths, freshly shaved, with his hair cut and slicked back, and dressed in the first new outfit his skin had enjoyed next to it in years, he no longer looked the ragged desperado who had set a respectable lawyer, his articled clerk and two secretaries on the trembling edge of terror. It was his intention to alight at Ashford, find some digs for a while – as little a while as it took – and buy himself a retreat out somewhere in the remotest aspect of Romney Marsh. But whilst, no doubt, he would from the start have been keeping a watch for unwelcome interference by the invisible puppeteer, that dread puller of strings who was indeed about to send him off dancing down another path, nothing is ever immutable, not least the plans that for the first time in his life he felt himself free to explore.

So it was that by the time the train huffed and puffed its way alongside the platform of his intended destination the deepening land of orchards and hop fields into which he rode would have felt and moderated the full tumult of his thoughts, and contented villages he'd have examined critically, as the train stopped at country halts, his eye suspicious and contemptuous at first, would have begun to absorb his rancour and rejection. And then of course there was the money in his pocket and the banker's receipt for a small fortune that he had folded into his wallet, which had already seemed to make everything a little less fraught and hostile. I did that, he had thought, watching the City of London slip away behind him as the train gathered speed, gleeful and still surprised that he had concluded the deal on the house and the family business without, it appeared, bringing disaster upon himself. Free at last his journey this time was not quite such a desperate one, and by the time he arrived his plans would have been cast in a different light.

Then there was also the matter of Rosalind Campbell.

The woman sitting opposite was insistent. Would he or would he not return her smile? She had walked twice past the compartment, the train already on its way, before eventually sliding back the door and indicating, with a small gloved hand, that she was inclined to take the seat opposite by the window, if that was acceptable. Fazakerly replied with an almost imperceptible shrug and a pursing of his lips, then fixed his stare on the vista of slate roofs and chimney pots that was beginning to glide past. Why had she come in here when there were other carriages, for God's sake? He'd had it all to himself.

"Oh dear," she said. "What a to-do."

What, was she ill? Oh, please no. His eyes were fixed on the railway embankment that raced past. He felt giddy.

"Children these days." She gave a small laugh, nodding towards the corridor, and for the first time he heard the babble of voices in the next compartment. "Seems like it's a whole school. They have the entire carriage." She tut-tutted to herself. "There, I mustn't complain. Don't want to sound like an old fuddy-duddy."

He saw her smile at him in the reflection from the window but he continued to stare out, despite the fact that they were passing noisily through a tunnel and all was black outside.

She was scared of him. That was it. Make friends and he wouldn't beat and rob her, that was her ploy. Typical. I don't want to know, lady. I have no interest in you.

He tried looking through her, his eyes focused on the pattern of the seat behind her head; he pretended to doze, his head in his hand, his elbow on the narrow window ledge, but the vibration and rocking of the coach over the rails made the pretence farcical, and uncomfortable. Perhaps she wasn't going far. Maybe she'd get out soon. Sevenoaks, even Tonbridge, that would be a relief. Fancy her striking up a conversation like that, with him, a stranger. What, was she one of these suffragette types?

"Do please excuse me," she said, suddenly leaning forward, her fingers poised as if she was about to tap him on the wrist, "but you are Miriam's younger brother, aren't you?"

He shook his head emphatically. He tried a smile. It felt tight and cold. Perhaps she'd leave him alone now.

"Oh, I'm so sorry. Do forgive me. I'm really terribly sorry." She pursed her lips, a flush of pink embarrassment mottling the skin at her throat. Then, with a sniff she persuaded herself of her fortitude and briskly opened her purse, withdrawing a card from a silver case, which she passed to him. "Please be assured I don't make a habit of talking to strangers," she said, "but you look a most respectable gentleman and I really was mistaken, you see, I…"

He looked at the business card. It gave her name, Rosalind Campbell, and the address of a law firm in Haven.

"There, I hope you can see I am not a Jezebel. I really did think you were Miriam's Adam. We are a respectable firm, sir, I assure you. Highly respected."

"I'm sure. Don't worry about it." He tucked the card in his inside jacket pocket. Perhaps she'd shut up now and leave him alone.

The train clattered on and Fazakerly drifted out across the unfolding green spaces. He thought of that other journey in a different place, his cold dead flight from the nightmare that was the Western Front. It was a long time over and since his arrival at Étaples he had not reflected upon it at all. He'd really travelled alone that time, completely alone. Without even himself for company. And then there had followed his slow resurrection, the months when he had, it seemed, been immersed in a society that functioned with him as its axis: all that attention, all those conversations. He'd enjoyed it then. Yes, thinking back he surprised himself by agreeing, he'd enjoyed the company. All that vibrant feeling of human animation recollected made him shiver with irrepressible pleasure, as for a moment he relived the exquisite glow of self awareness, the easy slow months when a new sense of himself had been gradually distilled from the thoughts and words exchanged with the medical staff, the orderlies, the soldiers who had stopped by to chat. It had felt good, there was no denying. Really good. Memories of the most trivial exchanges warmed and relaxed him. The books too, hardly a gem amongst them but they'd set his thoughts running. There had been so much to catch up with, the life he had missed shut up in that house, the colourless monotony of trench warfare;

there were a million other refractions from the dimensions of his expanding world that he'd suddenly yearned to catch. All those conversations, like this, sat by the window, the lively exchange of views, discoveries and speculation with Hermione...

A guillotine came down on his reverie. All of the threads led to the same knot, the silly bitch, surely she'd known that. He saw her bright fresh face hovering outside the compartment's rain blotched glass and shut his eyes against the reflections from his mind. Must stop this unravelling. What did she think she was doing, filling him up with all that junk? His mother's junk, too!

"You can't blame me, missy," he whispered, his breath misting the windowpane. "Nothing I could do. Nothing anyone could do."

He opened his eyes and saw the Campbell woman's face mirrored in the glass, then came a sudden jarring discord followed almost immediately by the slam of a large bore gunshot and he jerked bolt upright on his seat, the compartment door thrown open and a howl of rushing wind coming from the corridor with inexplicable menace. Then, as soon as it had come, the noise subsided and the train settled back on a smooth course after its fit of braking and lurching over points. The sliding door to the compartment closed itself again, slowly this time and with no reprise of the report that had startled him.

Fool, he grimaced silently. It can't have been that extraordinary a din. She didn't seem to have heard it, Miss Suffragette over there. She'd have been up on her feet if there were anything untoward going on. Just the door, idiot.

He glanced across at the woman on the bench seat opposite. Miss, or was it Mrs Campbell - he couldn't see any wedding ring – was sitting back in her corner, enjoying not the abundant delights of the Garden of England, which turned and turned again its carousel in a grand parade, whilst they trailed through it behind a streamer of white smoke, but lodged at an angle in her seat, with her eyes fixed upon the compartment door, she seemed intent on listening to something beyond the jostling noises of the carriage and the occasional shrill of the train's whistle.

Yes, she's afraid of me, thought Fazakerly. Silly woman. She's hoping the guard is doing his rounds. What on earth is she going to say to him? That he looks like her uncle? Come and join us, my dear, it's been a long time? What's she doing with a business card like that anyway? Why would a clerk be given something like that? His suspicions made some big leaps. Law firm, law firm, what was his mother's lawyer called? In a sudden sweat he was rifling through his jacket pockets, looking for the note of account that had concluded his recent transactions. He felt certain he knew the name but he had better make sure. He had it in his hand, the contents of his pockets spilled out across the seat. *Bull & Fallin*, it was headed. Yes, as he remembered thinking, it didn't sound like lawyers, but then did Kitchener sound like the name of a Secretary for War? Well yes, it did, rather. Kitchener, kitchen knives, butcher - Jesus, I'm all over the place! He caught at the scrambling thread of irrationality. Here it was in black and white: *Bull & Fallin*. No connection with the name on her card. Except that both were in the business of practising law. And didn't they all stick together, that lot? Freemasons, weren't they? You were bound to find a lot of the brotherhood in that world. That's how they kept their power, of course, being at the heart of the matter, in with the law of the land. They were some of those very people who pulled the biggest strings of all. That was it then. She'd been sent by them to spy on him. Of course, it was so obvious: they know I know about the wine.

But why reveal her hand?

His question and the dilating phantom of paranoia were brushed away by the appearance of a man in a heavy dark coat who walked slowly past the compartment door, looking as if he was dressed for another season. His tread was laboured and uncomfortable, but he carried rather than leant on a walking stick that swung against the wooden door.

The woman in the corner had her face hidden behind a newspaper.

Fazakerly read the headlines in front of him then looked away. I don't want to know, he reminded himself. It's all lies. He turned his gaze back once more onto the fields and woods that slipped by, thinking how it was going to be so easy to vanish into that quiet green distance, not long now surely, he'd soon be riding over the ridge and onto the marsh. Another world. Away from the lies and deceit, no-one telling him what is and what isn't, no-one setting him up for a fall just to nourish their own designs. No more, he sighed.

Mile after mile flew away and he settled at last into the promise of things to come, whilst the rags of history blew away over the carriage roof, wrapped up in the hurtling billows of smoke from the locomotive. His uninvited companion remained engrossed behind her newspaper and he no longer felt oppressed by the memory of her importunate looks. Soon he would be free of her. His thoughts ran cheerily over images he remembered of remote locations glimpsed on his passage across the marsh to Ashford. Out there he'd be free. Not long now. The train was slowing again and he was wondering which stop it would be when the compartment door was pushed open and the man in the dark coat came slowly in. He'd put on a tweed cap, which he pulled down over his eyes with a sharp tug. Fazakerly thought he was about to doff it in greeting but instead he shuffled to the window then back to the corner seat by the door, his pace suggesting some difficulty but the walking stick offering no relief, he had the handle hooked over his forearm and it swung free of the floor. Two deep-set eyes peered across at Fazakerly for a moment, made their searching assessment then disappeared under the peak of the cap. Fazakerly found himself staring and was not sorry to notice that the heavy coat had swept onto the floor some papers and other small pocket items from the seat where he had carelessly unloaded them. He busied himself with the diversion of gathering them up, reaching down for a pencil and the woman's business card.

"Do allow me," she said, the toe of her shoe holding fast the small card, making him sit back, feeling awkward. She crouched to pick it up and handed it to him. He nodded. Her face had lost its smile, her lips tight, her eyes penetrating. The look she gave him was neither fear nor anger; but there was something equally urgent going on, he couldn't make it out, only the slight furrowing of her brow suggesting caution. He opened his jacket to pocket the card and she flinched, ever so slightly but enough to make him hesitate. He turned the card and glanced at it, looking back at her as he did so and seeing the tiny movement of her head, her bottom lip drawn tensely under her teeth. It was not the same card. At least, if it was the same card she had given him earlier he had no idea how she'd had time to write upon it without him noticing. He looked up at her, eyebrows raised in question and again she shook her head, her eyes making quick arrows in the direction of the man in the dark coat, who hadn't moved during all of this wordless dialogue. As if she could read his thoughts she let him see the corner of the original card crumpled up in her fist, nodding at the card in his hand, where she had written in capitals PLEASE HELP - I AM SERIOUSLY IMPERILLED.

Imperilled? Imperilled, what sort of language was that to use outside of a cheap penny romance? He felt the light draining away from the sky. I'm a free man, he thought. It's not my fucking peril. Desperately, he looked through the window as the land raced past. Ashford. Come on. It can't be far now. Let's be having you.

The train continued to slow, shaking itself down its whole length like a wet dog as the brakes were applied again, the view outside the window obscured by gusts of white steam. It came to a halt and doors banged. The air cleared. He craned to read. Pluckley, said the big letters on the station fence. Not Ashford, then, but close, he might even alight here and beg a lift.

She was still staring at him when he looked back. He shrugged and wrinkled his nose appeasingly, but she was not going to let him go, drawing his gaze with a deliberate but discrete movement of her head and shoulder in the direction of the other occupant of their compartment.

There was whistle, a squeal of spinning wheels, steel on steel, and the train moved on once more. As he watched the small platform disappear from view Fazakerly felt panic rising. He was wheezing, though no sound came from him, and there was a rope around his wrists with another pulled tight around his ankles, binding them together. A halter twisted through the sleeves of his jacket, crossing tightly over his back where the knots dug into his spine and the yoke stretched over in a loop around his neck. It was tightening and he couldn't breathe.

She spoke brightly: "Not far now, darling. Soon be home."

What? Is she talking to me? Fazakerly looked across at the man in the corner by the door, who had jerked upright at this outburst but seemed intent on keeping his purpose private, his cap was fallen so far forward over his face he could only peer out sideways like a lizard. The tug on his fetters invited Fazakerly to be more attentive.

"Shall we be on time?" she pressed.

"Oh, next stop. Won't be long." God, what was he doing. How did I say that? His lungs felt shrunken and tight. I'm a fucking free man, he screamed, stretching against the tethers and ties that bound him.

"Good. Next stop, you say? Splendid. Did I tell you that Daddy will be meeting us? And I dare say he'll have that wretched man Ransley in tow. There was a Revenue meeting this morning."

"Yes. Yes, you did mention it." Had she? When? Oh shit, he didn't know this woman. He'd just shaken off one and here was another on his back. What was going on and why couldn't he stand up?

Now she was up, reaching up for the leather document case she had slung in the luggage netting above her seat. That too bore the name and address of the company described on her business card, in letters of gold. The man in the corner had his eye on the case, it was the only thing about him that showed any sign of movement.

"Mustn't forget this," she announced quietly, sitting down next to Fazakerly this time, the case wedged tightly between them. "Look!" she cried, so close to his ear that his jaw dropped, but not so startled he didn't miss the dark coat rising up simultaneously on the periphery of his vision. She was pointing out something in the distance, her voice low in his ear.

"Thank you, thank you. Now, please just stay close until we are away from the station. There's usually a policeman on duty near the gate. I don't think our friend will try anything if he thinks you are with me. He wasn't ready for this."

Fazakerly by now felt as girdled as an Egyptian mummy. She had her arm crooked through his, holding him tight against her. Grimly, he reflected, obviously, neither was I.

They were both surprised on turning back to find that the compartment was empty and they were alone, but neither made any attempt to move; to look out into the corridor might be tempting fate. The train was approaching its next stop and both, each for their own reasons, were eager to disembark without incident.

"Ashford!" Porters hastened along the platform chivvying the confluence of arrivals and departures, an instant confusion of people who scurried through the eddying whorl of pungent smoke that swirled from the engine, it swept departing passengers from carriages and lifted up the skirts and coats of those who climbed aboard.

Hearing the cacophony of doors being opened and doors slammed shut, Fazakerly strained at his leash.

"Wait," she insisted sharply. "Stay on the train. Everyone says it's easy to be lost in a crowd but he knows that too. He might be hiding out there amongst all the hustle and bustle."

Without releasing her hold on his arm she urged him to the door and they looked out. The party of school children had left the train, leaving a deep silence throughout the carriage. Not a breath, not a footstep came. Then the window was down and she had hold of the door handle, they were outside and Fazakerly felt his bonds loosen with the jarring of his feet on the platform.

A whistle blew, once, twice, three times, insistently, and he ducked. Gas alert! Gas alert! Voices cried alarms and he could hear the slamming of a battery of doors that deafened him with its orchestrated thudding, the infernal throes of a machine reaching for a point of discharge, a sound as of gears thrashing, or was it artillery, the rumble of a tank, and as the locomotive prepared to shoulder its load with a great hissing and grinding of metal on metal he took off, bent double and at a run for the safe shadows of the station building.

Country air, he felt it fresh on his face, his breath quick in his throat. He was unshackled at last, unharmed. Every restraining thread – gone. The woman had let go his arm the moment he'd run and he turned with his back against the sooty bricks of the waiting room wall to see if she still pursued him.

It had barely moved yet, but the train had made clear its determination to depart, there was a brief shunting movement between the couplings and Rosalind Campbell was forced to take a step forward, then another in quick succession. The man in the dark coat stood in the open door at the end of the carriage. He had Rosalind's document case under his arm and was hauling himself up into the moving train while she held on to his walking stick, all the while beating frenziedly at his other arm with which he sought to pull himself aboard.

Fazakerly watched in horror. Let it go, let it go, he urged, soundless words that he forced into flight. Let *me* go, for God's sake, don't do this to me. I'm not here, I am really not here. He felt himself on the verge of weeping.

She was almost running now, side-stepping, red in the face, and there was a loud whistling from an official with a red flag, the only individual who seemed to have noticed what was going on, but the train had gathered pace and Rosalind's crab-like gait made her stumble and lurch, it was only by hanging on firmly to the walking stick that she kept herself from falling. The end of the platform was a rapidly decreasing number of yards away. Its height from the track was a modest few feet but it may as well have been a precipice that swept towards her.

All of that no longer mattered. With a snap and a click that was audible only to her and her assailant the shaft of the walking stick came away in her hand, the thin blade it had concealed striking like a line of white light that severed the space between them as she lost her footing and threw out her arms like a high diver launched into space. Fazakerly too swore he was flying. He was picked up on a wire and thrown across the platform, his whole weight barrelling into her while he twisted to scoop her up and back and away from the scything thrusts of the sword stick. Then she had her arms around his neck, she was hanging on to him and he was keeping her from falling into the race of the accelerating train; he felt the weight of the whole world dragging him down and down until the carriage door slammed shut.

"It wasn't me. I would rather have been away from there, as you can imagine. But like I've been saying, come too close to people and they'll pull you in. Change you. Anyway, that's how I came to build the Round House. Maybe that's how you came to be caught up in my life too."

Now it was Stephen's turn to laugh:

"Come on, you've been telling porkies, haven't you. All that James Bond stuff, you were making it up. What, are you trying to tell me you'd turned over a new leaf?"

"She didn't make up losing the sight in one eye, I can tell you that. He just caught her with that blade. It wasn't immediate, it didn't look so bad right there and then, but she was blind in that eye within a twelvemonth."

"Oh come on. This is all too much. What, are you trying to test me? I'll have you know that researching iconology doesn't mean I'm looking into the meaning of fairy stories!"

"I'm trying to explain. How we're connected. Haven't you been listening? I'm trying to throw some light on what happened between you and me. Anyone else would be grateful. But if you're not interested...."

"OK, but what does this little melodrama tell me about the Round House? You're really trying to make up for Hermione, aren't you? Suddenly, Mr Fazakerly the hero!"

"Listen, will you. It was her land. After I got her home – well, I couldn't just leave her there, could I? – we got talking. She had a house on the front, here in Haven, right opposite the beach. Hadn't meant to get off the train at Ashford, of course, that was just a ruse, so we had to arrange transport. Anyway, I had to give the police my name and address and she made it easy for me, said I was her brother. She must have taken a lucky guess at my situation, or something like. I thought I was lucky, anyway, given my circumstances."

"Fortunate."

"Like I said, she had this piece of land and, after we got talking, well, long after that, she agreed to sell it to me. But that was a while later, as I said. In the meantime I had nowhere to stay and she had this big house."

"And the law firm? I suppose that made the sale easier, her being a lawyer. Come on, in those days?"

"No need to sneer. She wasn't. But she wasn't just a clerk, neither. She was aiming for the top, working her way up. Don't forget we'd had our first woman MP the year before. Oh yes, it was all change from there on. She could have become a barrister, though I fancied she'd be better as a magistrate, the eye patch would have looked a bit too rough for the high courts of law."

"Oh yes of course, the eye patch." Stephen hooted. "And I suppose the man with the sword had a wooden leg and a parrot under his coat."

"No. Just money. Sewn into the lining. He was travelling through to Dover, for the boat, only she'd been up delivering evidence about him on behalf of her firm, something to do with the Excise, and he ran across her at the station. Thought he might persuade her to give up the documents she was bringing back. They got him though, stopped the train at Westenhanger, he was carrying too much to make a run for it. Silly bugger really stitched himself up there.

Anyway, enough of this taradiddle, all I was meaning to say was that you never can tell, you have to keep a hold of yourself or something else will come sneaking up on you and grab you by the ring in your nose. Like you. Wasn't that something like what happened to you?"

He's wandering, thought Stephen, and this is going nowhere. It had nothing to do with the affair that had brought them together so fundamentally into this weird state of conflict and dependency; it wasn't doing anything to make sense of the last ten years of his life. It was just an old man fancying that he could see meanings in a series of events where in truth there was only serendipity. How much was imagined and how much borrowed, he wondered.

"I have to go." Stephen stood up to leave.

"No wait, I did go looking for a place down on the marsh but I got to thinking, I was more likely to be conspicuous doing that than if I just settled down quietly in an ordinary little seaside town. I wasn't known there. I could just become part of the background. I read a story about that somewhere, something about a purloined letter. People won't notice something hidden in front of their noses. On top of that, she gave me some credibility. She was respected in the town after all, and that sort of rubbed off on me. I lived in her house for a while you see. All above board of course. I had the top floor all to myself - well, me and the birds."

"The birds?"

"Yes, you know, the seagulls. They'd found a way into her loft. Gawd, what a racket. But she didn't mind, said they made her laugh with all their cackling and calling. We'd have to shout at each other some times, over the noise. I suppose that's what she counted on really. Didn't want any guests to stay too long. A bit like me really. Best on her own. A fine woman, but I was glad to get away, relieved to be able to pick up my own threads once again.

- TEN -

STEPHEN PARKED HIS OLD Morris Minor next to the promenade and sat with his hands clasped around the top of the steering wheel, his chin propped in his knuckles. The split windscreen misted but he wasn't looking out. Watching the sea was always an act of recuperation that he could depend upon to lift him out of himself, he'd come there on autopilot whenever he needed to think something through, but today he was in a daze and his spirits wouldn't rally. How many extremes of emotion can a person go through in a day, a week, a month, and not feel one's enthusiasm for any more wrung dry? Discovering the old man, he had been shot way up there into the stratosphere, so high he believed he'd be able to look down and see into every dark recess of his assumed ignominy that before had been concealed by ignorance and the observance of polite conduct. And now, today, it was all overshadowed again. He had learned a lot about the old man, true, but he'd expected so much more from this new liaison. More fool him. He should have known it was too late to go seeking answers. Ten years on and the world had changed. Memories had reinvented themselves. Fazakerly had been old even in 1957 - he'd certainly looked it to an eleven-year-old boy, probably much older than he really was - and now, after a further ten years shut away with just his thoughts to trouble him, he was bound to have lost the plot. To explore the meaning of things with him could produce no meaning. All that twaddle about rescuing a damsel in distress. Pure invention. Just trying to balance his guilt about that ghastly business in France. He's looking for absolution, thought Stephen. Plain addled, he decided; I can smell it, he's rotting away just like this wreck of a car.

They hadn't known of course, his parents, they hadn't realised that a trauma not faced up to at the time becomes a psychosis waiting to happen. Oh why didn't they deal with it properly? Why didn't I?

Of course, he knew the answers just as well as the questions. They had done what they believed was best according to the prevailing rules of play. And him? He was only a child then. Innocent maybe, certainly bewildered, though he hadn't felt innocent at the time. He'd mixed it with the undertow like every other kid. Didn't everyone at that age? It was an accepted pattern. Sure, theirs had been dark deeds let loose to run amongst the alleys and streets of a quiet seaside town, all in the imagined peace following an apocalypse, yet there were rules of engagement, a strict understanding that this world was separate and sealed from the comfort and order of hearth and home. It was never meant to appear large on the radar of adult consciousness. And while the social order of children free to play in a world so recently rid of the devil had its own jostling communities and tyrants and vicious wars, none of it was meant to mean anything. Not at the close of day when doors were locked and curtains drawn, when they would gather in safe confidence around the levelling congregation of broadcasts from the wireless, or dance the domestic waltz of hobby and craft and picture book, their secret wild places abandoned for the night to fill with the new dews of adventure. The assignment of meaning was left to the adult world after all. You couldn't expect an eleven-year-old to rationalise human behaviour.

Fazakerly was right about one thing though: this matter of sovereignty, the phoney claims for independence of the human spirit, it all struck a chord. Yes, Stephen had been intending that to be a main feature of his research, it would be a topical controversy, his provocative exposure of the visual images of Western ideology being shaped to peddle falsehoods. So what if it was an unwitting process, it just went to prove that nobody was that free. All that stuff on the radio this summer, just more of the same. A whole youth culture turning on and tuning in and dropping out. Or so it was said. They were just being manipulated. It was big business. And all those swaggering declamations to promote free love. Free for whom? The old man hadn't described it like that, of course, he had been digging away at something a lot deeper, something more primitive, but it was all the same thing, it was all about influence and control. Nothing good would come from trying to run away from it.

That's how they fucked me up, he groaned. They should have let me face up to it good and proper, and now I'm not really sure at all what was going on.

When the garage door slammed shut he'd been left with a big gnawing feeling like indigestion, but it was more in his head than his chest or his stomach. He hadn't wanted to go home. It didn't feel right to go home as if nothing had happened and knowing it was probably still happening, he could hear Marcus's exhortations continuing even as he passed out of the driveway and turned up towards the sea front. Better to hang about a bit, not too far away, just to make sure that the kid came out in one piece. Oh shit, surely he didn't mean that, they wouldn't do anything really awful, would they? No, it was just a bit of a lark. After all, it wasn't as if they were setting fire to Humphrey himself. Stupid mongol, it was his own fault anyway; he'd known what they were like. He was just too greedy for his own good.

Perhaps he should wander round by the hotel. Like as not he'd run into Nola. She'd be bound to ask him if he'd seen Humphrey, she always did when she met any of the kids around there; not as if she really wanted to know, just making the point that she had one of her own and he should be properly acknowledged. It's about all she did say, as far as Stephen could remember. Or if on this occasion she was in one of her uncommunicative moods, when she stood and stared with red-rimmed eyes into the space beyond the end of her cigarette, then he could easily slip it in to start the conversation, just mentioning Humphrey's name would be enough. That would do. She was known to chat with everyone who went past when she was out for one of her cigarettes, and she was always out for one of her cigarettes. All nonsense of course, her conversation; it never made any sense.

No, he pulled himself up fast, he couldn't possibly do that. He'd be implicated. If something terrible happened he'd be guilty by association. He knew all about that from school. *If the culprit doesn't own up right away you will all suffer.* Class punishments. Oh bugger it. He'll be all right, the stupid mongol.

Stephen kicked a stone along in front of him disconsolately. It was a large brown pebble thrown up from the beach, smoothed and rounded by a million tides. He imagined it was Humphrey's dark-skinned arse and he took a running kick. 'Wah!' he mimicked, "wah-ah!"

"You, boy," he heard the accusation in her tone before he could place the voice; it sounded too educated, what would be regarded as posh in that part of the town. "Leave the stone alone before you decide to smash any more of my windows and come here."

He was sure he hadn't deliberately smashed anybody's windows, not even old Marble Gamble's, but she wouldn't have seen him anyway, not then, not when he was hiding in the undergrowth from Warren and the others. It had been important to keep his head down with all those rocks being chucked about. Well actually he couldn't have done any smashing. The glass was already gone. They'd been having a war game in the bombsite behind her back yard, that's what it was, and they'd ended up shooting spud gun pellets through the broken panes. Warren had said to wait and see if the witch would fly out. Not that any of them believed in witches, of course.

Stephen followed the woman's voice as she called out to him again; she was standing in her open doorway, squinting down at him from the top of a steep flight of stone steps. Holy fit! – it really was her, Marble Gamble, and if she wasn't a witch she was still as scary as hell.

Not that she was wrapped around with a sleek black cloak. There was no pointed hat, no stars or pentagrams, and absolutely no sign of a broomstick. Maybe not, but this witch was no less identifiable from her drab housecoat that bulged in all the wrong places. How many rats and toads did she have tucked under there, and what deformities was she hiding? It was said she'd been stuck halfway when changing back from something eldritch and preternatural. This hapless housecoat was no more fortunate. It had once passed for better than post-war utility but was now as shapeless as any ration book compromise. She'd managed to fashion it into a crude envelope, enclosing her person with the help of a judiciously tight length of braided silk pulled from a curtain or a dressing gown; which was a blessing, thought Stephen, for a breeze had blown up, her white hair wafting hither and thither upon it like smoke and perilously secured to her head by the elastic of her pink eye patch.

"Boy, are you of a mind to help me?" she called. "If you are, do make haste."

So he was not in trouble. All the same, the prospect of helping old Marble Gamble was not something he relished, whatever she wanted. But hey, she wasn't really a witch. He knew that. You never heard of witches being burned any more. She was just an old woman, a bit creepy, but he'd never heard anything really bad about her, nothing like kidnap, torture and murder, and he could run faster than her if need be. Just so long as there weren't any spells. He took a deep breath and mounted the first step.

"You're not going in there are you? She stinks you know." He heard Warren's voice as clear as if he was standing at his shoulder, remembering how he'd waited here once before, he'd been selling mackerel caught by hand in a glut off the beach and he'd inadvertently dallied in front of her house.

"No, she's gone to find some money," he'd replied. "She wants to buy a couple of fish." He'd wanted Warren to go. The situation was already difficult but things were bound to become too complicated now. "I'll see you later."

But Warren had scented one of those moments. It was a gift better than gold and the leer that took hold of his face told of his sudden anticipation of wealth. This was an opening for a long and oft-repeated tale of daring in which he would secure his notoriety as the local Perseus, he would be slaying the Medusa in her lair.

"No, that's all right. I'll wait for you. I won't let her turn you into a toad."

Warren had plucked a mackerel from the bucket in Stephen's arms and skipped up onto the first step. "What a beauty!" He grasped it by the tail and whirled it around and around. "Look at those colours, eh!" The luminous silver and green-blue scales of the fish glittered, jewelled arcs that he made swell across the afternoon light.

"I'll take two, please, young gentleman," she had said, appearing at her door.

"Nah, lady, just the one. One for one and all for all," shouted Warren, letting fly the bright fish that shot a slippery trajectory over the steps and slapped heavily against Marble Gamble's forehead.

"Enjoy the fish supper," he had called, hooting, turning in triumph, elated; then with a sharp cry of pain he'd jumped, then he'd hopped, painfully limping with tears in his eyes, desperately hobbling away and frantic that Stephen shouldn't be able to watch him blubbing around the corner.

"Fucking witch," he had confided later. "Did you see her throw that spell at me? How else would I break my ankle, I was only one step up from the road."

I wonder if she remembers, thought Stephen, surely she recognises me. She may have been brooding on the indignity of that moment ever since, and today the time has come for revenge. Is this a trick to catch me too? He continued up the steps, feeling foolish that he might have been snared and equally so just for thinking that way. But he was grateful at least that Warren was not around today.

Despite what they all said amongst themselves, it didn't stink in the house, not when he reached the front door, or in the hall. True, it felt old and poorly maintained; the floral wallpaper that in better days had stretched a glorious trellis of roses from floor to ceiling was reduced to a faint tracery in dull monochrome, and the once vigorous orioles and waxwings that climbed amongst its tapestry of swirling foliage were all drained of life. She led the way through this dismal arbour to the back stairs, one hand pressed down on the handle of her walking stick and the other reaching out for balance, her fingers splayed against the passing wall, certain he would follow, turning only when she reached the back of the house, where she leaned heavily against the banister and gestured to the floor above.

"It's my birds," she said, in a quiet, not unkindly tone, "the naughty things have been poking their beaks into places where they shouldn't. I don't mind them finding shelter in my loft but when it comes to spreading their roost to the rest of the house I have to draw the line. Be a good boy, would you, and show them out. I can't climb these stairs today, not with my leg playing up again. I haven't been up there for some time, actually."

Whether this apparent frailty was a ruse or not, Stephen quickly decided that her civil manner made her all the more repulsive, not in the sense of her being unclean, but repellent in the same way that he reacted to anything made grotesque by unnatural combinations or associations. Like the salmon pink prosthetic limbs displayed in the town's one surgical hardware shop. He'd run with a shudder down that street. It wasn't just that the colour was an unfortunate mockery of human flesh, it was more to do with the leather straps and articulated steel-pinned joints that made them so hideous, the intention that this curious mosaic of materials could be thought to pass as human. However noble the engineering, he wanted to throw up whenever he saw them. With Marble Gamble it was not so much her crumpled physique, she was an old, old woman after all, not just the eye patch, nor the heavily bandaged leg under wrinkled stockings that nursed deformities described by Warren in terms both nightmarish and lethal - images which he was desperately trying to suppress - but the way in which all of her physical and thereby manageable ugliness was invested with an unsettling incongruity by the fine and undeniably cultured distinction of her speech. It didn't fit. This shambling old baggage and a voice from the BBC, no way was that anything but weird. He felt it cast a thrall over him, nevertheless. It was a voice of authority.

"What do you want me to do," he asked, his own tiny voice strangled by apprehension.

"Here, take this." She handed him a small wicker basket containing a hammer and a crumpled paper bag, in which was an assortment of nails. "Up there. I suspect the sash has gone, I heard something come crashing down last night, and since early this morning I've been aware of them flying to and fro. Just shoo them out, they won't hurt you, then nail the window frame in place so that it won't drop again."

"Just that?"

"Just that, boy. Why, whatever else?" He heard her laugh as he ascended the stairs: "While you deal with that I'm just going to boil up a nice mess of bats and toads..."

There were three closed doors at the top of the stairs but he knew which one he was seeking, he could feel the strength of the sucking draught that rattled the newspaper used for insulation under the runner. When he turned the handle the door was drawn in by an invisible hand, which made the hairs on his neck stand on end, then the rush of air subsided and he could see that the old woman's reckoning had indeed been correct: the top window had fallen, the frayed end of the rope sash visible where it wagged in the breeze outside the pane. There were no gulls in the room, which was a relief, although they had made quite a mess on the child's cot that stood against the wall opposite the fireplace. The chimney had been sealed with a thick wedge of folded newspapers and when he closed the door behind him he felt the rush of air begin again, the open window creating an alternate flue under the door. To keep the birds out, I bet, smiled Stephen; how long ago had she been up here to stop up the fireplace?

He made short work of the repair, tapping in more nails than were necessary to secure the window, though looking down from his perch on the dressing table he had frozen for a moment, his sphincter going rigid, seeing how high he appeared to hang over the tangle of undergrowth that had colonised the bombsite below. It must have been her kitchen windows they'd bombarded. Spud guns would have never reached this high.

Recollections of that episode brought him a wave of shame. Here he was in her house, after all, trusted to work alone, and she hadn't been so unkind as to mention any past wickednesses. The precipitous view also reminded him of his desire to make a quick exit and he jumped down, items from the dressing table clattering onto the floor as he skidded the lace doily from its smooth surface.

"Nothing broken, nothing broken," in haste he sought assurance, impatient with himself as he hurriedly gathered everything together, a photograph in a small silver frame, a child's teething ring, a bottle of furniture polish and a duster, rearranging them as best as he could remember on the cloth that he smoothed back into place. The photograph was apparently very old, a full-length image of a young man and printed in shades of brown. It was hard to make out his face, the contrast had faded over the years, but from his posture it was possible to see he was quite jaunty and Stephen was sure that he was grinning at the photographer.

"All done. Let's go," he urged himself, wondering if he could just slip out unseen, then noticing again the crusting filth left by the birds, he took up the duster and quickly wiped the cot rail. There was something about a child's bed. He couldn't just leave it like that.

There were no toys in the cot, no clothes, no teddy bear, although it was made up ready for slumber, but at the foot of the crocheted and rather damp coverlet a large soft-covered book had been thrown down. It had *Scrapbook* printed in a simple script on the front, but someone had crossed the word through and written above it in fine swirling copperplate the line *Spring Offensive – where the Buttercup had blessed with Gold,* the name Wilfred Owen added in another hand, in tiny letters, bracketed as an afterthought. The book had stiffened with time and from long exposure to the air of an unheated room, but he carefully cracked back the covers. Despite the suggestion of the title written on the front there was nothing here to do with anything intimating warfare, nor buttercups come to that. In fact the contents had been stripped almost bare. A number of pages had been torn out, or whatever had been stuck down on them had been rudely removed, leaving the rough gummed corners of what seemed to have been photographs. Just a few fragments from old newspapers remained pressed between the stiff card pages, so ancient that the dark chunky print from the reverse had mixed with the pictures and captions that had been cut around and preserved for some obscure posterity. He carried the book to the window for better light and found amongst the fragments a brief report of planning applications approved by the town council, there was no date given, a lengthy piece of solid type describing one day's proceedings at the County Court and a photograph of a man being held by a policeman blessed with heavy side whiskers. In the next fold of the pages were more indistinct pictures in yellowing newsprint of a smart young woman dressed in the sort of business clothes that he'd seen his grandmother wearing in old family albums. Most curiously, there was also a more recent black and white photograph of Mr Fazakerly's house.

"Weird!" he gasped.

Stuck firmly inside the back cover he found another picture. If the stark tonal contrasts were not enough to suggest that this was a scene from well in the past, the old fashioned costumes of its subjects left no such uncertainties. But old as it was, the clarity of the image itself had remained sharp, and Stephen found himself looking at the same smart young woman he'd seen in the cuttings, only this time she was seated in a garden, dressed completely in black, her jacket, long slim skirt, her blouse with a high collar and the broad-brimmed hat pulled down against the sunlight, its shadow hiding half of her face. All in black, or so Stephen assumed from the deep uniformity of the dark shading and the contrast her outfit made with the long string of shiny white buttons that ran from her waist to her neck. A man stood behind her, his hand on her shoulder. It was evidently a fine, sunny day, the summery sunshine reflecting from the round lenses of his spectacles, and the wrinkling of his brow as he squinted in the light endowed him with an aspect of mirth that was at odds with the woman's air of solemnity. Someone had drawn a deep diagonal line from corner to corner of the photograph with scissors or a knife.

A sudden noise from outside drew Stephen back from his fascination with this odd jumble of memorabilia. None of it made any connections for him, even the picture of the Round House had ceased to be out of place amongst the random collection of uninteresting cuttings. It was hardly as weird as he had first thought. Old people were like that. They gathered stuff about them for reasons best known to themselves. His grandmother's sideboard was stuffed full of all manner of things whose value was known only to her: creased photographs of people with no names, a teaspoon with *Casino Margate* engraved on the handle, champagne corks whose romantic pledges to rendezvous with their wire cages had never been kept, porcelain thimbles, theatre tickets and odd bits of wax, stuff like that. And not just old people, either. Stephen was an avid hoarder of cinema tickets, not to mention his flags of the world bubblegum cards. The only difference was that, whereas he could swap his collections, this was all junk. He picked up the photograph of the Round House once more, wondering who had taken it. Perhaps she had done it herself, old Marble Gamble. It was just down the next street. She'd have been bound to be interested in it. It was, as his father had said, a local folly.

The noise outside the window came again, he could hear shouting, a lot louder and with manic insistence, and looking out he was just in time to catch a glimpse of Humphrey bowling down the far end of the alley that ran along the back of the bombsite, already a safe distance from Marcus and Paul, who were locked in a struggle just at the top of the slope nearest their house. They were both hollering and gesticulating furiously, Marcus sucking at his wrist and looking white in the face, but with some apparent presence of mind he was intent on maintaining a restraining grip on Paul's arm, the younger brother dancing with rage and brandishing the air rifle.

Stephen ran, flinging the scrapbook into the cot and thundering down the stairs. He had forgotten all fear of the witch and her ugliness. The door behind him hadn't finished slamming before he reached the hall and he had run through the front entrance and down the steps to the road before she emerged from the kitchen.

The sound of his footsteps receding along the sea front was all the goodbye she received.

"I take it you don't have time to stay for a cup of belladonna," she cackled in a dutiful, witch-like whine. She waited for a moment, her head on one side. "No, you won't be coming back for dinner, either. Men," she sighed, "it seems we'll be dining alone, Rosalind. Another night *toute seule*."

The hearse had pulled up directly opposite his car but Stephen hadn't noticed. It was only when the rear door was closed upon the coffin that he sensed movement over the road and looked up. He was parked across from old Ma Gamble's house. There was a man standing in the open doorway, calling to someone inside the house. The driver of the hearse was leaning against the bonnet of the vehicle, smoking a cigarette.

"Tell them to get a move on," he said to Stephen as he approached. "She may not be in a hurry but I am."

Stephen paused at the bottom of the steps. Even though it looked as though she had gone at last, he knew that the uneasy sensation he was feeling would always persist about this house. It was a shivery, eerie breath of shadows that darkened the whole house front. Just standing there with the light made wan he could feel all those old macabre reverberations from the stories they had told to scare themselves. Come on, he spoke out loud, come on, disconcerted to find himself climbing up the steps on tiptoe and twitching from a childlike frisson of anxiety.

"Better late than never," snapped the long haired man holding the door.

"Pardon?"

"The key, gimme the key. Hey, Mick, leave it," he shouted down the hall, "forget it will you!"

"I'm sorry…"

"You will be, mate, if you muck me about," the man was wiping his hands on a grimy cloth; "filthy in there. I ain't going back. Here, you are from the old dear's solicitors, aren't you?"

"Sorry, no. I was just passing and I wondered whether this was old Ma, I mean Mrs Gamble who'd died."

"Gamble, Gamble? Oh yeah, gotcha. Look, that tosser in there has lost the key and I can't lock up. You're supposed to be the joker from the solicitors' with a spare. I ain't going back in. There should have been someone else here in the first place, someone in authority. Not right us just doing a removal job all on our own. I just hope nothing's gone missing."

Mick thudded down the hall at a run.

"All right then? Are we off?"

"I'll give you all right! Look," said Long-hair to Stephen, "I shouldn't do this, ok, but we have to get back. Our band is playing tonight – and don't," he grimaced, "don't ask if we're called The Undertakers, 'cos we ain't. Someone else got there first. Anyway, we'll lose the gig if we don't get away sharpish, so can you just hold this door shut for a bit, make sure nobody goes in. There's someone on his way with a key."

"Are you sure?"

"Of course I'm sure. I phoned didn't I?" He waved vaguely towards the red telephone kiosk on the sea front. "Agreed? By the way, you a friend of hers or what? Only, if something goes missing."

"Oh. Yes, quite close."

How long he had before the messenger with the spare key arrived was an unknown and it spurred Stephen over his reluctance to enter the hall. The hearse had sped away at an unseemly pace, leaving him in sole possession of the house for maybe a minute, perhaps a little more, but there was no room for delay. He'd have to be quick. He couldn't risk being locked in inadvertently; neither did he want to be discovered taking a look around somewhere he shouldn't be in the first place.

It was much as he recalled it inside the house. His last visit had been brief but he recognised the bleached remains of William Morris wallpaper that lined the hall and continued all the way up to the first floor, just the ghost of a grid plotted in regular intervals by spidery grey bird legs and dark spectral beaks, some smudges of pink and green in between, and on the hall floor and up the stairs the same runner, now threadbare and uneven. Only it really was filthy, as the long haired man had said; it was in a state far worse than squalid.

Stephen fought back a shudder as he became conscious of the extent of the changes that time had wrought. At some point in the last ten years the birds had extended their domain from their fastness in the loft, eventually taking command of the whole house, the success of their migration made obvious by the depth of foul droppings that covered every surface. The acrid stench of guano made him double up. He took a deep breath as if he was diving underwater only to find himself gagging on the putrid air with which he'd filled his lungs, but he kept going, slithering forward over the mess that had accumulated on the stairs.

A pool of fresh vomit glistened on the floor of the landing. No wonder Mick had been keen to make a quick getaway. But some relief from the foetid atmosphere was to be had when he opened the door to the room with the cot, finding the air inside musty but of a less toxic prescription. His repairs to the window had lasted well and there was no sign that the gulls had found another way into this room. Could it be that no-one had come here since that day, ten years ago? He shut the door behind him, noticing as he turned back that the hammer and bag of nails were still there, but not as he'd left them. He was convinced he'd just abandoned them on the lino by the dressing table. Seeing the way they'd been replaced neatly in the wicker basket made him more certain: the basket stood smack in the centre of the fancy doily, deep in a layer of fluff and next to the photograph in the silver frame, which had been placed face down, its stand folded flat.

She'd been up, then. A long time ago, it would seem, but somebody had been to tidy. Whoever it was had been into the room had also removed the scrapbook. In fact, the cot where it had lain had been stripped bare.

"Damn!" Stephen punched the air in exasperation, his eyes darting about the room, but a quick search under the cot and in the drawers of the dressing table brought no sign of either the book or the bedclothes.

Stuffing the photograph into a pocket, he took another deep breath and slipped out of the room, struggling to keep his balance on the mouldering carpeting without touching the faecally encrusted banister. The stink made his eyes water and by the time he reached the front of the house he was ready to liberate his entire lunch.

A party of herring gulls wheeled over and around the house while he squatted against the coping of the parapet and swallowed great gulps of sea air. Whether they missed their dead patron or were just angered by the day's repeated invasions of their space, their fierce calls were far from friendly and Stephen was on the point of fleeing their swooping disputations when a bright red Mini with a Union Jack painted on its roof pulled up behind his own car. The driver, a tall young man not that far off his own age, having prised himself from the front seat sauntered around the front of Stephen's Morris and began to show a more than passing interest in the number plate; then he spun on his heel with a nod and crossed the road, walking with an exaggerated show of self-importance.

"Thought it was you," said Warren, looking up. "Recognised the plate. That old rust bucket of yours!" He unhooked a large key from a ring at his belt and glanced quizzically from it to the lock on the front door. "Here, what you doing anyway? Not still flogging fish are you."

Stephen laughed. "You remember that, do you? No, I was just passing. In fact, I'd better be on my way."

He ran lightly down the steps then turned, the back of his left hand raised to his chin and his elbow crooked, the other arm outstretched and pointing, as with a diabolical wiggling of his fingers and a mad grin on his face he called back:

"Hey, Warren! Watch how you go. I put a spell on you!"

- ELEVEN -

HE WASN'T DUE to start work until midday but Stephen couldn't wait. The duty nurse was irritated at having to rush his medication but Fazakerly beamed warmly, introducing her to Stephen with such a generosity of compliments and felicitations that she was embarrassed into making schoolgirl blushes and scuttled away with promises of coffee and biscuits.

"Good to see you," he smiled broadly, rubbing his hands together as if in confident anticipation of a rewarding conversation. "I'm told I'm doing well, young man. All is on the mend at last."

"So you find our meetings helpful?"

"No - well yes, but that's not what I meant. Had a bit of trouble," he lowered his voice, "you know, below the waterline." He motioned with his eyes. "Not very tasty. Had one of those bag things fitted. Something wrong with it too." He blew out his cheeks. "Cor, I'm glad that's been taken away. What with the nasty niff. Here, it hadn't bothered you, had it?"

Stephen looked out of the window. I've smelled worse, he thought, putting on a face. Oh yes, much worse. He smiled to Fazakerly, pulling up a chair, looking him up and down. The old man certainly seemed improved, both in body and spirit.

"Thought I'd make it an early visit today," he said, as if an explanation was needed, "thought I'd catch you whilst you're fresh."

Fazakerly laughed. "At my age that'd be little short of miraculous, but I appreciate the thought."

"Ah well," continued Stephen, his smile full of salve, "I wouldn't be so rude as to insist you admit how old you are." He winked. "Tell you what though, I bet you aren't as old as this chap." He pulled the photograph in its silver frame from his jacket pocket.

Fazakerly clutched the picture in both hands, his eyes screwed up as he concentrated.

"Relative of yours?" he asked. "Grandad? Here, fetch me my spectacles, will you. I'm all right with distance but... haven't had time to put my contact lenses in today." He turned to check that the nurse had gone. "Actually, I've been going without. One of the young doctors – he's a bit evangelical – doesn't appreciate it's not something I want at my time of life. Marvellous things they may be, but too fiddly for an old soldier like me."

Stephen rummaged in the bedside cabinet drawer. It was a tip, an unpleasant confusion of boiled sweets and coins, through which several opened bags of mixed nuts had recklessly spilled their contents, but there was nothing as paramount as a spectacles case.

"Here we go," exclaimed Fazakerly, teasing a fine gold chain from under the pillow in his chair, and with a tug the gold-rimmed spectacles sprang out. To the boy Stephen they had always made a fiercely haunted face, peering luminously from the Round House windows, though for a number of contradictory reasons they now seemed less a cause for unease.

"John Lennon glasses!"

Fazakerly chuckled: "Thomas Fazakerly glasses. Had these a long time without any trouble, but I'm supposed now to hang them round my neck when I'm using them. Hah! –

bet I look like a bloomin' librarian." He hooked the wires of the spectacles around his ears and defiantly let the chain make absurd loops across his nose. "Worse than doctors' receptionists, librarians. Here, let's see now."

He stared in silence at the photograph in the silver frame. His expression didn't change, his face was alert with excited interest, like that of a child with a new puzzle, but the colour bled from his cheeks so dramatically that Stephen was relieved when he heard the sound of the nurse returning with a tray.

"Don't know if he deserves that," Fazakerly remarked bleakly.

The nurse offered Stephen the tray with the coffees.

"I said," Fazakerly cleared his throat, "there's some here who don't deserve such hospitality."

The nurse regarded him quizzically for a moment, touching the back of her hand to his brow. She looked at Stephen and nodded reassuringly.

"He'll do," she said; then breezily: "Mr Fazakerly, isn't it good of your young friend to give up so much of his time?"

Fazakerly ignored her until she had gone. "So what's your game?" he snapped. "And where did you get this?"

"House clearance. I take it from the face you're pulling you can tell me who it is?"

There followed a long still silence during which the old man stared blindly through the walls and Stephen tried to stifle the sound of the coffee gurgling in his throat. Could it be that his suspicions really were going to be confirmed? Wow, what a turn up that would be. But he'd rushed it, and now he was horribly afraid he'd tipped Fazakerly over the edge and - Oh Jesus! - perhaps this was what a stroke looked like. The irony of what he had done clubbed him with its dull mace. Ten years on and he'd finished the job. Hadn't Fazakerly been waiting for this?

"She's gone then." The corpse that was not a corpse let out a long breath. "Free at last." His ebullience had dissipated; his eyes behind the exaggerating lenses were closed.

"She?"

"There's only one of these pictures. It's all I had, all I could find in our London house. My mother didn't believe in keeping photographs. Sentimental, she said. I had it taken the day I joined up. They told me it was a fancy print, the brown picture, a commemorative. I remember laughing, thinking how there was no way I was going to forget that day. My way of escape, see. I left the picture behind when I moved into my Round House. She was keen I didn't take it, said it would be company for her in that draughty old place on the sea front."

"She?"

"You're playing games, sonny. Don't do that. You know who I'm talking about. More than you're letting on, I'll be bound."

Yes. He had it now. Now he could be sure. But it hadn't been until yesterday, not until the young undertaker had made the leap that had taken him so much longer. God, I'm so damn slow, he reproached himself. Was it only the kids who knew her as Gamble?

"There were other photographs – where I found this one - but they'd been destroyed. There was just one I remember that I could make out clearly, a portrait of a couple taken in a garden; oh, and another one of your house that looked more recent, though in fact that was a while ago too. When I first saw them, I mean. They're both gone now."

"Best thing, when all's said and done. All dead and buried long since, all of that. And now her as well, you say."

"So I believe."

"A good woman that. Didn't deserve me. Deserved better. No good for women, me. I mean, look how I let her down with all that business on the train. If I hadn't been so minded to look after my own bacon we'd have got away without any trouble. But she didn't hold any blame against me, not even losing her sight in that eye. She just said it was human nature. Well, I couldn't run out on her after that, although in retrospect I bet there's many a time she'd wished I had."

"So you stayed on there for quite a while then."

"Long enough. Here, pass me my notecase." Fazakerly crooked his finger at the shiny brown wallet on the top of the cabinet, taking it from Stephen with a flicker of distrust. "Between you and me, right?" He unbuttoned the wallet and thumbed through the pockets. "I'm not known for presence of mind but I did think to grab this from the house when they came for me. Nothing else of mine survived the fire. Except me, of course." He hooked something shiny from the wallet. "First anniversary," he declared, offering Stephen a small black and white photograph.

Stephen turned the photograph in his fingers. There was no date or any other kind of inscription on the reverse, and its irregular shape suggested that it had been cut from a larger photograph. The image on the front included just the head and shoulders of a woman in a broad-brimmed black hat, and in formal pose a man wearing the sort of Thomas Fazakerly spectacles that were now all the rage.

"My garden," exclaimed Fazakerly. "Just think, that was my wonderful wild garden." He frowned at the picture. "I don't know why I looked so bloody cheerful."

"Well, if it was a celebration…"

"Look, I haven't been entirely straight with you. Didn't want to drag all this up again. Not something of which anyone would be proud. Yet we buried it then and all things considered we thought it best that it should remain buried, but that's been no help. What happened damn well happened and that was just another thing I hadn't planned." He took another long look at the photograph of the man and the woman. "But there's no point in denying it now. Perhaps if I tell you the lot you'll be a bit more understanding."

Fazakerly drank his coffee from the saucer, deep in thought. "It's always too late, isn't it? Always the wrong time. What you do and what you're supposed to do, they never quite meet. All these rules, that's what makes it so difficult, especially when underneath there's nothing but disorder." He frowned and grabbed Stephen's hand. "Like I've been trying to tell you, they're other peoples' rules and you don't want to forget that."

"But there's always an element of choice."

"Hark at you!" the old man squawked, "had a lot of that, have you? Don't you believe it. Ever played those pinball machines? I love 'em. If I ever get to heaven that's all I'll do. But that's what it's like, life, and if it isn't rules that's flinging you around the table it's some other force. You think you're on a straight run then, wham! – someone hits the flipper and you're shooting off in a different direction altogether. There are rules how to play, of course, but they're not really the point. I just like to keep sending the ball whizzing."

"I'm getting a bit lost here."

"It's simple. Let me tell you. When we picked ourselves up from that station platform I could tell I'd been flipped good and proper. If it had been purely down to me I'd have been out that gate and away like a ferret down a rabbit hole."

It wasn't that she needed him to help her any more; it wasn't a matter of her feeling grateful. She may have clung to him for that brief moment as they fell but it was Rosalind who pulled him to his feet and felt for broken bones. Even then, even after he was identified in her own conspiracy as her brother, he could have gone his own way, he could have bade farewell and picked up the carefully imagined path into self-styled anonymity that he had convinced and committed himself to walk since his escape from France, probably long before that. No-one could accuse him of being mercenary, either, it mattered not that he had arranged no place to stay, he'd survived far worse predicaments than that.

After the police had satisfied themselves that they had asked enough questions to fulfil their competence and produced a doctor to exempt them from any liabilities of a medical nature, pronounced fit to travel and exhorted to make a hospital visit the next morning, Rosalind asked for a cab to be called. As if he had consented to adopt the mantle of her brother, whom he later discovered had been lost at St Julien, near Ypres, Fazakerly held the door for her then followed into the rear seat, looking more like a man who was accustomed to chaperoning his sister than the vagabond masquerading as a hero in his new suit of clothes.

She didn't question him, there seemed to be no need of questions between them, she simply instructed the driver with her own address and settled into the leather upholstery, her eyes closed as the enervation born of excitement crept over both of them and they passed the ensuing ten miles in silent contemplation of the unfathomable but quickening necessities that had brought them there.

It could have ended with that ride together, but she had weakened visibly by the time the cab pulled up at the bottom of the stone steps to her house and he quite naturally guided her to her door, without coming any closer to understanding what to make of this diversion. Perhaps it was having shared with her that glimpse of death's roar, when the steam from the locomotive hissed its call of seduction and the wheels of the carriage threatened to crush what seemed to be their asphyxiating last minutes into the track. It was not the kind of analysis he was capable of making. He was unconscious, a sleepwalker buried beneath the coils of line that had snagged him the moment she sat down opposite him in the train. All he could think at that moment was that it would be futile to resist. He'd make sense of it later.

She was sick that night, the nagging ache from her wounded eye become the noise of thunder in her head, and by the morning, after running in his shirt to the town square in search of her doctor, he found himself thinking that there was no harm in staying a while. He'd introduced himself as the lodger, pointing up the stairs to a top floor he had yet to explore, and the doctor had seemed pleased that there would be someone on hand, there being no kin.

"You talk about choice," said Fazakerly, "there was no element of choice at all. I wasn't on the make. I didn't need her money, if she had any - and how would I know when we'd only just met? I wasn't after her – you know, not in that way –

and once she was on the mend I started travelling about a bit on my own. I only tell you this to show I really was still set on having a place of my own down on the marsh. She even helped me out with that. Once she was well enough to go back to work, well, being in that line of business she came to hear of opportunities, and I'd go and look a few places over on her recommendation. But I found that things had moved on, as they do. Something had happened, though the only part of it I remember clearly was how so quickly everything went downhill; then of course how just as quickly we were picked up again. Talk about being all at sea! Anyway, I didn't see any choice in all of that. I was just on a roller coaster. The only way I can describe it now is that it felt as if there were new layers of meaning that got in the way, it was like there were new patterns to be understood, things I hadn't taken into account before and that I had no choice but to decipher before I could move on. I shouldn't have let myself be diverted in the first place, of course; that's when it all started to go wrong again."

It was as if he had slowed in his flight and all the baggage tied behind him had eventually caught him up, slamming him in the back. His new companion, recovered from all but the slow and invisible creeping blindness in one eye, had for public purposes and to keep their intercourse unassailable, determined to cement their relationship as one of landlady and lodger. This rationale was as much an explanation to herself as for anyone who might pry, and it did not prevent her from enjoying his company in a house that previously she had shared only with the gulls afforded shelter in her loft.

Their evenings were easy at first, with much to talk of, as may be expected when there are two intelligent strangers thrown together, each with a lifetime's chronicles to exchange. But the more doors were opened upon his past the less willing he became to risk spending time with her. For Fazakerly there were too many uncomfortable echoes beginning to crowd in for him to hear his own thoughts coalescing; they gave him no room to sift and judge before he might express himself with impunity.

When it came, her tearful narrative of the loss of her brother, made more potent by readings from a handful of letters he had sent from the front, was the anvil upon which Fazakerly's carefully reconstructed sensibility was sundered. Descriptions of glorious country summer days populated by desperate men in respirators and goggles, the screaming rush of air torn by trench howitzers, a landscape of broken trees and broken bodies all tossed together in a grey muddle of wood and bone, these were all images of a dead world he thought he had left behind him. She wept silently at her brother's last report, he was taking his turn in a watch from a ruined farmhouse, and amidst the monotonous rattle of a machine gun from the German trenches he had been entranced by the sight through a window of an apple tree, just the one tree in a field yellow with buttercups, the ground pitted with craters that had been quickly colonised by the surge of bright flowers. Evidence of the eternity of life, he had remarked with chilling fatalism, but for Fazakerly the image reprised the numbing blast of his own consciousness expiring on a foreign wasteland, and he suffered the certainty that he would have to relive the torture of that experience all over again.

The veneer of optimism he had laid down during his sojourn on the marsh began to peel back, revealing the cracks and splinters of the damaged frame beneath, its dissolution serving to compound his old despair at the futility of human purpose, and before he completely lost even the inclination to scorn his new confidence in forging a different life, it frightened and depressed him further to witness how rapidly and completely the black drain of his past life could well up again, poisoning the fresh reservoir he had made of his spirit.

Beyond that point, with his thoughts fractured, he resumed his soulless journey from Torhout, driven to retrace his steps and start again, taking to walking late into the evening, it mattered not where so long as he felt the distance being set down again. It was in any case more comfortable than sitting in the drawing room of that tall narrow house, raised up there above the road and with its large window open on the sea, from where on clear days he could not avoid the sight of the French cliffs gleaming in the sun just twenty miles away. But eventually, his perambulations too succumbed to his growing obsession and he would take a spy glass, climbing whatever hills or convenient structures he might encounter to peer across the water, looking, searching for any trace of that which he had convinced himself must surely come after him.

Their conversations became a burden to him. Rosalind's bookish education and her formidable aspiration to be one of the first amongst her sex to become an accredited lawyer were at first a magnet, her tales were scrupulously ingenuous, and soon forgetting his shallow contempt for the suffrage movement he had listened rapt as she explained the struggles and debates nationwide that had led, only the year before, to the passing of legislation that would allow her to bring her professional ambitions to fruition. But when he reached the point in his descent from the balance of reason where argument was an undertone submerged by the voices in his head, at which juncture he lost his faith in the substance of the daily commonplace, when he felt the ground beneath his feet beginning to break up, her words began to part around him like a stream around a rock. His days then were given over to solitary manoeuvres along the coast, where his own noisy progress across the screeing heights of shingle was drowned out by the growing echo from other footsteps, and he would hasten to the top of a rise like an automaton in step to the crunch of military boots in a compound. Returning from these miserable excursions late in the evening he could no longer sit and absorb her earnest and well-meaning geniality, for he saw another woman in her chair, a woman whose crisp white uniform dazzled the darkness he had gathered around him, whilst so agreeably she sat reading from a book or speculating with radiant optimism on the opportunities the post-war world would bring.

Rosalind was of course aware of the changes that were being wrought in him. Intuitively, she also knew that somehow she herself had touched the lever that had released him into this spiral of depression. He had mentioned Hermione in terms that gave no clue to the fatal end of that relationship, but the parallels in their situation were enough for her to signal danger. It was unfortunate for both of them that with her rationale thus confined to an imagined sorrow and the easily conjured tale of regret and lost affections, she unwittingly muted her own strength to support him, being unaware that the terror pursuing him was a far greater spectre than what she expected was combat fatigue or the memory of a failed romance.

They were caught in a maze of their own making. Fazakerly's need to be away before he lost sight of the exit that only months before he had drawn in the centre of his plan was, if only he could know it, obscured by the undeserved credence he was allowing those demons whose debilitating visions he was fleeing; whilst Rosalind's own sense of her contribution to their predicament, that she had, for selfish reasons she would not admit to herself, delayed his departure from a mission that was elemental and vital to his survival, would if explained to Fazakerly have cast him further into depression.

So it was a salvation for both of them when the key that unlocked this impasse was forged during one of his frenzied reconnoiterings, the desperate vigil on the roof of the Martello tower that led to his chance meeting with the military architect. Having coaxed Fazakerly down from the tower the architect's immediate thought was to return to the roof and continue his own researches, but concern at Fazakerly's severe state of agitation persuaded him to change his plans and instead he delivered him back to the tall house on the sea front. As Fazakerley conceded all those years later, their conversation on this short journey had already wrought a change in his demeanour by the time Rosalind opened the door to the architect's urgent knocking.

That she was able to render real and material assistance to the feverish discussions sparked by this new association was a source of pleasure to Rosalind, for she had a genuine debt to pay, and she was quick to realise how the Round House, which they began to plan that very night, the three of them seated around the big octagonal table in her drawing room, offered possibly the last best chance of redeeming her friend's sanity. It was also a source of more intimate reward for Rosalind, for while the architect sketched and scribbled, and Fazakerly fed his ruler with dreams, the knowledge that this physical embodiment of his psychological redemption might be set down not so far from her own lonely eyrie, on land she made it known her dear brother had worked hard to secure, warmed her through with a rich infusion of other, more arcane sentiments.

"Is this all a dissertation on misogyny or what? Because that's what I'm beginning to think."

"Miss who?" Fazakerly peered about him, deep in reverie.

"Women. Why you hate them. You do, don't you? First there was your mother, who you say was some kind of inebriated gorgon, then there was the poor nurse in France – and I'm still pretty shocked by that, I can tell you, since you've reminded me – and now we have another scheming Sibyl plotting to ensnare you, or so you make it seem to me."

"Started your studies again, have you? Don't give me Sibyl; there was nothing of a Sibyl about her. Though I know what you kids used to say, damn your eyes. I told you, I'd moved on by then. I may have been a bit down but I hadn't lost it completely. It was too lonely out there on the marsh, I've told you that, and I felt exposed just walking about. Setting up like I was some kind of noble savage in the wilderness wasn't a realistic option in the years following the war, there'd have been too much going on around me. I'd already overstayed my welcome – things were getting quite lively by the time I left my little hut on the beach. So I really did think it would be easier to lose myself in the town, and what I decided had nothing to do with what she wanted. She just helped it happen, that's all. And it worked too, it made sense, except for you blasted kids coming round from time to time, poking into my business."

"OK, ok, keep your hair on."

"Well just don't go bringing your amateur psychology into something you don't understand. Hasn't helped you much has it? It wasn't women who were my problem, they get clobbered just as much as the rest of us. None of us could know where the next wind was going to be blowing from, and that's as true today as it was then."

The Round House was like a great wooden raft they both clung to when together they surfaced from Fazakerly's troubled depths. Even as an idea and before the plans were approved it had become a shared possession, although Rosalind was wary of intruding too far upon his idea of it as a refuge from a world from which she had no intention of disengaging. It was safe ground too, there were no pangs of history to poison their enthusiasm, and she took care to speak only of their current obsessions with design and what they hoped for in the construction of this exotic monument to survival - which is how dramatically she interpreted his vision.

As the project advanced she collected together the evidence of its authenticity: a copy of the land exchange, the planning notice from the local newspaper, contracts with builders and builders' merchants. The architect too made a photographic journal of the construction; he mentioned that he would include it in a book he was writing, although Fazakerly extracted from him a shaky promise that he would confuse the reader with respect to its exact location. He proudly presented the two of them with a set of dated and numbered prints, all of which Rosalind pasted into her own record of their venture. Until the house was completed, she thought, it would provide Fazakerly with an unarguable proof that changes really were being made, and she would make sure that he could look forward with renewed confidence instead of back.

Fazakerly stayed on at her house, he had nowhere else to go and in any case they were now confidential partners in a private adventure. He had not and would not have judged it appropriate to venture any firmer bonds between them, and she never voiced her notion of their friendship. If the Round House was their passion it had no room for critical reflection, and he rarely conjectured where they might be travelling together. Quite uncharacteristically, he felt no need for circumspection, being buoyed simply by the fair prospect she had painted of the unchallengeable expedition of his plans.

To claim that they became lovers would be a deceit. He felt no love for her and if he had suspected that he might he would have shut himself away in the safe isolation of her top floor for the duration of the building project. The very concept of love for Thomas Fazakerly was something he would liken to a fog of suffocation, a dense entangling cloud, which as the unwary breathed at its edges would quickly disarm them with its soft inflaming filaments, this fair enticement from the wayward ends of its never ending tangle of bounds fast overtaken by threads become tethers, like serpents that would insinuate themselves and sew and seam and stitch tight their victims, enfolding and embracing and squeezing until there was no need of further breath at all.

Whilst, he allowed, even as committed a sceptic as he might yet be beguiled by a uniform or a voice of authority – those familiar camouflages of the powerful that he railed against – the consequences of his foolishness would be limited to transient hurt, such as the loss of time or money, and his sentence would be temporary, whereas beguiled by love he knew he would lose the right to his own will.

But as each day with glee they watched the building rise, the Round House assuming its unique form, beam over beam, rafter over joist, a tall huddle of spars that rose above the building site masting the circumference of its swelling presence, and seeing their own fiesta of joiners and carpenters and glaziers gathered to make a tremendous conviviality of creation, when the day's work was done it was its own intoxication to walk as one, arm in arm, the two of them blithe in the evenings' airy rooms, the house made resonant by the promise of the celebration its completion would bring them.

"I was walking on air. Her too, I reckon. I remember, we couldn't keep from going round to take a look. It was a good time, I can say that."

"For both of you, then, especially as it …"

"Yes, I was able to put everything else to the back of my mind. Heady times, heady times. None before like that, none since."

"But surely, the photograph…"

"That's right. You're so right, lad. I was coming to that. Gawd, I was dumbstruck when she told me she was expecting. Totally buggered. In fact, I wished afterwards I'd been a bit less obvious about how shaken I was. That must have sounded unkind. But here was I, on the verge of having my own place to go to, where life was going to be so simple, so sure that for the rest of my natural I could get along without the need to bother anyone and no-one'd bother me, and she goes and slings that at me."

"But still, you did the right thing."

"Did I? It didn't look that way some of the time. She seemed to think we'd wed, do it quick so no-one would put two and two together, but I wasn't having it. Christ, and her a lawyer, or about to be. It suddenly dawned on me what I'd got into there."

"I don't know what you mean."

"That business in Étaples. Never really understood that, but I couldn't deny it had happened and that I'd been a part of it. Had to put it down to the way things were then, what with the war and everything. We were stripped down to our basics. It's the only way to survive in a time like that. You stop functioning as a civilised human being. You ask your father what happened in his war, it wasn't just the Russkies that went ape in Germany. Well that's what I made of it. Didn't help much, didn't make me feel any better; I didn't like to think I was behaving according to type. But what else could I think? I wasn't a well man either, not after Torhout. Then, with Rosalind…"

"Yes?"

"Well, for a start it wasn't bloody 1967. There were rules of engagement, so to speak. People weren't just having their way with each other like they were sharing a cigarette. And here was her, poised to join the establishment, some of the very people I was trying to avoid, and trailing all her woes about her dead brother. What do you think I mean? I was about to be crushed. Hung drawn and bloody quartered for daring to break out."

"Oh come on!"

"No, you listen. This was serious emotional warfare. It wasn't just that she was about to tie me down with more ropes than the Lilliputians could throw over a man, it was the way in which every other Tom, Dick and Harry was going to pile in. Open season. If you think it was tough when you were a kid you want to know what it was like when I was a young feller. It might have been all right for King bloody George's old man to have kept a string of fillies but quite another matter for the likes of me to have just one in a small town – and one where I was trying to melt into the scenery, so to speak. They didn't use such polite terms as *out of wedlock* neither."

"But…"

"I was about to be put on display, I knew that. Whatever I did, they'd know me. I wasn't one of them, I'd only been there a matter of months. A tinker, they'd say, a pikey's in town, lock up your daughters. Oh there'd be plenty of chatter I can tell you. Well, I suppose I could have lived with that, but her, what do think they'd have made of her? She was a professional woman, one of the first, but don't think that meant she could take the sort of liberties they do today. You don't want to believe everything you read about the smart set between the wars. That was just the privileged class. No, here was her career gone out the window, not just her reputation as a woman of good honour."

For Rosalind the feeling was one more of joy than shame. To be aware of this brought with it possibly even greater surprise than realising the truth of her condition. It shunted everything else aside. The series of calamities that her otherwise fortunate life had thrown at her, not least the loss of her brother and the encounter that had led to her failing eyesight, followed so swiftly by having to assist in piecing together Fazakerly's broken mind, all had contributed to a growing sense that fate was cheating her, with all the good things that life had offered turned over, soiled, broken. Everything felt like a betrayal. Her disillusionment extended to her career, which was still in its infancy. She would never make it, she knew that; others, in years to come maybe, but secretly she had often admitted to herself it was too early in the game for her. And it was a game. She'd seen that all too clearly, working in the company of lawyers. Fazakerly was right about that. It was all a construct, the law; it had no intrinsic meaning other than to regulate and rule. It was the machinery of power. She would never have subscribed to Fazakerly's notion that this was just the surface of a universe in which fate looked more like a formulary, but the scales certainly seemed weighted against her. If anyone had thought to ask her to describe her outlook on life, honestly and without qualification, just one word would have sprung to mind: disappointment.

Yet throwing herself into the building of the Round House she had found herself attached to the flow of other, simpler rewards. That it provided the platform for the revival of Fazakerly's mental faculties made it doubly satisfying, and she saw in the construction of the house a metaphor not only for his own recovery but also the new vigour for life which their collaborations were bringing her. She hadn't looked for anything more, but considering her new situation she found it less a predicament than one more unexpected elevation in the uncertain and ever-changing landscape. It was not unwelcome. Life had assumed a new dimension and she had no inclination to shrink from it and seek out her old habitat of regret and discontent.

She had some capital, a small family income, and the proceeds from the sale of the land on which the Round House was being built. She determined she would survive, come what may. Her education and a small degree of financial independence provided some compensation, for they bought her a buffer from the tongues of the mean-minded. Not that for once she expected the world would leave her alone altogether.

Fazakerly was horrified by her equanimity. Seeing how resolved she was to brazen out her situation, whatever he decided to do, he fully expected she would make a public proclamation of their shame, so determined was she not to falter in the face of anticipated disapprobation. But it was not enough to persuade him that he must make an honest woman of her.

"You relented, of course. Eventually."

"Eh? Were you there?

"You mentioned your first anniversary, remember!"

"She was such a determined woman, Rosalind. Very mindful of others too, very thoughtful. She didn't flaunt herself, probably because of her breeding – it wouldn't have been seemly – but I also like to think it was in deference to me and my stupid anxieties about what everyone would say. I never heard any tongues wagging, mind. Not that it was obvious - you'd never have known to look at her and of course there are ways of disguising these things. She started getting bits and pieces together, though – you know, for the child – a cot, stuff like that. Had it brought by a carter down from London so no-one would be any the wiser. You know, putting it off as long as she could. Didn't make a big thing of it with me, either, didn't make me go and look, but I knew what she was up to. Sheer wasted effort. After all, what could she expect, that they were really going to leave her alone? Only royalty are allowed that sort of license. But as I say, she was an independent woman. She had plans. She never said, not outright, but I was pretty certain she was planning to pass off the child as the orphan of a relative or some such. It wouldn't have been the first time. You'd be amazed what sort of private arrangements were made between family, even neighbours, in those days. Some may have believed her. Under those circumstances it was best I kept my distance from any preparations she was making. It might have complicated matters if I was seen to be associated with them."

"But you did relent. Of course you did."

"Not in my nature. Not then anyway. What was the point when it was all beyond my control? I'd known that from the start."

She'd known what was going to happen. It was not so much the ache in her womb - that had been little more than a whisper of restiveness after their customary evening walk to the building site – but from the first caution that she heard in the accent of her body she had felt the dread pall of loss that came to stand expectantly at her bedside throughout the early hours of the sleepless night. It was an all too familiar figure but at first she refused to let herself recognise this silent spectre. Things were different now. Life was always going to be difficult, she accepted that, but she was vehement in her relish for the fight.

By midnight she could not deny the physical torment and the bitter taste of blighted hopes.

She hadn't made a sound. She hadn't wanted him to hear her pain. If she'd cried out the sound would have stuck him like a knife and he would have slipped further away, beyond her grasp forever. At the same time, hearing her, he would have come to her, she knew that; to hold her gently and not without concern, bathing the agony from her forehead, even breaking their confidence to send a neighbour for her doctor and knowing that by doing so he was placing the testimony of their guilt into a network of passing hands. But he would already be out of earshot, his feet over the step of that special place they had come to inhabit together; their secret would be sparks on bitter tongues lighting the nighted streets and he would have wanted to leave before the clamour drove him insane. She couldn't use her pain to secure him, not then, not in that way, just as down the long empty years she would not berate with her grief. It was not through her blind obedience to any ritual female subservience in the world of men, she had thrown off those shackles long ago; it was more fundamental than that. That night, she knew, was a new betrayal come upon her, it would always be so, the roll and tumble of light and darkness end over end, and this was just another disappointment that she had been too joyful to imagine might be waiting for her. That's how it would be from now on, there was no other greater disaster that would be necessary to convince her of that absolute.

Finding herself staring into the stark truth that she had not wanted to share with him brought her closer to the man who stood with her now in the deep summer's night, watching her stoop with the lifeless bundle, her face and the pristine shawl as white as each other in the moonlight. Closer yes, but despite her anxiety not to drive him away they were parted for all time, for even as she felt the compelling weight of his nihilism she was unable to take as a faith that which would require her to deny her self. It was the best she could do to respect his belief in the tensions that had brought them both to this place.

She had borne the pain alone, knowing instinctively that it was to be an end and not the beginning she had made all her own, she would suffer no-one but herself to witness it. Certainly there could be nothing she wanted that might be gained from calling out to him; it would have brought only his resentful servitude. None of it required explanation: the finality of the small dead hope that she wrapped in a shroud made from comforts that had been meant to nurture it was indubitably hers to claim. He had pressed no jurisdiction there and would now be released from any obligation. Would he, she wondered, rejoice at the irony of this, her tragedy?

There was no coffin, only the simple shawl to accept the soft shovelling earth and she was glad that she could not hear death's cold fingers rapping on the wood of her child's tomb. As dark earth filled the hole she watched the moonlight retreat from the small white promise that had failed to bloom, the last faint edge of the shawl concealed as he worked his spade, wordlessly tipping the soil into place, finally replacing the rough turf, which he carefully pressed level with the shadowless surroundings of the unmade garden. Her thoughts remained unspoken.

She was weak and it was all she could do to remain upright whilst he finished his work, glad to be lifted and carried into the sweet scented wooden rooms of the Round House, the roof newly installed and the house made whole, where the aromas of pine and oak, rosewood, walnut and maple, she could not remember all the names of the timbers they had selected, had been captured and warmed by the sun in a great wooden pomander. He moved a bed under the south-facing window and next day waited at the road to send away the tradesmen who were arriving early, bent on completing their final labours, while she began her recuperation in the light from the summer sun, the air in the room made an atmosphere of spice that sent her dreaming.

On another occasion she would have made merry of their entrance, but this further irony she also kept to herself in bitter silence, the knowledge of herself carried over the threshold to his bed in the house they had made together.

It was the last time she entered the Round House. On the first anniversary of the building being made habitable they met in the garden for the occasion of the architect's celebratory visit, it had been long agreed that he should join them formally to salute the completed building. They had always planned to have a traditional ceremony to mark the roof going on but Fazakerly had delayed their celebration, initially out of deference to Rosalind's unexpected ill-health and then publicly exclaiming that he wished first to set the garden to rights. So it was agreed that they would meet when the house was made whole by its landscape, a year hence from the last shingle being tapped into place. However, it was she who insisted on keeping the precise date, for it was she who had a ghost to lay.

Fazakerly had been right to delay the visit. Not that the house itself would have failed to fascinate many months before, but his vision of it as a refuge in the midst of a wilderness was made manifest by the garden that he had raised around it, a deserted but not desolate scramble of grasses and wild flowers that rose in quiet waves against the walls. He brought out chairs in front of the house for them to sit and enjoy the rewards of this tranquillity, which together they had conceived and engineered. Mostly, he wanted them to bask in the golden light from the myriad buttercups he had nursed across the space where there might otherwise have been a lawn.

Closing her eyes for a moment Rosalind could still see the warm glow from the crowding flowers pressing through her eyelashes, their brilliance making no moment of her failing sight. The field of gold was unbroken. There was nothing to remark the tiny grave hidden somewhere beneath her feet and, but for the grief she held tight within herself, there was no evidence of what they had done that night. Silently she searched but the flowers covered everywhere, she had to tiptoe for fear of crushing their cheerful petals underfoot.

The architect was setting up a camera on a tripod. He wanted pictures of the house and its unusual wild garden to complete his photographic journal of their achievements. Rosalind was to pose in front of it with Fazakerly, his partners in this extraordinary design.

Fazakerly was in unusually high spirits. He brought out chilled lemonade in a porcelain jug and toasted the three of them with exaggerated flourishes of his long arms that took in the house and its grounds. Rosalind watched him, angry at herself for indulging his good humour, yet never before had she seen him beaming like that, never so youthful-looking; he was nothing if not suffused with delight from having made this special place. Could it mean he was mended, she wondered, had he shaken free from whatever haunting past had brought nightmares into her house?

Once she would never have doubted. Free as he'll ever be, that was the concession she could make, she was reluctant to utter contrary thoughts on such a fine day, though it was not easy to acknowledge that he'd moved on when for Rosalind it seemed she had yet to draw breath and think about leaving the old pieces of their lives behind. Could it really be, the falsehood and deceit that he railed against, all that web of pretence in which he said most people took refuge from the harsh authenticity of truth, was he really so free of all that himself? Her resentment searched for a place to settle but sitting in the middle of this extravagantly wild garden her thoughts made her feel crabbed and sour in a way that she knew she found unattractive in others. It was meant to be a glad day and despite what she had thought to make of it, the sad truth of her loss from the year before was not something she wished to dwell upon. She knew now that it would remain inviolate beneath the gaze of all who passed and looked upon the golden surge of flowers.

The camera popped and the architect clapped his hands together approvingly, the afternoon's rituals were almost over. It was the most splendid of outcomes, he was suggesting, such a fine idea to wait until they might see this special house in its full defining context. He waxed lyrical about proportion and symmetry and perspective. He was keen to compare it with his other commissions and launched into an earnest report of all the projects he had undertaken since the war, all but admitting they had provided him with a way of making amends for the many deaths he had aspired but failed to prevent with his ingenious military earthworks. As his oration fixed them like a congregation Rosalind's thoughts turned to her brother, whose land she had provided as the host for one such restitution.

"And here we are," the architect was saying, "in these more peaceful times, able to enjoy the fruits of our labours. It really makes you think, doesn't it, as we sit surveying all of this, how not so long ago others less fortunate will have looked upon similar splendours with very different eyes. How does it go, I've been trying to remember, that piece by Owen? – *Hour after hour they ponder the warm field* – and the rest, I'm thinking of the buttercups of course - you'll remember."

"I remember," she said, "*where the buttercup had blessed with gold their slow boots coming up.*" She looked at Fazakerly as she recited the rest of the stanza, the expression in his eyes hidden by the glow from the garden. She was troubled that the words of the poem left her with such a sinking feeling.

- TWELVE -

IT WAS BECOMING quite a story, though not exactly
the kind of tale that Stephen had been looking for, that first
time they'd met, when he had come face to face with a dead
man and found him – once he'd recovered from the surprise –
as good as alive as himself.

More to the point then had been the unexpected
prospect that this hale corpse could quite possibly be the key
he was missing, that discovering Fazakerly alive could be the
one chance he might have of unlocking the enigma of his own
young life. But now, how many times was it that they had met
– half a dozen, probably more? – and he found himself no
nearer to the truth about what had happened on that late
summer's afternoon all of ten years ago. Sure, he'd learnt a lot
about Fazakerly, a lot of stuff dredged up from the depths, but
he'd still not come any closer to the bottom of his own private
well.

In the cold light of day it all struck him as completely
insane – that's when he could find the wit to think about it
objectively. Well, he'd been there, hadn't he, all those years
ago, right there at the centre of it all, and yet from a
remarkably short time afterwards he'd found himself unable to
piece any of it together properly in his mind – not in a way
that made sense anyhow, not so that he could pack it away and

move on. And thinking about it again now, still none of it made any sense. It was just too ridiculous. To think that a whole chain of experience could be removed in such a way, just sliced out of his memory and hauled off into some unreachable place. Because that's how it had seemed to Stephen then, and that's how it felt now, as if someone had snatched it away before he'd had enough time to take it all in. For good or ill, someone had deliberately bundled it away out of sight, leaving him wondering just what it had all been about.

It's like the whole experience was part of a conjuring trick, he thought, and the only concession that this interfering prestidigitator had left him – for it was easier to think of the imagined perpetrator in that way, much less daunting than to believe he had been deceived by a larger conspiracy – was a disquieting sense that just for an instant he had touched something momentous, something that his unreliable memory could subsequently reconstruct only as a formless and fading but powerful significance, leaving him guessing, never having had his part in it explained.

He'd hoped that having found Fazakerly's demise to be a lie it might be possible to cast a new light on his memories, perhaps take off some of the pressure he'd been under for so long and let his brain get back into gear. For a start, with Fazakerly not dead there'd be less for him to fear, if that was the problem, for there'd be less risk of bringing any reckoning upon himself should he succeed in pasting together his scattered memories in a way that might deliver up some less than pleasant answers. Even better, working together they might find themselves able to shuffle the pieces in an entirely different way, testing each other's recollections until they had assembled a clear picture upon which they could both agree.

Stephen brightened. He might seem obtuse in the manner of his story telling, but the one fact that Fazakerly was not trying to avoid was that he had been there on that fateful afternoon. And surely, *his* ought to be a very singular take on the whole event. He'd owned up to, even relished, having been there, hadn't he, right there at centre stage, so why not? And then again, thinking back to the description of his rescue, there was no doubting it had been executed with undeviating professional élan. He'd been plucked unharmed from the destruction of his seemingly inviolable domain with such a flair of speed, and with such precision. The old man's impression was one of having been rushed away deliberately and unimpeded, his passage from all that he knew into a place that was entirely unknown having been rapid, unchecked and exact. So it was not improbable to suppose that he too had suffered from the same feeling of displacement as had Stephen, that his memories too would be ruled by an implacable sense of having been wilfully and surgically removed from history, rudely taken without any option and filed away thereafter in a state of suspended animation.

Who knows, maybe it was the frustration of that very experience that made him behave so obtusely: the suspicion that some one or some thing had carefully tweaked him out of the burning frame of the moment in order to incarcerate him in the safe but slow time of the nursing home. Hadn't he described himself in those sorts of terms to Stephen? Or was that what Stephen had imagined, letting his mind subversively fill in those gaps again, having discovered Fazakerly in what he'd observed was a state of preservation, all wrapped up safe and sound in the clean white antiseptic room of the nursing home, and making the wrong connection, the old man become a motif, he was seeing him like he was the main feature in a local history society's time capsule? Thinking back to their earlier conversations he did recall Fazakerly at more than one point suggesting everything was a pretence. Was that meant to be a giveaway?

The trouble was, if Fazakerly had really thought of it in those terms, he'd surely have worked out this whole conundrum before now. Just knowing what was real and what was not, he'd have cut through the fog; and he'd had the advantage of not having been a child when it all took place, he'd have been able to understand the codes that adults use to conceal the truth.

Stephen's hopes slithered from pillar to post. The fact remained that none of it yet was any the clearer. When it came down to the truth, if ever truth were to be known, all he'd got from Fazakerly was a damningly ignoble account of his life as a young man, starting somewhere around the time of the Great War, and tricked out it had seemed with the conceits of fiction as a deliberate device to soften the grittier and less gallant moments. That and all his wacky metaphysical stuff about free will, or the lack of it. Worse too was his irritating insistence that Stephen had still to explain himself, to come clean – at least that was the undertone of his entreaties – that Stephen was somehow obliged to give an account of himself and why he had come to choose Fazakerly as his – what did he think? – victim. How paradoxical was that!

Then there was all this stuff about Marble Gamble. Quite a turn-up and all very absorbing – plausible too, come to think of it – but it didn't bring him any closer to the truth about himself. That's if the little dramatic episode triggered by the photograph had anything to do with truth, and Stephen couldn't find a reason to convince himself why it should or why it shouldn't. Whatever the veracity of her part of the story, it did little to help jog his memory, it didn't shed any light on his own traumatic evening in Fazakerly's garden all of ten years ago, and it would need a big jog after ten years. It felt like a physical block sometimes, everything was so clogged up in there after a whole decade of unrelieved mental wrestling, so much so that at times he would be overcome by a feeling of spiritlessness, picturing his brain cells choked and fused with a thick accumulation of scar tissue.

It was not that he'd forgotten the general account of what had happened, not the sequence of events. He wasn't that witless, he was sure of that, and he'd been able to run through every frame of that day so many times since, like it was captured on film. But somewhere along the way he'd mislaid the essence of what had happened, and without that feeling to give his memories an extra dimension of meaning, the flat statement of facts they depicted didn't make much sense. No matter how many times he repeated the bald catalogue of events it didn't reveal the purpose of what had gone on, or why it had happened at all, and in time it was at risk of becoming a meaningless mantra that he intoned just to remind himself there were things left undone. More recently, running through it all in his head, over and over, he'd been left with the impression that he'd been only an onlooker, not the fully paid up transgressor of his earlier recall. Then just when he thought he'd caught a glimpse of the fuller picture offered by this more panoramic lens, the whole unfolding sequence would tail off into a colourless empty space, incomplete and before he had set the focus upon it all. Oddly enough, his strange conviction that the entire experience had been deliberately removed from sight had provided Stephen with an unexplained source of comfort when he was a child, although it was a rationale that he'd alternately welcomed and resisted. In later years it only worried him.

Fazakerly, on the other hand, seemed to have less trouble remembering the feeling of things, allowing of course that there were a lot of gaps in what he chose to relate. He wanted to blame everyone else for what had happened too, as though he had no exercise of choice in anything; either that or he'd run and hidden from the truth. There were so many contradictions and, to top it all, the thought that Fazakerly might be playing a game of concealment unsettled Stephen, for it was too close to his own experience. He'd had enough of gazing into a mirror anyway, and he had no wish to find Fazakerly staring back at him, whispering that they were two of a kind, both equally adept at playing that game. Trouble was, whilst he didn't want it to seem like that, with no other answers he was beginning to wonder if it was indeed what he had been doing all of this time.

Stephen went on with the routine of his morning chores in silent contemplation, attempting, as he had done all those countless and fruitless times before, to recall the substance of that entire fateful day. The trick was to bring it back without letting his imagination sabotage what little he might still claim to be memory. It was true, he'd admitted a long time ago that there was plenty he might have wanted to forget, it had been a most uncomfortable day, but it was curious, thinking back, how much he had not managed to explain or even thought to question. How he'd ended up in the witch's house, for instance, and not been afraid, was one aspect of the day that had seemed quite natural at the time but which struck him now as wholly bizarre. Warren would have said she'd hypnotised him, put him under the watch of her evil eye. What a shame. If they'd known what he now knew would they have been any kinder towards her? He suspected not. He'd made up his mind never to tell Warren the truth about Rosalind Campbell; better to keep the myth going than have him snigger over her sad affair with Fazakerly. Come to think of it, he'd never mentioned to anyone what he'd discovered in that upstairs room, not until yesterday morning's conversation with Fazakerly.

Of course, that little moment of excitement upstairs in her secretive back bedroom had been overtaken by the larger events he'd first spied through the window.

"That fucking little mongol!" Paul was dancing up and down, his fists clenched. His face was crimson and he was on the verge of spilling tears of rage.

Despite his stepbrother's fury, Marcus was preoccupied by more immediate concerns of his own, but he had enough presence of mind to keep one foot on the air rifle, holding it flat and hard against the gravel path. With his free hand he repeatedly pushed his stepbrother away, over and over and over, but making no lasting impression on Paul, who kept stubbing away undaunted with his boot at the stock of the gun.

"Cool it, cool it, will you!" Marcus spoke in short sharp breaths, more intent on sucking at his other wrist, which bled remorselessly from a mouth-sized wound. "Let's sort ourselves out first, then we'll do for him."

"I'll sort him out, just let me have the gun," Paul kicked hard again at the rifle butt, trying to dislodge it, but succeeded only in raising his own temperature.

"Not here, stupid. What, with all those loopy housewives watching out their kitchen windows?" Marcus jerked his head towards the ugly backside of the sea front terrace, where shadowy faces seemed to peer from the netted windows backing on to the bombsite. "C'mon, we need to think this through. How many did he take, anyway?"

"Two, as far as I could make out. But I don't know what else he might have nabbed."

"Well, before we make any greater fools of ourselves let's go and see. Oh shit, look who's coming." Over his brother's shoulder Marcus had caught sight of Stephen careening around the corner to the passage. "Say nothing, right, say nothing." He folded his arms to conceal the wound at his wrist, calling out breezily: "All right then Spas, come back for another look at our human fart machine, have you?"

Stephen was too winded to reply. He bent over with his hands on his knees and took deep breaths.

"Aw, look at him," sneered Paul, "right little Ben Dover, he's desperate for a dose of the same." He snorted scornfully, irritated and spiteful at the interruption. "Shame, innit, looks like he's run all the way and now it's too late. Missed the show, Ben, you dozy fucker."

"What happened to you?" All of a sudden Stephen felt strangely composed; it was the sight of the two Gregorys gripped by an unlikely state of agitation.

"That fuckin'......Oof!" Paul doubled up at Marcus's elbow jabbing in his throat.

"Nothing. Was it Paul? Just a bit of a misunderstanding with Humph, that's all."

"I meant your arm. You've got blood all down your front."

"Oh. Right." Nonchalantly Marcus held the wound out in front of him, hoping to look casual, but there was something about the sight of it that...

"Shit, grab his other arm!" Stephen caught Marcus as he slumped in a dead faint, his head on one side and his knees bent and boneless like those of a plasticine model. "Come on, we'd best try to get him home. Might even need a doctor."

Paul had insisted they take his brother back to the garage, avoiding the front door to their house. Rather implausibly too, thought Stephen, when he could hear what Paul was saying, for he had jammed himself under Marcus's armpit and was breathing heavily as he shouldered the weight of the older boy, who was still in a daze.

The first story he tried was that their mother was not at home and hadn't left a key. A little closer to their front gate and with an even greater show of reluctance to enter the house, Paul was suddenly full of concern that Mrs Gregory couldn't stand the sight of blood and, with a morbid vengeance, he foretold scenes of tearful hysteria were she to witness what had happened to Marcus. Their short but slow journey was peppered by a long list of his objections and he ranted incoherently all the way along the passage behind the sea front terrace; but most of it was not about Marcus, their mother, or whether they would need to call a doctor once they were safely home. Mostly he fulminated about Humphrey and how he would do for him as soon as they had settled Marcus. He had reclaimed the gun the moment Marcus keeled over and jubilantly brandished it as they walked, raising it aloft, his menacing display accompanied by lunatic whoops and snarls. By the time they reached the garage he'd abandoned his brother to Stephen, who was by now too exhausted to remonstrate.

It was probably hearing these indiscretions that roused Marcus from his faint, although the eye-watering stink of petrol that hit them as they entered the garage may also have had something to do with his rapid recovery. Whatever the reason, he was no longer a completely dead weight by the time Stephen lowered him onto the big black inner tube that in less fraught moments they'd used as a raft on the sea, and he sat and shivered while Stephen tried to catch his breath in spite of the foul air.

Seemingly oblivious of his stepbrother's plight, Paul went straight to delving in his collection of military paraphernalia. He had first to pile boxes one on top of another in order to climb up to his platform in the rafters, for the rope ladder lay in a jumble on the garage floor, then after much thrashing about in the darkness above him Stephen heard a cry and was just in time to catch a soft bundle that came flying out of the shadows towards him. In the field first-aid kit that Paul had thrown down he found webbing and bandages, enough to stem the flow of blood and strap up Marcus's damaged wrist, though to his unpractised eye it seemed inadequate for such a large wound.

"You might need plastic surgery," he ventured, nervously, knowing the Gregorys and thinking that later he would somehow be blamed for the lasting effects from this hastily improvised treatment.

"Nah – I'm getting Spastic surgery." Marcus was quickly regaining his wits, but he shivered uncontrollably, showing little of his infamous self-confidence, and he didn't object when Stephen suggested that he might need painkillers.

He'd pulled himself upright on the edge of the old lorry inner tube, fully awake now but frighteningly pale, and with an uncharacteristically hunted look in his eyes. It was plain too that Paul's loud and nonsensical dissembling was bothering him more than his wounded arm, the facile moment when his stepbrother theatrically discovered from his watch that their mother was, after all, not yet expected home, drawing looks of pitiless contempt.

"Painkillers, Paul? You got painkillers up there?" Stephen's request brought only a torrent of curses from above his head.

"Paul! Get me some fucking aspirin!" A short silence followed the older brother's outburst then Paul stood glowering before them.

"Aspirin?" He shrugged and pouted defiantly, first lost in vacillation and then feigning further surprise when reminded that he did after all have a key to the kitchen door in his pocket.

With Paul sent for aspirin and a cup of water it didn't take long for Stephen to realise how much things had changed between the two of them.

"If you find she's home early, don't whatever you do encourage her to come out here. Fucking dickhead," gasped Marcus, when his brother was gone. "Fucking Nazi dickhead. It's all his stupid fault. Look at it. Thank Christ they don't put the car in here."

It was only then that Stephen was able fully to take in what had happened in the Gregory's garage, the wreckage and utter disarray to which they had returned going a long way to explaining the two brothers' state of agitation. At any other time Marcus would have grinned at the look of horror on his face.

"Yeah, he's totally lost his marbles, ain't he? You see the state he's in?"

Worst of all was the extent of damage done to the actual fabric of the building. One of the rafters had been snapped completely in two, its split and splintered ends hanging down at a sharp angle just above the level of his head, and with one of its supports gone Paul's platform hideaway leaned in toward the centre of the garage. With the collapse of the platform, all manner of military paraphernalia had come tumbling down, and in a display of theatricality, an old army blanket from his stash had unrolled and caught on a spike of the broken rafter. It dangled inches from the concrete floor, which glittered with the strewn shards of several broken bottles and a scattering of gleaming rifle shells.

In the centre of the garage, the crate that Humphrey had been made to use as his lunch table lay smashed like firewood and around their feet a broad wet stain had exploded across the floor and up one of the walls, blackening the concrete beneath a spray of glassy splinters. Stephen imagined he could see fumes rising from the spate of spilled petrol even as it dried, evaporating snakes of gas writhing away in search of a spark.

"He did all this? Just to get away from you and your experiment?"

"Nah. My dickhead stepbrother. Well, the roof at least, though all of it's his fault, in a manner of speaking. Still, what would you have done if you thought someone was gonna fuck you with a milk bottle?"

"What?"

"Humph – turned out he wasn't in the mood for a bit of auto-da-fé. Thought we were some sort of perverts."

"It really stinks in here!"

They both winced at Paul's shrill voice and the grinding crash of the garage door being opened to its full extent. He propped it up with a clothes pole to let the air clear, the incoming draught catching at the loose blanket and dislodging it further so that it dragged across the floor. As he handed over the aspirin and glass he saw them watching him.

"What've you been saying?" He glared at Marcus. "Thought we were keeping it on the QT."

"I've been thinking." Marcus sipped at the edge of his glass. "Listen, there's no way Humph'll come anywhere near us for a while, not after all this, so our good mate Spas, here, he might be able to do us a favour."

Stephen cringed inwardly at the thought of becoming further embroiled. "But if he wasn't responsible for all this damage, why..?"

"Molotovs. He's got a couple of my Molotovs, the little fucker. And whatever else I don't yet know." Paul dredged through the broken glass with the toe of his boot, separating out the live ammunition into little brass-coloured heaps. "Yep, I reckon he's taken about half a box, half a box at least, maybe a dozen - perhaps as many as two dozen shells." He whistled and looked expectantly at his stepbrother, his hands rammed defiantly into his pockets.

He glared belligerently at Stephen: "You're gonna have to find him."

Stephen blanched at the picture forming in his mind. They expected him to go after a half-wit with a pocket full of live ammunition?

"Hang on though." Paul was suddenly alert again and scrambled back up the teetering pile of boxes, the platform bowing precariously under his weight. They heard him dragging something heavy out of the farthest corner above them. "No, it's all right. He didn't get the mortar."

His face appeared over the edge of the sagging platform, a look of triumph glowing in the darkness; he was dangling a short and smoothly shaped silver tube with a pointed nose at one end and fins at the other, which Stephen thought resembled a tiny space ship. "Found this on the ranges. Would you believe they'd just left it propped up in a foxhole, the wankers? What a beauty."

"Fuck it Paul, you never told me about that!" The aesthetics of ordnance were completely lost on Marcus, who was suddenly on his feet, pulling himself up by Stephen's arm and quickly making for the open door, still tugging Stephen by the sleeve and hollering at his stepbrother.

"You cretin. Just get rid of it. And when you've done that you'll have to clean up this mess or we'll be deep in the brown stuff once the old man gets home. Get a bucket and wash all this petrol out. Put some sand down. Come on," Marcus clung to Stephen's arm, "let's talk outside, down the alley. It's fucking crazy in here. And don't switch the light on", he called back loudly; "the air in here's so rich the whole place could go up. That blanket of yours is soaked now, it'll be like a wick."

They crouched in the alley, their backs against the link fence that enclosed the bombsite, hidden from onlookers by the fireweed that crowded over all of the tumbled hollow where not so many years before there had been smart houses.

"It was only a bit of a lark. But he wasn't having any of it." Marcus pulled a stem of grass through his front teeth, screwing up his face as he thought back. Things had never gone this wrong before.

"Maybe we should have burned the place down, then nobody would have been any the wiser. Perhaps we should just go back and torch it now." He waited, expectantly, as if an answer would appear from out of the air.

"No, things are bad enough. As I was saying, he wasn't playing, just stood there and howled. So Prat Features back there decided to top him up, as he put it, said he was going to stick one of his Molotov's up Humphrey's arse and fill him up with four star. I mean, it's all very well having a laugh with a plate of baked beans, but this was serious." He grimaced, his hand cupped around his damaged wrist. "I always thought I was the hard man but, Jesus, even I felt a bit scared then, it was obvious he meant it, kept muttering on about how H was just sub-human scum, how he and his mates would clean up, that's how he described it, once they were regulars they'd really clean up."

"So Humphrey wrecked the place when he heard that, is that what you're telling me? He was scared shitless."

"No. No, hold on a minute. I don't think he understood, you see, not really, not at first. We'd never done nothing like that to him, not before, just mucked him about a bit, so he wasn't expecting anything worse this time. But it was still all Paul's fault. He went stupid. Kept zipping and unzipping his fly right in front of the kid's face, dancing about like he was some kind of poofter and taunting him with his dick out and such, so when he stuck the bottle up Humphrey's arse the kid thought he was being well and truly buggered. That's what Paul wanted him to think, of course."

"So why didn't you stop him. He takes notice of you."

"I dunno. I just didn't. Don't ask me why, I simply don't know." He threw the grass stem up into the air and it blew back into his face, making him blink sudden tears. "Well, that's how it is sometimes. Why do we do anything – or not?" He spat out a stream of green saliva. "Anyway, that's all bye the bye, 'cos you should have seen the strength in him, Humphrey I mean, he just ripped his way out of the rope ladder once he felt the neck of that bottle in his rectum, and he was going for Paul as if he'd pull him apart too, with his bare hands. You should have heard him, wailing and screeching, tromping all over the stuff on the floor like a zombie. Buckled both the rims on my bike. I swear his eyes were red like the Devil's and all."

"That's when he pulled the rafters down."

"Yeah. Sort of. But that was Paul's fault. He was trying to get away up the ladder and Humph had his fingers stuck like meat hooks in his legs, hanging on, he was shaking him like a terrier with a rabbit. That's when the rafter came down, and the platform with all Paul's stuff, the bullets and all the rest."

"So the two of you, you couldn't handle him then? He really is that strong, sort of like Clark Kent, sort of superhuman only you'd never know just by looking at him."

"Hey, more like Gargantus. You should have seen it." He painted a banner in the air in front of them. "*Humphrantus, Scourge of Humanity.* Hah! I can just picture his gormless face on the front of a Tales of Suspense. Anyway, there was just me to handle him then. Paul had got up there in the roof somehow, heaved himself up out of reach; like a fucking Junior Leaders assault course, it was. That's when H turned on me, so I whacked him with my catapult. I had to. Like I was facing the creature from the pit. Got him right between the eyes with a marble. Point blank. He just stood there for ages, like he was pole-axed, then instead of crumpling in the time-honoured way he went totally nuts."

"Your arm."

"Yeah. I reckon there's a bit of me on the garage floor somewhere. It was when he went for the bottles; he was pulling them out of the crate and smashing them on the floor. I thought any minute the place would go up in flames so I gave him a bear hug from behind and…well, he took a big bite out of me." Marcus held up his arm. A slight red mark had appeared through the bandage. "Not much I could do then, he was totally wild. Ran off with a couple of them in his mitts. There was no stopping him. We went after him when we could but as soon as I saw Paul had brought the gun I…"

"You mean he's got two of your brother's petrol bombs – his Molotovs?"

"You got it. That much we are sure of…"

"But he's an imbecile."

"So they say. That's why we need your help. Find out where he is and maybe we can ambush him before anything worse happens. We need one of those tranquilliser darts. You wouldn't happen to know where…"

"Shouldn't we tell someone? Isn't this a matter for the police?"

"Hey, are you kidding? Think! Where did he get the stuff in the first place? And since when are the rozzers going to listen to a couple of kids anyway? Nah, they'd be straight round to spill the beans to our parents."

"OK, but maybe his mother, Nola, maybe she could speak to him."

"C'mon, she doesn't have a clue. Not about anything. She lives in another world. After all, that's how she got Humph, innit? I mean, who normal's going to want to give someone like her a good poke?"

"I don't follow."

"Never mind – if you don't follow I'm not going to lead you by the nose. You'll have to ask Humphrey. He knows what I'm talking about, I'm pretty sure of that. Hey, he never did answer your question, by the way. You know, about him chasing the old geezer on the bike. So you've a lot to ask him about when you find him."

"I never said…"

"Course you didn't. But think about it. He's out there running around the town like a human bomb and you're the only one can stop him. There you are, see. You're the real Clark Kent! What's the betting he's down at Blackman's right this minute, demanding jamboree bags with menaces. Off you go, get a move on. It's Superspas to the rescue!"

Stephen didn't know which was worse, the thought of tackling Humphrey on his own or not managing to find him. Either way he was mixed up in some deep, deep trouble. Perhaps he should just go home. It had been a pretty disappointing day all round. Yes, a really dirty day, it had left him with a dry, sour taste in his mouth. He cupped his hands to his mouth and nose and exhaled heavily, finding his breath rough with a stale mixture of catarrh and bile. Was that the taste of fear or recrimination? Either way, he should just excuse himself from it all. Go home and shut the door on the day. Shut the door on the Gregorys, more like, and for good. No-one at home need know. In fact he didn't need to say anything when he got home. He could just go home and get some tea. The Goon Show might be on the wireless later. What day was it?

He cheered himself with that thought. Yes, he could easily go home and shut the door on the whole business of today. No-one would know what had been going on. Well, only Paul and Marcus, they knew; but they wouldn't tell.

Would they? One never could know with Paul and Marcus. But surely they'd really not want to be telling anyone; it would mean big trouble.

Trouble, oh, the sound of the word rumbled in his head like a great boulder bearing down. There could be trouble anyway. Supposing word got about, suppose Humphrey blew himself up, which he might; someone who'd been stupid enough to drink from one bottle full of petrol wasn't going to be any more careful with the two he had carried away. That's if he didn't know the risk, of course. But then why take them at all if he didn't understand what they contained, what he might do with them? Could it mean he wasn't so daft as he seemed?

Mmm - so it wasn't over yet, not if Humphrey was bent on revenge. That, then, was the real issue, and trouble wasn't the word for it; there was no denying that Humphrey had been put through hell that afternoon and he'd be coming back for them. Including me, shivered Stephen. I was there. I shouldn't have left him alone with them. And now I'm to suffer the vengeance of Humphrey.

It would definitely be far worse than the return of Gargantus.

Yet he knew that if ever he was interrogated there would be no explaining it. His interrogators would know that, but they wouldn't have listened to his pleas, they wouldn't want to hear him protest that he couldn't have run home and reported that a half-wit was being tortured in a garage down the road. They wouldn't admit they'd have not wanted to know. Those kinds of things didn't happen. Not amongst kids. Not with nice kids in that neighbourhood at least. Or worse, they'd have made such a big deal about it, whoever *they* were, for there was a whole army of authorities that would want to take a view, that he'd have *really* paid for the consequences. Yes, that would be it. There'd be such a to-do that he'd end up being marked as a pariah for ever and ever.

Still, Paul and Marcus, they couldn't dump it all on him, could they? They'd be the ones having to explain how the garage had been wrecked, wouldn't they? There'd be no getting away from that. If their father saw what had happened in the roof of his garage, and if the place still stank of petrol, well, he'd soon put two and two together, especially if Humphrey blew himself up. That was for them to deal with, then. That let him off the hook. Course it did.

He doesn't know me, does he? Stephen faltered, trying to remember if he had ever spoken to Mr Gregory. Because if he did, and knowing how the minds of parents worked, wasn't he, Stephen, somehow to blame, not having done anything about it?

It all went round and around and he was trapped in the middle. But that wasn't the half of it.

Worse was all that other stuff. He didn't even like to think about it or attempt to give it a name. Picturing the particular misadventure that Marcus had just described made his blood run cold. All that pervy business, it had started with them taking down Humphrey's shorts, of course, and he'd been there, although he hadn't thought anything of it at the time, not in that way at least, not when it was just a stupid farting game. It was just the way things had happened, and he'd thought no more of it than it was just stupid Humphrey farting for his supper, so to speak, and they were all having a laugh. Just a grubby little kid with a fat arse who'd do most anything for a plate of beans. Well, almost.

He fished in the murky pool of his conscience. Sure, he'd felt a bit uncomfortable, he knew that; he'd been concerned for the boy, he'd be the first to admit it, but he knew he was a touch over-sensitive that way and after all, it was just something they did. It didn't mean anything. Humphrey and what they did with him was simply the way of things for kids in that town. Any town. No harm was meant and everyone knew it didn't really matter when H was such a mongol, so long as he never came to actual bodily harm. Stephen wracked his brains in search of anything really gross that he might be able to recall from previous adventures. No, his conscience was clear, there was nothing there that did any more than make him shrink a little. It was all kids stuff. None of it meant anything, there'd been no lasting damage as a consequence. But now with this other stuff, Paul and that crazy business with the bottle...

Stephen's head swam. God, what would his parents say about that? Just imagining what they might think made his head ache and his eyes filled with a hot and salty torment. A monster, that's what they'd call him. A filthy homo. He was no better than Paul - his nasty little friend, they would say – they were no better than those disgusting homos who lurked in the public bogs. Hmmm. So is that what he got up to when he wasn't at home?

Filthy little beast needs locking up.

Oh God, what would his parents think if they could know all the rest of what had been going on that afternoon? And not just that afternoon. All of it seemed so much worse now that he looked back, all of it, his association with the Gregorys – all black and squalid. Whether or not he'd been there all the time that particular afternoon he was irrevocably associated with these people, these degenerates, as they would call them. Oh Jesus, he sighed, he knew exactly what it would be like, they would see it all as so much worse than even he now pictured it in his horrified mind's eye. How would he ever excuse himself? He'd crossed the divide to a place they had never known to have existed and he was certain they'd allow him no way back once they discovered its bitter authenticity.

He had no choice then. Marcus had known that. He was smart, that Marcus, he always knew the limits of possibilities, always understood when and where to engage with the adult world. He'd known: the three of them would have to sort this out for themselves.

Stephen's half-hearted resolve did not erase his fear, the big fat heavy fear of being found out. Though what might be found out and used against him by whom, that wasn't clear even then. It was just the thought of letting them in to his disgrace, that's what burned like acid in his belly, owning up to his parents that his world could not be explained simply as down the beach or over the recreation ground or – so glibly – round at so-and-so's house. He hadn't got it under control like Marcus. He'd always known that, and knowing it was part of the fascination. Marcus could step back and forth between both places invisibly, and he would do it without leaving telltale footprints all over his parents' world from the secret dirt on his soles. In Marcus's world the rules of engagement were clear and the larger universe had nothing further to say to him. Certainly it had no place to play. When he'd finished there he could walk away, let it all go on of its own accord, picking it up again later, tomorrow, or next week, without having let anything drop. Even this afternoon's business in the garage. He'd find a way to absorb the shock of it, surely he would. But for Stephen it seemed there was now an unstoppable rupture in the wall of his secret childish world, and the terror that he had begun to notice as a welling sickness in his gut was born from the realisation that this other world had become too big to shut away, too swollen and shapeless for him to file it away safely in his compendium of life's account.

Numbly, he'd reached the bottom of Queen's Road, and was about to turn the corner by Blackman's sweet shop before he concluded with dismal certainty that there was no other option for him other than to go along with Marcus's plan. His feet had recognised that already, he'd left Marcus sitting in the alley minutes ago and they were still taking him further from home. It was decided. But where should he search for Humphrey?

Across the road old man Fazakerly was lifting his bike down onto the pebble path that led from his front door. The pieces of blue and green glass that hung from his porch still swayed and tinkled where he'd passed beneath them and Stephen looked up, catching his eye for a moment. The afternoon light flashed on the faces of the slowly spinning lozenges and Fazakerly turned back, watching them turn and nodding to himself, a look of deep satisfaction on his face.

Old Ma Gamble's not the only witch in town, thought Stephen.

He drifted across the road and hovered by the gate, fascinated as always not just by the house but by the contrast of the reckless wilderness of garden, set between the unremarkable order of a neighbour's crew-cut lawn and the gloomily curtained facade of the funeral parlour on the other side. Was it as wild and unkempt in the house, he wondered? He stared at the large front window but could make out only the ordinary dark shape of a chair back. Of course, what did he expect to see? A sorcerer would be the last person to leave his secrets unconcealed. But mysteries there had to be; what else were those bobbing glass shapes over the door meant to protect? That's what he found most curious about Fazakerly's place, not just the unexplored wilderness or the strange brooding presence of the house itself. Those watchers over the door, they had always been scary – all the kids agreed on that – especially the big one over the door, the big blue eye...

"Oye!" The old man set the latch on his front gate. "Hop it." He swung his leg over the saddle, not looking at Stephen. "Don't want to see you here when I get back. Savvy?" He rode away, the spokes of his bicycle ringing like tiny bells.

But Stephen wasn't paying him any attention, for he'd caught the briefest glance of sunlight on another glass surface, back across the road, a momentary glint of light atop the high brick wall that concealed the hiding place against Blackman's shop. He squinted in the afternoon sun. Sure enough, he could make out the top of someone's head, thick dark hair over an equally dark forehead and large black eyes watching him. No, he was mistaken; the head was turning away from him, the wide eyes following old man Fazakerly as he cycled away past the funeral parlour. Then came another careless twinkle of reflected light as the bottle held in the watcher's hand was removed, the mop of hair disappearing down behind the wall.

What a relief. He'd found Humphrey and it seemed that no harm had yet been done. So easy. Hah! He whistled through his teeth. Now he could go home and shut it all away. He just had to fetch Marcus, that's all, tell Marcus where to find the boy, and he could slip away. He'd be home in ten minutes, surely. There would be time for a bath before tea. He'd be able to wash away this awful grubby feeling that had taken hold. They didn't need him to parley with Humphrey, either; he'd trapped himself in the narrow place behind that wall. He was a sitting duck and all they'd have to do would be to wait. He'd soon be fed up with hiding. Failing that, a couple of Fry's Five Boys or a Mars Bar would bring him out. Time was on their side. Humphrey wouldn't want to stay there once the sun set and the creepy crawlies came out. He'd been terrified of creepy crawlies since Marcus put mealworms in his Wellingtons. Bloodsuckers, Marcus had called them.

Stephen's spirits soared.

"Listen, I've only about half an hour. I'm on my lunch break."

Stephen took the newspaper away from Fazakerly's lap. The old man was red eyed from dozing in the full sun under the window. He said nothing but stared at Stephen with an apparent lack of recognition.

"Something I wanted to ask you. Something important. Please, are you listening?"

"Got a cold. Can't see too well today."

"But you can hear me, can't you? It's me, Stephen."

Fazakerly nodded very slightly and rolled his eyes from side to side. "The food in here's gone to pot. Like war rations." He gestured at the unfinished meal on the trolley next to his chair. "I've eaten better rats."

"OK, ok, I'll see what I can do. But listen. These past ten years, well, right from the beginning, didn't you try to find out what had happened? You keep asking me now why I was involved, but didn't you want to know then? Didn't you ask anyone to explain?"

The strain of recollection on the old man's face made him look suddenly much older than of late. He thought silently for a long while, licking his lips with a dry tongue.

"I thought I said. It bared me to the world, that fire. It wasn't just my house I lost. I felt uncovered. My soul was naked to the world. Horrible. All that I'd laid down, all that distance put away, snatched up into the sky in a cloud of smoke."

"Yes, it was terrible. I remember. But didn't you want to find out? You know, why it happened and who had done it? At the time?"

"Oh, I know who done it. So do you. But you're right, what I really want to know now is why. Never bothered much with why in those days. It was enough of a struggle without pursuing that particular thread. We'd never get very far through life if we bothered with why. But now, well, you're right, what it was had brought you there is something I would like to understand before I die. Not then, I admit, didn't try to find out then, I was just content to be away from it all, here behind these walls."

"Post traumatic stress."

"Eh?"

"Why you didn't go after the truth. Until we met this summer."

"Call it what you like, I'd just had enough. Seemed to me the game was up. I'd seen you hanging around my house, I remember it clear as day. Seen you a few times actually, creeping up my garden path, you and them others, poking your snotty little noses into my affairs."

"We thought you were a wizard or something. They were just dares. We meant no harm."

"And that other one. The pot-bellied kid with the long hair. Little bastard, always hanging about; even followed me. Well, you saw him attack me, as I recall all too clearly. That was your plan I suppose. Distract me. Get inside my house. What did you expect to find? Had somebody been speaking?"

"Nothing of the sort. Humphrey was…"

"Humphrey?"

"Yes. The pot-bellied kid. He was a bit simple. At least that's what we thought, but I'm no longer sure about anything we thought then, as kids."

"One can't. Be sure about anything, that is. There are bigger forces at work. Which brings me back to my question.

The one you won't answer. Why? What was it all about, my house being taken from me like that? Whose idea was that then?"

"I don't remember it being anyone's idea, actually."

"As I thought, you were the instrument of larger forces, and here you are, all of ten years later, been sent by them to finish me off." He looked Stephen up and down, his red eyes accusatory, his thoughts gathered in one of those rare moments of focus. "The watchman, were you? Ach," he sighed, "well, I suppose I'd had a good run for my money. My partner in crime was right about that, she promised me it would work out better for me if I lived in the town. But it became too easy after a while, that's what did it. Life went on. There was no trouble. That's when I got careless. I forgot my responsibilities. Around about the time the war ended – your father's war, that is – I thought I might try my hand again, take part a bit more. A long time had passed and there'd been no trouble – forgetting the war, of course, though that weren't my trouble, not this second time around. But what a silly bugger I was, I got caught with my guard down."

"So you came out of hiding."

"Enough of your cheek! Thomas Fazakerly wasn't in the habit of hiding. Not likely! Just stepped out of the arena for a bit, that's all. Best place. Sit back and watch the rest of them make fools of themselves, I thought. Only, it gets a bit lonely."

- THIRTEEN -

ON VICTORY IN EUROPE DAY he awoke with a shiver of warm anticipation, it was powerfully reminiscent of when as a young man he would have been stirred from sleep by the first draughts of early summer air, prescient, sweet and full of promise. He could feel the sap rising in his bones in those long departed youthful days, the taut, urgent madness for change that would come swirling out upon the world, feverishly searching for a place to gain entry. It would wash over him like the rush of a spring tide, he would find himself quickly submerged as it surged around and within him, beating in his blood, enjoining him to feel rash and free and dangerous, and without a care except for the unimpeded assurance of his fulfilment.

Could that madness be upon him again, these many years on? Surely not now.

The light of a bright May morning streamed through the broad window and, despite his reluctance to let prying eyes observe his rude gladness, he tugged at the catch and stood pressed against the glass in his greying vest, letting his hunger feast open-mouthed upon the fragrant air that flowed in through the gap he had made.

How long he stood there was measured only by the progress of a spider across the torn blackout, for the house had no clocks to tick away the hours and Fazakerly had long since gone without a watch. What care for marking time had a man who had stepped outside of its blind passage? Yet last night, yes, last night had remarked the passing of a significant moment that not a man living could turn his back upon. John Snagge on the wireless: unmistakeable, that calm and authoritative establishment timbre, but with his speech made jagged on the airwaves last night, cut by an uncharacteristic edge.

That'll be the end of him, thought Fazakerly. Unforgivable. That insufferable lot at the BBC will have been listening in; they'd have noticed his faltering delivery to be sure.

But come on, it was all over, it really was - five or, crumbs, was it six years? They would surely forgive him the catch in his throat, bearing news like that. Hey, a spell had been broken, for God's sake; it was curtains for Adolf, everyone knew that, and the enormity of another bleak interlude of death was already made history. Or so it would seem.

Not that they would let it go so easily. From the very beginning this unpalatable dish of war had been served up to a credulous nation. They'd made it easy – so easy to be gulped down with lashings of the poignant sauce of heroism – and with the momentum of the whole dark festival cheered along by the phoney celebration of a cause célèbre, the community of justice had been served. Well, maybe. Maybe this particular cause was less dishonest than the last time around, but there could be no-one who would regret its passing, surely not. Fazakerly frowned contemptuously. Pah! No, no chance. They'd make the most of this moment, wringing it dry, today, tomorrow and further down the years. The powers that be – *that be*? Christ, he raged, with his fists tightly clenched, did they have divine right or what?

They'd have it all planned though, to be sure. How to make the most out of the moment. How to get back on top. No doubt about that. It would have all been long prepared. Then again, did that matter when maybe it really was over at last? Think about it. Maybe it was different now; for this time the Devil himself, no less, had been scourged.

No. There was no energy left, no desire amongst the survivors to take time out of their glad relief and glance askance at the other demons who would profit quietly from his removal. And don't anyone doubt it, plans were already in motion, and there'd be no resistance, not a chance, not from amidst that crazy euphoria of ardent salvation.

They'd not realise it, the poor saps, not for a long while at least, but just as they were taking stock of the lives they thought they had lost, these so-called survivors were about to be marshalled all over again. Without pause for breath. It would be easy. They'd won their freedom but they'd forgotten what it was like to be free.

These bitter thoughts dried upon his tongue and he wiped the sour rime away with the back of his hand. Let them, he thought, it's not been my war. Never again for me. I do have that.

Outside in the whiskery garden a plump tabby cat leapt carelessly for its breakfast and the scolding blackbird that exploded from the grass threw a brief flicker of shadow into the room, dislodging his darker mood. Fazakerly felt the spark of his reverie touch him again and he scrambled half-dressed upon a chair, quickly taking down the blackout from the bedroom window, shaking out the dust and desiccated insects that had accumulated there over the past six years, tearing away the fragments of lace curtains that had rotted unwashed and untended from end to end of the neglect and glare from successive wartime summers. He ran through the house, stumbling from window to window in a frenzy until, with all ten casements thrown wide, the Round House resembled a buccaneer's rig with its gun ports agape, the flaking panels of its curved flanks matted with the scum of battle and a never-ending journey, it had been unpainted for so long and buffeted by a succession of winter south-westerlies.

But this was not a day designed for fighting, or for embarkation on distant voyages, and the only artillery to be heard now was from the rise of scrub and gorse behind the town, where men and boys sought rabbit and pigeon for the pot to feed the day's celebration of peace in our time. A clatter of shotguns, infrequent and stuttering, echoed across the quiet patchwork of streets and gardens right up to the sea wall, where it was discharged upon the sea, having first passed through Fazakerly's north-facing windows and been despatched thence to all points of the compass east, west and south from the array of open and unencumbered chambers.

Peace had hung in the air for some days, but the long awaited news that the Devil had been vanquished had not come until the ebbing hours of May Day. What crazy dances would have been made around the merry pole had confirmation of Hitler's death been reported just a few hours earlier. Then last night came the announcement that tomorrow would be fêted as Victory in Europe day, it would be a public holiday, with the simple promise of festivities made the occasion for further conciliation, the authorities generous in granting room for everyone to dance on through the joys of yet another holiday declared for the following day.

Fools. Dupes. Fazakerly scowled his heavy-footed way into the bathroom. Such a bounty they'd been granted. Hah! What sort of nonsense was that? Could it be that which had played on his mind during sleep? Finding that the invisible strength of early summer might still touch him had been extraordinary enough a revelation, although it was neither an unwelcome nor unfamiliar discovery, and even to know that he might feel relief at the prospect of war having ended did not pass beyond the realms of belief, but the promise of merriment and carousing, to order and by dispensation no less, what a nonsense.

Me? I'm free of those bastards.

He snorted, instinctively raising his free hand as he tensed, his other hand whisking his razor furiously in the bowl of cold water, glancing guiltily and catching his look of shamefacedness staring back wide-eyed from the shaving mirror. A solid line of dust impacted his wrist where he had stifled the sneeze, dirt gathered from the wreckage of his skirmish at the windows.

What nonsense, just the dust, that's all. Why should he be ashamed? Just startled by the moment. It was after all a time of great and momentous change.

Fazakerly's single storey Martello was constructed entirely from wood. He had admitted no brick or stone save for the chimney and the hearth. Wood, he explained, was alive, and long after curing it would continue to sing whenever the wind pressed close against its curves. Summer and winter alike, the warming and cooling of the sun would cause the shingles of the low vaulted roof to tick and shuffle through an endless cycle of tumescence and deflation.

For Fazakerly, the house resonated with all the buzz from the natural world, it was plugged in to the untrammelled source of life, and he had always anticipated that its construction would be a source of comfort.

"More simply than that," he had exclaimed to the architect, with a look of secret satisfaction, "you can hear who's coming. It's not the same with stone, nor brick or concrete. Masonry deadens the senses, it buries you, but with wood I can know what's what."

He sometimes felt that sitting by an open window he could hear night fall, the collapse of an immense hush of darkness pierced by the ringing scintillation of stars, though it was the changes made in the air around the house that he heard, in that period when the wind from the cooling land is stilled and the night breezes off the sea commence their shift to come wafting over the shingle with clangourous breath. Daybreak was a more raucous affair, full of glad rudeness.

He could hear movement in the earth too, beneath his wild garden, a sound sometimes like his own heart beating, an echo of himself from the hollows of a realm he had chosen not to explore, but it was smothered by a comfort of grass and the burnished crop of buttercups. It was too faint to suggest anything more than a passing flicker of memory's unease.

There were voices on the path outside, slowly approaching; he could see the two women, hesitant in front of the house. They had stopped to wonder at the design of his wilderness. They'd be here to complain, of course. Now the war was over there'd be plenty to complain about. Plenty of time now, oh yes. They'd be setting the world to rights again and that included him. Christ, they don't waste time, these people. What would it be now, letting down the tone of the street? Good Lord, woman, there's a whole bomb site to tidy only a street away. Does he need some help with his garden? Let them try to help!

A ringing from his glass sentinels told him they had arrived at the door and he grinned as he imagined them ducking the bright pieces that swung overhead from the open porch. Yet the knock that came was brave and maybe a fresh draught of the mood that had awakened him helped him decide that it deserved an answer. With his hand upon the latch he quietly cursed the morning for his sunny demeanour.

The older woman was cheery, not intrusive at all, although he was certain she'd have plenty of gab to exchange with neighbours over the garden wall, especially now she'd had the courage to draw him out of his keep. She wore a housecoat, come straight from her chores, with an incongruous blue straw hat upon her head; it suggested she had been trying on her outfit for the holiday when she had been flushed out by a sudden tumult of excitement. But that's why she was here. The street party. Surely he would join them. Would he not? And did he have something to contribute? Something salted away for, well, if not a rainy day, this day, this joyful exalted day of celebration that they had all known in their heart of hearts must come sooner or later.

Fazakerley could feel the cold irons tightening around his ankles and a halter locked with a silent snap around his neck. They don't waste time, these people. Why can't they leave me alone?

He hardly heard the mantra. So nice if you can join us. It's such a relief, isn't it? So good to know it's all over. For all of us. Good times ahead now. Her head bobbed and wagged over the full crescent of her smile.

He hardly heard her, for she was looking beyond him into the house and he found himself wedged in the space made by the open door, his arms spread over his head to block her view. He didn't want her eyes boring through the residue of his life that had settled there over the years, didn't want her voice wandering into his private rooms, to go licking at the dust that swarmed in the velvet sunbeams, or whispering to the memories that sat hunched in dark corners. He craned over his shoulder to make sure, just to check she hadn't slipped anything by him, that there was nothing there that might be glimpsed or teased into view.

Her companion had walked on around the outside of the house whilst she spoke, and now stood by an open window. With his chin on his shoulder and his eyes popping Fazakerly could see her silhouetted against the bright light, across the far side of the living room and framed by the ragged drapes that he had yet to remove. He had seen her before, though he could not quite remember where or when, a young woman, maybe still in her teens, twenty or twenty-one at most. She wore a white dress and a pale, flat expression on her face. No, not a dress, it was a coat, a uniform, like a doctor's but not quite the same. She seemed to be staring at him, surprised perhaps to be discovered peering in at his window, but as he threw her a look of challenge her gaze remained fixed, her eyes wide and their aspect deep and indecipherable. She seemed to be someone poised at that instant before darting away, her next move undecided, waiting for that tipping moment.

The breeze through the window raised her hair then came scurrying in across the room, pulling the inner door closed and eclipsing the tableau of the girl at the window. It brought him that thrill of sweet air in his nostrils again and he turned back with a smile.

Lemonade. Yes, he would bring lemonade. He had some stone jars hidden away somewhere. Several jars, he was certain. Might be a bit stale by now. Maybe not. It wouldn't matter, it was vintage lemonade. He laughed at that and the woman in the blue straw hat beamed and patted his arm.

She was the girl from that hotel. Not a doctor at all. He'd spent the morning worrying at the fragment of recall that at last had become an entire image. White overalls, white shoes, like golfer's shoes with a broad fan of tongue. He put down the boots he'd been polishing absently for nigh on an hour. Yes, he'd seen her pushing the wicker bins into the yard at the back; they were much too large for a slight girl like that to be heaving about but she was seemingly impassive as she laboured. Indifferent too when assailed by the contemptuous propositions of the laundry boy, who carelessly toiled each creaking bin up the ramp to his van, winking and nodding his lascivious head, letting the fresh laundry fall short of her arms as he tossed her the brown paper packages just so she would have to run and bend and kneel in the dirt. In silence she bore his empty wit, or hated him for it. It was impossible to tell.

Simple. That was it. There was something simple about her. Some may have described her look as vacant, he had heard the children in the street speak scornfully, but in hindsight Fazakerly remembered how, cycling past, he had remarked to himself her look of fresh naïvety.

When he found himself smiling he picked up the boots again and gave them a vigorous rub with the old chamois pad. Get a grip, Thomas.

And as suddenly the thump of a bass drum made him sit upright, the introductory skirmishes of Colonel Bogey that followed, rasped on a brass euphonium, declaring that his reverie was indeed over.

Oh what nonsense, Thomas, they've got the town band out there now, playing military music of all things, how crass is that on a day of peace, and look, you've gone and shone your boots like a man who is shamelessly desperate for admission to the rank and file. What did I tell you, Thomas, it goes on.

He pulled them on all the same. Pah! I'd stick out like a sore thumb if I *didn't* go. Then he clumped around the house with large self-conscious footsteps, closing the windows, peering out suspiciously at the crowd he could see drifting together in the street. Hmph. Now I'm invited I'll have to go. Don't want to be conspicuous by my absence. His old tweed jacket hung from the back of the kitchen door and he snatched it from its hook as if he was being hurried, then he threw it down and went rummaging in the drawers of the tallboy in his bedroom. A clean linen shirt, that's what was called for - no collar, he could go without a collar, it wasn't a formal do. He fastened the shirt buttons and smoothed out some creases with his long fingers. Fine. He hesitated before gathering up his jacket again. Why not? If he was going to put in an appearance then let's make an entrance. That'll show them.

He took from his wardrobe the navy silk blazer that she had bought him. He hadn't worn it since that day, the last time she had visited. He had kept it shut away like a reproach he felt was undeserved, something of her to remind him, something of which he did and didn't want to be reminded. Rosalind and the architect and him, that sunny afternoon when they gladdened the Round House with their own celebration, and he had smelled the bitter poison burning in her.

Pah! I'll show you. I'll show you all. He donned the blazer and shivered with delight at its crisp, smooth touch. There. It's done. He crossed to his dressing mirror and admired the dark figure who stood erect in his room. His hair was long and greying, and his round spectacles emphasized an apparent look of wise disengagement, but middle age had not dealt him a poor hand. Hmm. He traced a faint whisper of stubble around his chin, making a mental note to strop his razor. Not now though; it gave him a certain rakish air that pleased him. Yes. He folded a clean white handkerchief and set it just so in the top pocket of the blazer, patting it upright, and looking up to check that it was straight he found himself smiling back from the mirror. Very good, Thomas. Right!

A bonfire was burning in the middle of the road and two air raid wardens in uniform ranged around it proprietorily, piling timber and keeping back the children who swarmed. Tables had been set along the pavement, heaped with hastily convened jellies, sandwiches and fruit, the impromptu incongruity of the feast made large by two pianos that had been dragged into neighbouring gardens, where a woman and a man, both with Union Jacks tied around their heads, competed with the band, which immediately struck up Land of Hope and Glory in a moment of coincidence that seemed to welcome Fazakerly to the fray.

"I don't think you'll want any of this," said the woman in the blue hat, who had appeared out of a throng of children in fancy dress. With blackout craftily turned that morning into costume they shrieked and whooped and waved their arms menacingly at a boy and girl who clutched hands at the centre of their circle. "Hansel and Gretel," she explained; "these others, they're the wild wood, or so I'm told. Goodness knows why. It's all a bit too German for my liking." She had hold of his arm and led him away. "It won't last, thank goodness. The blancmange is made with dried milk and saccharine and I imagine that will quieten them down in a while." She smiled approvingly at a small child with a leg iron who sat on a giant brocaded cushion and dangled a pompom from a stick. "Miss Muffet. That's better. Someone had the bright idea of them all doing fairy tales. Well, I know it isn't quite…"

Fazakerly ducked beneath the huge Union Jack that billowed across the pavement.

"Here, said the woman, I'll park you here with Nola. Drink?"

It was only then that Fazakerly remembered the lemonade he had promised, left languishing in the scullery cupboard. He could see the six creamy earthenware jars in his mind's eye, but he wasn't going back for them. The girl from his window - no, he reminded himself, the girl from the hotel - stared at him unsmiling from under a severe brim of thick black hair. He attempted a grin and felt it compose itself mischievously into a leer, but she didn't appear to notice, she was looking through him, not staring at all.

The woman in the blue hat reappeared with a pewter mug, which she passed to him, the head of stout tumbling over its rim. "Ooh, that's lively," she laughed; "not the usual watery stuff. Thank goodness we have our own brewery in the town. I imagine that some of the parties being held elsewhere will quickly run dry and then there'll be no end of trouble. Nola? Do you want anything, dear? As it's a special occasion?"

Nola shook her head, slowly, without looking at anyone in particular. She seemed fascinated by the red, white and blue cotton bunting that bobbed on string, tied in a zigzag from the lamp-posts the length of the street.

"No. Simple pleasures, our Nola," smiled the woman who now held the blue hat in her hand. "Anyway, I must be off. My sister queued this morning for bread - two hours she was down there at the bakery. I can't expect her to be stuck indoors making the sandwiches all afternoon. There'll be some sort of stew as well. Down there, see?" She pointed at a tumble of tarpaulins on the corner in front of the Co-op, where steam and grey smoke rose in the bright sunlight. "Anyway, ta-ra for now. Be good."

The girl, for she was only a girl, he could see that now, briefly creased her face in the faintest of smiles. Fazakerly thought back, trying to recall when first he'd seen her at the hotel. Late teens. She can't be any more than that. He remarked the fresh, pale skin of her throat, not a fault or blemish, not a line, her eyes deep and dark, as if the pupil had absorbed the iris, despite it being a bright sunny afternoon. Her cheeks reddened, a mere trace at first, then her neck grew florid and rosy.

"I'm sorry." He lowered his gaze. He had embarrassed her. Come on Thomas. You of all people. Don't stare.

She was watching him when he looked up again. She had regained her poise. "Nola," she said, unexpectedly, and with practiced charm held out her hand. He took it carefully. It too was pale – surprising, considering the tyranny of hard graft to which he imagined she was condemned at the hotel.

"Thomas," he replied, grandly raising her hand to his lips and brushing the skin oh so slightly.

She giggled.

He handed her the pewter mug and with only a moment's hesitation she drank, her eyes wide, the foam from the beer on her nose and she was trembling with laughter.

He gave her the clean white handkerchief from his top pocket and nodded down the street. She had drunk every last drop from the mug.

"Come on," he said, pulling her up from the garden wall where they had perched, "let's go and find another. And you can have one on me."

The beer tent was a hole in a tall privet hedge, with a canvas canopy for shade and the barrels stacked on trestles in the garden behind it. A chevron of old dining chairs roped together across the pavement formed everyone into a queue, at the head of which a man in uniform dispensed ale and stout into whatever receptacles were presented.

"No charge," he said, brushing aside Fazakerly's proffered half crown; "on the 'ouse. Company's paying. The brewery. For the moment anyhow."

He squinted pointedly at Nola. "Sure you want some for her too?"

"Isn't it free for ladies?"

"There's nothing going there mate. You're wasting your time." He caught Fazakerly's fierce glare. "She's mental, mister, ask around if you don't believe me."

"And you'd know, would you?"

The soldier, having filled the pewter jug, took the newspaper wrapping from a pint glass and filled it from a barrel labelled Best Mild. He held it up to the light before passing it over, hesitating. "There you go. Don't say I didn't warn you." He stared at Nola and pursed his lips, at last letting go his hold on the glass and leaning close to Fazakerly. "You'd do better elsewhere, if you take my meaning, 'specially on a day like today. Dapper looking gent like you."

Fazakerly drew her away with his arm around her shoulders and they were immediately swept into the confluence of several large contingents of party-goers who were madly herding through an open gate, all pressing as close as they could around an open window where a wireless had been balanced on the sill. Its volume was turned up to maximum and Fazakerly flinched at the crackling and screeching that preceded the unmistakable voice of Churchill, his three o'clock address to the nation booming across the heads of the hushed merry makers. He listened, captured more by a fascination with the practiced thrall of the man's speech than he was interested in the meaning of the words, his attention set all the while on Nola's rapt face. She didn't see him; she was transfixed by the radio's spell.

"The German war is therefore at an end. Long live the cause of freedom. God save the King!"

Pah! Before the national anthem could gain full strength he swept the girl back through the gate, feeling the looks of disapproval raining down on his back from those who stood dutifully to attention, many in salute. He grimaced, partly in anger and partly in satisfaction. What did I say? It goes on, Thomas, it goes on as before. As I knew it would. Freedom my arse!

Finding the adults preoccupied a gang of youths had commandeered one of the tables set up for the jolly feast and dragged it into the middle of the road. With the air raid wardens having judged the premier's broadcast a good time to go and refill their pint pots, unchallenged they'd boldly planted it astraddle the slow burning bonfire, and now they clapped and whooped as a boy in shorts he'd long outgrown goose-stepped along its length, strutting and kicking the bowls of trifle, custard and tinned fruit high into the air, his index finger across his upper lip in mimicry of the vanquished Führer. Amidst the sizzle of burning dessert he suddenly stopped and pointed.

"Hey, it's Nola Numskull!"

They ceased clapping and rounded on Fazakerly and the girl, their eyes bright with sport.

"No-la, No-la, No-la," came the chant, then a hail of sandwiches.

"Mister!" cried a raggedy child at the front of the throng, "don'tcha know she's a dumb-dumb?" He hurled an apple that barely missed Nola's cheek.

"Ninny Nola," called the boy in the inadequate shorts. "You wanna watch her, guvnor. Hey Nola, g'is a kiss." He laughed and the others roared at his audacity.

The girl shrank into Fazakerly's shoulder, her arms up around her head. She said nothing, as if saying nothing might help her attain invisibility.

"No-la, No-la, a shilling an' you can roll 'er." The young impersonator was stamping out a rhythm on the table top, red sparks spraying with every beat from the embers around its legs, and the others started clapping again, their rough childish voices joining the taunt. "Nola, Nola, a shilling an'.."

It seemed to Fazakerly that natural forces conspired with his fury just at that moment, for as he ran and flung the contents of his pewter mug in the face of the Führer a fresh lick of flame shot all the way up one of the table legs and the whole rude performance lurched sideways, the table leg splintering with a shrill crack, the boy tipped off balance and already hopping on one foot backwards from the shock of a face full of warm beer, his eyes wide and accusatory; while the members of his pubescent gang were flung back as one in the opposite direction, their hands up to their faces to ward off the shower of sparks anticipated from his fall into the glowing cinders beneath.

"The little blighters."

"Was he hurt?"

"I suppose they're all grown into model citizens now. You probably know them as those grown-ups who never put a foot wrong. A few more years and they'd be paying rent, working all hours, a wife, kids mewling all night. Didn't think of that, did they? All cock-a-hoop. Or then…"

"What?"

"Maybe that's what it was all about. Their last cry of freedom, against all odds. A last spasm of true consciousness. I shouldn't have minded them if I'd known that's what they were doing. All the same… Nah, I'm getting maudlin'."

"But was he hurt? And what about Nola?"

By now, Stephen had all but given up on his quest for answers. True, Fazakerly's stories still had something of a ring of authenticity that fascinated him, but he felt himself no nearer to explaining the meaning of this bond that held them. And now the old man was really beginning to irritate him. All this pseudo metaphysical stuff was becoming so laborious. Let this be his last visit. He'd be away soon, back to his studies, back once more to a place with focus. There wasn't going to be any light at the end of Fazakerly's tunnel and he was beginning to feel he'd be better off getting back to the way it had been.

"So was he? Was there trouble?"

"Oh, there was trouble all right. But not with those stupid kids. Little blighters got off with having their ears boxed. All that mess too. Soon as they'd finished genuflecting to God Save His Privileged Self the mob from the garden could've scarcely drawn breath before they were back swilling ale and scoffing down all that grub they'd put together. Didn't take kindly to some of it going to waste. Rationing I suppose, that would have been on their minds. No-one tolerated waste during the war. But their anger didn't last. A bit of hearty slapping that's all. They were too euphoric to be meting out punishment. Those kids got off lightly, I reckon; the boy too, just sent packing to change his trousers." He laughed, suddenly and triumphantly. "The seat of his pants was smoking, I do remember that."

"So he was all right. And Nola?"

"Ah now, that's a different kettle of fish altogether. Like I said, there was trouble."

"Trouble."

"Yes. Well you know how it is with women. They have moods, and you're supposed to be a bloody mind reader and know why they have 'em, or what it is you've done to make them have 'em. They just flare up without warning. If you ask what's up or if you ignore them it's one and the same."

"Is it?"

"Of course. It's your fault. But it wasn't like that with Nola. No moods. I suspect she'd never had one. Didn't have the capacity somehow. She was brilliant. Placid."

"Isn't that a contradiction?"

"Look, Dr Smartarse, she could be both, couldn't she? I was there, wasn't I? As I was saying, she was a bit frightened by those kids. Who wouldn't be – a young woman, I mean. But soon as they'd gone, soon as we walked on, so was her fear of them. No sobbing or shaking, no carping and recriminations. Hung on to me though. I suppose I was a bit of a hero, being older too."

"Oh no, you're not going to give me the old Mills and Boon bit now are you? I think you've said enough already for that to be implausible."

"Mills and what? What are you talking about? No. No nothing along those lines. What me, romance? Hah!

No, but she was definitely in some kind of a trance, I can tell you. Whether it was the beer - pretty unlikely I can tell you, though, war beer being what it was, you'd more chance of getting drunk from the kitchen tap - or just the mood of the day, I didn't know. But she wasn't like other women, that's for sure. Serene, I called it. Didn't have much to say, just held on to my arm. We passed a couple leaning in the shadows of the hire car garage, a man in uniform, a lance corporal as I recall - don't know why that should stick in my mind - and a young woman wrapped in his arms, her brittle laughter was echoing all around the dark old loft of that place, the silly trollop. Well, that did it. 'Nola's a good girl', she said that crisp and clear, shaking her head as we walked away. Those kids had got to her sure enough. That's what I was thinking. Just that. But it might as well have been her calling card, all she felt it necessary to tell me. She didn't venture any more about herself. She didn't have a word to say about her work, though I did ask her. But I was so taken by the look of her. So uncomplicated. That's the word. Makes me think now of these Polynesian girls you see on the nature programmes: unsophisticated, just the look of nature about them and nothing else. Of course, she wasn't brown like them. Pure, but pale like the aristocracy keep themselves. All the same, there were no moods, no being difficult."

"So she wasn't trouble, then. Not like other girls, you reckon. But didn't they say she was simple? Didn't the kids say that?"

"Not them, oh you didn't want to be listening to them, they were just being unpleasant. Just kids. But yes, she was simple all the same - I mean, in an unsophisticated way. A blank canvas. Took to me, though, and me to her an' all. I mean, here was someone with no strings to tangle me. I could feel that right away. No baggage. A free spirit, that's what I saw. It was a real joy to behold. I felt liberated. Here was someone I didn't have to avoid for fear of getting caught up in all their rules and prejudices and beliefs and paranoias and…"

"Just like that. You knew."

"Of course, she'd had no education. That was soon evident. As we walked I asked her what she thought would happen now, with the hostilities over, but she just smiled. Didn't have a point of view, you see. Didn't seem to know why it had all started in the first place. I took that as a plus. Well, you see, I knew straight away that for once I wasn't going to have to put up with any of the old ritual humbug – you know, all that false correspondence the human world uses to fool itself. All that background noise, all that deceit they use to make sense out of what they think is chaos. It didn't frighten her, you see. Oh no, there was no dark void for her that needed pasting over. Mmmm, I remember now just how glad I was not to have the usual claptrap thrown at me. You know, I'll admit this to you, right there and then I thought I'd been handed quite a jewel. I'd had an uncut gemstone plonked down right here in my hand."

"But those kids, the ones who were so unkind. They seemed to be suggesting she was a right baggage."

"Like I said: they were up against all odds. Somehow – whether they could've told you that or not at the time – still, somehow they could tell she wasn't condemned to a future like theirs, so she was bound to be a target for their frustrations. That's how I look upon it and that was the sum of it"

How many years was it he had shut himself away? All through the war, he knew that for certain. And before? How long had it been? Twenty years? He couldn't remember. The continuity of life behind the walls of his Round House did not admit the finite measurement of years. Only the interlude of war had provided the defining limits of a start and now an end. And here he was rolling on again at liberty once more.

His mind drifted to contemplation of that perfect circle, the ring he'd drawn around himself. Perfect to him, anyway, in the manner of its construction. Not an edge or corner on that house of his to catch at the ropes, ratlines and bands that flailed across the exploding moment of consciousness, all those thoughtless snares trailing from the whirling chaos that propped up the temple of time. That's how he pictured it in his head. A fantastical great disc of rushing confusion, and him at its centre, untouched. Yes, it was well designed for skirting life's vortices, his house.

His architect had listened carefully, sincerely, when he'd recounted that story by Poe – one of his favourites but it wasn't the best known – agreeing at last that the advantages of perfect symmetry were truly drawn from science and not the imagination of a lonely mind. Together, they'd found no mystery in that, and with the Round House built there would be no quick descent into the maelström swirling past his safe encompassing walls.

Nola had not shown any recognition when he retold the story, merely staring wide-eyed with a look of delicious horror as he described Poe's vision of the terrible swirling torrent, the descent of one man into a nightmare of cloud and water that swallowed everything eventually in its deep black maw. She'd never heard of Poe, and whilst Fazakerly relished passing on the thrill of the late author's dark images, he was unaware that each day of her life had been defined by confrontations with events whose mystery and imagination were all the more threatening to her in measure of their drab ordinariness.

It neither surprised nor disappointed him that she'd not heard of anyone else he mentioned that afternoon, as first this and then one more story led to another, and quickened by his own enthusiasm he was happy to have to begin each one at the beginning. Oh what a fine time he could look forward to, etching colour onto this blank canvas. Eagerly he talked on, it had been so long he had forgotten the joy of it, hearing his own voice ring out alive from the remembered pages of the books he had read, a renewed passion quick in his hands that articulated each tale and the sun's brightness sharp in his pale eyes, as silently she sat with him upon the sea wall, her fingers tracing on the blue horizon a squall of herring gulls that lifted on the breeze, swirled up from the lattice of ironwork that rose through the small peaks of breaking waves. It had been so long since he had enjoyed a moment like this. Solitude had been a necessity, not a fulfilment. How long had it been? Rosalind, were our evenings spent like this? No, he sighed, no, that had all been too intense a game from the start. Their lives had been brought together with so much impact it could never have been sustained. Christ, when I think of it now – now that was a maelström all right, I didn't have a chance to gather my wits about me. Smashed together, we were, thrown all a-muddle, and I didn't see it coming. No, he shook his head emphatically, it wasn't with Rosalind he had shared these safe and gentle joys of literature; their evenings together had been made fast and then quickly rent asunder by desperate and imprisoned passions all their own.

He reeled in his unseeing gaze from the heat blurred horizon, brought back from muddied reminiscences by a noisy roiling of water around the stark geometry of military defences below them. The structure leaned insensate into the rising tide, red with rust, the sun through the incessant swell and splash of the sea making the metal of the scaffolding glisten as though it dripped with blood. Soon, the explosive mines attached at intervals to this infernal construction would be removed and there'd be a welcome anticlimax with no bloodshed. Would tears be shed for the hours wasted on its making? He felt the wry smile rib his face. Well, better the effort lost in that case.

Way back, he'd watched it all being planted in the sea during a low spring tide, the improbable cases of concrete mixed and poured in haste, the fresh steel already corroded in the salty air of the yard, long spikes left standing proudly drowning as the turning waters seeped back up the beach. Then the branches, limbs and stems attached in the following days, hurriedly erected between the tides, until as far as the eye could see, east and west, making a perfect study in perspective, an angular thicket of pipe and bracket and bolt marched the length of the shallows down the coast, its lethal fruit just visible beneath the surface at high tide, on the south side, facing always to the sun, always to France.

The white movement of the gulls filled his eye and he found himself staring silently at the girl, who had stopped her sky writing, his hand tight on her wrist so that the breeze could not catch and take her into the air, away from him. But she was tugging at him now, the sound in her throat both a question and a screech of pain, and he tightened his grip as the hem of her well laundered overall flapped open and she prepared to take flight, he was sure she would swoop away across the glistening beach in the company of gulls and he would never know, never know...

They were off the wall now and straining at each other like children in a crazy whirligig across the beach, she was pulling on his arm in merriment, as quickly turned from fear to gaiety, spinning him round until they collapsed in a tumble of her laughter onto the slick bank of stones that fed the oncoming tide.

A large wave broke heavily over the submerging rust raw cordon, the salty blood-red flash of light that assumed mastery of his inner focus fixing a sudden sharp fringe to the silhouetted whiteness of her outstretched arm. In a moment, looking back beyond her into the distance of the sun-dewed sea, he saw the birth of the wave, watched it roll and rise all the way from the continent, lifting and gathering mass as it bore down towards his briefly gay haven. No, not Rosalind, it hadn't been Rosalind, but further back, a place he might have deceived himself was an imagined memory, as most memories become and most imagined undertakings are remembered. The hiss of fast surf cascading had him on his feet in an instant, his boots unsteady in the screeing shingle, his back against the groyne and holding on to the girl now for support as the crash came and spume scattered across the beach.

His eyes opened after a tightly pressed eternity, finding the wave had subsided into an enervation of froth and foam. It was being dragged broken and noisily down the longshore, an ache of dissipation over the crush of jostling pebbles and he had been touched only by a glancing mist of droplets, which left cold and salty tears upon his cheeks.

There had been no tears on Hermione's face, only a look of disbelief.

Shit! How could the memory of that face be so clear? He grabbed the girl by her hand and they took off across the beach, his boots sinking deep into pits of uncertain shingle and her white shoes lightly bearing her like a ghost above him up the slope.

Don't you come back to me now. Don't you go looking at me like that. His voice yelled in silent pain at the surfacing memory. They'd been uncertain times; that's what she'd written to his mother. The world had gone mad. Her very words. Well, you... the silly cow should have known. Me too. Don't you come the innocent with me, girl!

He was bundling Nola up the sea wall, he had one arm around her waist and another gripping an ankle, and she was hoisted in a scramble onto his shoulders, tipped forward onto the promenade above. In his haste she'd become wrapped in the trailing edge of her overall so that she couldn't stand upright, she was trapped in its stiff folds, one foot caught in the turned up edging until a button came loose and he saw that she had grazed her knee on the rough concrete. But now he too was over the lip of the wall, a safe rise away from the wound of the sea, scrambling to his feet and hurrying her across the road.

He cursed silently as they scurried away. You fool, Thomas. Oh what a fool. How many years? - and in one sorry afternoon you tear it all down. Where was she, where had he hidden her so ineffectually? But the memory of that face began to blur once they'd turned into Queen's Road and the sound of the surf faded behind him. He could see the Round House, his Round House, at the end of the road, and there came a surge of warm comfort that quietened his step. The golden glow that bloomed around the house seemed to reflect from its distant walls. Did he imagine that? No, that was real enough.

Hermione was long gone. A grey mist of memory that had coalesced on the stiff, salty summer air and been blown in on the tide.

He relaxed his hold on the girl's wrist. She had been running to keep up, unprotesting. She looked up at him expressionlessly, hooking her arm in his, a brief smile sketching a question on her face, she was still hurrying to stay abreast of him.

As they approached the corner a jumble of festive riot shut out the ambiguous landscape from which they had fled, and turning into the full force of the celebration they were almost immediately bowled over by a juggernaut of several dozens of individuals who waved and thrust their legs into the air in unison, performing a long straggly conga along the middle of the road, orchestrated at its head by a Scotsman in full Highland dress. The drone of his bagpipes hung over the long line of clutching dancers like a spell from a smokestack and they clung to his unerring march like the children of Hamelin.

Nola's eyes were immediately alight with the reflection from a hundred laughing faces and without a glance at Fazakerly she broke free to join the last of the line, her bright whiteness the tip to its long ragged tail.

"A joy to behold, that girl."

"So she wasn't any trouble, after all."

"What, Nola? No, she wasn't any trouble. I watched her for a while as they wove up and down the road. I think evening was coming on by then, or so it seemed, the sun was on its way down the sky, but they just went on and on for ever. It must have been early evening when…

"Anyway, I was getting hungry so I gathered some bits and pieces from the tables – no-one was eating by then – and I went back for another pint. I actually managed to pick up a couple of quart bottles and had them filled. Good stuff and all, for a change. That cheeky gink who'd served us earlier had gone, only I'm sure he'd have been less obliging, free beer or not.

"By the time I got back the conga was breaking up, they were all gasping and clapping each other on the back. You know how it is with people like that. Some of them were nosing around my front gate so I told them to bugger off and went and sat on the lawn with my spoils. Well, I say lawn, but as you know it was mostly weeds, mostly buttercups at that. That's just how it was. Yes, just because we were all pals together after the war they thought they could take liberties like that, poking into my affairs. Anyway, that bloody bagpipes stopped bawling, bloody curse they are, and with the Pied Piper dropping off his entourage it wasn't any time at all before Nola came tripping along to my gate; she'd got a taste for the place that morning, I suppose, and me too of course. Took to me, I could see that."

"So you reckoned."

"Hmm. Anyway, there were still some nosy parkers looking in over the gate so we went and sat against the wall of the house where it was still warm in the sun. The grass was long there and what with a couple of old currant bushes we weren't overlooked. Quite a spread I'd brought back. I fetched some cups for the beer. Quite a picnic, she thought. You should have seen the smile on her face."

"So. No more spectres of Hermione then."

"I didn't hear you say that. Anyway... So, that was that."

"All's well that ends well."

"That's what they say. Thought we'd sit back and watch the fireworks when it got dark, it was warm enough to sit out. Only..."

"It rained?"

"Poor girl, there was blood all over the inside of her overall. My fault of course, I'd been somewhat ungentle shoving her up the sea wall. Silly bugger. Her left knee was a right mess. She didn't seem to be too bothered but I couldn't leave it, I went and brought a basin of water and some disinfectant, and a clean towel too. There was a bit of trouble."

"Trouble?"

"Yes. Don't you listen, cloth-ears? I already told you. She was like a bloody wild animal, I had to use all my strength to hold her down or she'd have bitten me. Her beautiful white overall: I had to stuff a sleeve in her mouth or else she'd have bitten my fingers right through. It was clean though, she was always dressed so very clean. Such a shame that it had been messed up; with the button torn off I could see her blood had made a right mullocks of the lining. She didn't seem to have noticed but it was streaked all up her thigh too. Such a pity. There she was, pure as snow herself, and as simple as the light that shone on her skin; and then that. All the way up to her sweet arse. But such soft clean skin she had, I couldn't fault that, I couldn't say otherwise. What a fresh and innocent girl, I'd thought all along. Still did. No complications."

Miz Stebbing always tell me I'll be respec if I keep clean an tidy and mine my peas n cues. I did'n mind about the clean an tidy cos I only had two changes of clothes in my wardrobe, an it was me what done the laundry checkin and bagging anyway, as well as my own ironin, but I could'n really do much about any peas and cues cos I was'n allowed in the kitchen garden on account it might mess my uniform and when I said this to Miz Stebbing she said it was unbecomin of me to speak smart like that an I should reflect on the delicate nature of my posishun. Then she give me one of her knowing looks and I unnerstood it was another secret I did'n need to unnerstand. Like the secret of the young men. She said I would never go wrong if I unnerstood about the young men an' all they wanted was to hurt me. That however much they might smile and tickle my fancy, unnerneath it all they wanted to hurt me, hurt me really bad so's I'd always pay, I'd be sorry to the end of my days, so I must be dee mure and firm at the same time an always say no thank you very kindly. Then they would respec me and go on their way. Why they would want to hurt me was a secret an Charlie always was kind to me when he brung the groceries with a speshul bar of choclit he hid in my breast pocket always with a wink an a chuckle, an other than the laundry boy who was sly anyway I din't see many young men so I din't unnerstand, but she was the boss so she knew better an I did xactly as she tol. After all she was the reason I had a roof over my head she said. She tol me I was a good girl an I tol Charlie who said he bet I was an all so I knew then that this was the best way to be and I was minded to tell other people that so I would have respec from them too.

It was'n too bad in the otel speshully with the war cos not many people come on holly day, there was too many exploshuns an those flying doodles that took away hole houses an even streets near us, which was scary but the days were easy enough with no-one on holly day. Then when the war stopped Miz Stebbing said we'd have a vick tree celebrashun because they had a vick tree in Europe (Europe is foren but spelled same as in English I saw on the newspapers in the lownge) for a whole day may be two which I xpec is a bit like a Chrismas tree only more speshul cos it isn't just for Jesu's birthday but for all the heroes from the war in Europe against the Nasties an it's for two days as well.

We was all going to sit around the vick tree for a party an Miz Stebbing tol me to stay close when she became an organ izer and went round our bit of town asking for donashuns. Cos I'm a good enough writer who she tort to write I must make the list of things that would be brung to the party. I am speshully good with my postrofees which is unusual and she tol the vicar who said wel done an she said it would be handy with writing numbers which don't have postrofees – e.g. dozens – which not everyone seems to know much to everyone's annoyance. She said it would be good practis for after the war when there would be new opertunitees for good girls like me who has a bit of educashun. Everyone would be invited so it would be a long list too. Even the funny man on the bicycle in the wooden house who scary me a little tho Miz Stebbing say he nothing to be frighted about he just a lonely sole who need a bit of joy in his life. He was not like Charlie or the laundry boy but a grown man with a bristly sort of face though not xactly a beard an his garden was the small wunder of that part of town, it was all golden flowers for much of the year until the summer was over altho Miz Stebbing's sister say it was a disgraceful of weeds. I did not see it much as I was in the otel but when I had to buy Miz Stebbing's oh dear under ordered meat or wretched boy no tomatoes in a hurry for dinner I would walk past very slowly and it was like a field made all out of gold. It made me go all glowing an dizzy an felt very nice.

I din't like the eyes watching me from his front door so I went to look at the flowers and he still saw me looking through his house but he seemed a nice man after all with a posh voice not like Charlie or the head waiter who Charlie said was an ignorant jock who could'n speak the King's English. I din't take any of his beer at first cos Miz Stebbing says to be careful with the demon drink just look at Mister Stebbing, but it was after all a speshul day when we had a bright future ahead of us all the free world said the man on the wireless, who must have known must'n he? I think even Miz Stebbing had had a few and would'n have minded me havin a taste. But he was so polite and not scary at all and I was dee mure and gave him my hand like they do in the films and he was dee mure back only a little cheeky but not so it was impolite and I knew he was a kind man and good frend to Nola. Good job as there was some fright full people let loose that day and just to make sure I said I was a good girl like I always did, but he was'n a young man so it was proberly not needed which is why he just smiled.

I think he was what Charlie called a man of the world, like Charlie said he was only I don't think he'd been any further than Ashford market, an a lady's man too like Charlie said was Mister Stebbing only different cos he was'n rough like Mister Stebbing was with the cook xcept when he looked after me when we met the silly childrun. I think he was a clever man I din't know what he was talking about most of the time but it sounded nice like in books you hear on the wireless and he looked very kind and thoughtful. But like clever people you have to be careful cos they sometimes have queer moments an he did on the beach instead of enjoying the lovely sunshine and the birds that were so graceful. He was a bit rough then though he could'n help it because he was being clever. And later of course.

But I did like to hear the stories he tol me speshully the scary ones cos they are after all only stories and showed he had a big imaginashun. He had a funny turn then but one has to xcept that with clever people cos it's on account of their supearia brains getting into gear. Miz Stebbing is always scolding Mister Stebbing for not getting his brains into gear becos he keeps them in his trousers, which is a mystry I heard often through their private staff only door. Certainly he not very clever he keep being caught with them down, I tol by Charlie. But my frend he very kind to me and was thoughtful when he take me away from the big waves that started up. It was'n his fault I tore my button off or scraped my nee. I just a clumsy madam as cook say. An he did'n tell me off neither.

Well, when we got back to the vick tree party the head waiter was marchin up an down blowin on his bagpipe with his kilt on from the war before the one we just stopped, oh what a surprise that was I could'n stop laughin, an everyone was dancin along behind him what my new frend said was a conga and sure enough they'll be doing the hoky poky next so he said did I want some food instead. But I joined the conga dancin and he just smiled and went for some food anyway an I felt safe becos he was there lookin out for me an becos everyone was just having a peace time celebrashun. I xpected if we did the conga long enough it might take us all the way to the vick tree what I had'n yet clapped eyes on, sadly.

I was so tired by the time the bagpipe stopped an there I was right next to my frend's house an I was dizzy with the dancin an the sunshine an even more now I saw all the lovely flowers again in his garden which I went in. An such a lovely man he had brung us a hole feest from the party an even take some cups from his house so that we had a picnic which I had not had proper before, only the occashunal sandwich and cup of tea at morning break in the yard. It was so lovely and I thought it good to have found such a good frend not a young man who want to hurt me good an proper or give me nasty scary looks like Mister Stebbing. Of course it would'n last it was only cos of the vick tree, that's what I thought, an Miz Stebbing even with her big smile also say don get your hopes up gal when things going well, but it did'n matter cos we was having a speshully good day after all an who knows what might come. That's what I always think. One must always be hope full after all. I don have time for the gloomy sort, I mean look at me.

It was very speshul to be sitting there with all the golden flowers around us which my frend say were his inspirashun and his salvashun, which I xpect was the way he thought on account of him being older and nearer to god. He was worried about my nee saying it looked a mess and mus hurt but I tol him it were all right an that the drink he gave me made it better already. We was drinking beer like grown ups now but I tol myself that was all right too cos I am a full grown 21, an anyway it was just for the vick tree was'n it. But this was beginning to annoy me now cos I still han't seen no vick tree yet but he said hush it no matter just enjoy your self you don really want to be part of all that nonsense. Then he got his brain box in gear again an said I mus be cleaned up I was such a particlar spessmin of whatever (something good by his expresshun but I can' mind the word) that he could'n bear to see me spoiled an he was meanin of course my nee which I had cut on the wall. Well I thought of Miz

Stebbing an how I mus keep clean an tidy so all right I said if you mus it will be for the good.

Then he come back with a basin with some of that stuff cook puts down the drane an sometimes in the greens to kill the bugs an he say let me help you my young lady, he was all like a real lord and gentleman it was lovely, an he wash my nee only it splash on my overall I think cos he had several cups of beer which make him frown so he dabbed it with a towel that had an Empire Made label an then he wash my leg with the same stuff an he rubs at the blood on the inside of my overall cos it was truly a mess an he angry with himself I think, he go red in the chops an he's puffing as he works.

That's when I thought I should be a bit more dee mure cos my overall was all hitched unseemly but I was feelin a bit woozy like the head waiter on a Saturday after clean up time an it did feel nice to have him wash both my legs so the blood was gone an I was beginning to look a bit cleaner although not tidier cos my button was ripped an my overall was all rucked up and staind with grass an yellow from the flowers by now. I was going to be infra it that's telling you young lady, that's all I could think.

But I was still a bit scared about not being as dee mure as I oughta when he suddenly looked at me like I imagin a young man or like Mister Stebbing does the cook an his eyes were all a poppin an I scream but he pushed me back down and stood there with my overall in his hand it was like a big white gost flappin above me an then its arm was stuffed in my mouth so I could hardly breath an I kicked my legs like the cat what got stomped by the dray horse an run an run but could'n no longer move Mister Stebbing had to put it out of its misery.

I tol myself this was a bad dream and I was goin to be put out of my misery too before I woke up an maybe I would'n but the golden flowers seemed real enough they was getting all crushed unnerneath my head and my arms so I thought I'd better lie still or there'd be trouble later not to mention it was a pity to see them destroyed. I could'n move much then cos he had both my wrists tight in his hands an his nee on my middle.

It was not long anyway until the sleeve was taken out of my mouth cos he just fell on top of me he was very heavy and there was a very sharp pain an he said No-la No-la about a dozen times like it was a chant then he weezed an shut his eyes an gave a cry like a little bird I think was most like a stone chat or maybe not a little bird at all but a hawk proberly. When he opened his eyes he was looking at the flowers again and I was dismayed thinkin there'd be trouble cos they were crushed but he was smilin and brushed my hair with his hands and said oh dear your clothes which I saw were more blood than I had thought possible from my nee. But he clean me again with the Empire towel an he said in a moment or two there'd be fireworks and we could watch under the light of the moon an then there were lots of what he called very lights an rockets in the sky an I began to wonder if I imagine what had happen it had not hurt very much so it may not be like the young men after all. He say I a very speshul girl an he glad he find me before I soiled by the (don know the word it sound like trip relashuns) of the world. An I said I not usually soiled only we seem to have a bit of a mess on our hands proberly cos of the demon drink which also the undoing of Mister Stebbing, so I am tol, he once said to Charlie that things were gettin messy. So I say not to worry Nola it all come right in the morning when everything get back to ship shape an bristol fashun.

Anyway I was wrong cos afterwards I have been sick an Miz Stebbing say I am a sickening retch of a girl which is xactly how it feels very truly, she mus know how it feel, an she says I will be sorry to the end of my days which is what she had warned me an now I am getting bigger an bigger I know she mus be right an I wonder how long before I burst. I see my new frend on his bicycle once or twice but he only stop once an say it is a sorry thing how we are all tied to the wheel of fate after all an he sorry he had'n realise his mistake before the vick tree celebrashun, tho I think he was putting his brain into gear then an I was not able to unnerstand him xactly. It is all too complicated for me to try to unnerstand and I have other things to think about now anyway.

"I don't believe you've just told me that. Why?"

"Why did it happen?"

"No, why tell me? Is it true or just another of your stories? I mean, do you really expect me to stand here and listen to stuff like that?"

"It's true. Sadly it's true. And I was truly sorry, though it was too late by then. But you had to know. It's what you wanted to know."

"It is? I don't think so. In fact, I don't think I want to know you at all. Don't worry, I'm not about to tell anyone, you can sink in your own pit of slime all on your very own. But I won't be coming back again. You're just a filthy old shit and I don't know why I didn't come to that conclusion a long, long while ago."

"Please. If you'd only listen. It really is what I've been trying to tell you all along. Don't you see? That there's no escape; not for me, not you, not anyone. I didn't realise before. I thought it was down to everyone else. All the stuff they make up. I thought if I could just step outside all of that I'd be free. But it's much deeper than that. It's in us, it's what we are; and we're in it.

"I tell you, I didn't mean her any harm, although I know I caused her grief, course I did, but she was a rare thing, someone without complications.

"Only I was fooling myself, thinking that. There was more than meets the eye. Always is. It's all biology of course. Everything we do, you trace it down and you find it's all just biology; the biggest damned web of them all and no-one can tear themselves away from it. I tell you now, boy, everything else is just make-believe. All pretence. All the lies that people prefer to the brutal truth of what we are and what we do. Stuff to make us feel better than the animals. That's the sum of it all and I wish I had understood it from the very beginning."

- FOURTEEN -

WHAT A WASTE OF TIME. Only it was a greater disappointment than that which burned him now; the hot shaming sense of the folly he had pursued was roasting him alive.

How naïve to think that after all these years of desperate but fruitless analysis he'd be able suddenly to make sense of it all. That he'd fooled himself, that's what hurt, that and the blast of shockwaves from Fazakerly's impenitent admission, the surprise he'd felt from the old man's declared outrage having filled his empty hopes with the weight of an immense and aching darkness.

Stephen reached the car park without realising he'd been running and the bright afternoon sun had flared around him as he burst out through the windowless door. For a moment he saw everything with the heightened polarity of cinema, his vision fragmentary, stroboscopic, black and white and black again, stilled now but his eyes continuing to smart under the same concussive tension that throbbed in his head.

He leaned against a wheel arch of the Morris Minor and immediately felt the hot metal scorch his thigh. Shit! It was all unravelling, and not in the way he'd anticipated. Perhaps there was no sense to it anyway, was never going to be. Perhaps that was it. Some things just happened, didn't they?

His head swam and instinctively he patted his shirt pocket. No cigarettes. He rummaged unsuccessfully for change in the pockets of his trousers, then remembered the emergency ten shilling note that his father had folded under the car's horn button. Enough to get him home when he'd drunk all his petrol money, that had been the gist of it. There'd be plenty of change from a packet of *Consulate* and anyway, obtusely he carried a spare can.

Opening the driver's door he recoiled from the exhalation of heat, in that instant losing interest in the money and the brief comfort of tobacco. Some things just happened – when you were kids, especially. You can't blame yourself forever for what you did or didn't do then. The rules were all different when you were a kid, and you had to get by without knowing all the passages and passwords needed to traverse the incoherent labyrinth of adult reason.

It was baking like an oven in the car and he swung on the open door. Not that survival wasn't a simple enough matter, despite that handicap, despite not having a map and compass, and you could get by without having to ask for directions. There was always a certain pattern to guide you when you were a kid: things happened, you made a choice, and there were consequences. Only this time the normal course of events had been hijacked, there had been a serious and catastrophic deflection of the natural consequences and he'd been waiting for them to drop on him ever since. Some day, out of the blue: wham! How was he supposed to get on with his life when it was all still out there somewhere, and heading his way more than likely?

Justice. That was something else they'd all understood as kids. One either suffered it, delivered it or took steps to avoid it. Natural justice was the reasonable and inescapable authority everyone knew was invested in the consequences, whatever they might be. Only he'd been denied even that, and he'd craved forever the clean absoluteness of justice deserved, however awful it could turn out. To receive it or confront it and, maybe, escape it, that was his due; but it had been denied him, it had been nimbly diverted into the maze of adult consciousness, and there, and there....

There, it had become unreal. It had been made into nothing more than an oblique reference. It had been absorbed and ameliorated by family love, a brief poisonous discharge of turbulence quickly sublimated by the discriminate decency that oiled the spaces between and within God-fearing communities. After all, was that not the decent thing? Was this not the way it had to be done, the devil having so recently been seen off and the field of his disgrace laid waste? Was it not right to preserve their belief that having won their well-being at such an expense of human misery it must be protected at all costs? At any cost? Consider: what had they been fighting for all those years? Satan may indeed be gone from Germany but let not any chink be offered in the very bosom of humanity. Let him not find means of entry here.

But was that really what he had been expecting from Fazakerly – justice?

That bastard, though, stringing him along, letting him think there was something he could reach for, some epiphany that might be his, if only... If only he had died that night, the creep. Now that would have been a sort of justice. He could have lived with that, knowing what he now knew. That would have put the tin lid on it for certain. But of course he wouldn't have known, would he? – not if the old man had died – and the fog of not knowing would as likely have been as dense as it was now.

He threw himself behind the wheel and slammed the car door angrily. The seams of the red leather seat had split under the weight of several previous owners and he wriggled awkwardly, trying to find a comfortable driving position. The air inside the car was still unbearably hot and smelled of petrol from the spare can in the boot. How hot would it need to be before it ignited spontaneously? Could that be what had happened at the Round House, something like that?

He knew otherwise of course, deep down, but the chain of memory had lost its natural sequence of serial events. No sense could be made of it when it had been severed like that, the pieces removed and dispersed amongst a darkness of contrived obfuscation. That's what he'd hoped for, of course, from the old man, something – some word, a fresh point of view – that would help him join all the pieces together again, so that he could go hand over hand, working back and forth along that chain, navigating the events of that day and afterwards, tracing his way over link by unbroken link until he understood exactly how it had all happened and why.

His hands were shaking as he fumbled with the ignition key. That bastard, to think that he'd sat and talked to him all through the summer as if he were a normal decent human being. To think he'd swallowed all that guff about the war and what it made men do. And all the time there'd been an insistent and self-righteous expectation that he had something to give him, some explanation that he, Stephen, owed the old man! As if he would. As if he'd want to. Let him rot.

The smell in the car had become achingly powerful and he wound down the window, the two-tone mewl of a siren reaching him with a sharp spasm of clarity before fading behind the hill. Ambulance or police, he couldn't tell, but the sound drew him back to the source of his anger. Was there any point in telling anyone? Probably not. Who'd want to do anything about it after all these years? Probably even Nola wouldn't want the truth to be told now, and those who did need to know would have known at the time, they'd have dealt with the knowledge in a manner appropriate to the time. That was the nub of the matter, he recognised that now. He too had been dealt with in such a manner, and wasn't that just as much a crime? Where was the justice in that?

An echoed reprise of the siren triggered a desire for music and he punched the button on the Motorola. The sound took him away from his anger for a moment. *My Generation*. The words of the song had drawn a deep line in the sand; we want something other than all that pretence. We do indeed. '*Why don't you all f-f-fade away?*' He turned the key and the little gold seal engine coughed into life. '*Talking 'bout my generation.'* Yeah, but that song had no more to do with truth either. Make believe, Fazakerly would have said, if he could have been persuaded to listen to the words of that particular anthem. It was no more subversive than Stephen's own brief dalliance with student politics, and like most everyone else he'd barely given it thought; it was all formulaic, transient. He flicked the off button. More pretence, and however loudly anyone insisted the times were a-changing the enduring flux of people's lives would have continued to boil and stream just underneath the surface in much the same way as it had since man first walked on two legs. It was only the preferences that changed, and whatever they might be you were left with the same book, only bound in a different cover. Preferred lies, that's what the old man had called it, hadn't he, and that was pretty close. He was so sure he'd exposed an elaborate web of self-deceit.

Yes, Stephen could go along with that. But to think it could all be traced back to biology, now that would be too easy, too much like an excuse, and he resisted allowing the old man any further credence. It was a claim that didn't seem to go very far in explaining his own circumstances anyway. There was to be no consolation of philosophy there and he felt the rush of anger come throbbing in his head once more.

His parents. His thoughts always returned to their role in all of this. Why would they have done that? Why close him out, and why didn't they fucking tell him the old man hadn't died?

He rammed the gear stick into first, forgetting there was no synchro, and the car bounced over the tarmac with a shrill squall of pain. Turning first towards Ashford, after a short distance that he would have been unable to recall he flung the wheel hard left, taking the old Lympne road that led to the marsh. There was nothing out here but grass and sheep and an invisible skylark, nothing more demanding than the tug of the breeze over the land from the sea, the whiff of distant spaces and the comfort of the turning seasons.

At the summit of Lympne Hill the road spilled over onto rough ground, a careless drift of melted asphalt and stones encouraged onto the grass by the wheels of cars parked for the view. Switching off the engine, Stephen let the Morris ease down the slope on the handbrake until he hung over the long escarpment. It was good to cling there, perilously close to the edge. He remembered how only a few months ago the brake had torn away from its rusty housing when he'd pulled up at lights on a hill. He took imaginary bets on the efficacy of the welded repair. Another reckless inch and he could be tumbling over and over all the way down to the canal. Just the thought of it seemed to tighten the rush of wind through the open window, the sound resonating with the thrill in his head and making his sight grow keener, glazing the vista that spread in front of him across the marsh so that it felt as if he were looking through the lens of a microscope. Out there it could all still feel raw and fresh. He knew it was only a feeling he had, his particular way of looking at things, but it was true the marsh had its own sense of otherness. It was a secret he shared with Fazakerly – he felt awkward acknowledging that – they both knew that out there it was a different world altogether. The place had its own geometry.

He shifted in his seat and traced the remains of the Martello towers, an irregular procession of symmetrical shapes which at that distance he could imagine had been hammered into the shoreline, giant pegs holding taut the jawline of the coast in its defiant curve against the sea. At the eastern end of the line of dark profiles Tower 13 shone in the sunlight. Someone had made it their home, painted it white and opened up its enigmatic face with panoramic windows. It rose bright and clear in the afternoon light that shone down on Marine Parade. Had that been the model for Fazakerly's Round House, the strange wooden retreat which he had built less than a mile further to the east?

As the Earth turned infinitesimally the afternoon sun mirrored in the tower's gradually spiralling windows and briefly it became a beacon, a steady torch of fiery golden light that seemed to draw everything in the landscape towards its reflection.

Humphrey did not appear again from behind the wall and Stephen was in two minds whether to go and haul him out or to run and find Marcus. It was unlikely that Humphrey would climb out, not for a while yet, he'd wait until he knew they were bored with looking for him, he had an uncanny knack for telling how long his persecutors' interest might be sustained. But if he did, if he took his chance and bolted, that would be Stephen's dilemma left bare and unresolved again. Worse: the Gregory brothers' contempt at being shown an empty hiding place was bound to be harsh and loud and inescapable.

Stephen stepped lightly across the road. Maybe Humphrey could be persuaded to come out without giving any trouble. After all, he'd spoken up in his defence, hadn't he? Perhaps, but what Stephen could remember of their last meeting didn't exactly fill him with confidence.

Still, a bird in the hand, so to speak...

He reached up and felt along the top of the wall, finding the brick coping damp and greasy as his fingers flexed for a sure hold, at the same time stealthily wedging a toe in the crack between two stones, glancing around to be sure no-one was watching, best to be sure before it became too obvious what he was intending. It was an unspoken faith that the existence of this hiding place had to be kept secret from adult eyes and he wasn't going to be the one to betray that covenant.

There was nobody in sight, nobody watching, only – bugger, someone had turned the corner by the garages and was ambling in his direction. Marble Gamble – now what was she doing here? He hadn't been that rude to her, not so she'd come after him, surely! Or did she know he'd been poking into the private things in her upstairs room? Course she would. Someone like her would know. Come to think of it, she'd most likely been watching him all the time, in her crystal ball or a magic mirror or suchlike. Well, she shouldn't have left all that stuff there for anyone to see. Indignantly he glowered down the road at her.

Yes. She'd seen him. He watched as she quickened her pace. Well, why should he worry? He'd left everything where he found it. All the same, if she was really on the warpath then he wasn't going to wait around, there was no point hanging on here, not if she was about to unleash some of her infamous malevolence.

That decided it. Marcus's sarcasm was a less worrisome prospect than facing the spite of the town's witch.

Rosalind watched him run full pelt up the sunny side of Queen's Road. The sight of him fleeing like that had made her doubly breathless. She'd already cursed her failing limbs for having lost the brown boy, as she called him, the Childermas, the other name for Humphrey that she shared only with herself, and now she was at a total loss where next to look. The din in the passage behind her house had been fierce enough to wake the dead and she'd looked up from her cooking to see Humphrey rushing away in panic, but whatever horrors he fled was not made clear by the view from her kitchen window. Then the other child, that rather strange, unusually quiet boy she had quite obviously terrified into mending her window, he'd come galumphing down the stairs immediately after. Something was up, something serious, and she was of a mind to find out. That Childermas needed a watchful eye kept over him, which his wretched mother seemed incapable of doing, and it was a matter in which she, Rosalind, had always felt naturally obligated.

Now she'd lost him and was beginning to feel foolish, the urgency of the moment having been mislaid. She'd caught up with him briefly by the Co-op, where she found him skulking around the warehouse door, fascinated by the two Teds who worked there playing split the kipper with a sheath knife, but at her approach instinctively he'd taken off again. And then, just as she'd discovered the other boy hanging around in front of the Round House, a boy who from his mad exit down her stairs she deduced would surely know what was going on, Thomas had come out of his front gate and, well, that had scuppered everything.

She'd ducked inside the garage door, left wide for the roaming hire cars, made a mental note of the number of pigeons that stared back at her from the high ledge on the far wall, and looked out again. Thomas Fazakerly was riding away, his back to her. She felt a thrill of mischief, imagining that she could send the pigeons after him – and the birds from her loft – she'd summon a great cloud of them to swarm and flutter about his head. That'd teach him. She could hear the gulls' raucous laughter filling the air as he swayed and swerved down the road.

No, it was too late for that kind of thing. She'd let her anger go underground many a year since. This was not the time to go digging around in the stuff of bitterness long since buried. But the boy, there was still the brown boy, Childermas, who might be saved. Only, there was now no sign of him, just the other child – he'd been standing at the road's edge, furtively peering across at Blackman's shop, seeming to be listening for something. He'd looked most suspicious, and when he took off like a bat out of hell...

She leaned against the wall, trying to stifle the wheezing rattle in her chest. Could that be the sound of somebody else's breathing? She held her own breath and concentrated: there was a faint susurration coming from behind the wall; she heard a brief but unmistakable scraping sound, someone moving awkwardly in a confined space.

"Boy – are you in there?" Of course he wouldn't answer. But I can't climb up there and pull him out. "Boy, can I help you?"

No answer came but she heard the tiniest sound like bottles chinking, a sound that seemed to echo in the road behind her, a musical tinkling of spokes as Fazakerly's old bicycle rounded the corner. Oh my – there was no time to run, no means of making herself scarce and covering her discomfort.

He allowed her an impassive glance, just once, a tiny nod of recognition, and fixed his eyes on his front gate. She watched him dismount, pushing open the gate with one hand whilst with the other he steadied a string bag hung across the handlebars. She saw him look back, it was most unexpected, and she was so engrossed by the difficulty of this sudden meeting that she didn't at first notice, she was so transfixed by the change in his demeanour that she wasn't immediately aware of the movement above her head, but the quick look of revulsion on Fazakerly's face made her turn, she had to screw up her bad eye in order to focus the other, finding herself staring into the face of the brown boy as he leapt down from the wall, a bottle of lemonade in each grubby fist.

The speed with which Fazakerly tore all the way up his front path left her staring, her mouth hanging wide open in wonder, watching in astonishment as his precious bicycle was thrown down, his hands shaking as he fumbled with his key at the lock, and the door hurled open with a crash that set the glass sentinels on the gazebo frantically bobbing. The boy, Childermas, was close behind him, silent in pursuit. There was something distinctively animal about the way he moved and Rosalind read from his gait the visceral certainty that this time his prey would be taken.

It was the worst outcome possible. Stephen scrambled up the wall whilst Marcus stood with arms folded, the bandage at his wrist a dull brown where the blood had finally stopped seeping, but in his heart Stephen knew that Humphrey would be gone. It had been a bleak and dismal day all round.

"So." Marcus turned his back and leant against the crumbling stonework. "So he was here and now he ain't. That right? So where is he then, Spas?"

Stephen looked down into an infinite tunnel of despair, the darkness at the bottom of the hideaway opening wide, a deep void that would swallow him, he could jump in right now and disappear.

"Well, he ain't in there is he?" Marcus's voice had regained its blunt edge of contempt. "You'd better stop wasting your time and get down here so we can sort this out proper. How about the other stuff – you know, Paul's equipment? Any sign?"

Stephen eased himself down behind the wall. There was no bottomless pit, nothing but loose rocks, sweet wrappers and a scattering of dog ends. Reluctantly he pulled himself out and jumped down to the pavement with a shake of his head.

"Nothing? Mmm. Come on then."

"What?"

"Well, we can't let him get away, can we? Fucking human bomb, he is. Anyway, if we don't get him Paul will, he's gone to find his crazy soldier pals."

"But.."

"Don't be dim. What's the betting Humph'll be over there, with his Daddy?" He nodded across the road. "He's always hanging around old man Fazakerly's place. I knew he'd get in there one day – and today's going to be it, more than likely. I gotta feeling. You saw him earlier on din'cha, what he was like with the mad old git? Jeez, imagine having him for your old man."

They adopted the crouching run of commandos and swept through the open gate, Stephen conscious of the breaking of a zillion taboos as they tiptoed on the grass to avoid the giveaway the pebble path would make. He closed his eyes as they ran, he'd never ventured here so boldly, never dared to confront the sentinels that watched suspended from the gazebo, not openly like this anyway, never imagining he could ever make so audacious and defiant an approach and not suffer some terrible consequence. He felt Marcus clutching at his shoulder.

"Watch it, Spas."

The older boy had pulled him up short of the gazebo and, opening his eyes, he saw immediately the litter of shattered glass on the veranda floor.

"Here." He found himself pulled sideways, deeper into the grass in front of the house. "And keep your head down." They crouched under a window and, before even he'd caught his breath, Marcus nodded at him expectantly. "Go on, then, take a look."

"You're sure it is his Dad, aren't you?" He'd heard the word and found the shock too great to accept it. It didn't help his disbelief to say it now. If it was true the thought was monstrous and he shuddered at what it really meant, all those echoes of normality overturned that he couldn't understand but which made the word taste sour. At the same time it suggested a way out of their predicament.

"Thought everyone knew that."

"But..well, if that's the case why don't we just go and knock, say there's been a mistake, you know, ask for the bottles back."

"Don't be a spas, Spas. When I say everyone knows, I don't mean *everyone*, not like Fazakerly would want it to be everyone, not the whole bloomin' world and his dog. Just us in the know, right." He tapped his nose in the manner of a spiv. "He'd have your guts for garters if you just went knocking and said 'scuse me sir, I don't believe I've had the pleasure, not formally, but I'm a good chum of your son, Humphrey. Come off it."

"But.."

"Oh no, too late for buts, here comes fucking trouble."

Paul came weaving through the grass; he'd donned a camouflage jacket and carried a pair of field glasses.

"Got him, then? S'pose you were right about him and the old man. Isn't that what you're doing here?" He pulled a face at Stephen. "Don't tell me it was you what made him run in there."

"Don't know yet. We were just about to take a look, weren't we Spas; we only just arrived." Marcus nudged Stephen with his foot. "Look lively."

"Hold on, this calls for a professional recce. Us soldiers know the drill."

To Stephen's great relief, and without a moment's hesitation, Paul stood up, leaned back and flattened himself dramatically against the house, his fingers spread for purchase and his cheek turned side on to the smooth wooden laths, slowly and supply extending himself to his full height alongside the window. He threw them a glance, just once, enjoying his audience, then hunching his shoulders he peered around the edge of the frame – and in a shot he had thrown himself back on the grass with them, his face bloodless, his lower lip jutting in horror.

"Holy shit!"

"What? What's in there?" Marcus was energised, but Stephen could think of nothing but flight.

"What d'you think? Let Spas take a look. It's right up his street."

"We'll all look, right."

Marcus had Stephen by the scruff of the neck as the three of them slid up the wall beneath the window, three heads craning over the wooden sill, two pairs of eyes wide that they might capture all of whatever there was to be seen and quickly withdraw, unnoticed, one pair of eyes half closed again for fear of what they might see and be punished by the knowledge.

"Holy shit indeed!" Their three voices hissed in unison, they were quickly tumbling in a heap on the grass, Marcus grinning, Paul too, now that he had got over the surprise. It was only Stephen whose face was frozen in a gape of horror, so stunned by what they had discovered he couldn't make out the other boys, they were just a blur. All he could see was the ghastly tableau they had witnessed in the middle of Fazakerly's parlour. It was indelibly printed on his vision.

"What did I tell you, Spas, there are real perverts about in this town." Marcus spat into the grass. "Eh, Paul?"

Paul had stopped laughing. He looked troubled.

"S'not right though, is it? These filthy bastards. Dad's guv'nor in the TA says they should all be given a whiff of gas." He clenched his fist in a spasm of anger, his eyes darting. "Well, I know how to sort them out. Just give me a minute."

He was away as quickly as he had arrived, the field glasses banging against his hip as he ran. Halfway along Queen's Road he passed Marble Gamble coming down the other side, she had Nola's elbow in a tight grip and was propelling her along inelegantly and breathlessly, leaning on her stick with her other hand. She had the appearance of a boatman having great difficulty punting an unwilling vessel down a shallow riverbed. The flurry of smoke from Nola's perennial *Woodbine* added a further note of incongruity to their desperate progress, as she stood her ground for long pauses to drag on her cigarette and wonder out loud, over and over, why she'd been snatched from the hotel yard. But Paul hardly saw them. He had something important to do. He was going to clean up good and proper.

"C'mon – cretin or not we'd better find out if he's all right." Marcus was pulling at Stephen's arm. They could hear sobbing from inside the house. "Old bastard, I betcha he's been riding around on that bike of his seeing who else he might nab." He shivered. "Yeah, who knows what's been going on here before even today. I always thought it fucking queer, him living in a daft place like this."

They stood up and, shielding their eyes from the reflections in the glass, peered in once more.

Fazakerly stood in the middle of the room, knee deep in a sea of rubbish. He was all but struck rigid, it looked at first as though he were fixed in place by the engorging piles of waste, yet his arms were still free, they were waving frantically in the air, their movements devoid of purpose or reason. With his mouth open and his eyes staring he appeared to be deep in a trance, and he couldn't seem to decide where he wanted to put his hands, he couldn't find a safe place anywhere to rest his hands. Not on the boy's head, certainly, he didn't want to touch Humphrey with his hands, he couldn't bring himself to extend that intimacy; but he was locked in the boy's embrace all the same, he was fixed to the spot, and Humphrey on his knees had buried his head in the old man's groin, he was sobbing, great gasps of roaring anguish racking his whole body, his head bobbing violently and his shoulders convulsing.

"Daddy, Daddy," he repeated, burrowing deeper into the folds of Fazakerly's trousers, "be my Daddy," his words lost in the hoarse rumble of sobbing that penetrated through the window.

"Fucking cocksucker," snarled Marcus. "Just look at that! Look what he's done to him. He's made him into a fucking cocksucker. Let him go, you old bastard!" He'd abandoned stealth and was hammering on the glass. "Hey, you old fucker, let him go! Homo! Pervert!" But Fazakerly appeared not to hear, he was turning instead towards an inner door, shouting now himself as the two women rushed in.

"Get him off me will you. He's a little devil. I can't make him let go of me."

"Holy Moly, look at that now!" Marcus's jaw dropped at the sight of the witch and Humphrey's witless mother marching uninvited into the forbidden territory of the Round House. "What did I tell you, there's something big going on here. Look, they're in it together. Fuck!"

Although scared that he would turn on her, with the advantage of her own fearful eminence Rosalind had managed to prise the child from his grip on Fazakerly's thighs and he had transferred his distress to his mother. Remaining on his knees he locked his arms around her waist and continued to sob with his face pressed into her side. Nola, seemingly oblivious of her role in this crisis, was struggling to stay upright as vacantly she fought to extract her cigarettes and matches from her overall pocket.

"Look, Spas, they're all at it, even his Mum!" Marcus had lost all of his illustrious poise. "This is..this is.."

It was at that point that Fazakerly seemed to notice them for the first time. His face was black, distorted with rage. Free at last from Humphrey's clinch he strode to the window and flung it wide, and would have stepped through if he had not felt Rosalind's restraining touch on his arm.

"You! This is all your doing," he bellowed, his long bony finger pointing, "I saw you hanging around, you little guttersnipe, yes I've seen you creeping around my house, interfering with things that don't belong to you. What's a man got to do to be left in peace?" He raised his fist at Stephen and shouted back into the room. "He's the ringleader, that one. You remember his face. Always skulking around on his own, spying on folk. These kids, they should be locked up." He thrust his head through the open window and glared at Stephen while Marcus crouched on his knees with his arms over his head. "I know what goes on; I see it all from here." He turned back and shook himself free of Rosalind. "Did you know what they were doing? Is this your idea of restitution? Why? I mind my own business, don't I, I keep myself to myself and...Or you," he barked at Nola, "they cooked this up with you, didn't they; what did you think you were up to setting that foul miscarriage of yours onto me?"

Fazakerly ranted and fumed, his knuckles white, his teeth bared, it seemed he was about to explode as he railed at Nola. "Look at you, not so long ago you were a picture of innocence, a real treat. Well, what are you now? And put that bloody cigarette out, you stupid little bitch – just look around you! I'll not have you doing that in my house. This is my home, remember!"

"Time to go, Spas," Marcus breathed in Stephen's ear. "Before he really goes mental."

They turned on their heels only to be met by Paul hot footing it across the grass.

"Told yer I'd deal with it." He waved a fat metal tube at them. "Here we are. This'll sort the bastard once and for all. Made it myself." He lay the tube on the grass and took a loose assembly of steel rods from a canvas bag. Stephen thought they had the appearance of brake calipers, taken from a child's bicycle. There was the business end of a rest for a fishing rod in there too, and it was all strung together with lengths of copper wire. He watched, mystified, as with a look of glee Paul used the device to prop the tube firmly at an angle, its empty mouth raised towards the open window.

"Here we go." Deftly Paul extracted the shiny mortar from his bag and dropped it fins first into the tube. "Bombs away."

The initial blast from the open window was disappointingly quiet compared to the thudding of young bones that Stephen heard, as all three of them threw themselves to the ground. There'd been an impossibly tense delay, as if their fearful expectancy of detonation had stretched out the moment with the saving grace of failure, then just a whooshing sound, like the rush of unseasonal wind through a heavily laden tree, followed by a hiss and crackle that sounded strangely liquid. And as soon as the first charge of burnt air subsided there came the regular clap of hurried feet running away over the grass, Paul's voice, angry, whining and out of countenance, in the background a metallic clanking that measured its jarring counterpoint to his awkward retreat; and Marcus, chivvying him along, sneering, calling him a dickhead and a let-down.

Stephen did not get up and follow them. He'd hit his head in the angle between the wall and the dried out summer lawn and the bruised gonging of his heartbeat had grown suddenly loud in his ears, he thought he'd been knocked unconscious by the explosion. The afternoon sky had darkened prematurely, there were cold grey clouds piling one on another, and he could tell from the gnawing in his belly that it was well past his teatime. Only, everything felt so hot, like it was the middle of the brightest summer's day, and it was so much easier just to lie here, he'd had enough of rushing everywhere so pointlessly. It was better in the end to let the world run its inexorable course. It made no difference in the end.

I'm not the gloomy sort but I agree what Miz Campull said, it was a great shame what had happened to that house an I was sorry to see it was worse inside than out. Ten years, she said, more than ten years this silly old fool had let it all slide – that's what she called him, silly old fool – since the war she said. I thought maybe it was cos of the war he'd behaved that way, I seen folk made worse by it, tho he was too old even then, too old to be on what they called active service.

So that didn't explain what he did, not to me nor the house, tho of course we all suffered. I xpect that's why the kids all hang about there, him havin let it all slide, as she said, it's a good place for an adventure. I did'n like what I saw inside tho, it was a fine old mess, an me being brung up to be clean an tidy it was a shock to behold. Anyway, I was glad to see all my Humphrey's friends, he very popular my boy, an I wish he just play with them an not keep bothering the old genulman. After all, the old genulman he not really been my speshul frend for a long time now an it not right he can' ride around the town on his own two wheels of fate without a daft boy trubbling him.

But Lord what a mess, my Humphrey was up to his neck in all sorts of rubbish, a hole heap, we could hardly see where the floor was under all that load of rubbish. How anyone live like that an not catch their death I dunno. What on earth would Miz Stebbing say if she could see, that's all I could think. An the smell was bad, I was soon gasping for a fag just to clear my nose. Poor Humphrey, Miz Campull try an try to pull him out of it, she say over an over we mus get the Childmas away from here, tho it beats me why she keep callin him that cos he was not born at Chrismas or anything, but she seem very fond of him. So I did'n ask, it not polite, speshully when she say he is a pity me of innosense and I know for a fact he turned out a real pity for me. So I respec her opinion tho he my speshul boy now.

Listen to me I'm wandering again as they say at the otel, there goes Nola off on her wanderings again, what a cheek they have but they mean well. Well, I did'n want to go near that place, speshully after what happened the first time, but she was making such a fuss, Miz Campull, that I thought maybe I oughta, cos I did'n want to think of my dear boy getting into any trubble. It was bad enough him just believing what he did which is the fort of Miz Stebbing's sister, her an her big mouth, which was not fair as I was already going to be sorry enough to the end of my days. So there we was, up to our oxters in old newspapers an books an maps, not to mention smelly stuff which mus have been dinners not eaten a long while since, it made me want to puke worse than the pig bins at the otel. I laugh out loud when he say don you two come in here and make my place untidy with your presents, cos it was so bad I was choking from the pong. So when I come over all faint an my mouth as parched as the proverbyul chinaman's jockstrap, which is what Charlie would say if it were him, tho why a jockstrap is'n a scotchman's an not a chinaman's I don unnerstand, it was a bit of luck when I see he had a cupple of lemonades on his dresser, an I remember he like lemonade, but he shout at me very sharp an say you put that down, that no good for you, girl. He a real meany, I remember when he pretend to forget the lemonade on vick tree day.

Anyway my poor boy was all histerical wanting his deserts from his natural father, which Miz Campull tol me is only natural, tho how she know that I dunno, it meaning the sort of speshul afecshun an protecshun an the dissiplin to be xpected of a man. It made me sad to see, since I could'n give him all what he needed on my own, seein him clingin to the old man for dear life till Miz Campull managed to pull him free. She is a power of a woman I can tell you. Invisible powers I have heard.

That of course is when there was real trubble cos with Humphrey out of the way my frend as used to be once could see the boys playing in his garden, an he went stone the crows what is this, what is going on here? I could'n tell why he make all that fuss, they was just some frends of Humphrey, nice boys, they always used to pass the time of day whenever they see me. They had a smart little space ship they was playing with, all silver, it look real fancy, an they did'n mean no harm I can tell you but they had to put it away quickly he was shouting so much, they hid it right quick in its box so he could'n see. Not quick enough, neither, I can tell you, good job Miz Campull was holding on his arm or he would have jumped through the window he was so mad. It was horrible to see the old genulman like that, speshully when he turned on Miz Campull who was only there to help after all, an I was feeling quite retched, tho glad too that he had'n tried to make an onnest woman of me, he'd have been no catch at all. A trial more like, proberly worst than Mister Stebbing. Anyway, I was shakin an Humphrey was cryin an I lit a fag to calm my nerves. Only that was a mistake cos he turned on me then an called me awful names and lashed out at me, he was red in the chops like that other time after the war, it was most unkind seeing how we was related, sort of, an he slapped me so hard it knocked the fag out of my mouth.

I was feelin stunned an right sorry for myself, an he just went on shouting and stamping, what a awful way for a genulman to behave an that was my last fag too, when Miz Campull said look there's smoke coming from the corner by the door an of course where there's smoke there's fire, an sure enough there was all too soon, I do not deny. It was scary I thought to myself how quickly the flames jumped up from the floor, they were in the nets in a flash, so to speak, and then onto the drapes. Do something, we mus do something, I remember is what she said, Miz Campull, just like Miz Stebbing do when she drops the milk or the dog does poo-poos in the kitchen an she all overcome an I am xpected to be quick on the uptake, which I can be, an I did'n care any more for his hot temper, not in such a situashun. So I grabbed the two bottles of lemonade, thinkin I not scared of you Mister, and pinged off the stoppers – just like that: Ping! Ping! I always love that sound, it a cheery sound when the springs on the bottles go ping – and in the batting of an eye I shook them out all over the nets and the floor where it was burning, putting the flames out. Only it din't.

Oh Nola, you are daft as a brush, I said, cos just then I remembered the look in his eye when him say not to touch, an I did wonder, but it was too late as everything went woosh an I felt my eyebrows go stiff an there was a nasty niff like with the turkey when we take the candle to it for the feathers at Chrismas.

Before I come to Miz Campull was bundling my Humphrey through the window, he a well built boy an it not easy, he was making silly noises too, puffs and squeaks, but out he went, then Miz Campull. The nice boy, the one who Humphrey's speshul frend, I think, he help her best he can, cos the others run away with their space ship going clonk clonk in its box, an good for them, but Miz Campull she a large lady, bigger than my boy an too old, too old to go jumpin through windows at her time of life, her being parshully sighted an all. The old genulman, he no help neither, he just hold his hands to his head and shout why, why, why, what have I done to deserve this, an such like. I xpec he having to deal with the trip relashuns of the world again, like he tol me a long time ago. Anyway, out she go too, the nice boy pullin some of the window away to help her, it was already burning real fast I could'n believe how fast the flames took hold an the window was all wonky. Silly havin a wooden house tho, everyone say so an I never would. Somebody should of tol him, the genulman, before it too late.

But this boy he was a strong sort an he made the hole wider, it look to me like the hole window about to come away, it shook me how easy it might come away. So Miz Campull, she sort of tumble down and then she bob up again, like a cork, it made me giggle, seeing her through the smoke, tho she had her serious face on. An as I look for my own way out she look all stern an tell the boy in no uncertain terms he mus disappear sharpish, she shouting most unlike her an waggling her finger at him saying this not the place for a boy like him, this not being his bizness neither, an that were true. My Humphrey he already gone, very sharpish, thank the Lord he such a bright boy after all.

So that left just me – an the old genulman, but he was'n thinkin of going nowhere, I could tell – an it was getting dark with all the smoke so I just jumped. In fact it so dark I nearly jumped on our young helper outside, he mus have been a bit shocked he had'n moved, an I don think he see me, proberly cos my nice white overalls were all dirty by now – would they ever be clean after this I ask myself. He was just standing with a piece of burnin wood in his hand, that he'd just pulled away proberly but I wish he'd put it down. Maybe, I thought, maybe he mean to light a way for me through the smoke with his torch, what a kind brave sole, but then I do have daft thoughts like that. Soft and soppy says Miz Stebbing, an more like sloppy on her off days. So I tell him to get away, I was runnin myself, I say this nothin to do with you, repeatin just what Miz Campull say, just get away, but he not hearin me. The fire was roarin an he look like he away with the fairies instead of getting away proper. Perhaps Miz Campull put a spell on him when she was doing her bobbin an tellin, they do say she has a way like that. Anyway, I hear the bells comin so I mus get away myself before the coppers come. I already got enough reason to be sorry all my days I don need any more trubble. He'll be all right anyway, he a good strong young lad. Nice fambly I'm sure. It very hot tho.

- FIFTEEN -

IT'S A CONDITION of being human that we have to find a reason for everything. We just have to have the reassurance that there's some cause or purpose inside all that happens or exists, and believing that is what separates us from the beasts and the birds. That's why we invented God, of course, to explain the inexplicable. The alternative, the possibility that things just are, is too frightening an option to contemplate, even worse than finding ourselves unable to explain all of the meaning we imagine is invested in our world. It simply doesn't sit easy with our level of consciousness.

I've grown used to it, myself, the not knowing, and it has turned out to be less and less important now that it occupies the greater part of life's experience. I don't pretend to claim wisdom, but with the accumulation of years has come the inevitable acceptance that I'll never begin to understand it all, not more than a tiny fragment of the whole it would seem, maybe not even that, not even those memories once thought to have been clear and rational testament of the immediate moment. And it doesn't seem to matter. I've actually stopped worrying about the need to find a reason for why, which is funny considering the career I chose: academe, critical thinking and a lifetime of research into the symbols by which we explain our world. Colleagues used to tease me, calling me a zealot and claiming I was on a taxonomical mission to make sense of the way we live.

Instead, it is enough for me now to blame it all on the *zeitgeist*, the way things were then, and I remember those times as a child in the nineteen-fifties with a deep sense of fondness, not fear or frustration. Even better, I've long since realised that my parents were persuaded to their behaviour by an unswerving and sincere conviction, not as conspirators but simply because of their belief in a society sworn to protect what remained of innocence. It was a belief that for a number of years sustained the right to childhood, as something valued and to be preserved in the aftermath of a second war to end all wars. It would have been arrogant and uncharitable of me to hold that against them for ever.

Recent research has brought me a greater sense of equanimity too. Not my own research, I hasten to add, but that which has legitimised the neurological condition known as ADHD. Finding that I am blessed with the impassively-named attention deficit hyperactivity disorder – and I mean to stress my positive stance when others might be tempted to say I had been cursed – has been something of a revelation, which although coming a little late in life has not been too late for me to reassess the phenomenon of my particular consciousness. Certainly I don't regard myself as having suffered from the condition, and neither would I admit to having been of a disorderly disposition! All those intensities of mood and perception, the torrent of sounds and images that inspired flights of hyperactive fancy, they were a joy and no less real to me now for knowing their source.

I didn't see Fazakerly again. I guess it was his own lack of charity that finally rendered him unfit for survival outside those institutional walls, and he saw no charity on offer in the world around him, only threats and disappointment. But that wasn't why I didn't go back. His analysis was too plausible for me at the time, that was the trouble, and I wasn't ready then to accept the chaos it implied. The prospect now is less daunting, when I'm no longer driven by the necessity of finding an explanation, and when his vision of the world no longer speaks to me of chaos but merely describes the way we are. As for his desperate assertion that there is no escape, that we are trapped in a web of associations and obligations, where if it were possible would he have us escape to? I never heard him tell me that.

Actually I did go back, in a manner of speaking, that hot afternoon in 1967, the Summer of Love. I was drawn in along with everything else under the spell of that beacon of reflected light. Watching those silent reflections radiating out from Tower 13 it felt like all the summer's heat was being sucked into a vortex and I convinced myself that if I made it out to the other side it would be into a new season, under a different sun, I'd reach a place where the air would be cooler and sharper. I'd be wiser too, perhaps. Yes I know, it was all very Sixties.

The heap of ash that once had been the Round House had long been cleared away, but when I parked the Morris alongside the broken garden wall it seemed that little else had changed in the decade since the fire. A painted notice board advised that the site had been acquired by a local firm and gave an address in Haven to which all enquiries could be made, but the paint had long since faded, suggesting that nothing urgent had been planned in the way of redevelopment.

I was surprised to find that the fig tree had recovered from the fire, having grown considerably, and was laden with green fruit. The grass too around the perimeter of Fazakerly's garden was tall and dense, its plumes heavy with seed, and the bushes that made a boundary had become wildly disproportionate. At first it seemed to recreate the atmosphere of those childhood playgrounds where whole blocks had been laid waste by doodlebugs, leaving wildernesses of rubble and fireweed, and stepping further away from the path the world beyond the vacant lot receded quickly so that I was free to engage my imagination once again. But there was no evidence that this place had become a playground. There were no trails through the grass, no disturbance to be found at all, and as I moved further into the centre where the weeds and grass abated I found an untrodden carpet of buttercups, each flower open and glistening in the warm sunlight. They had spread across the black surface where the house had stood so that only a slight unevenness betrayed where they covered the events of that distant afternoon.

Looking out over that empty space and trying to remember how it had appeared to me as a child, before the fire, I found myself struck less by the tranquillity of all this secluded abundance than by an oppressive feeling of desolation. It was then that I relived the uncomfortable feeling of being somewhere where I should not be, that I was an intruder, unbidden and unwelcome. It was time to go and I looked for the shortest route to the path.

The flowers grew close and, hearing a voice call out to warn me, I was aware of being overly cautious about where I put my feet, suddenly fearful that I might crush some of those glorious petals. Marooned, I looked about me for the owner of that voice but could see no one else in the garden. It was more than unsettling, the sense that I was not welcome here had become almost palpable and the heat from the sun that the flowers threw back at me was stifling. I even had the childish notion that if I ventured still further I would find it extremely difficult to retrace my path: one more step forward and I would smell the soles of my shoes burning, for somewhere under that cloak of gold the inferno still raged.

It came to me then that it was the heat from the wreckage of Fazakerly's house that sustained all this wild profusion of growth, not the benign reflections of a sunny afternoon. This was no place to run and hide, no childish sanctuary. There could be no cries of unbridled adventure expected here, and no-one these days who would dare to come and pluck the green figs.

Returning to the gate I looked back and thought no more to recognise the thrilling invitation of a glad wilderness. The golden carapace that spread almost the length and breadth of Fazakerly's ruined domain begged, no demanded, to be left alone.

"Stay away," it called; "leave me be."

Acknowledgements

Sources for this book have been, on the whole, my own memories of growing up in the 1950s and 1960s, which have provided much of the context. Background which I cannot have supplied first-hand has been derived from the memories of others, as well as from some texts. Chiefly, these have been Norman Longmate's *How We Lived Then*, a compelling record of home front experiences from the second world war; the fascinating *Letters From A Lost Generation*, being the first world war correspondence of Vera Brittain and four friends, edited by Alan Bishop and Mark Bostridge; and the pictorial celebration of *Romney Marsh* by Fay Godwin and Richard Ingrams, which captures the otherworldliness of that region in both word and image. Readers will also be familiar with the brief quotations from Wilfrid Owen's *Spring Offensive* and The Who's *My Generation*, and will have recognised from several allusions the significant motifs contained within Edgar Allan Poe's *A Descent Into The Maelström* and *The Purloined Letter*.

Notes

Printed in the United Kingdom
by Lightning Source UK Ltd.
135349UK00001B/153/A

9 781847 533708